# A PERFECT CORNISH ESCAPE

Seven years ago, Marina Hudson's husband was lost at sea. She vowed to love him for the rest of her life — but when kind-hearted Lachlan arrives in Porthmellow, should she really deny herself another chance at happiness? Tiff Trescott was living life to the full as a journalist in London — until her boyfriend's betrayal brought it all crashing down. Fleeing to her cousin Marina's cottage, Tiff feels like a fish-out-of-water. And when brooding local Dirk wins a day with her in a charity auction, she's thrown headfirst into Cornish life. This summer promises new beginnings for both Tiff and Marina. But are they too good to be true?

PHILLIPA ASHLEY

# A PERFECT CORNISH ESCAPE

*Complete and Unabridged*

# CHARNWOOD
Leicester

First published in Great Britain in 2020 by
Avon
London

First Charnwood Edition
published 2021
by arrangement with
Avon
A division of HarperCollins*Publishers* Ltd
London

*A catalogue record for this book is available
from the British Library.*

ISBN 978–1–4448–4650–8

Published by
Ulverscroft Limited
Anstey, Leicestershire

Set by Words & Graphics Ltd.
Anstey, Leicestershire
Printed and bound in Great Britain by
TJ Books Ltd., Padstow, Cornwall

This book is printed on acid-free paper

Dedicated to all the brave volunteers who
save lives at sea

# Prologue

## September, seven years ago

Marina pressed her back against the door of the wooden building, seeking shelter under what remained of its porch. The coastal lookout station had been left to the mercy of the elements a decade ago, but now she was desperate.

Hail battered what was left of the roof. When she'd set out on her walk an hour before, it had been a fine evening, blowy but with hardly a cloud in the sky. She hadn't bothered with a coat. She hadn't expected it to rain and almost hadn't cared if it did. The little things — getting caught in the rain, getting soaked to the skin — didn't matter.

Nothing seemed to matter any more, not now Nate was gone.

Marina had headed out for her walk straight after work. The new term had begun at the college where she taught English. It had been the beginning of the summer holidays when Nate had vanished but that was two months ago and she couldn't stay on compassionate leave forever. Her students needed her, however much she might feel like curling up in a ball howling, or spending her time here, looking out over the coast, hoping, waiting, praying . . .

She'd been drawn to this spot even more in the few months since Nate had vanished in his

1

fishing kayak off the cove below the abandoned lookout station. The station had once been well equipped with powerful binoculars, which enabled the coastguards to watch and listen in to the marine traffic passing by. They could see for many miles, and alert the search and rescue services to anyone in trouble, not only shipping, but local fishermen, windsurfers, divers, even walkers on the coast path.

Once upon a time, they had watched and logged every vessel, person and incident, large and small, because one day their vigilance might save a life. It had saved lives . . . but not Nate's.

The station had been closed long before Nate disappeared. The fishing kayak was a new 'toy', one of many, and purchased from a mate at a knockdown price. He said he was going to flog his catch to the fancy restaurants in Porthmellow, Newlyn and St Ives. It would be a nice little earner, he said, and give them some extra income while he got his real business — one of them — off the ground.

She'd told him to be careful, hiding her dismay at yet another of his schemes. At least this one seemed to involve little outlay or risk. Nate had been born and brought up in Porthmellow and for a brief time before she'd married him, had worked on a fishing boat. He knew the sea well, and she'd thought it was one thing he respected.

Not enough. A storm like this one had been forecast when he'd set out in the kayak from Porthmellow Harbour for a fishing session. Even today in the murky conditions, Marina could see the place he liked to fish from, near a rocky outcrop.

The battered craft had been washed up a few days later, minus the gear and minus Nate.

If the station had been open, he would *surely* have been spotted. Someone would have been watching out for him and surely seen when he got into difficulties. Those eyes would have known he was in trouble and alerted the coastguard and the RNLI. A lifeboat or helicopter would have been scrambled, and he might be here now. She might have been tucked up safe and cosy in their cottage, sharing a glass of wine with him in front of the fire and dreaming of a brighter future.

Their marriage hadn't been perfect. Far from it. Nate had debts, and he wasn't always the most considerate of partners and they had their spats. He could be thoughtless, he wasted too much time and money on crazy schemes, but she'd loved him.

They'd had an argument about his latest 'plan' the very morning he'd been lost. Marina had taken on some extra private tutoring to help keep a roof over their heads and she'd begged him to try and look for permanent work — he'd turned down a job offer from Porthmellow Sailing Trust because he'd pinned all his hopes on the fishing kayak. He'd claimed he could 'make a mint' supplying fresh fish to the local restaurants.

Marina squeezed her eyes shut, letting the rain blow into her upturned face. She wanted to be wet and cold; she wanted to feel she was alive in some way — or was she punishing herself? If they hadn't argued that morning, if Nate hadn't

3

set out angry and distracted . . .

'I'll show you!' he'd shouted, snatching up the keys to the boatshed in the cove. 'I wish you'd bloody believe in me more!'

At the time, she'd been upset and called after him: 'Then give me something to believe in, Nate! I've had precious little so far.'

Now, she would give everything to snatch back every bitter word, every row they'd had in their two years of marriage. No matter what had passed between them, she loved him and missed his handsome face, his funny jokes, his enthusiasm for life, his touch, his warmth in her bed. She felt as if her heart and soul had been ripped from her body and cast into the sea along with Nate. The torment was unbearable and yet she went on living every day. It seemed wrong that the sun rose in the morning, and the rain fell from the sky, and the world turned — and yet it *did*.

She so badly longed for answers; she felt she might die if she never found out what had happened to him that summer morning. Yet as each day passed, she began to realise that she might live with the agony of uncertainty forever.

'Why did you do it, Nate?' she called out. 'Why did you have to leave me on my own?'

Her plea was drowned in a rumble of thunder. She hammered her fists against the door of the station in frustration, and, tiring, rested her head against its peeling wood. Its very presence added to her agony. What business had it standing here, abandoned and ramshackle? It would be better if it had never existed because in its present state, it was worse than useless.

4

Still all she could think was that if someone had been watching the day Nate set out, maybe she wouldn't have been standing here in the storm, tears mingling with the rain, drawn to the spot where she lost him. She might have some answers, instead of being doomed to look out over the cove forever and never know.

As the lightning flashed and the thunder crashed, she called out to the sea and the storm.

'Nate. I love you, and I always will,' she called as the thunder shook the station. 'Wherever you are and no matter what happens, I swear, I'll never stop loving you.'

# 1

## April 2020

'Marina! Quick. There's a body washed up in Silver Cove.'

Marina yelped as a droplet of boiling water splashed onto her bare skin. Abandoning the kettle in the staff area at the rear of the lookout station, she strode into the control room, sucking her hand.

'What? Where?'

Gareth's eyes were glued to the telescope in the lookout station. He could hardly get his words out. 'Down there at the western edge, by Cormorant Rock. Look, it's rolling around in the surf.'

He pulled his face from the scope and swung it towards Marina. 'Here. Have a look for yourself.'

Marina hesitated. Gareth's shout had unleashed memories that had swept her off her feet and left her tumbling over and over, powerless to do anything except hope she broke the surface again and could breathe.

He hopped up and down. 'Go on, look!'

Marina felt sick but Gareth couldn't have been more excited if a mermaid had been washed up.

'Shall I call the police?' He snatched up the radio handset.

Marina composed herself. 'Hold on, Gareth.

Let's make sure of what we're seeing, first. And if it is something sinister, remember we're talking about someone's loved one.'

'Yeah. It's just . . . I've been doing this for four months now and I've never seen anything . . . you know . . . It's quite exciting.'

Ignoring him, she pressed her face to the eyepiece of the high-powered binoculars. They were so powerful you could make out the name of the lifeboat in the station at Porthmellow a mile away and see that Craig Illogan, hauling in his lobster pots beneath the lighthouse, was wearing a red beanie hat today.

So she ought to be able to tell if the object rolling to and fro on the shingle was vaguely human or not. From two hundred yards away, she ought to be able to make out its face. If God forbid, it had a face — or once did. Fighting down a flutter of panic, Marina fine-tuned the scope and looked at the object again. It certainly *looked* like a body: right size and weighty, and it was clothed, but it was being tossed around by the waves, and never stayed still long enough to tell for certain. And yet, she was almost sure that the object wasn't human.

She could almost feel Gareth humming with nervous energy by her side. She had one more look, to make doubly sure it wasn't a person.

'Is it?' he hissed, still sounding worryingly excited. She decided that it wouldn't do any harm for him to learn a lesson.

'I'm not sure . . . I think we should make a closer inspection. In fact, I think you should go down and check. Tide's going out so you'll be

8

safe as long as you take care on the steps.'

'B-but shouldn't we call the police or the coastguard or the lifeboats?' Gareth had turned several shades paler in the past ten seconds, but, given his excitable behaviour moments before, Marina knew this was the time for her newest recruit to discover what their role as volunteer coast watchers really entailed. Even if that meant a baptism of fire — or salt water in this case.

'Don't want to get them out on a wild goose chase — there's a swimming race at Porthmellow and they'll be flat out helping with safety for that. I think we can handle this. You can, Gareth. You said you wanted to do something more exciting than making the tea and writing in the log.'

'B-but — what if it is a . . . a real body?'

'Then you'll be able to tell pretty quickly and radio me and we can get the emergency services involved. Off you go, take the radio and be careful. Sooner we get this sorted the better.'

While Gareth scooted down the steps from the eyrie of their lookout station, Marina ran the cold tap over her scalded hand, thinking about the object washed up on the rocks. It could have been much worse. It could have been some poor drowned soul and, to be fair, it did very much look like a body. When Gareth had shrieked from the control room, for a moment she *had* wondered, before she'd focused on the object rolling in the waves.

Gareth emerged at the bottom of the staircase and picked his way between boulders. He'd joined the Wave Watchers a few months ago and was a student at the local college where Marina taught part-time.

Gareth was very excitable and a little too keen for 'action', but the group couldn't afford to turn down a willing recruit and Marina was hopeful that he'd calm down once he'd gained more experience.

She'd never forgotten her vow to Nate and, four years previously, had finally found a way to honour his memory. In the early days, she'd been too overwhelmed by grief and hope to focus on anything but praying that Nate might come back. She'd no idea how she'd got through every hour, let alone each day and, of course, she'd had to use what energy she had to deal with the police investigation.

After his disappearance, it became apparent that Nate had been in debt up to his eyeballs, that he'd re-mortgaged the cottage. Marina had always suspected he had a few secrets but had had no idea . . . Had he taken his own life to escape his problems? Or was it simply a tragic accident — from venturing out in a storm to make a few pounds from fishing?

As she began to rebuild her life, she discovered not all the pieces could be found, and the result could never be the same. However, the Wave Watchers offered a new way to fill part of the gaping hole.

She'd become fixated on the disused lookout station that had once been run by the coastguard and manned round the clock. Cuts to their funding had meant they couldn't afford to keep it open so, along with similar stations, it had been closed and fallen into disrepair — but, in her heartbreak, Marina had decided to change that.

Fundraising to restore the building and equip it with the technology required had given her a new sense of purpose and brought her into contact with some amazing people. She'd never thought she could get it off the ground at all until she'd discovered a national charity of coastal watchers who helped to support the station with some apparatus and training. However, the day-to-day staffing was entirely down to a team of around thirty local people who gave up chunks of their time to watch over the seas within sight of the station. They kept an eye on everything within view — be it divers in trouble, a yacht drifting with no engine, a child on an inflatable blown out to sea or walkers cut off by the tide.

She'd finally cleared Nate's debts and, with a legacy from her great-aunt, she'd also managed to pay off the mortgage on the cottage. She worked four days a week at the college these days, and had dropped her private tutoring to give her more time to spend at the lookout station.

Everyone in Porthmellow, and most of all herself, felt it was a fitting tribute to Nate. It had been an emotional day when, surrounded by a crowd of friends and neighbours, she'd unveiled the bronze plaque on the wall of the station that read:

*In memory of Nathan Hudson*
*Forever in our hearts*
*From his loving wife, Marina,*
*and the people of Porthmellow*

11

Despite the lump in her throat, even now, at the reminder of her loss and of the circumstances that led to the re-opening of the station, Marina was proud of what she and the people of Porthmellow had achieved and the difference they had already made to the lives of those they helped. It meant the world to her that she could help prevent another family going through what she had.

Her radio crackled. Gareth's voice was a squeak. 'Jesus. Christ. Ewww!'

'Gareth! Are you OK?'

'No. I'm not. I almost threw up. It's not a body, it's a dead seal and it's all chewed up and rotten and manky. It's tangled up in seaweed and some old clothes and there are *things* crawling all over it. Crabs and sea creatures with far too many legs. And it stinks!'

'But it's *not* a person.'

'No. No, it isn't.'

'Then we should be very, very grateful. That poor seal probably died of natural causes and the body got tangled in the clothes off the container ship that was wrecked in the spring. I'll come and take a look myself once you're back here.'

'I was sure it was a real body.' Gareth sounded mutinous.

'Thankfully not, and let's hope we never have to find one. Come back up. I'll make you a cuppa and we'll talk about it.' She cut off any further protest.

Marina wrote down the incident for the record and ladled an extra spoon of sugar in Gareth's tea. For good measure she spooned some in her own, too. Even though she'd known within half a second that it hadn't been a person washed up in the cove, that moment had been enough to send bad memories flooding back, even after all these years. Today had shown her that the past was always lurking like rocks below the surface of the cove, ready to catch her out when she least expected it.

# 2

'Oh f-f — ' Tiff Trescott bit off an expletive just before the old couple reached her. She was flat on her arse on the cobbles of the quay opposite the Harbour Café. Several people had seen her go over on her ankle and crumple to the floor but the pensioners had reached her first. The other locals, two teenage girls in wetsuits, were too busy laughing themselves silly.

'You all right, my maid?' An elderly man gazed down at her.

'You went a right purler.' A lady with a walking stick reached her, voice full of concern.

The old man offered a gnarled hand to her.

'Thanks, but really, I'm fine,' she said, catching sight of her trolley case which was teetering perilously close to the harbour wall. 'I must rescue my bag before it falls in the water.'

'I'll get it,' said the lady, making off at a surprising speed towards the suitcase

Tiff tried to get up but her ankle protested, shooting a sharp pain up her leg. She let out an audible wince and the smooth soles of her heeled boots struggled to gain purchase on the stones. She groaned inwardly; the last thing she'd wanted was to draw attention to herself but there were now half a dozen people watching the little scenario from the terrace of the nearby pub. Clearly, she was the best entertainment they'd had in months.

The old man's hand was still extended. He

winked at her. 'Come on, before you go arse over tit again, eh?'

Interesting turn of phrase, thought Tiff, finally accepting his help and finding herself surprised at how easily he pulled her to her feet. She felt rainwater seep through her jeans. Oh great, wet knickers as well as a twisted ankle: just what every woman wanted.

Despite feeling slightly shaken, not to mention her sore ankle and damp bum, Tiff put on a brave face. 'Thanks. Very kind of you.'

'No bother, maid. Happy to help a damsel in distress.' He let out a cackle.

Tiff didn't think she'd ever been called a 'damsel' and at thirty-nine, she felt she'd long passed the stage when even the most generous of people would describe her that way, not that she'd ever really been the delicate-lady type.

'Here's your case. None the worse.' The old woman passed her the suitcase.

'Thank you so much. I don't know what I'd have done if it had ended up in the harbour.'

'It'd have gone straight to the bottom, very likely,' her husband chortled.

'But it didn't, Troy,' the lady said in some exasperation. 'So all's well that ends well . . . I couldn't help noticing the label on your bag, my dear. Are you Tiffany Trescott? Marina's Tiffany?'

'Tiff to my friends,' she said, staking her claim early to be known by her new nickname.

'I'm Evie, by the way. I know Marina pretty well. We both do.'

Troy whistled. 'You've been away a long time, maid.'

'I haven't been back too often,' Tiff replied, which was an understatement. She'd only been there a couple of times in a decade.

Her parents had moved away from Cornwall when Tiff was still in nappies, to a large house in Oxfordshire where her father had become a surgeon. Her mother had been a barrister and Tiff had been packed off to school from the age of seven, only coming back to Porthmellow for some of the school holidays.

She had fond memories of the times she'd enjoyed there with Marina. Even though her cousin was a few years younger, she seemed to have more freedom than Tiff did. They'd wandered around the village, the beaches and coastline. Marina had loved to hear about Tiff's shopping and theatre trips to London while Tiff had enjoyed the gossip about the local boys and eyeing up surfers on the beach. She might have kissed one or two, as well . . .

Although she'd only been back to the town twice since childhood, she'd seen Marina from time to time in her London home. Her ex London home. It was only a tiny one bed in an unfashionable suburb, but it had been her haven from the cutthroat world of journalism.

'I've been living in London for a very long time,' she explained.

'Oh dear,' Evie said, as if Tiff had confessed to having been in Wormwood Scrubs.

'Eh. You don't know Foxy Seddon's cousin, do you?' Troy asked. 'She lives in London.'

Evie rolled her eyes. 'Course she doesn't, Troy, there are millions of people there.' She peered at

16

Tiff. 'I do remember you though. You used to stay with Marina's family in the school holidays sometimes, didn't you?'

'Yes, I did.' Tiff maintained the smiley eye thing but braced herself. She'd known a few locals would remember her but she hadn't anticipated meeting a couple who knew her background, and probably every detail of her childhood, within five minutes of arriving in Porthmellow.

'Nice to see you back,' Evie said. 'Is this a holiday?'

Evie was so innocently direct that Tiff couldn't be offended by her question.

'Sort of. I'm here to recharge my batteries and visit Marina.'

'Ah, yes, come to think of it, she did mention you were coming for a break. Well, she'll be glad of the company after that terrible business with Nate.' Evie sighed. 'Anniversary of his disappearance comin' up too . . . I can hardly credit it's nearly seven years.'

'Time certainly flies,' Tiff replied crisply. She couldn't believe it had been so long since Marina's ex had vanished either. Even though Tiff had thought Marina's marriage had been heading for the rocks, her cousin had naturally been devastated when Nate had disappeared, feared drowned.

'I warned him not to take that fishing kayak out, not with a storm brewing up,' Troy said gloomily. 'But he wouldn't listen. He thanked me and smirked; thought I was an old fart probably, but I know these waters like the back of my hand. I work for the Harbour Commission, you know.'

17

'Wow,' said Tiff, picking up her bag again. She suspected Troy was about to relate his life history and she was eager to reach Marina's and relax with a hot bath and a cool glass of wine. She'd warmed to the couple already, but she didn't really remember them and certainly didn't want to reveal too much about herself as she guessed they were lynchpins of the harbour town and knew everyone's business and history. Luckily, Evie unwittingly came to her rescue.

'We have to go, Troy, or we'll miss the arrival of the birthday girl.'

'Girl? Daisy Seddon is eighty-five, Evie!'

'She can still be a girl. We all deserve to be girly from time to time, don't we?' Evie chuckled, sharing the joke with Tiff, who warmed to her all the more.

The chimes of the clock tower rang through the air, and Evie let out a squeak of horror. 'Oh, it's already seven. We'll be late for this birthday party. Come on.'

'Yes, best be off,' Troy agreed. 'Oh, Tiff, are you off up to Coastguard Terrace now?'

'Yes . . . '

'Would you mind taking this up to Dirk 'n' Stormy's for me? It's on your way to Marina's place.'

Tiff wasn't sure she'd heard right. 'Dark 'n' stormy?'

Evie's eyes crinkled in delight. 'Dirk 'n' Stormy, my love. Dirk Meadows, he's the lifeboat mechanic, you see. Don't worry, only post it, if you don't mind.'

'Right . . . ' Tiff didn't see at all. 'OK, I get the

18

Dirk part . . . I presume the 'stormy' is because he's on the lifeboat crew?'

Evie giggled. 'Oh, Lord no. It's because he can be a bit up and down. Tumultuous, you might say.'

'A moody bugger,' Troy put in.

'Oh, go on, Troy, he's not that bad.' Evie smirked. 'He's always more than civil to me and he fixed our car for nothing. Kept cutting out, it did.'

'It was the turbo sensor. The local garage was flummoxed and our son was in Scotland on business or he'd have done it. Dirk stepped in; what he doesn't know about a marine engine you couldn't fit on the back of a stamp,' Troy said, in wonder.

'And there's plenty of women who'd be more than ready to put up with his moods if they could only get close enough. He's a bit of a hunk,' Evie added mischievously.

'He needs a shave more often. Scruffy bugger,' Troy said, with a raucous cackle that echoed around the harbour.

'He lives two doors down from Marina's place at number nine. It's a little white cottage near the end of the row,' Evie said. 'So if you wouldn't mind putting it through his door, it would save us hauling our ancient bones back up there. It's a pack of flyers for the fundraising day we're holding in aid of the lifeboats and the Wave Watchers.'

'The Wave Watchers? You mean the volunteer group who run the coastal lookout station?' Tiff said.

19

'Yes, Marina's lot,' Evie replied.

'Of course I'll deliver them,' said Tiff, figuring that by posting a few leaflets, she could help out Marina and get herself down in everyone's good books as a nice, helpful person.

'Grand. Mind you, go easy in those high heels. It's steep and slippery.' Troy grimaced at Tiff's boots as if they were glass slippers.

Tiff hesitated then smiled. She wanted to fit in, and anyway, she instinctively liked Evie and even Troy had a weird kind of rustic charm. 'I'll be extra careful.'

'Thanks, you're a star. See you around very soon, then.'

Off they went, leaving Tiff gingerly making her way up some steep steps to the top of the town. Her boots were wet through and the soles were as good as ice skates on the cobbles. She made a mental note to buy something more practical as soon as possible — not only because she'd break an ankle if she didn't, but also to make herself more unobtrusive.

The suede boots, a well-loved sample from a shoe designer, were a vestige of the old Tiffany, one she couldn't quite bear to part with, but she might have to resort to trainers or flipflops from now on. Or, God forbid, *Crocs*. The idea sent a shiver of delighted horror through her. She shuddered at the thought of herself in chunky rubber clogs. She wasn't sure she could go that far.

Puffing like a steam train, she dragged herself and her case up the steps between the houses, finally emerging on a lane high above Porthmellow. She paused to get her breath; no amount of skipping up and down the stairs in the Tube could have prepared her for the lung-busting climb from harbour to top — and no amount of imagination on the train here could have prepared her for the view spread out below her.

It was picture-book perfect, and luckily for her the rain was clearing away to the west. The harbour was unusual, with two square basins — an inner and an outer. Three of its sides were lined with pastel-coloured cottages, gift shops and eateries.

The cobbles glistened in the shafts of sunlight, and the cries of seagulls, and halyards clanking on the masts of fishing boats and yachts were clear even from her lofty viewpoint. Beyond the harbour entrance, whitecaps danced on the sea. No wonder Marina loved this place.

Tiff hadn't expected to be so transfixed. Down below, she'd felt pissed off and tired by her journey, irritated by her inappropriate footwear, and disgruntled at having to be in Porthmellow at all.

The climb to the top had probably boosted her serotonin levels and — ha — given her a fresh perspective. Beyond the houses tumbling to the steep sides, the rest of the Penwith peninsula stretched out to Cornwall's far west, blurring in a blue haze of sea and sky. Wait a minute . . . She pulled her polarising sunglasses from her bag. There was a white shedlike structure perched on the top of the cliff about half a mile away towards the east.

Was that Marina's lookout station — where she and the other 'Wave Watchers' hung out? At

21

the thought of why Marina had re-opened the station, Tiff told herself to grow a pair. No matter what had happened to Tiff herself, Marina had endured far worse and was still going through the mill because Nate had never been found. He was dead, of course, Tiff thought grimly, but what a horrendous thing to have to face up to. Tiff wasn't sure she could have handled any of it.

The realisation made her all the more determined not to be an added burden on Marina. She'd make herself useful, try to be cheerful company and then leave her cousin in peace once the heat had died down in London. As it would, she was certain . . . then she could find a new job on a decent newspaper and get on with her life.

With her breath almost back to normal, she bumped her case onto Coastguard Terrace and wheeled it to the end, looking for number nine. A third of them didn't seem to have numbers, preferring unfathomable names like 'Chy an Mor' and 'Kerensa'. And, to further complicate things, several of the cottages could be described as 'white', the shades ranging from mucky dishrag to celeb tooth. Some even had numbers: a fourteen, an eleven with a ten next to it, which totally defeated all logic of odd and even being on opposite sides. In the middle of the numbered cottages was a pallid dwelling with a wonky sign that read 'Sod Hall'.

How hilarious, thought Tiff, regretting her agreement to be a good Samaritan. She could, of course, always post the envelope in a post box, with 'Dirk 'n' Stormy, Porthmellow' on it, though it wasn't stamped which meant Dirk would have to drive miles to the sorting office and pay extra postage.

The idea of riling the mythical beast of Porthmellow made her smile and brought a satisfying image into her mind. She pictured Dirk: craggy, with days of stubble, in greasy overalls, a wrench or some other tool of choice in his hand.

He sounded like a kind of pound-shop Heathcliff . . . and she had no idea where his lair was.

'Ah.'

She'd already wheeled her case a few metres when she spotted it. The cottage was almost at the end of a row, but on the 'wrong' side of the street for the odd numbers, and calling it white was pushing it. Tiff would have described it as grey-ish, like a storm cloud, and, judging by the oily pong, it had been very recently re-painted.

There was no number but that didn't surprise her as it had probably been removed while the masonry had been rerendered. However, a number nine had been daubed on the wheelie bin along with a peeling Lifeboat sticker. Tiff didn't need to have been a top newshound to sniff out that this was Dirk 'n' Stormy's lair.

She deposited her bag on the gravelled strip of front 'garden' and took out the envelope before climbing up the stone doorstep. Now, if only she could locate a letterbox . . . or any orifice in which to deposit the envelope and accomplish her mission.

OK. She could accept that Porthmellow didn't

have any logical sequence to its house numbers, but no letterbox? What was this? Some kind of initiation test that incomers had to pass before they could be allowed into the local pasty shop?

'Oh, for f —'

The door was wrenched open, taking her by such surprise that she almost fell backwards. Classical music drifted out of the hallway; the 'Flower Duet' from *Lakme*, sweet and lilting — quite the opposite of the face that glared down at her.

'Can I help you?' it growled.

A figure filled the doorway, his dark hair almost brushing the lintel. It was clear he wasn't her man because instead of mechanic's overalls, he wore black tux trousers and a white dress shirt which was gaping open to reveal a tanned chest, sprinkled with dark hair . . . and, good God, one nipple was pierced by a discreet silver ring. In one hand he was clutching a black silk bow tie, the real kind that comes undone under eager fingers.

'Yes?' he said, his brow furrowing as Tiff teetered on his doorstep, clutching the manila envelope to her chest.

'I'm looking for Dark. I mean Dirk. *Mr* Meadows,' she said firmly.

His indigo eyes took her in with one sweeping glance. 'Good for you but if it's double glazing, I've got triple, if it's loft insulation, I'm warm enough. If you want to convert me, you'd have better luck with Satan.'

'In that case,' she said, deciding she'd definitely keep hold of the letter, 'I clearly have

24

the wrong house. Sorry to have disturbed you.'

'You *have* disturbed me.' The voice was a bit growly but definitely not Cornish, more RP.

'Well, I'm sorry, but it was a genuine mistake. I'll leave you to . . . ' Tiff took the opportunity to give him a head to toe stare, as he'd been so ungracious. 'Do whatever it is you're doing.'

'That's exactly the problem. I wasn't doing it. I can't do it.' He waggled the bow tie in front of him, obviously agitated. 'I can't get this bloody thing to work, you know, tie up. Got so hot doing it that I unbuttoned my shirt.'

'No. They can be tricky. If you're not used to wearing black tie,' she added wickedly.

'I think it's fairly obvious I'm not. This get-up is hired.'

She raised her eyebrows dramatically. 'Wow. I'd never have guessed.'

Was that a bead of perspiration glistening among his chest hair and the evening sun glinting off his nipple ring? While annoyed by his rudeness, she was irritated by her reaction to him even more. Since when had she been so easily thrown off kilter by a handsome face? She'd met better-looking men in her former life, though never one who seemed so little aware of it.

'Well, good luck with it. Thanks for your time.' Reluctantly, she tore her eyes from his impressive torso and turned away, still holding the envelope. 'I was hoping to deliver this envelope to Mr Meadows, but it looks like I'll have to drop it in the nearest post box, which is a shame because I don't have any stamps — '

'Wait a minute!' he called after her. 'What's your business with this Dirk Meadows?'

Ouch, that was direct, she thought, but then, she was used to people being 'direct'. Unless someone was chasing her down their drive, screaming expletives, she was rarely intimidated.

'I'm afraid I can't tell you that,' she said sweetly. 'It's personal.'

'In that case, you really had better come in.' He pushed a lock of hair out of his eyes. 'Actually, *I'm* Dirk Meadows.'

Tiff raised an eyebrow. 'Are you sure?'

'Of course I'm sure.'

'Then why didn't you say so right away?'

'Because I thought you were trying to sell me something or make me see the light.'

'As you said yourself, I don't think there's much chance of that,' Tiff replied tartly.

To her surprise he gave a wry smile that suited him very well. 'Apologies. I probably was a bit brusque but I'm late for a function due to this bloody thing.' He waggled the bow tie again.

His voice had softened, still craggy but not as rough. Tiff hesitated half a second, deciding whether she wanted to be caught or not. She was a little late herself but Marina wouldn't mind and, besides, there was something about Dirk 'n' Stormy that was bugging her — beyond the fact he was six feet four of brooding hotness. His comment about not needing loft insulation had been hilariously accurate.

'Um . . .'

She stopped, hovering between tottering off and turning around. 'Yes?'

26

'Um. You, er . . . look like the kind of person who knows a thing or two about, er . . . clothes.'

'What are you trying to say?'

'That you seem to be well, um — turned out — and, er . . . ' He stepped down into the street in his bare feet, the bow tie thrust out, a plea in his voice. 'Would you mind tying this damn thing for me?'

Tiff burst out laughing.

'Please?' he added. He held out his arm in mock gallantry, and Tiff swept past him into his sitting room.

The cottage was decidedly not a lair. Simple furniture, mostly scrubbed pine or light oak, an eclectic mix of old and contemporary or re-purposed. In seconds she'd absorbed his possessions and tastes, used to forming an opinion very quickly on what people's homes said about their penchants and character . . . or what they wanted you to *think* about their taste and character. The place was neat and tidy, with quite a few prints of Porthmellow and the sea hung on the white-washed wonky walls. In fact, the only thing out of place was a pair of black socks abandoned on the coffee table among a stack of magazines about classical music and, unsurprisingly, marine mechanics.

'Actually, an elderly gentleman called Troy asked me to give you this.' She handed him the bulging envelope. 'Something to do with the fundraiser day,' she added. 'I'm on my way to visit my cousin and I was going past. He and his wife said it would save them walking up here.'

He took the envelope. 'Troy and Evie know

everyone in this town. Not much gets past them.' He put it on a dresser by the door. 'Thanks.'

Maybe she'd lingered a fraction too long on his sitting room. He had the ghost of a smile on his lips by the time she finally spoke again.

'Would you still like me to . . . ?' Tiff nodded at the bow tie.

'Yes, if you wouldn't mind.' He handed it to her, brushing her fingers fleetingly. He had nice hands and nails for a mechanic, she thought. Big hands but clean, short nails and instead of engine oil he smelled of a subtle woody cologne that, if she wasn't mistaken, might even be Creed.

'I'd better button up my shirt first,' he said.

'Probably a good idea.' She nodded, willing herself to stay cool as those impressive pecs and nipple ring mercifully vanished from sight under the snowy cotton. He fastened the top button and took the tie from her, threading the silk under his collar but leaving the points sticking up.

Tiff wasn't short herself — at five feet seven she considered herself on the tall side of average — but she had to reach up to tie the bow tie. She'd done many of them, for student mates, colleagues, boyfriends — and Warner of course. The last one she'd tied had been on New Year's Eve before they'd both set off for a big political bash. She'd been so happy, so in love — and so naive to ever have believed that he might have felt the same way.

'Are you OK?' he asked, a flicker of concern in his eyes — or was she imagining it?

28

'Yes. Yes, of course.' She recovered herself and leaned closer to his neck, feeling his warm and minty breath against her cheek. Luckily the tie was long enough, and she secured it first time.

'It's a lot easier if you think of it as tying your shoelaces, rather than an actual tie,' she said, tweaking the ends of the bow until it was as good as she was going to get it. It wouldn't have done to spend too much time in such close proximity to him and it was with relief that she was able to take a couple of steps back.

'There you go. Do you want to check it in the mirror?'

'I trust you.'

She took a moment to study his face, now an unexpected truce had been called between them. It was as tanned as you'd expect, with lines enough to reflect his outdoor lifestyle and perhaps a fair bit of frowning. When he'd shoved the lock of hair out of the way, he'd revealed grey at his temples, though his hair was still thick and espresso dark.

Unexpectedly, her ex, Warner intruded into her mind. She'd felt an instant pull of physical attraction to him when they'd first met, too, although perhaps not as powerful as the one she felt for this stranger. Tiff thought she could be in trouble here, if she allowed herself . . . but she wasn't going to do that, again, ever. Letting down her guard was what had got her into trouble in the first place and lost her her job, her home and her reputation.

Letting down her guard was why she was in Porthmellow *now*, in Dirk's sitting room, on the way to throw herself on the mercy of her cousin.

'I'd better let you get to the ball, Cinderella,' she said, moving away from him.

Dirk let out a laugh. 'It's no ball. It's a fundraising gala dinner for the lifeboats. A necessary evil.'

'Oh, come on, it can't be that bad.'

'It depends on whether you like these sorts of things. I expect you'd be in your element at one.'

She frowned. 'What makes you say that?'

'You've obviously been to a lot of black-tie dos.'

'As a matter of fact, I've been to way more than my share but that doesn't mean I enjoy them,' she shot back. Not any more, thought Tiff. In fact, she hadn't been to a smart do for a while and never wanted to again, but perhaps if she went to one with Dirk, she might change her mind . . . Immediately, she reminded herself again that post-Warner she should steer clear of any event that involved the company of charming, handsome men. Not that Dirk was charming, but he was dangerously handsome.

'I can't stand them myself.'

'Come on, you might surprise yourself by enjoying the evening,' she murmured, unhappy associations cooling her desire to banter with Dirk. She was suddenly weary after her journey and eager to be gone.

'I doubt it . . . and I must leave now or I really won't make the dinner.' He was brisk again; the temperature had dropped by several degrees on his side too. 'Thanks for tying this,' he added. Tiff took the hint, and was half relieved, half disappointed at his coldness. They'd been almost

30

flirting but the storm clouds had come back over for some reason.

'No problem,' she said, deliberately choosing a neutral reply instead of, 'A pleasure.'

He showed her out and shut the door with no further words of thanks, and certainly not with a 'see you around', which was odd when he knew she'd be staying nearby.

On the rest of the short walk to Marina's house, Dirk filled her mind as her suitcase rattled over the stony pavement. She had a good memory for faces and names, honed by twenty years as a reporter and journalist on various regional and London papers and magazines. Even as she'd grown older, she still had the ability to search through her mental filing cabinet when a story or a person triggered a spark of recognition. Often a face would jog a feeling, an emotion, more than an instant name to go with it. She'd picture the person in a situation; tragic, comic, joyous or dramatic . . . how she had felt when she'd seen that face and heard or read their story.

Dirk was definitely sending out tragic and dramatic vibes and they had nothing to do with his amusing nickname. Tiff was convinced she'd seen him before but couldn't for the life of her think where.

# 3

'Woohoo. Muscadet. That's a blast from the past.' Tiff thrust out her glass as Marina produced a slender bottle sheened in condensation.

'It goes very nicely with the hake I bought from the harbour fish kiosk,' Marina said, amusement tingeing her voice as she poured Tiff a glass. She'd told Tiff she was ready for some wine herself after her experience with the 'body' earlier that day at the cove.

Tiff savoured the crisp, lemony Muscadet before swallowing it. 'And it's very nice. You're spoiling me.'

'Yeah. You look like you feel guilty,' Marina replied, pouring a glass for herself. 'I'll put the oven on. I got the hake ready earlier. I wrapped it in pancetta . . . I hope you like it?'

'I love it. Now, you really *are* spoiling me. It's lovely of you but I don't expect special treatment.'

'Good because you won't get it. I thought you might be ready for a treat after the journey. I'm going to pop it in the oven with the potatoes.'

Refusing any help, Marina scooted into the kitchen, leaving Tiff alone in the sitting room. She curled up on the sofa, admiring the quirks of the cottage. Nothing was straight; not the thick walls, the floorboards or even the windowpanes. Marina had told her before that it was very old, having been an ale house and a smuggler's haunt

— then again, wasn't every old cottage in Cornwall?

Marina and Nate had bought it a year or so after they were married. Tiff had been there only once in the past seven years, while Marina had visited her in London a few times.

They'd kept in touch regularly by phone, however, and when Tiff had lost her job that horrible day in January, the first person she'd thought to call had been her cousin. Marina was someone she could trust to listen without judging her, while also being unafraid to be honest with her in the purest sense of the word.

Tiff's memories of Porthmellow were among the happiest of her life, although she'd never imagined she might actually live here. Her mother and Marina's father were siblings, and both had been brought up in Cornwall.

She and Marina shared a love of words: after leaving university, Tiff had got a place at a newspaper training scheme and worked her way up to features editor of the *Herald*, and Marina had worked hard to get her PGCE and was now an English lecturer at a local HE college. But that was where the resemblance ended. Although they were cousins, they could hardly have looked more different.

Marina took after their maternal grandmother and wasn't much above five feet, with blonde curly hair she usually wore in a ponytail, especially when she was 'on duty' in her Wave Watchers 'uniform' of trousers and sweatshirt.

Tiff's DNA was dominated by her father's side of the family. She was five feet seven in her stockinged feet, willowy, if she said so herself, with hair that her mother insisted on calling 'Titian' but Tiff regarded as simply 'ginger'. Sometimes she spiced it up with a vibrant red or aubergine colour, to annoy her mother even more, and she kept it in a sharp bob. Although that would probably change now she was in Cornwall. She certainly couldn't afford her favourite stylist at her London salon and she wasn't sure she'd ever be brave enough to set foot in the Harbour Cutz place she'd passed earlier.

As for their personalities, it would be too simplistic to say that Tiff was the savvy, hard-as-nails cousin and that Marina was soft and homely. It was true that Marina was innately kind, always putting other people first — to the detriment of her own wellbeing, in Tiff's opinion — but Marina was no doormat and was straight talking and firm when she had to be. She'd been the first to offer Tiff a home for the summer while Tiff licked her wounds, and had put her in touch with the editor of the local lifestyle magazine.

Marina was a lovely character but she did care so very much about people. She tended to give them the benefit of the doubt, while Tiff's first instinct was to naturally suspect and question others' motives.

Tiff had always thought that Nate had taken advantage of Marina's good nature, but Marina had been besotted with her handsome husband and wouldn't hear a word against him. When Tiff visited, try as she might, she hadn't warmed to him. He'd sneered at Marina's enthusiasm for her students and community life and made snide remarks about her appearance, which he'd passed off as 'banter'.

Privately, Tiff had longed to tell him what she really thought of him, though she'd tried to be civil for her cousin's sake. From the looks Nate had given her when he didn't think she or Marina were looking, she knew their distrust was mutual. He knew that she'd seen through his larky 'wit' and that under the tan, the earring and the whole piratical charm crap was a lying git. He was no Jack Sparrow, that was for sure, and one evening, Tiff had seen him round the back of the pub, kissing another woman.

On the train back to London, she'd agonised over whether to tell Marina. She'd still been wondering whether to reveal it when the news came through that Nate's kayak had been found washed up on some rocks at the foot of Silver Cove.

Tiff had dropped everything to come down to try and comfort Marina, and had even told her boss to feck off when they'd wanted her to do a story on the tragedy — which had probably done her no favours, though she didn't care. She'd stayed for a week, helping to support Marina and the family while shielding her from the press as best she could. How ironic . . .

She couldn't stay forever though, although she kept in touch, and Nate's body had never been found. Tiff had moved on, and so had Marina. It was hard to believe that the seven-year anniversary of his death was coming up in the summer, and with it, the time when he could officially be declared dead. At least, that would bring financial and legal closure for her cousin, and perhaps be the final piece of the jigsaw in her emotional recovery.

Marina returned from the kitchen, the aroma of herbs and garlic wafting in from the open door.

Even though Tiff and Marina hadn't spent much time together since leaving school, they soon settled into the easy familiarity they'd enjoyed as children and teenagers. Tiff found herself unwinding while she asked how her aunt and uncle — Marina's parents — were getting on. They now lived and worked in north-east Cornwall so Marina didn't see them as often as she liked.

It was therapeutic to focus on other people's relatively normal lives and Tiff enjoyed hearing about Marina's college job, the Wave Watchers and local characters. She was intrigued to find out more about the forthcoming joint search and rescue fundraiser with the local lifeboat station, though she didn't discover much more about Dirk. She didn't want to appear too interested in him and risk being teased by Marina. They soon moved on to Tiff's new job.

'It'll be a change working for the local mags,' Marina said, sounding positive as ever.

'They pay peanuts but I'm grateful for it, and with the rent coming in from my flat, it'll cover the bills. I obviously intend to contribute my fair share here.'

Tiff smiled, feeling a little guilty keeping a couple of titbits from Marina. One of them was that she guessed Marina would find the additional income of a 'lodger' useful, even if it was only short-term.

Her other secret was less altruistic. One of the editors at the *Herald*'s rival paper had agreed to help her out on the quiet. Tiff planned to string stories for them while she was in Cornwall. Her name might be mud but she could still pass on tip-offs if she found anything of interest in the area. And that, along with writing and editing the local lifestyle mag, would be better than nothing and keep her from going insane.

'What exactly happened, Tiff?' Marina said gently. 'It must have been pretty dramatic for you to have been sacked. I know you didn't want to go into the details until we were face to face, but maybe it would help if you got it off your chest. After all, you know all my darkest secrets.'

Tiff was touched. She didn't have a best friend in London with whom to share her 'darkest secrets'. She had colleagues and contacts, and rivals — and a lover. Now an ex-lover, who she'd naively thought had become so much more.

'We were going to move in together . . . ' The words slipped out as an extension of her train of thought.

'You and this politician?'

'He wasn't a politician himself, just an 'adviser' to a Cabinet minister. He even joked about being a lackey. That's what I liked about Warner: his refreshing lack of ego, his selfdeprecation, unusual from someone in his position, I can tell you. Now I know that it was all an act. He's a massive dick like all the rest of them in

37

that place: women and men.'

Marina frowned. 'I'm sorry you've had a rough time. What happened, lovely?'

'Marius Woodford-Warner happened. Though he's known as 'Warner' by his friends — or fellow snakes, to be more accurate.' A memory of some of the snakes sprang to mind. She pictured Warner playing for the House of Commons staff cricket team with a bunch of the other lackeys, most of whom she couldn't stand. She now regretted every wasted Sunday admiring him in his whites while trying not to nod off and eating curling cucumber sarnies in the pavilion. Most of all, she regretted falling for him so hard that she'd been blind to the real truth; that he'd only been using her.

'Are they all snakes?' Marina asked. 'Aren't some of them trying to do the right thing?'

Tiff admired Marina's ability to think well of others. She'd been like that once: believing too much in people. These days she didn't trust anyone within a five-mile radius of Westminster. 'A lot of them start out *trying* to do the right thing. Plenty end up actually doing it, until they decide to climb the slippery pole to high office. It's fine and dandy to have principles until you have to actually make a choice between country or party or career and then integrity almost always goes out of the window.'

'You don't usually write about politics, Tiff — I thought you were interested in human-interest stories and women's page stuff. How did you get involved in this?'

'I was tempted by a story. I thought I'd got a

38

big scoop about Warner's boss. We had a codename for him. Mr Blobby — I think you can tell who I mean . . . '

Marina wrinkled her nose. 'I do and you're right. I wouldn't trust him as far as I could throw him either.'

'Neither did Warner. He said he secretly loathed him too, but it was all a ruse to get back at our newspaper for trying to expose his boss's dark dealings with a big rail developer.

'Warner handed me a scoop and I walked right into the trap. He claimed that Mr Blobby was taking backhanders from the rail company in return for big government contracts and said we could expose him together. What he — and Mr Blobby — *actually* wanted to do was discredit my newspaper in the most public way possible.'

Marina gasped. 'Are you saying he got close to you with this in mind, all along? I assumed it was all going well between you right up until your break-up.'

'I — I'd like to think there was something real between us at the start, though perhaps I'm deluding myself. I'd known him a few years and we started seeing each other — casually at first — the year before last. Then he got a promotion and was busier and busier. I just thought he was working longer hours but, with hindsight, he did seem to grow more distant. The more I look back, the more I know I was taken in by him but didn't want to recognise the truth: that he'd begun to see me as someone he could use, like everyone else around him.'

Tiff paused, refusing to give in to self-pity, or

worse, tears. She would *not* shed tears. Not in front of Marina, who had far worse things to deal with. 'Silly old cow,' she added lightly, wincing at her own naivety.

That was the worst of it. Tiff, the savvy and unshakable smartest cookie in town had been conned. She was ashamed to have been duped, and deeply hurt. Worse, the experience had left her insecure and betrayed.

'I'm gutted for you, hun. Anyway, you're not old,' Marina said, jumping to her defence. Tiff could see her cousin was genuinely worried about her.

'Well, I bloody feel it!' Tiff laughed. She was only a few years older than her cousin but, despite Marina's recent troubles, she still had a young, almost cherubic face at thirty-six. Her blonde curls were tied back in a messy ponytail, and she wore hardly any make-up, not that she needed it with the almost year-round golden tan from a life spent outdoors. Tiff had an armoury of expensive cosmetics, many of them free samples, and she'd needed them lately just to look human.

She thought again how lucky Nate had been to have a loving partner like Marina. Despite her own problems, Marina was still happy to provide a haven for Tiff and a sympathetic ear.

'So, what did Warner do that landed you in so much trouble?' Marina asked.

Tiff sighed. 'He showed me a 'smoking gun' of emails between Mr Blobby and the rail company, 'proving' they were offering him bribes. I was convinced they were genuine, so we published the story.' Her voice tailed off and she cringed at the mistakes she'd made in trusting her ex.

'It turned out they were fake and Mr Blobby threatened to sue the newspaper. We had to grovel and print a retraction and they agreed not to go to court if we made a large donation to his charity of choice — and if I was sacked. In the end, the editor let me resign. He said it would make it difficult to run stories about Blobby from then on unless we were absolutely water-tight. No one at the major London newspapers will touch me for now, possibly forever.'

Marina's eyes widened in shock. 'Surely not forever? You must have friends you can trust who would bail you out.'

She shook her head. 'I have colleagues, contacts, acquaintances — but no one I absolutely trust, or who can be seen helping a pariah. No one will employ me for a long while, that's for sure. I don't know . . . No one feels sorry for journalists. It goes with the job.' She'd been so busy working and networking that making and keeping real friends had somehow been lost along the way.

'I feel deeply sorry for the way you've been treated by this vile bunch of people. And I'm angry too, my lovely.'

Marina's sympathy touched a raw nerve, and Tiff smiled gratefully. 'I should have known better, and it could be even worse. At least I do have a job — of sorts — now.'

'Working for *Cream of Cornish* won't be that bad,' Marina said.

'You're right. I'm lucky they let me freelance

for them at all. Thanks for asking your friend to take a chance on me.'

'She was pretty gobsmacked when I told her you were coming down here for the summer and looking for work. She didn't think she could afford you.'

Tiff laughed. 'I'm happy to take the going freelance rate.'

'I think she's a little bit scared of you.'

'*Moi*? Why on earth? I'm harmless!' Tiff sniffed the air.

'Wow, that smells amazing.'

'Oh, yes. It'll be done!' Marina leapt up.

Tiff got up too. 'I'm coming to help you serve it up and I'm doing the washing up.'

They sat around the small table in the dining area at the end of the sitting room. It overlooked a small patch of garden from where there was an uninterrupted view of the sea. However, on this cool late April evening, which would probably be warm enough for drinks at a pavement café in central London, the wind was cold and biting. Marina said she'd light a fire after dinner, but for the time being, they sat at the table, enjoying the pancetta-wrapped hake, which was topped with a spicy tomato sauce and served with new potatoes and samphire.

Tiff helped herself to a spoonful of samphire dressed with lemony butter.

'Wow. Samphire. Is it from a local fishmonger?'

'Actually, I got it from the bar on the other side of the town.'

'The *bar*?'

Marina smiled. 'Loe Bar. It grows at the back of the beach. And the potatoes and fish are local too.'

Tiff sighed in pleasure as the hake melted in her mouth. 'I can see it's not as uncivilised here as I thought . . . ' she said during bites.

Marina laughed.

'On that note, I met some of the local characters on my way here.'

'Already?'

'Yes, Troy and Evie, who I vaguely remember from some of my holiday visits. She was a local teacher, wasn't she?'

'Mm. Mrs Carman. Been retired for years though.'

'Nice lady. Funny too. Her husband asked me to deliver some leaflets for a friend. They hardly know me but they took it on trust that if I was a relative of you then I must be OK.'

'You can relax here, Tiff. You can rely on people.'

She smiled. 'We had some good times here, didn't we? It'll be fun to revisit them,' Tiff said.

'What, ogling surfers? Perhaps I should be more discreet these days.'

The Muscadet seeped further into Tiff's veins. She waggled her glass. 'Remember the time I got you drunk on cider at that beach party and had to half carry you home. Your mum and dad were furious.'

'I was only sixteen!' Marina laughed.

'I've always been notorious. I bet people are gossiping about me already. I'm probably already known as the snooty Londoner who wore stupid shoes and fell over on the harbour.'

Marina nodded and grinned. 'Some people might remember you but I doubt very much they will have any inkling about why you lost your job. Soon, you'll melt into the background and be no more interesting than fishing quotas. Although, saying that, they're quite a big issue here . . . hmm . . . you know what I mean.' Marina topped up her glass with the dregs of the bottle. 'Unless, of course, you're going to give them something juicy to talk about?'

'No way.' Tiff wagged her finger. 'I'll keep my head down and live a blameless life henceforth. Write about the opening of the new dental surgery, extol the virtues of seaweed body wraps and eulogise about the local eateries, even if the food is crap.'

'Actually, Gabe Mathias's new place is pretty amazing.'

'Is it now?' She raised her eyebrows in interest. 'I had heard he left London to run a little place down here . . . Hmm. I must try it out some-time.'

'He lives just up the road in Clifftop House,' Marina said. 'But don't get any ideas. He's engaged to a mate of mine, Sam Lovell, and while there was a story in that once, it's all in the past now. They've gone through enough without someone raking up muck about their private lives.' Wow, the warning in Marina's voice was real.

'I wouldn't dream of muckraking.'

'Good. Stick to the dentists and body wraps.'

'I won't be digging up dirt on your friends and

neighbours, I swear! I want to be useful, you know, integrate closely with the local community.' Tiff tried to cross her heart. 'Anyway, I already have made myself useful. Those leaflets for Troy and Evie Carman that I mentioned, I gave them to one of your neighbours on my way here.'

'Really?'

'Some lifeboat person called Dirk 'n' Stormy.'

'Dirk?' Marina sounded surprised.

'Mmm. Quite a character . . .'

The image of Dirk leaning in his doorway with his bare torso on show threw her off kilter and wine sloshed onto her linen top, wetting her bra. 'Damn.'

Marina threw her a tea towel and Tiff dabbed at her top.

Marina smirked. 'You know, if you really want to integrate and help the community, I have the perfect solution.'

'Really?'

'Yes. You could help out at the fundraising day on the harbour. All the money will be split jointly between the lifeboats and the Wave Watchers. There should be quite a few visitors because it's May bank holiday weekend.'

'OK,' Tiff said, slightly regretting her offer. 'What kind of help?'

'Running the tombola, selling raffle tickets, fetching and carrying, publicity . . . a woman with your skills could be very useful and we need all the money we can get to keep the station going.'

Tiff envisioned herself standing behind a table

full of cheap plonk and out-of-date chocs but hid her dismay with a wobbly salute. 'Aye aye, Cap'n.'

'And,' said Marina, picking up Tiff's empty plate, 'Dirk will be at the fundraising day, if you need an added incentive.'

'Really? I'm not interested, obviously.' She pretended to inspect her nails before giving Marina a wry smile. 'Once upon a time I would have been but not at the moment. I feel . . . a tad battered and bruised, if you know what I mean.'

'I do. Even though it's been years, there's been no one since Nate. It's been hard to let go.'

'I'm sorry, my love.' Tiff squeezed Marina's shoulder. It was so much easier to turn the attention away from herself and pretend Marina needed the comfort way more than she did. 'But what about the lovely Dirk? How can you resist him?'

Marina laughed. 'Very easily. We've been friends for a very long time and he's showed no interest in anything more in all the time I've known him.'

'Hmm. That's not a definite 'no' then.' Tiff searched Marina's face for a hint that she was hiding a secret crush on her hunky neighbour.

'It's a definite 'not likely'.'

After ushering Marina out of her own kitchen, Tiff loaded the dishwasher and cleared away the other pots and pans. Dirk was etched on her mind and, pre-Warner, she might not have been backward in coming forward — but she really meant what she said about being battered. Dirk was hardly the man to soothe her. She had a

46

feeling he would be . . . challenging.

She would try to 'integrate' with the community, but as for integrating closely with Dirk 'n' Stormy? Judging by the terse reception she'd received, it was more likely that Elvis would turn up in Porthmellow singing with the town band on a Sunday night.

# 4

'So, this is the marine radar and the automatic ship identification system. We have radios to communicate with vessels and call the coast-guard. And, of course, we have these.'

Marina had been surprised and delighted when Tiff had accepted her offer for a tour of the lookout station. She showed Tiff the high-powered fixed binoculars that they used in addition to their portable sets and how to fill in the shipping and incident log, along with the procedure for reporting possible emergencies.

Tiff had listened intently, asking pertinent questions. 'Can I try those huge binoculars?'

'Of course.' Marina helped her adjust the focus. 'Can you see anything yet?'

'Can I see *anything*? Bloody hell. These are amazing. You could see a pimple on someone's arse with them. They're better than a long-range lens.'

Marina rolled her eyes. 'Hey, don't get any ideas.'

Tiff pulled her head away from the twin eyepieces. 'I won't.' She added, sombrely, 'Wow. The responsibility. Not sure I can handle it. Get something wrong and you could kill someone.'

'Not *kill*. Not unless you ignored a Mayday from a vessel that couldn't get hold of the coastguard or some obvious sign, like a lilo drifting out to sea or a windsurfer in trouble.'

'That still sounds like a big responsibility.'

'It is, but you learn not to miss anything. It's amazing what you can train yourself to notice, if you're looking hard enough in the right places. Remember, there was no one here for years before we re-opened the station so anything is an improvement.'

Tiff slid her a sympathetic glance. 'It's wonderful that you got the place back open. I'm sorry I haven't been here before. Now I'm here in the flesh, I can understand exactly why you wanted to do this in Nate's memory.'

'It wasn't only for him. If I — we — can save even one person by being here, then it'll be worth every minute I've spent begging for money to keep it open or sitting in here in hail, rain or shine.' She broke off, almost breathless at the intensity of her statement.

Tiff smiled ruefully. 'I knew it meant a lot to you but I've only realised how much now I'm actually here, seeing you in this place, hearing how you feel. I don't think I've ever seen you as passionate about anything. You're different, you know,' Tiff went on.

'What do you mean?'

'I probably shouldn't say this but . . .'

Marina laughed. 'You never normally hesitate to say what you think.'

'I know you adored Nate and were devastated when he disappeared, but I see a new Marina here before me. It's as if, and forgive me for saying this, my lovely, you have emerged from his shadow and into the sun yourself.'

Marina hid her intake of breath.

49

'You're not offended, are you?' Tiff said.

'N-no . . . not offended. You think so, really?'

'Yes, I do. I'm not saying that losing Nate wasn't a terrible thing, the worst thing anyone could have to face, but now you've blossomed despite that awful event. You have bloomed from the ashes, my lovely, into this strong woman who knows what she wants and gets things done. Yet you're still the kind, compassionate cousin I always knew.'

'Stop it, Tiff. I'm not some kind of Mother Teresa.' Marina felt tears sting her eyes.

'Don't worry, I know you're no saint.' She laughed. 'But I do think it's time that this new Marina should — and you can tell me to mind my own business . . . ' There was a guarded humour in Tiff's tone.

'Not that it would make a scrap of difference.' Marina laughed.

'Yeah. What I'm trying to say is . . . well, isn't it time that you thought about *you*?'

'You mean I should start dating again?'

'Not necessarily a relationship. Just someone to have fun with — and maybe hot sex.'

Marina gasped. 'Like who? I know almost every guy in Porthmellow and I'm not interested in any of them.'

'Is there no one who's even tickled your fancy in the past few years? What about some of the Wave Watchers?'

Marina snorted. 'The men are either pensioners, students or gay. Ew, I love most of them to bits as fellow volunteers but I can't imagine dating any of them.'

50

'Have you ever tried to get back out there again beyond Porthmellow? What about the Internet or Tinder?'

'I've been fixed up with guys by well-meaning friends at dinner parties a few times. I tried a dating site once but after one meet-up where the guy turned out to be a trawlerman with halitosis and a secret life as a druid, I gave up.'

'A druid with halitosis? Oh my God!' Tiff dissolved into laughter, then became more serious. 'If it's loyalty to Nate holding you back, you've more than honoured his memory. You deserve to be happy,' she said. 'Again, I mean,' she added hastily, as if Marina might assume she meant she wasn't with Nate.

Marina remembered the vow she'd made after Nate had first vanished.

*I'll never stop loving you . . .*

She'd held fast to that, but it didn't stop her craving love again, did it?

'I'll admit, it's been hard not to feel disloyal to Nate . . . but if I met someone special, I'd give them a chance.'

'Really?'

'I mean it, but I *haven't* met someone yet,' she said, although Tiff had made her look at her life in a new way. By sheer force of will, she'd ignored the pain, conquered her grief and raised the money to re-open the station. Tiff might be right, although Marina hadn't thought about her life after Nate in this way before.

Someone had once told her that there was always a sun in a relationship . . . Nate for all his faults, had been lively and popular, at least with the people he didn't owe money to. He could be charming, funny and was the life and soul of any party. She'd seen herself as the anchor in his life, she'd thought, content to live in his shadow.

It was ironic that his death, while almost destroying her at first, had seen her emerge out of that shadow and into the light. She'd had to force herself to peer out of the darkness, step by painful step. She might never have dared, without the motivation of the Wave Watchers project. It had replaced Nate in her life. She was its rock and it was hers.

But was it enough?

She returned to the task in hand: showing Tiff how to look out for potential trouble, which was a far easier job than delving into her deepest hopes and fears.

'Look, I can just make out some divers in the water by the island,' she said. 'We make a note of when they descend and keep an eye out to make sure they resurface by the dive boat and not too far away. Can you see if you can spot them through the binoculars?'

'Hang on . . . these take a bit of getting used to.'

Marina chuckled to herself while Tiff tried to adjust the sights. She was sure that she hadn't expected to have to actually *do* anything in the lookout station, but Marina had other intentions. If her cousin was going to stay for the next few months and was keen to help out, the most useful thing she could do was volunteer.

Marina wouldn't push her too hard, of course, but she thought it would be a good way for Tiff to make new friends, to distract her from the turmoil of the past few months. Marina recognised a woman hiding a deeper pain under a veneer and, whilst Tiff's veneer was thicker than most, she was still pretty sure there was more to her cousin's escape to Porthmellow than she'd so far let on.

'Got them?' she said, thinking that Tiff had gone quiet. 'I think you're looking in the wrong place . . . '

'I can't see the divers, I have to be honest, but I *have* spotted something else that might be of interest.'

'What?'

'See for yourself.' Tiff straightened up and nodded at the binoculars with an arched eyebrow. 'About a hundred metres out from the shore, halfway to the dive boat.'

Marina looked. She quickly located the safety buoy attached to the divers and followed a line from their RIB towards the beach. A few seconds later she saw a man swimming out to sea. She could tell he had no wetsuit on, only a pair of red swimming trunks.

'Did you mean the guy swimming?' she said, still tracking the man's progress. His front crawl was measured and steady, his feet creating tiny splashes as the swell lifted him up and down.

'Yes. Where's he going?' Tiff asked.

'Mmm. I don't honestly know. Occasionally people try to swim round to the next cove to see the seals — which is a dangerous idea anyway — but he's heading right out to sea.'

'You don't think he's going to do anything

53

stupid? It must be freezing in there.'

'A balmy eight degrees, actually. I don't know what he's doing but it does seem strange. I suppose he could be training for a triathlon . . . '

'Maybe he thinks he's Poldark?' Tiff offered. 'Or a merman?'

'He's certainly something unusual,' Marina said, watching the swimmer growing smaller and smaller as he swam further from the shore.

'Should we put him in the log?' Tiff offered. 'I can do that.'

'Yes, please. We'd better keep a close eye on him for now too.'

'Surely he'll have to turn back soon?'

'You'd hope so.' Marina wasn't sure. The man was ploughing through the waves, and was now almost as far out as the dive boat, but a hundred metres to the west of it so he obviously had no intention of boarding.

She watched him for a few more minutes. He didn't seem in difficulty but he was alone. She was debating whether to call his presence in to the coastguard, when she lost sight of him momentarily. Her heart was in her mouth for a second but she quickly spotted him again. To her relief, he had turned around and was heading determinedly back towards the cove.

Very relieved, she took her eyes from the scope.

'Should we call someone?' Tiff asked.

'I was about to report it to the coastguard but he's coming back in.' She hesitated. 'I still think I might nip down and have a word with him.'

Tiff raised an eyebrow. 'Is that part of the job?'

'Not strictly speaking, but occasionally I do warn people. I don't want to be a killjoy but . . . '

'Better to be safe than sorry?' Tiff smiled then her face fell. 'Hey. That means I'll be up here on my own!'

'Only for a few minutes. You can contact me by radio if you need to. I'll hurry.'

By the time she reached the beach, the swimmer was out of the surf and halfway up the beach. Marina then saw what she couldn't see while he'd been in the waves and she had to stop herself from drawing in a breath. His board shorts showed off a stocky, athletic physique that was more like a rugby player's than a swimmer.

However, it was the scarring over his shoulders, neck and one side of his face that almost stopped her dead. The flesh was livid and thickened, like the roots of a tree. She thought of turning away for a moment, because she felt as if she'd invaded his privacy. She hoped he didn't think she'd trotted down here to gawp at him.

He'd already spotted her walking towards him so she smiled and met him halfway up the steep shingle near the top of the beach.

'Hello,' she said brightly, eager not to sound hectoring.

'Hi.' There was a puzzled expression on his face. 'Everything OK?'

'Yes. I'm from the lookout station on the cliff.'

His gaze swept over her 'uniform' and flicked briefly to the station before resting on her again. It was calm and clear. Hazel eyes, light brown hair, a quietly handsome face that was unremarkable apart from the scarring. His accent was most definitely not local, with a soft Scots brogue.

'Aye. I see,' he said, with a hint of a smile that evaporated quickly. He seemed amused by her for some reason. 'And you're sure there's nothing I can help you with?'

Marina was a little taken aback that he thought she was the one who needed help. She sensed he was trying to take control and was used to doing so.

She focused on his eyes and kept her tone friendly but confident.

'I'm fine. I popped down here because I wondered if you knew that this cove isn't a great place to swim? In fact, there are some dangerous currents around the cliffs and some rips on either side of the beach. You were only a few metres away from one.'

He listened intently, without commenting at the end of her little speech, which almost threw her off her stride. She pressed on. 'Porthmellow's main beach is a much better place for swimming. There's RNLI cover too, at the weekends.'

He waited before replying, allowing the silence to stretch uncomfortably but Marina decided to play him at his own game, waiting pointedly for a response.

'I prefer to be away from the crowds,' he said eventually. 'But thank you for the warning.'

'OK.' She resolved not to hassle him further — he was an adult, after all, and she'd done all she could to prevent another accident. 'If you prefer to swim in peace, there are plenty of quieter coves within a few miles without such treacherous rips and currents, if you're planning on staying around. You can ask at the surf lifesaving club next to the beach or come up to the lookout station if you want to know more.'

'Thanks. I'll do that. Very kind of you.' That brief smile again, his tone unfailingly polite but edged a clear signal that she should back off.

'No problem. It's what we're here for. Enjoy the rest of your day.'

There was nothing more she could do. With a nod, he turned his back and took the steps back up past the station, quickly but not hurriedly. She hung back for a few seconds before following behind, with his face and his manner imprinted on her mind. The scars looked like burns to her. Poor guy. She checked herself. By his manner, the last thing he wanted was pity or sympathy. She shook her head as if that would dislodge the reckless swimmer from her mind.

She turned off the path before he did, up the steep steps marked 'private' which had been cut into the cliff to give access to the lookout for staff.

Tiff was waiting at the door. 'Wow. I saw everything through the binoculars. A merman! Am I imagining things, or was he unimpressed by being told off?'

Marina broke into a smile at the idea of the tough-looking man on the beach being a merman. 'Firstly he didn't have a shiny tail, and secondly, I didn't tell him off! And he was civil enough but yeah, he clearly wasn't in the mood to have a chat.'

'Those scars on his face are nasty, poor guy.'

'Yes, and it was hard to see past them . . . God

57

knows how he got them,' Marina said.

'Hmm.' Tiff's lips twisted as she mused. 'He looks exmilitary to me. Super fit, short haircut, very upright.'

'So, you took a very close look, then?'

'I thought that was our job?' Tiff said archly.

Marina smiled. The man had been strangely compelling. She sobered again at the thought of his injuries. 'Whatever happened to him, it must have been bad. He told me he likes to swim away from the crowds and I don't blame him if people start gawping at him.'

'Is he local?' said Tiff.

'I don't think so . . . I don't recall seeing him around Porthmellow, and he had a Scottish accent. Funnily enough, he didn't have a rucksack or a towel with him, though. He walked straight up the cliff path in bare feet so I suppose he must be staying nearby, unless he parked his car on the top road.'

'Hmm. Curiouser and curiouser. Gosh, there are a lot of intriguing people in Porthmellow. Far more than I ever dreamed.' Tiff had a wicked glint in her eye that set off alarm bells for Marina.

'Remember your vow,' she warned.

'Don't worry, my halo is still in place! Anyway I have to interview a conservatory company tomorrow so that should bring me down to earth.'

Marina laughed. 'Talking of work, we're having an auction at the fundraiser and if you happened to come across anyone who might donate a prize, that would be brilliant. We only have a few lots so far. The best is a meal at Gabe's restaurant, and, between us, the others are a bit uninspiring. I thought while you're working at the mag, you might persuade the advertisers and traders to donate something.'

'What kind of lots are you looking for?

'Oh anything. Vouchers for a haircut or salon treatment or a meal in a pub or café. The farm shop has already offered a Christmas turkey . . . though it's a long way off . . . and Bryony Cronk has offered to trim a dog free of charge, though some people won't consider that a prize, more so a curse. Bryony's a bit heavy handed with the clippers, so I hear, and she can be . . . um . . . quite opinionated. I'm seriously wondering if anyone will bid for it . . . '

Marina broke off, seeing Tiff shaking with laughter. 'Stop it, you rotten devil! It's not that funny.' She grimaced, though holding back the giggles herself. 'It won't be funny at the fund-raiser when we only have half a dozen lots and no bids on some of them.'

Tiff exploded. 'I'm s-sorry. It's j-just so funny. The idea of a turkey voucher in M-May and some poor pooch having to endure a seriously bad hair day courtesy of this Bryony person. Oh, I do love the quirks of small-town life. The idea of living here is so delicious.'

'The idea, yes, but you'd go nuts, surely?'

Tiff wiped her eyes. 'It's lovely, in so many ways. But you're right, I couldn't handle it permanently — though, certain aspects of it are, I admit, very alluring . . . '

Marina cottoned on immediately. 'Like Dirk?'

59

'Now, did I even breathe a word about him?'

'You don't have to.' Marina smirked. 'But you know I'm sure he'd be *very* grateful if you helped us out at the fundraiser any way you could.'

'Really?' Tiff's eyes gleamed. 'OK. Don't you worry about the auction lots. Leave it with me. I'll see what I can do.'

The rest of the shift was fairly uneventful. Marina showed Tiff how the marine radar was used, and they kept an eye on a couple of teenagers who seemed to be about to scramble down a closed-off section of cliff path. Other than that, the drama was confined to the peregrines' aerial display around the cliffs and a brief visit by a family of seals.

'They look *exactly* like wet Labradors,' Tiff declared, laughing at the whiskered heads bobbing up and down a few metres off Porthmellow Point. She was glued to the telescope and Marina smiled to herself. The delight in her cousin's voice was amusing and touching. Seals were almost daily visitors to the cove but it was refreshing to see them through the eyes of a visitor, and especially one as hardened as Tiff had become.

Marina was sure that her cousin's shell remained in place; she was almost certain she'd heard only part of the story. She hoped Tiff would open up eventually, but in the meantime, she was enjoying the company and the contribution to the household finances was welcome. However, their house sharing arrangement couldn't last forever. Tiff would have to make a decision about her next move — and so would Marina.

Resting her hands on the desk, she gazed out

over the ocean, aware that her decision would have to be taken sooner rather than later, no matter how painful. She'd accepted that Nate was dead several years ago and, as far as she could without a body, she'd gone through the grieving process to a degree.

They'd had a funeral of sorts, a humanist service with the scattering of flowers into the sea.

The seventh anniversary of Nate's disappearance was coming up in the summer, and she could then trigger the legal process to have their marriage dissolved. It would bring a finality that was hard to take. No matter how much she'd accepted Nate's death and mourned him, she didn't relish writing The End on his story. It was so final, so absolute.

'Marina?' She turned to find Tiff's hand on her shoulder. 'You were miles away.'

'Was I?'

'Or maybe not so far away after all?' Tiff nodded at the grey shingle of the cove a hundred feet below their feet. She must have guessed that Nate had been occupying her thoughts.

'No . . . ' She smiled at Tiff. 'But I can get it all sorted soon. Take another big step forward. I'll always love Nate, even if he did leave me with such a mess, it felt like my heart was wrenched out when he disappeared . . . when he *died* . . . '

Marina glanced down, realising she'd been twisting her wedding ring round and round. She'd lost a bit of weight over the past few years, from worry and holding down several jobs. She'd had to sell her engagement ring at one point, along with a favourite necklace he'd given her.

Things had grown dire and she was on the verge of defaulting on the mortgage and had refused point blank to take another loan from the family.

She couldn't help but wonder whether it would have been easier if she'd had children, because, while things would have been even tougher on her and them, she would at least have had a vital piece of Nate, something to live for. Instead, the Wave Watchers had provided that comfort and purpose.

They walked home together, though Tiff insisted on taking a detour and 'nipping down' the steps to the wine merchant's in town for a bottle to celebrate her arrival. Marina wondered if she'd be so enthusiastic by the time she'd climbed back up to number four Coastguard Terrace. On her way to the house, she nodded a hello to Dirk who even managed a brief smile. She also spotted another familiar face: the swimmer from the cove was letting himself into number one, though he now had jeans and a hoodie on.

He saw Marina and nodded even more briefly than Dirk and without the smile. Clearly, he was not happy to have been spotted by her again. Well, fine, but she wished him good luck with trying to avoid her when he was staying two doors down. He didn't know that yet, of course, as he'd shut his front door by the time she'd gone into her place.

Despite his reticence, she was left hoping that she would get to know more about her intriguing new neighbour before too long.

# 5

On the following Friday evening, Tiff held forth about her first week working for *Cream of Cornish* while she helped Marina plant some summer flowers into tubs in the cottage garden. Tiff could kill a houseplant with a single glance but it was obvious Marina loved her little patch. Only a hedge and the coastal path separated it from the cliff side, and its slight downward slope meant you could see over the low shrubbery to the sea. From the vantage point of the terrace, you could look down the coast to the Lizard one way and Porthmellow Harbour on the other.

Fairy lights were strung along the trellis and the patio held a small bistro table and chairs. On this sunny evening in late April, the indigo sea sparkled in the sunlight.

Tiff held a plastic tray of flowers while Marina emptied compost into assorted tubs and pots.

'I don't mind the 'office' in Porthmellow even if I've seen stationery cupboards bigger than that place. I don't mind bumping my head on the sloping roof above my desk every time I stand up. I don't mind driving on the main roads, even if they're packed with tourists, but I have *no* idea how you cope with these narrow lanes!' Tiff said in awe. 'I clipped the wing mirror on the company car on a hedge today. I was late for my appointment at the bloody Bed Emporium because of the traffic. I thought I'd left ages to get to Truro after I'd interviewed some oyster farmer in Mylor but the sat nav took me down a track that claimed to be a public highway. Highway? I've seen wider bike lanes! And for the love of God, *how* many potato trucks can one county have? Ye gods, I must have been stuck behind every single one of them.'

'The roads do take some getting used to,' said Marina, her shoulders shaking with laughter as she filled a second pot with compost.

Tiff watched as Marina dug the soil over with a trowel. She might make light of her first week, but it had been a culture shock in more ways than one.

She'd expected to tootle about sleepy byways, maybe stopping off for a sneaky coffee at a sea-side café or a potter in a gallery in between jobs. However, the reality had been very different. Her boss certainly wanted her pound of flesh and had Tiff trundling around from Launceston to Land's End, 'interviewing' everyone from double-glazing manufacturers to cider makers.

Writing the endlessly upbeat, sycophantic prose about the companies — all of which were important advertisers, of course — wasn't the cakewalk she'd assumed. Much to Tiff's disgust, the 'clients' also had a say in the final copy, which went against her principles. The air had been blue as she'd tapped away on her laptop, eulogising about patio doors and cider varieties.

However, there were compensations. At least she was occupied, earning a little money and the working environment was an absolute stunner. She'd been amazed at the effect the sea and wild moorland had on her, forcing her to stand and stare in a way she could never have done in London.

She'd even pulled over a few times, simply to breathe in the fresh air and the views even if it did mean she was late. And, she thought wickedly, she could always blame the potato lorries . . .

'Tiff?'

Marina's voice penetrated her musings.

'Sorry?'

Marina stood up, gloved hands on hips. 'Are you ready to put the plants in?'

'Yes, of course. I was miles away.'

While Marina filled the other pots with compost, Tiff planted the geraniums, and told Marina about the results of her other mission: the auction lots.

'It's not been as easy as I thought to find anything decent. Of course, if I was in London, I'd just pick up the phone or take a few people to lunch, but I don't know the clients here well enough yet. I . . . um . . . did manage to get some vouchers for a bikini wax, a mackerel fishing trip and a photography workshop.'

'A bikini wax? That's a great start,' said Marina, sounding delighted, but Tiff was far from happy. Having seen how much effort Marina put into the station, and how welcoming she'd been, she wanted to pull out all the stops.

'Hmm. Maybe, but I really wanted to get something far more exciting for you. I'll reach out to some of my London contacts, even though I haven't heard from any of them in a while. Don't you worry, I'll sort it.' She threw what she hoped was a confident smile at Marina. 'Anyway, enough about that. Have you found out any more juicy details about the merman in the cove?'

Marina stood up. 'Merman?'

Tiff wasn't fooled by Marina's feigned lack of interest. 'The guy we saw swimming in the cove?'

'Oh, I see. Not much, and nothing juicy. He's called Lachlan . . . McKinnon or McCann or something Scottish. The post woman told me and she talks at a hundred miles an hour so I didn't quite catch it. He's a mate of Aaron Carman — that's Evie and Troy's son. Lachlan was apparently in the RAF in Scotland, but Aaron was in the army, so I don't know how they met each other. The post woman isn't sure how long he's staying, but the estate agent said they'd let the cottage on a long lease so I'm guessing six months or even longer. I think he's joining Aaron's security company. That's it, I'm afraid.'

Tiff laughed. 'You should come and work on my paper. You seem to have found out plenty. Any clue as to what happened to him or how he was injured?'

Marina shrugged. 'Not really. Lots of theories but all speculation. Anyway, it's his business. I feel a bit sorry for him, to be honest, the rumour mill is red hot.'

'At least they won't be talking about me any more.'

'I wouldn't bet on it. The woman who runs the chip shop was trying to find out who you were and how long you were staying.'

'It really is a small world. I wonder how long

66

Mr Something-Scottish will stay?'

'I've no idea,' she said briskly. 'I need to pop to the garage for some more vermiculite. The garages are behind the houses on the other side of the road so I'll probably be a few minutes.'

*Vermicu-what?* Tiff had no idea what Marina meant so she concentrated on digging tiny holes for the young geraniums. It was strangely therapeutic, pulling them carefully from their trays and patting the soil around them, imagining them blooming in a few weeks' time.

Tiff's mind drifted once again to another of Porthmellow's intriguing men. She'd now spotted Dirk three times on her way into and out of the cottage and once in the post office in Porthmellow. He'd inclined his head a millimetre to her on his way out, while she queued to post a birthday parcel for her father. Every time she saw him, he had a greater impact on her. He seemed taller, darker, and more delicious — like a chocolate tasting session where each sample was more delectable than the last. Her mouth watered at the very thought of him.

She knew she should dismiss him from her mind — she hadn't come all this way to fall for another man — but it was becoming very difficult. Maybe she could take up swimming in cold water, like Lachlan Something-Scottish. And on that matter, he was intriguing — not as intriguing as Dirk of course, but it was clear that Marina had warmed to her new Scottish neighbour. Tiff hoped so, in one way, as long as Lachlan didn't make matters worse.

First impressions of him hinted at someone

pretty intense and Marina deserved some light-hearted fun. Judging by the reception Marina had received on the beach, he wasn't the most sociable of neighbours.

Tiff patted in the final geranium and straightened up to stretch her back. Mm, maybe she could gently nudge Marina in the direction of someone else. Marina was still young, attractive, kind and vivacious, there must be at least one single guy in Porthmellow to help her move on from Nate.

'Evening.'

Tiff jumped and swung round to find Dirk standing barely a few feet away. The top of his chest was visible above the wooden fence, but fortunately he had a T-shirt on. His sudden appearance so close to her set off a Catherine wheel low in her stomach, swirling and shooting sparks of lust.

'What are you doing there?' she blurted out, fighting for her composure. 'I mean, I didn't expect you to be next door . . . '

She heard a faint meow and momentarily Dirk disappeared, only to pop up again with a furry bundle in his arms.

'I'm watering the plants and feeding the cat for our neighbour Gwen,' he said, stroking the tortie cat with a finger. 'She's in hospital for a few days so she asked me to look after the house and Bumble here.' Ensconced in Dirk's arms, Bumble looked like a cat who'd got a whole pint of clotted cream complete with a strawberry on the top.

'Oh, I see. Sorry, I didn't mean to be nosy,' she said.

'Really? I thought that was your job. Professional nosiness.'

'I hardly think freelancing for *Cream of Cornish* counts as professional nosiness,' Tiff said haughtily.

She met his eyes as Bumble rubbed her cheek against Dirk's stubble. Tiff went shivery. She wouldn't have minded being Bumble right at this moment. Then she came to her senses. He'd been very blunt. 'I'm Marina's cousin, just here to enjoy her company over the summer and to have a change of scenery while I'm between jobs,' she said.

'Of course you are, and I'm sure you'd never *dream* of digging around in anyone's life,' Dirk said, running his hand over Bumble's fur.

'What do you mean?' Tiff demanded.

'Isn't that what all journalists do?' he asked, while Bumble purred loudly in his arms.

Tiff on the other hand didn't feel like purring at all. She was too full of indignation at Dirk's implications and her body's treacherous reaction to him.

'If you don't mind,' Tiff said coolly, trying to hide her annoyance at his rudeness, 'I need to get on with this planting. I'm sure Bumble needs her litter tray emptying.'

He turned his eyes on her. 'I've already done the dirty work.'

'Good for you,' Tiff muttered, crouching by the tub again so she didn't have to behold the monumentally annoying hotness on the other side of the fence. The way he said 'dirty work' had almost made her gasp.

'Enjoy your gardening,' he said. 'Probably a good idea to stick to geraniums rather than potatoes. I look forward to bidding on the bikini wax.'

'What?' Tiff glanced up sharply but only glimpsed the back of his head before he vanished. All that was left was a whistled rendition of what sounded suspiciously like 'Mars' from *The Planets* suite. The bringer of war . . .

Out of nowhere, an image of Dirk's face flew into her mind. She'd seen him in a photo, devastated and broken . . . on a dark night but with lights all around him. It was a photo taken in London. The full picture was within her grasp but she was also distracted by his taunts about the auction.

She'd half-feared he'd heard her whingeing to Marina and now it was obvious he'd overheard some of their private conversation. Mind you, she had been rather vocal and forthright.

'Right, Mr Dirk 'n' Stormy,' she muttered under her breath. 'You just wait. I'll show you.' She was a doer, used to using all legitimate methods to get what she wanted. Snaffling a knockout 'money couldn't buy prize' for the auction should be well within her reach.

Marina returned with the vermiculite, which turned out to be a bag of magic growing grit, and Tiff tried to focus on the petunias. However, despite her best intentions, she couldn't help but wonder what exactly *did* turn Dirk on and, more importantly, what lurked beneath his clearly angry shell.

# 6

Marina had only the birds for company when she went straight from work to do an early evening stint at the lookout station. Gulls wheeled overhead and she could hear the distinctive cry of the choughs as they flew around feeding their babies on the cliffs. Term was in full swing again and she'd been lecturing that morning, before attending a faculty meeting and doing some marking.

Her fellow watcher had called in sick at the last minute, and while she didn't really mind having the station to herself, it was obviously more tiring to keep watch alone. When the station had first opened all those years before, she'd found herself dwelling a lot on Nate and what might have happened to him.

From time to time, she also found the swimmer from the beach — though she ought to think of him as Lachlan — stealing into her mind. She'd seen him a couple of times from a distance but no other acknowledgement apart from the nod. This was unusual on Coastguard Terrace where all the permanent residents knew each other, and even some of the second homers had become friends. But he'd already demonstrated that he wanted to keep himself to himself and that was fine.

So she almost did a double take when he appeared in the sights while she'd been scanning a collapsed section of the coast path for walkers.

She put the binoculars down and looked at him with her naked eye. This time he wasn't in trunks, but jeans and a hoodie. He came from the direction of the Lizard and was obviously heading back to his cottage. Or so she thought. Instead of walking in front of the station, he vanished which could only mean one thing.

The path ran directly in front and below the station, with a short detour up to the building itself. Most of the time, they left the door open, welcoming visitors, most of whom were happy to leave a small donation for funds. A few seconds later, she heard him climb the steps and reappear in the doorway. After rebuffing her invitation, he was the last person she expected to visit.

'Hello!' he called from the lobby next to the staff area at the rear of the station. 'Am I disturbing you?'

'No, come in!' she called.

He walked into the operations area, where Marina smiled a welcome, wondering what he wanted. It was such a surprise to see him after he'd brushed off her previous attempt to engage with him.

'You're on your own up here?' He scanned the room as if someone might be hiding.

'Yes, but only for this shift. The retired coastguard who was supposed to watch with me has gone down with shingles, poor guy. It's not ideal, but otherwise the station would have to close . . . We seem to keep seeing each other from afar,' Marina said. She held out her hand. 'Marina Hudson from two doors down.'

Those hazel eyes were watchful as he shook

her hand in mock solemnity. His voice even in offering his name was measured. 'Lachlan McKinnon. Your new neighbour from the far north.'

'Hello, Lachlan.'

At least she didn't have to think of him as Lachlan 'Something-Scottish' any more. She liked his name, kept wanting to say it out loud and found his accent was as soothing and rugged as she imagined his home might be. His hair was thick and curly, the colour of a chestnut, and he was taller than she'd recalled, but he *had* been up to his ankles in pebbles on their first encounter. She wondered how much he knew about her circumstances — probably more than she knew of his.

'I'd heard your first name . . . Aaron Carman told me,' he said.

'I knew your first name too.' She smiled, deciding not to tell him that the post woman had told her. 'Word travels fast in a small town like Porthmellow. Trouble is, it's not always that accurate by the time it reaches me.'

'I can imagine . . . ' His eyes lit up with curiosity. 'What else have you heard about me?'

Marina hovered between tact and honesty and decided that Lachlan would respond better to the latter. 'Almost nothing, other than you were in the RAF military police and you've come to work with Aaron.' She smiled. 'Excuse me for stating the bloomin' obvious but Porthmellow is a long way from the Highlands.'

He smiled. 'Aye. In every way.' His eyes darted around, taking in the equipment. She wondered if he was giving it a professional appraisal. Although they were reasonably well equipped, it couldn't possibly compete with a military set-up.

'Did you find somewhere to swim?' she asked, breaking a silence that had gone on a fraction too long for comfort. Maybe he was ready to leave now he'd introduced himself properly . . . funny how much she hoped he'd linger a little longer. She wanted to know more about her new neighbour.

'Yes . . . I asked Aaron and he made a few suggestions. In fact, I came up here to thank you for your advice. I'm sorry I was a bit offhand when we met down in the cove the other day.'

Marina almost dropped the binoculars. An apology. Wow, and he'd bothered to come by and tell her. 'Oh . . . I see. I have to be honest, I'd wondered if you thought I was being a busybody.'

'No.' He grimaced. 'OK. I'll admit I wasn't in the most receptive mood for health and safety tips that afternoon, but I hadn't long been here and let's say I was out of my comfort zone so I headed out for some exercise to try and sort my head out. I probably shouldn't have swum in a strange place alone . . . ' His gaze held hers. 'Although fortunately for me, someone was watching.'

A hint of warmth stole into Marina's cheeks for no reason whatsoever.

'That's our job,' she said hastily, reminding herself as much as him. It was her job to keep an eye on people. Thank God he couldn't see the secret tucked inside her: she'd thought about him a lot since that afternoon; his face, his manner, his body . . . way more than she should have. Wave watching shouldn't be a licence to ogle, she'd reminded herself a dozen times, but Lachlan had stirred feelings in her that she'd thought had vanished along with Nate.

'You're all volunteers here, then?'

She nodded, keen to move the conversation on to her work. 'Yes, though some people think we're employed by the coastguard. When they hear the truth, they often think we're mad to give up our time for nothing.'

He laughed softly. 'Maybe we are.'

She noted the use of 'we'. 'Have you been involved in something like this yourself? Coast guarding, I mean?'

'Not as such . . . not by the sea, anyway, but I was a volunteer in a mountain rescue team while I was serving on the RAF base near Aviemore. It was a while ago now . . . ' He took a closer look at the marine radar, resting his hand on the desk next to the shipping log. 'This is quite a set-up.'

Marina was convinced he was being generous but didn't want to pass up an opportunity to tell him more about the Wave Watchers now he was interested in the station. 'Would you like a mini tour?'

'Aye, as long as I'll not be disturbing you?'

'No problem. I can still keep watch while I show you around.'

She showed him the equipment and told him about the duties of the volunteers. Unlike most of their visitors, he had some idea of how the radar and visual equipment operated and seemed genuinely interested. Before she knew it, over half an hour had passed by, during which she'd broken off to give a local weather report to a fishing vessel and kept an eye on the movements of a couple of anglers casting off the rocks off the cove.

While she did her duties, Lachlan looked out over the waves, quiet and watchful, as if he was searching for something — or someone — just as she had in the days and weeks after Nate had first gone missing.

She turned to him and explained what she'd been doing, showing him the observation log, and he asked her about some of the incidents they'd helped with.

'I can't believe you managed to re-open and equip this place on your own,' he said. 'When I was a volunteer with the MRT, even though we had professional support from the RAF, they still relied on donations and people to keep going.'

'I should think it was tough working in the mountains. Out in the snow and gales,' Marina said.

'Sometimes . . . ' He hesitated, a little wistfully. 'You get on with it though,' he resumed firmly. 'Did you raise all the money to re-open this place?'

'God, no. It wasn't only me,' she protested. 'Loads of people in the town helped — local businesses, the WI, the Fisherman's Institute, friends, neighbours, students and colleagues at the college where I work. Almost everyone chipped in or helped somehow. I could never have done it or kept it open on my own. It's a constant battle to raise enough to keep going and to get enough volunteers to keep it open during daylight hours. I'd never have dreamed of doing something like this before . . . ' Her voice tailed off. 'Before I realised how much of a need there was for someone to replace what the coastguard used to do.' She had no intention of volunteering the real reason why she opened the station. If he asked, well, that was different and she'd deal with it.

He blew out a breath. 'It's good going. Respect to you. I know the effort you must have put in and still do.'

'It doesn't feel like an effort. I enjoy it, in all weathers,' she replied, realising instantly what a strange thing that was to say, considering she'd started doing it because of losing Nate. She smiled and her next words tumbled out of her mouth before she could chicken out. 'You could volunteer for us, if you're interested . . . you'd have to do the training, of course, but we can do most of it here and with your background in SAR you'd probably breeze through it . . . if you're staying in Porthmellow for a while, that is.'

He hesitated. 'Thanks for the invitation but I'm sure I'd be no use to you in this situation.'

'Actually, with your background and experience, I think you'd be exactly what we're looking for.'

'Thanks, but I'm not sure what my plans are yet.' He checked his watch, unnecessarily as there was a huge clock on the wall. 'Sorry, I have to be off. I've a meeting with Aaron before dinner.'

Marina knew she'd cast the net too soon.

'OK. Well, you know where we are if you change your mind.'

He smiled. 'I'm afraid I'm not likely to . . . forgive my bluntness, but I'd rather be honest with you now. Thanks for your faith in me all the same. I'm flattered.'

'I didn't intend to flatter you,' she said.

She was answered with another smile that could be covering any emotion from irritation to pleasure.

She'd no idea what he was thinking but one thing was certain: he was eager to be out of her way. It was a shame, after they'd talked for so long. She'd enjoyed his company, his physical presence and the strange sensation that he was a kindred spirit, though that was entirely based on her gut feeling.

'You know, there's a fundraising day in aid of the lookout station and the local lifeboats a week on Saturday,' she said. 'If you fancy coming along with Aaron, we'd love to see you? His parents are helping out and there'll be an auction at the end. You could bid on a Christmas turkey, if you like.'

He laughed. 'A turkey? Wow. That's . . . tempting. In that case, I'll see what I can do.' He checked his watch again. 'Now, I must be going. Thanks again for the tour.'

'See you around, I expect, now we're neighbours,' she said,

'Aye, I expect you will,' was the simple answer before he strode out of the door. He seemed to be a mercurial man and despite what he'd said, she had an inkling he wanted to join in community life, but something was holding him back.

He left Marina wondering about him even more, to the point, in fact, that she was finding it hard to focus on the job: keeping people safe.

With dusk starting to fall, and clouds making the evening gloomy, she locked up the station and threaded her way through the gorse to the cottage.

Lachlan was on her mind all the while, which she found a pleasant distraction from the drizzle that had moved in from the Atlantic. OK, so he was simply the 'new kid in town' and like every attractive fresh arrival in Porthmellow, he was bound to hold an exotic mystique, if you could call the Scottish Highlands 'exotic'. And yes, he *was* single, according to Evie, although that was one nugget of info she obviously hadn't let on to him.

She was single too, she supposed, as her mother and friends had reminded her lately — but that didn't mean 'unattached'.

She was still attached to Nate's memory, even now seven years after they'd been ripped apart. Despite what she'd heard on the grapevine, even if there was no 'significant other', Lachlan McKinnon might be attached to someone too. He hadn't given any reasons for leaving his Highland life for Cornwall. He didn't seem much older than her, so he couldn't have retired . . . maybe the 'accident' had been the reason behind his move.

She might be imagining it, but she thought they had a connection — or was that simply her reading too much into a visitor's polite interest, after a solo shift in the remote station? After a lonely few years, isolated in her grief and recovery?

Whatever had caused his scars, she had a feeling they weren't much different from the ones she still carried inside from losing Nate. They had that much in common . . . and she wondered, could there be more? He had agreed to come to the fundraiser, or more accurately he hadn't said he *wouldn't* come. After his firm 'thanks, but no thanks' to joining the Wave Watchers, she'd have expected a refusal if there was no chance of him turning up at all.

Even on their brief acquaintance, she had a feeling he wasn't one for soft-soap or flannel even if it was to save someone's feelings . . . and he certainly wasn't a charmer or joker, as Nate had been.

Musing on some happier memories of Nate — the good days when they'd laughed and had fun together — she let herself in and hung her damp coat on the peg in the cottage hallway. On finding Tiff pacing around the sitting room with her phone clutched in her hand, her focus switched immediately to her cousin.

Tiff stabbed off her phone and tossed it on the armchair. 'Sh-shi — !' She bit off the expletive on seeing Marina.

'What's up? Are you OK?'

'Yes, of course. Why wouldn't I be?' Tiff retrieved her phone from the side of the chair cushion.

'No reason . . . you just seem a little bit stressed out?'

'I'm fine.' Tiff grinned. 'Apart from haring around the county. I need a weekend off. Now, how was your shift at the lookout? I thought you'd be tired and I made a spag bol. Well, actually, it's only the bol that's done. I waited for you before I put the spag on.'

'Aren't you hungry?' Marina asked, pleased she didn't have to prepare a meal.

'Not really. I went to a pasty factory at lunchtime and I'm afraid I rather over indulged at the tasting session.' She rubbed her stomach. 'I'll be the size of a trawler by the time I go back to London.'

'Thanks. I'm ravenous.'

★ ★ ★

A little while later, she tucked into her dinner, while Tiff toyed with her spaghetti before pushing her plate away.

Marina cleaned her plate and considered finishing Tiff's leftovers but it seemed rude.

'Busy day?'

'Yes. I'm knackered. I'd never realised how exhausting it is, having to be nice to people.' She sighed. 'I can't afford to upset the magazine's customers but if I have to feign interest about another conservatory manufacturer or hand-made soap company, I might go mad.'

Marina laughed. 'I'm sure no one can tell you're anything less than fascinated about their products. Talking of the advertisers, I'm going to a meeting about the fundraiser tomorrow night. We're finalising the list of auction lots so we can advertise them online and whip up interest. I don't want to hassle you but how are you getting on with potential prizes? Any luck with your London contacts yet?'

'Oh, fine. It's all in hand.' Tiff waved airily. 'I'm waiting for a few people to get back to me, that's all.'

'Great. It's wonderful that you managed to get the fishing trip and bikini wax, but if you could find something that would create more of a buzz, that would be amazing.'

'Like I say, it's all sorted.' Tiff's smile was confident.

'I'm sure it is. In fact, Dirk told me you had the situation in hand.'

Tiff's eyebrows shot up. 'Dirk? When? What *exactly* did he say?'

'Not a lot . . .' Judging by Tiff's shocked expression, Marina wished she hadn't mentioned her fleeting chat with Dirk outside the lifeboat station earlier that day.

'Well, he obviously said *something*.' Tiff's voice turned silky, putting Marina on her guard. She'd seen her cousin in defensive mode, like a cobra about to strike. She was glad she'd never been on the receiving end of a Tiff Trescott expose.

'I can't recall his exact words,' Marina said carefully. 'And I wasn't recording them,' she quipped, trying to lighten the atmosphere, but Tiff had folded her arms in expectation. 'I mentioned the meeting and he said: 'Oh good, I'm looking forward to hearing about the amazing auction lots. I hear Tiff is all over them.'

Or something like that.'

Tiff let out a snort. 'I bet he is.'

'Look,' Marina said soothingly. 'If you're worried about letting us down, you won't be. We're already very grateful for the prizes you've got. If there's anything else you can do, well, that's a bonus. Don't let Dirk wind you up — '

'Ha! Wind me up? I don't care what he thinks.'

Marina felt bad about mentioning the prizes again but she did have to report back to the committee so they could add the big lot to the web page and programme. There was plenty of time, of course, it would only take minutes to add the items to the social media, but the sooner the better in terms of getting the word out. She had wondered what Tiff was working on . . . a signed cricket bat from the World Cup winning team, perhaps? Tiff had said she'd interviewed one of their wives the previous year and they got on like a house on fire. Or a signed copy of JK Rowling's new novel? Tiff had contacts in publishing . . . Or maybe a London theatre weekend? Tiff had been to premieres in the past.

Hmm. Maybe those were all a step too far. It wasn't fair of her to hope for so much. She resolved to manage the organisers' expectations that evening, and have a discreet word with Dirk, if she could do it without Tiff getting to hear about it. Otherwise, her life wouldn't be worth living. One thing was for sure, there was definitely an 'atmosphere' between her cousin and Dirk. Marina wondered if those two had bumped into each other more often than Tiff let on.

Tiff made a pot of tea and joined Marina in

the sitting room. She was amused to find that instead of her usual mug of builder's, Tiff brought a tray with china cup and saucers, and a plate with a slice of lemon on it. She felt she'd gone to tea with the queen and that brought a smile to her face.

Tiff poured the tea into the cups, which Marina and Nate had received as a wedding present from his great aunt. 'Erm, I hope it's OK for me to mention this, but how are you feeling about the anniversary of Nate's disappearance coming up this summer?'

'Mm, mixed feelings really. It still hurts, but I've prepared myself for this for a long time now and it does mean I can get a lot of legal ends tied up. Actually, my solicitor has been in touch and asked if I'm ready to set in motion the legal process to declare him legally dead.' Marina could say the word out loud now. She'd made herself say it out loud if only to inoculate herself against the impact of the word.

'I think that's very brave. And very sensible.'

'I admit that I couldn't bear to face up to the finality of it until a couple of years ago but now I want it all over. Things weren't perfect between Nate and me, I can recognise that.'

'No . . . ' Tiff murmured before taking refuge in her tea. She didn't contradict Marina so Marina assumed she was being tactful. 'I'm here if you want to talk — or scream or cry.'

Marina smiled. 'I think I've done enough of that over the years. I want to have — that horrible word — 'closure' and move on.' Unexpectedly, Lachlan slipped into her thoughts again; his silhouette staring out over the sea ... Why, when she'd known other local men for years, had she been so struck by one who'd only been in the village for a few weeks? 'This tea is lovely, by the way,' she said brightly.

'You think so? It was a free sample from one of the companies I visited near Truro. They actually grow it here — can you believe it? They gave me a taster pack and I have to admit, it's delicious. There are some perks to the job. Hmm, maybe I can wangle some more for the auction.'

'Great,' Marina replied. She and Tiff continued to chat about her 'duties' at the fundraiser, but, however much she tried to concentrate on the tombola and bric-a-brac stalls, she couldn't help wondering if Lachlan would actually put in an appearance.

★ ★ ★

Marina didn't have to wonder when she might see Lachlan again for long. She finished work early on the Wednesday and had been to post some documents back to her solicitor when she saw him with Aaron and Evie Carman outside the newsagents on the harbourside.

Evie beckoned her over and Marina needed no extra encouragement. It was a fine afternoon, with a gentle breeze blowing. Both the guys were in shorts and T-shirts, and Marina couldn't help discreetly admiring Lachlan's physique.

'Afternoon, Evie,' Marina said cheerfully, adding a friendly, 'Hello,' for the boys.

Evie kissed her cheek. 'Afternoon, sweetheart.'

85

She turned to Lachlan. 'I expect you two know each other?'

'We've met a couple of times.' Lachlan shared a look with Marina as if he wanted their encounter in the cove and station kept between them. Evie was lovely and a stalwart of the village but perhaps a full-on introduction to the centre of village life wasn't what he needed when he was new and obviously liked to keep himself to himself. Marina felt a bit sorry for him.

Evie rolled her eyes. 'I should hope so when you two live virtually next door. Be getting to know one another a lot more from now on too.'

'Mum!' Spotting Aaron cringing behind his mum's back, Marina smiled broadly. Evie was known for her good-natured matchmaking.

'I'm sure we will,' she said.

'Now that Lachlan's joined Aaron in his security business, they'll make a great pair. He needs the help because he'll be busy now that there's a little Aaron on the way.' Tiny Evie puffed with pride. 'Have you heard that Ellie's expecting?'

'No . . . no, wow . . . congratulations to you both!' she said to Aaron. The news that Aaron's partner, Ellie Latham, was pregnant came as a surprise.

'It's early days. She's only twelve weeks,' Aaron said. 'So, we haven't told many people, have we, *Mum?*'

Evie patted her son's arm. 'She'll be fine.'

'I won't share the news, if you don't want me to,' Marina said, delighted for Ellie and Aaron, who seemed madly in love. Yet there was a corner of her heart that was thinking 'what if . . . ' She definitely wanted children of her own one day.

'It's OK. Everyone will know, sooner or later.' Aaron shook his head and put his arm around his mum. 'And it is wonderful news.'

Marina could see him swell with pride himself, and he was a huge man to start with. Lachlan stood quietly by, a half smile on his face.

'You'll come to the fundraiser, Lachlan?' Evie said brightly. 'Everyone will be there.'

Lachlan's lips parted. Marina could tell he wasn't sure and wondered if it might be a step too far to expect Lachlan to join a big community event so soon.

Aaron stepped in to rescue him. 'It might not be Lachlan's kind of thing, Mum. Give him a break, he's only been here a couple of weeks.'

'Long enough,' Evie said. 'It'll help you settle in. I'll introduce you to everyone. They'll all be at the fundraiser.'

'*Mum,*' Aaron pleaded.

'It's fine, Aaron,' Lachlan said. 'Thanks for the invitation, Mrs Carman. I'll try to drop by if I possibly can,' he said, sharing a glance with Marina.

'Great. I knew you'd want to join in! And do call me Evie, for goodness' sake, Mrs Carman makes me feel so bloomin' ancient! I can't believe I'm mum to this strapping fella.' She hung onto Aaron's arm and he smiled sheepishly before kissing her cheek. 'He's my big handsome boy and now I'm going to be a nanna again.'

Aaron grimaced but it was clear he adored his mum.

Marina laughed and caught the eye of Lachlan who had a smile tugging his own lips. It suited him, making his eyes crinkle as he exchanged a glance with her. He was obviously as amused — and perhaps touched — as Marina was by Evie's love of Aaron and his embarrassment.

'Come on, Mum. We'll be late for Gem's tea party,' Aaron said, adding, 'It's my niece's birthday.'

'Say hello to Gemma from me,' Marina said, knowing Aaron's sister from her school days.

'And you must come round for one of my shrimp creoles soon,' Evie said, finally releasing Aaron.

'I'd like that,' said Lachlan, and Marina wasn't sure whether he was only being polite or not.

Evie turned to her. 'That goes for you too, Marina. We haven't had chance to catch up for ages. It's about time we had a good old get together.'

'Thanks, Evie,' Marina replied, feeling a little awkward that she'd been included in the invitation. It was a vague offer, however, so it might not happen.

Evie went off, on Aaron's arm, leaving Marina and Lachlan alone together.

'Evie is lovely. She and Troy are both wonderful people who do so much for the town,' she said.

'So I hear.' He smiled. 'Evie loves her boy.'

'Yes. His face was priceless when she called him handsome.'

He laughed. 'Aye. He knows I'll not let him forget that when we're back in the office together.'

Marina smiled, heartened by his sense of humour. 'I can imagine . . . so, *will* you come to the fundraiser?' she ventured.

He shrugged. 'I hope so. I'll see how busy I am.'

A little deflated by his response, she pushed on anyway. She'd grown used to not taking no for an answer since she'd had to find funds for the Wave Watchers. 'I'll be looking after a stall and helping with the auction. Evie's our auctioneer, you know, and believe me, you do *not* want to miss that,' she said.

He smiled again, so she pressed further. 'You could drop by quietly on your own, you know? A small place like Porthmellow can be a bit much if you're new and everyone knows each other and their business. I can see it might not be the most attractive proposition but the fundraiser might be a way of getting the introductions over with in one go.'

'You mean like a baptism of fire?' he asked.

He did that thing again. Looking at her intently and listening as if it was a technique to make the other person say more than they wanted or needed to. She gambled on him being unable to resist her throwing down the gauntlet. 'I mean, yes, it probably *would* be a baptism of fire, but if you're up for the challenge, why not?'

'OK, you've persuaded me.' He smiled, with a piercing look that went straight to her core. 'I never shy away from a challenge.'

89

# 7

'Roll up, roll up! Welcome to the Search and Rescue Fundraiser! Come on, folks, make sure you visit all the stalls, buy lots of tickets for the raffle and don't forget to stay for the highlight of the day: our auction!'

Tiff winced as Evie's voice purred over a loudspeaker next to the lifeboat station. Not that she didn't think Evie was doing a fabulous job of whipping up interest in the auction. Quite the reverse: Evie was ramping up the anticipation to fever pitch, which only served to make Tiff's stomach swish like a washing machine. At the moment, it was only on a 'delicates' wash, but it wouldn't take much to set it going into a spin.

This was a little seaside fete, she reminded herself, not a swanky London charity ball. There was no pressure . . . although, seeing the locals behind their stalls, trying so hard to raise a few pounds for the Porthmellow Lifeboat Station and the Wave Watchers, she couldn't quell her butterflies.

Luckily the weather gods had been good to them, and by eleven a.m., a healthy number of holidaymakers were mingling with the towns-people. The fundraiser was being held on the quayside outside the station. Everywhere was bedecked with blue and orange bunting and a large canvas sign had been hung from the station entrance announcing the event.

*Porthmellow Search and Rescue*
*Fundraising Spectacular*
*give generously to our coastal lookout*
*and lifeboat crews*

Well, 'spectacular' was probably pushing it, but it was very charming. She would have genuinely been looking forward to it if . . . well, it was too late to worry now.

The whole thing was quite retro and reminded her of her old school fete with its hoopla and a 'splat the rat' sideshow. There was a second-hand bookstall, bric-a-brac and refreshments were being sold from the ground floor of the harbour office. It was an overcast breezy day, cool for the time of year. Tiff was in jeans, a white shirt and padded gilet; she didn't do fleeces — ever. Her bob was rapidly growing out so she'd added a silk scarf to keep it out of her eyes, and ditched the designer boots for low-heeled leather ones, hoping she wouldn't stand out too much.

For now, anyway.

She made her way to the tombola stall and helped Marina put out the 'prizes' and the drum containing the raffle tickets.

'Good grief, the last time I saw one of these was at the school fete,' she said, sticking tickets on a bottle of vodka that had a price ticket on it marked 'Porthmellow Super Booze'. The price was improbable by 2020 standards. 'Is there even a Super Booze in Porthmellow these days?'

Marina wrinkled her nose. 'It closed at least ten years ago. Nate used to go in there.'

'I hope this is still fit for consumption.'

'Apparently anything over twenty per cent never goes off,' Marina said. 'Slap a ticket on it. We need all the prizes we can get.'

'Has Lachlan put in an appearance yet?'

'Aaron said he'd promised to drop by after he'd done some work at the office. I hope he pops down.'

While they finished setting up, Tiff discreetly checked out the townspeople and holidaymakers, willing to give up their spare time and precious cash to help fund the lifeboats and Wave Watchers because it mattered to their community. She wasn't naive; they doubtless had their own problems and disagreements but for today had set aside their differences to help a common cause.

Now she had more time on her hands, she could make her contribution to the local community, help out Marina and get one over on Dirk at the same time.

However, so far her every effort at securing a standout headline lot — even *one* — had come to nothing. She'd hoped for a backstage pass to a gig, or front row tickets to a West End show, or hospitality at a sold-out sports event — anything that money couldn't usually buy and would create a real stir in Porthmellow. She'd contacted a dozen people in London, yet all but two hadn't returned her calls. She was obviously persona non grata and her editor — or Warner — had made her too toxic to even speak to. Or maybe they were simply so busy, with their eyes on the prize, that a request from an ex-colleague was at the bottom of their priorities. She knew the feeling.

Two friends, however, had responded positively and said they'd see what they could do, although they'd both warned it was very short notice. One was a young reporter whom Tiff had mentored and supported during her early career and was now entertainment ed at a glossy magazine. The other was an 'old school' editor, a blunt northerner, who Tiff had always got on well with. She was the one who'd agreed to pay Tiff to string some stories, and she had been outraged when Tiff had been sacked.

However, when neither had got back to her that morning nor replied to her messages, she'd known she had to admit defeat and confess to Marina that she'd been unable to deliver on her promises.

'Don't beat yourself up,' Marina said. 'We wouldn't have had three of the lots without you.'

'I know but I wanted to help you. I was sure I could call on my old friends — well, they're not friends, clearly. I just wanted to make this a big success. Now I've let you down, and I don't let people down.'

'Please! You had no time to set things up.'

'I kept on saying I could do it. People have a right to be disappointed.'

'No one will be disappointed. I — um — managed their expectations in case things didn't happen. They're all too busy dealing with their own stalls and work anyway.'

Marina was right. She was overreacting and if it hadn't been for recent events with Warner, she might have not been so agitated. But he'd shaken her confidence; the total capitulation of her own editor and even some of her colleagues had stunned her. She knew she operated in a cutthroat world, but fellow editors and journos were meant to back you not throw you under a bus . . .

That's why she'd had no choice but to offer herself as an auction lot.

And now she was regretting it almost more than anything she'd ever regretted before.

'Tiff. Are you OK?' Marina broke into her thoughts. 'You've gone very pale. Are you nervous about running the stall?'

'No . . . not about this.' She chewed her lip in anguish. 'Oh God, I have to tell you something.'

Marina frowned. 'What's the matter?'

'I've put myself up for auction as a star prize. I felt so guilty about letting everyone down. that I suggested it to Evie last night. She thought it was a brilliant idea but now I wish I'd never done it!'

Marina's eyes widened then she burst out laughing. 'That's inspired! People will love it.'

'I won't!' Tiff wailed. 'What if no one bids for me? Or someone horrible bids for me? I'm not much real use beyond writing scurrilous stories. Oh God, why did I do it!'

Marina hugged her. 'Because you're a good person who wanted to help. But you shouldn't have felt bad about the lots. You've helped already. Oh, Tiff, I'm sure everyone will be kind to you and you'll raise lots of money.'

'I wish I was as optimistic as you . . . Oh my God, it's Dirk.' Tiff caught sight of his tall figure hovering nearby. She nodded a 'hi'. 'Well at least one person will be happy,' she said to Marina, cursing inside.

'Dirk?' Marina laughed. 'He'll be amazed and delighted you're up for sale, I'm sure.'

'Don't say that,' Tiff muttered. 'He'll probably pass out with laughing.'

'No, he won't, and I bet he'll be very impressed.'

'That's not why I offered to auction myself,' Tiff insisted.

'Hmm . . . ' Marina said. 'Try not to worry. Concentrate on running the tombola for now . . . '

Trying to take Marina's advice, while ignoring Dirk, Tiff pulled a face. 'Please don't tell me that's a tin of mushy peas up for grabs?'

'Some people like mushy peas . . . '

Tiff rolled her eyes and tried to throw herself into running the tombola while Marina returned to rat splatting. She recognised at least a couple of dozen people who had introduced themselves to her over the past weeks, and whom she'd seen on several occasions, as was the way with small town life.

While people queued for their turn, the locals asked how she was settling in, joking about whether she missed the bright lights. In fact, she thought, she'd had more conversations with her near neighbours in three weeks than she'd had in three years with the residents of her London street. She hadn't thought it mattered, and frankly while she'd been zoned in on her job, frequently had her phone clamped to her ear while rushing to her flat to avoid wasting time on the briefest exchange.

Since she'd lost her job, and Warner had scuttled off like the cockroach he was, she'd noticed how lonely it was to walk into an empty flat, having seen or spoken to no one all day. She'd also realised that her life had been consumed by work and that her spare moments had been spent in Warner's company and his bed.

Life had been hectic, and the start of their relationship had been exciting, full of flowers — if not hearts. Looking back, she realised how he'd started to withdraw from her as he'd climbed the political ladder.

Should she have seen his betrayal coming? Was she too wrapped up in the moment to have taken his 'Working late again' and 'Sorry, I can't make dinner' more seriously?

There had been precious few people she could trust during and after the fallout.

She used to have friends outside of work too, but everyone was so focused on their careers that some of them — from university and the classical music society she used to belong to — had fallen by the wayside. It was hard to believe she'd once found time to go to concerts and the opera almost every week. Everything had been swept away by her long hours and devotion to getting a good story.

Tiff returned her attention to taking people's money, twirling the drum and handing out the occasional bottle of wine, chocolates or bath gift set. She'd discreetly replaced the mushy peas with a packet of Thornton's Continentals she'd bought out of her own pocket from another stall, and was delighted when a bowling club friend of Evie's won it.

96

It was a fleeting moment of pleasure in a morning where nervous tension had tied her stomach in ever tighter knots at the thought of what might happen at the auction. Had she let down the little community by not securing a 'proper' prize? No matter what Marina said, she felt awful and her mind churned.

She saw Dirk laughing with Drew, the man who ran the sailing trust. She was under no illusions, they probably weren't talking about her, but she wasn't imagining the fact that he glanced her way a few times. After she'd spent an hour on the stall, Dirk sauntered up, unable to hide a smile. It was her first really close-up view all day. He was in jeans and a dark blue lifeboats polo shirt. It wasn't exactly a uniform, but close enough for parts of her to do melty things that were very inappropriate in a community setting. Mind you, he could have turned up in sandals and socks and she'd have still fancied the pants off him.

His eyes swept over the stall. She'd re-stocked a few prizes from spare donations but things were looking a bit desperate with a bottle of HP sauce one of the prizes. 'Hello. How's it going?'

'Pretty good, actually. Can I interest you in a ticket for the tombola?' she said cheerfully. 'There's a still a bottle of wine left? I'm not sure it's a vintage I've heard of or how long it's been in someone's cellar, but it might be OK to add to coq au vin.'

He switched his focus from the stall to her. Tiff felt the temperature soar. 'How can I possibly resist?' he said and dug in his jeans

97

pocket for some change.

He handed over a pound coin, still warm from his pocket.

Mentally longing for an internal fan, Tiff twirled the drum. 'There you go,' she said breezily. 'Good luck.'

Dirk delved inside and pulled out a pink ticket. 'Ah. Lucky me. Sixty-nine.'

'You're joking!'

He frowned and held it out for inspection. 'No? Why would I be? Look.'

Tiff took the ticket and sucked in a breath. It was indeed number sixty-nine. 'Oh, I see. Right. Hold on, I think you have won something . . . ' Mortified by her innuendo — and that he didn't seem to have got the joke — she made a meal of scanning the table. 'Aha. The trio of red-hot sauces is yours.' She handed over a pack of bottled chilli sauces.

'Thank you. I'll treasure them. Anyway, I must get back to the station. It's my turn to show people round the lifeboat.' He seemed about to leave, but then added, 'And I'll see you for the auction, of course?' His eyes glinted wickedly. 'I can't wait to find out about all these exciting lots you've wangled.'

Tiff held onto her civility by a thread. 'Ah, well, I don't think you'll be disappointed,' she murmured.

He rubbed his hands together. 'Can't wait.'

'Argh. That infuriating . . . ' Tiff muttered to herself, already wishing she hadn't risen to the bait. It remained to be seen if Dirk would be disappointed by her 'lots' or not. Either way, he was bound to find her predicament hilarious.

She could see his head above most of the crowd all the way back to the lifeboat house. She pulled a flask of water and downed half of it, though what she really needed right now was a hose-down and a stiff drink, preferably with lots of ice.

# 8

Marina searched the crowds as the sun climbed higher in the sky. She was well into her second hour on the splat the rat stall, but there was still no sign of Lachlan. She hadn't realised quite how much she wanted him to turn up — for his own sake as well as hers — or how disappointed she might be if he didn't.

On the upside, her sideshow was doing a roaring trade.

The 'rat' was a small furry beanbag with a woollen tail and it was her job to drop it down a piece of plastic drainpipe fixed to a painted wooden board. The goal was to whack the 'rat' as it shot out of the tube before it hit the ground. Each go cost fifty pence and there was a small prize for anyone who scored a direct hit.

She'd done the job before and was getting quite good at releasing the rat in such a way as to create maximum surprise for the punters. Like most fairground games, it was actually much harder than it looked because, even if the player was totally focused, they could easily miss the rat. It was also very addictive, and people often tried many times to hit the rat, resulting in a very nice build-up of funds, while families and friends egged each other on.

Once or twice, she had to admit, she'd been more focused on the possible sighting of Lachlan than defeating the customers, so two teenagers had gone away gleefully clutching their prizes. They were only bags of Haribo and Percy Pigs, but hey, everyone loved to win.

From the moment they'd opened, they'd had people of all ages, from toddlers to a ninety-year-old lady from the sheltered housing, eager to have a go. Marina had been lenient with what counted as a 'hit' for the tiny ones and the older lady.

'Hello, Marina. How's it going?'

'Oh, hello, Craig.'

Her latest punter was Craig Illogan, one of Nate's old fishing — aka boozing — mates. He wasn't a bad bloke but he'd encouraged Nate's drinking and wilder schemes. Today, he was with his wife, who Marina liked, and their son and daughter, who were both at Porthmellow Primary School.

'I used to be really good at this when I was a lad,' Craig declared, holding the stick as if it was a baseball bat. 'Watch and learn, you two.'

'You always say that, Dad,' the little boy muttered.

His wife rolled her eyes and exchanged a smile with Marina.

After half a dozen fruitless splats, Craig was sweating and red in the face, but Marina refused to let him win just to feed his ego. He finally gave up, disgruntled, and she invited the children to have a go. She gave them some tips on how to catch the rat and managed to ensure they both scored a direct hit.

Craig's daughter jumped up and down in delight. 'I splatted the rat! I splatted the rat!' the little girl said.

'Me too. Hit him right on the nose. Did you see it, Dad?' the boy shouted

'Beginners' luck,' Craig muttered, earning himself a telling off from his wife.

And with that, the kids skipped off with their sweets, giggling and teasing their dad, while their mother told him not to be such a bad loser.

'Hi there.' Lachlan stepped from behind the stall.

A frisson of pleasure rippled through her. 'Oh, hello!' she said, feeling flustered. 'I didn't see you.'

'I've been here a moment. I would have come forward sooner but you were busy with that father and his family. He was getting frustrated.'

'Oh, yes . . . Craig. That's typical, I'm afraid, but he had every chance to win.'

'Too many chances, if you ask me,' Lachlan said.

'Hmm.' So, Lachlan really had been observing carefully. With the crowds and her attention focused on defeating Craig she hadn't noticed him. 'He's always been the same. His own worst enemy.'

'So he's a local?'

'Friend of Nate's actually.' She took a breath. 'Nate was my late husband.'

His mouth opened and closed before he said, so softly she could barely hear, 'Ah . . .'

'He drowned in a boating accident seven years ago.'

'I'm so sorry for your loss,' he said. 'And for speaking out of turn. I didn't mean to disrespect the man, if he was your husband's friend.'

Lachlan looked crestfallen so Marina took pity on him. It was always a difficult moment, hearing news like hers. She had no intention of elaborating on it and making an awkward situation worse.

'Please don't worry. You're absolutely right. Craig goes over the top and he can be insensitive to his family, let alone others.'

'Even so, I should keep my opinions to myself,' he said, unable to conceal the dismay in his voice. Marina was used to people's reactions but upset that Lachlan clearly felt so guilty about his comments. 'Please don't worry about it,' she repeated. 'And I'm so glad you could make the fundraiser,' she added, keen to change the subject.

'I told you I couldn't keep away,' he said, obviously relieved she hadn't taken offence. He softened the compliment with a smile so she wasn't quite sure if he was serious or not. She wasn't sure about anything as far as Lachlan was concerned and she had a feeling he kept his cards very close to his chest. And what a chest it was . . .

Quite apart from their difficult conversation about Nate, she'd probably underestimated how nervous he was of meeting people en masse. Anyone new was bound to be an object of curiosity at first, as Tiff was probably finding, and with his obvious injuries, their curiosity could well cross the boundary to intrusiveness.

'The lure of the tombola and the splat the rat stall were too much to resist?'

He laughed. 'Exactly . . . Aaron's a good bloke and I'd not want to let his mum down.' He held Marina's gaze. 'It's not as if I can hide away forever, is it? I'd have come earlier but I had to deal with a problem with the office IT systems.'

'It's OK to hide sometimes . . . as long it's not forever.'

'No.' He glanced around. 'How's it going?'

'Pretty well. The good weather helps and we've got lots of grockles as well as locals.'

'Grockles?'

'Tourists.' She laughed.

He raised his eyebrows. 'Do I count as a grockle?'

'Not if you live here.' *Not if you plan on staying for any length of time*, she wanted to add.

He took in the blue and orange bunting flying from the lifeboat station and the BBQ stand, which was being run by Marina's fellow Wave Watchers. Smoke spiralled into the air and the smell of hot dogs made her nose twitch.

'Have you eaten yet?' he asked.

'No time.'

'Aaron's gone to the barbecue. Shall I text him to get you something?'

'That would be great. Thanks.'

Marina was grateful for a slight lull in custom while people focused on getting something to eat themselves so she could have a precious few moments to chat.

Lachlan looked around him. 'You know, this reminds me a lot of the family days at the base and in the town. We'd have stalls like this and a hog roast, and we'd open up the hangars so the families could see what we did and have a look around the aircraft. My sister's kids loved it . . . .'

He gave a wry smile. 'The weather was never this good though. It was usually raining, or about to rain. That's the Highlands for you.'

She was pleasantly surprised he'd shared even a snippet about his background and for a few minutes they spoke about Scotland, leading Marina to wonder if he missed his homeland, despite any unhappy associations. He must surely miss his family, especially the nephew and niece he'd mentioned. At no point did he even hint at being involved with anyone on the base in the romantic sense.

She could, of course, simply ask Evie, but that would really be stepping over the line. She'd have to be patient and wait for him to tell her, unless any more information came her way by chance. Yet even if it did, she would still want to hear it from him directly. She wanted to hear from him full-stop.

She felt drawn to him and wasn't quite sure why. Maybe it was because of the empathy she felt for him, or the fact that she thought he had a body that was fit in every sense of the word — reflecting whatever he'd been through with an austere beauty that fascinated her. She'd seen more of it than most people in Porthmellow . . . and she didn't have to know him that well to have physical feelings for him every time she glimpsed him from afar or, like now, when he was close enough to touch . . . It was strange to feel the pull of attraction again. She hadn't experienced it since Nate, since the 'honeymoon' days when they'd spent a lot of time in bed.

Her face warmed at the memory and the

association with Lachlan. It unnerved her to be so powerfully drawn to him when he was so unaware.

'Here you go. I'm starving.' Aaron returned with the hot dogs and stayed to eat them while his partner, Ellie, went to see her sister on the wild foods stall.

Marina accepted gratefully, having not eaten since breakfast, and took a fifteen-minute break while she ate the hot dog. As soon as she'd finished, she re-opened the sideshow with a warm glow of pleasure when she realised that Lachlan showed no signs of leaving yet.

Aaron rubbed his hands together. 'Right, mate. Let's have a go at splatting this rat.'

Lachlan laughed. 'Not sure I'm in a fit state to splat a marshmallow these days, but I'll try anything once.'

Marina smiled to herself and got ready, determined to do her best to thwart them.

Aaron went first and missed all three of his goes before handing the splatter — a toy plastic baseball bat — to Lachlan. Marina watched him carefully as he waited at the bottom of the pipe to whack the furry rat. She was determined not to cut him any slack, and managed to defeat him on every round.

'One more for luck?' she urged, ever mindful of raising as much as possible and having an excuse to keep him there longer.

Aaron missed with his next three turns.

'Damn! I thought I had him!' he groaned. 'I give up, for now. I'm off to see how Ellie's getting on.'

Lachlan still seemed in no hurry to leave and hung around, smiling while a couple of guys from the local pub swaggered up and were also defeated. It was hard not to admire his biceps as he stood, arms crossed, waiting for his turn.

'Another try?' Marina asked him, half wishing she could leave her post to talk to him properly.

'Aye.' He grinned. 'Why not?'

He took the bat and she poised herself with rat at the top of the pipe. He really was a sight to behold. Eddies of desire stirred low in her stomach. She had a serious crush on him.

'Yes!'

The rat's tail had slipped through her fingers while she'd been ogling him and he'd hit it right on target.

She let out a cry of frustration then covered it with a laugh. 'Well done! Direct hit. Percy Pigs or Haribo?'

He laughed. 'Thank you, but save them for the kids.'

'We're next!' Two young girls lined up and Marina had to concentrate.

Lachlan drifted off. She saw him chat briefly to Tiff and buy a ticket for the tombola but he soon returned and stood nearby chatting to Dirk Meadows. Evie started to make an announcement about the auction, but people's attention had been drawn by something in the skies over the sea. They shaded their eyes and started to point at a large red and white helicopter.

'Now, everyone!' Evie announced. 'Here are our friends from the coastguard. Someone needs their help and our Wave Watchers and lifeboat crews are proud to work alongside them as volunteers. This is what we're raising money for — to help our friends in trouble.'

Evie's voice, strong though it was, was lost in the whirr of the rotors and engine. The helicopter was almost directly overhead and some people had their hands over their ears. Its rotors were a blur high up against the sky.

She turned to see Lachlan, a few feet away. He was transfixed by the helicopter; his arms were stiff by his sides. He seemed frozen but she could see the gleam of sweat on his face, and he was grey with terror. She'd seen something like it once before, a man having a panic attack on the steep edge of the cliff path . . . Lachlan was petrified.

She moved quickly, trying to reach him, but a second later, he was off, pushing past people hurrying towards the town. She followed as fast as she could, making her way past families.

'Excuse me! Sorry. *Sorry!*'

The crowd thinned as the helicopter circled in a pattern she knew well. It was searching for someone near the lookout station . . . but that wasn't her concern right now. There were other volunteers available to help if necessary.

It was Lachlan she was worried about, but she'd no chance of catching him — he was running along the quayside faster than she could ever hope to. Plus, she realised that in her desire to help, she'd left the sideshow and the cashbox.

This was crazy. What did she think she could do to help him, anyway?

He vanished from sight into one of the steep

108

alleyways between the shops that led up to the top of the town. She guessed he was going home where he could feel safe.

Her attempt to draw him into the community again had backfired. Cursing herself, she hurried back to her stall where she found Aaron waiting.

'What happened?' he said. 'I saw you race off. Everything OK?'

'I'm fine, but Lachlan isn't. I think the helicopter freaked him out.' She looked up but the aircraft was flying away now, south-west towards the Lizard.

'Jesus. I hadn't realised. I thought he was doing OK,' Aaron said.

'What do you mean?' Marina asked.

'He was involved in a helicopter crash at his base . . . but I don't know exactly what happened. He may be a mate but he's not comfortable talking about it, to say the least. I tried to get him to open up but he made it very clear I should back off, so I respected that.'

'Oh no.' She heaved a sigh. 'I'd no idea. I didn't mean to make things worse for him. I ran after him straight away but I shouldn't have. He probably wants to be alone.'

'It's hard to know what to do for the best, so don't worry,' Aaron said kindly. 'Even so, I'll pop up to the cottage and check on him. Thanks for letting me know.'

However much Marina wanted to make sure Lachlan was OK, she couldn't leave her stall again, and anyway, if he didn't want to talk to his buddy, then he certainly wouldn't open up to a relative stranger. She returned to the sideshow, hoping to at least check he was OK as soon the opportunity presented itself.

He wasn't the only person who wasn't enjoying the event. Over by the tombola, Tiff was anxiously scrolling through her phone and looking almost as grey as Lachlan had.

# 9

Tiff's tummy was officially on the spin cycle. Every ten minutes or so, Evie gave a countdown to the auction and before she knew it, it was two p.m. with an hour to go until her big moment. She checked her phone from time to time, hoping that salvation would come in the form of a message from her contacts, but there was nothing. She'd really hoped they'd swoop in last-minute with something to save her from total humiliation but it looked like it wasn't her day. Or year, in fact.

'Only one hour to go till the auction, folks. Make sure you're here outside the harbour office in good time. You don't want to miss out on that Gabe Mathias cookery lesson or our *amazing* surprise lot, do you?'

Tiff grew hot and cold at Evie's dramatic announcements. Was it too late to back out and beat a retreat out of town? Where would she go if she did? She was trapped behind the tombola stand, wishing she'd never had her desperate idea to offer herself as a 'lot' that morning. It had seemed like her only way out at the time, given there was no prospect of anything more exciting. However, Dirk's sarcastic comments — not to mention the sight of hundreds of locals and tourists all gravitating towards the auction area — had given her second thoughts.

Who would want her anyway? What if no one

made a bid or she went for the reserve price Evie had suggested? What if she ended up with someone . . . just plain *weird?* Looking around at some of the locals, that wasn't too unlikely.

At ten to three, Tiff closed down the stall. There was only a dried-flower arrangement and a tin of Spam left so she packed them away whilst she considered a final attempt at escape.

But deep down she knew there was no going back now. She dragged her leaden feet over to the lifeboat station where someone had positioned a chair and desk on a small dais for Evie. She had a sheet of paper in her hand and a microphone lay in front of her.

Evie spotted her. 'Are you all right, dear? You're very pale.'

'Just a little apprehensive, Evie. I do hope no one's expecting too much. I'd hate them to be disappointed.'

'Oh, don't be silly! Of course they won't be.'

Tiff smiled weakly.

Dirk handed Evie a gavel. 'Here you go.'

'Thank you, Dirk, my love. I think we're almost ready.'

'No problem. If you need anything else, you give me a nod.' He climbed down off the dais and walked past Tiff. Just as she thought he was going to go past her, she felt his breath on her ear.

'I can't wait for this,' he whispered.

She flinched but was too stunned to reply and Dirk was already gone.

'Come on, folks! Auction starts in five minutes!' Evie bellowed.

Trying to blot out Dirk's presence, Tiff attempted to lurk unobtrusively at the edge of the throng. However, as more people joined at the rear of the crowd, she found herself hemmed in at the front, only a couple of metres from the dais and right under Evie's eye. She'd no idea where Dirk had gone.

'Hello!' A hand on her shoulder told her Marina was right behind and the man beside her moved to let Marina stand next to her.

'Are you OK?' Marina whispered.

'Absolutely bloody marvellous,' Tiff hissed back. 'Apart from feeling like I'm on my way to the guillotine.'

Marina laughed. 'It's not an execution.'

'Mm. How's your day been?' Tiff asked to distract herself from her impending humiliation.

Marina hesitated and Tiff saw something — doubt? — flicker in her eyes before she brightened. 'Um . . . ' she said, 'it's going better than I'd hoped. We should hit our fundraising target, with a bit of luck. Thanks for all your hard work.'

'Thank me after it's all over and someone has bid for me,' she said.

Marina grinned. 'Oh, they will. You'll cause a sensation, I'm sure.'

The rap of the gavel drew their attention. 'So, that's a Christmas turkey sold to the Smuggler's Tavern for fifty pounds.' Evie looked at her clipboard. 'Next lot. A bikini waxing session kindly donated by The House of Payne.'

'Oh my God,' Tiff muttered as the crowd erupted with laughter. 'I still don't know why for

113

the love of God anyone would call a beauty salon that!'

'Because it's run by the Payne family?' Marina said innocently.

Tiff rolled her eyes. 'This place is nuts . . . I'm nuts. Oh God, it's almost time.'

Marina laughed. 'You'll be fine,' she said yet again, but Tiff's heart was hammering like she'd run the hundred metres, leaving Usain Bolt in her wake. Come to think of it, there was still time to do that . . . Her phone beeped. She scanned the message and a grin spread over her face, followed by a groan and a mutter. 'Now you bloody tell me!'

Cursing, she grabbed her notebook from her bag, scribbled a message and handed the torn-out page to Evie while the 'winner' of the waxing session collected his voucher. Evie frowned then nodded.

'Ladies and gentlemen, boys and girls, we have an additional lot, courtesy of Tiff Trescott and it's for you music fans. She has managed to get hold of two tickets to the sold-out Ed Sheeran gig at the Eden project — with VIP backstage passes.'

An excited buzz rippled through the crowd, making the hairs on the back of Tiff's neck stand on end.

Evie raced off-piste, clapping her hands together in excitement. 'But first I have an even better prize. Our very own Tiffany has offered the ultimate auction lot. Ladies and gentlemen: Tiff has offered *herself* as star prize.'

'No!' Tiff squeaked. Evie had misread the

note. The Ed Sheeran tickets were meant to *replace* her as the main lot. She thought of scribbling another note to Evie or leaping on the dais to grab her, but it was far too late and would only attract everyone's attention. Holy Mary, why had she even offered the auction lot . . . ?! If only she hadn't been so desperate to prove Dirk wrong.

There was silence, followed by confused murmurings then bursts of laughter. Tiff felt eyes lasering into her back, and a stage whisper: 'Oh my God. Is it her?' a woman said.

'That posh redhead from London,' another replied within Tiff's hearing. 'Something funny there.'

*I am actually bloody here*, Tiff wanted to shout, but tried to fix a smile on her face.

'Come up, my dear,' Evie called. 'Don't be shy.'

Tiff wished she could magically vanish in a puff of smoke, but it seemed her only special power was making a massive tit of herself. She shook her head at Evie, but Evie smiled.

'Come on, let all these lovely people see what they could be getting.'

'You have to go.' Marina gave her a little push in the small of her back. 'Knock 'em dead. I think you're amazing.'

People either side of her moved away slightly and Tiff found herself in a tiny gap in front of the stage. Somehow, she contorted her face into a grin and lifted a hand in a wave, before dragging her feet the two steps onto the dais.

'A big welcome to our star lot: Tiffany

Trescott!' Evie cried, and a smattering of applause rippled through the audience, accompanied by a few whistles. 'Now, Tiffany has offered to spend a day at your beck and call. She says she'll do anything within reason: gardening, housework, shopping, DIY, cooking, chauffeuring, pet sitting . . . you name it.'

Tiffany cringed. She could whip up an omelette and change a plug, but she'd never had a pet in her life, and as for gardening — planting the tubs had been at the edge of her skills. She could write up a storm, of course, and knew her Latin declensions, and she was pretty good at shopping . . . and if you wanted her to find out someone's deepest secrets or stir up trouble then she was red hot at that . . . but none of that was probably much use in Porthmellow. In fact, she really wondered what use anyone here could find for her. She'd never felt so *exposed* in her life.

Marina smiled and mouthed: 'You'll be fine.'

Tiff scanned the crowd for Dirk, still grinning like an idiot despite feeling like an unwanted sack of potatoes.

'Now I'm going to start the bidding myself here. I could do with putting my feet up for the day,' Evie said.

'Thirty quid!' A deep local voice boomed from the crowd. It was a fisherman in yellow waders, a pint in one hand.

'Fifty!' Evie said. 'Thirty is an insult.'

'Too bloody right,' Tiff said through gritted teeth, wanting to hug Evie but hoping an OAP wouldn't have to use her pension to spare her humiliation.

116

'Seventy-five.' That came from a woman near the lifeboat station. Tiff recognised her as the owner of a local hotel. She'd written a feature on it the week before and the woman was forthright but quite jolly. It might not be too bad working at the hotel for a day — and Tiff was definitely not above cleaning toilets.

'Ninety. I need someone to help me empty the slurry pit at the farm.'

'Now, Trevor, that's generous but I can't see Tiff muck spreading, can you?'

It was at that moment that Tiff caught sight of Dirk, stepping out from the front of the lifeboat station. He was at the back of the crowd but her height on the dais gave her a good view of him. Their eyes locked and his firm jaw might have slightly dropped.

'One hundred!' Hotel woman shouted and Tiff's shoulders slumped in relief. She'd decided that working for Joanna was the best she could hope for and smiled at her, willing her to keep bidding. Meanwhile, out of the corner of her eye she could still see Dirk, lurking near the back of the crowd. He must be having an absolute field day.

The bidding went up, whipped up by an almost breathless Evie. Gabe Mathias offered a hundred and fifty, and Tiff telegraphed him a look of unbridled joy. Working in his kitchen for the day would actually be enormous fun, and she could get a story out of it. This might not be so bad after all . . .

'Any other bids?' Evie called; gavel poised.

Silence, head shakes from the audience.

'Joanna?' Evie nodded to the hotel owner.

Joanna shrugged in regret. 'Out of my league, I'm afraid.'

'OK. Looks like Gabe has won. Thank you for the very generous bid, Gabe. Going once . . .'

Tiff's shoulders sank with relief with the realisation that she wouldn't be gutting fish or muck spreading.

'Two hundred!'

Heads turned, twisting around, standing on tiptoes.

'Did you say you'd do anything within reason?' Dirk shouted from the edge of the audience.

Despite her layers, Tiff shivered from head to toe. The idea of being at Dirk's beck and call was both horrifying and worryingly sexy. 'Within reason,' she said, hoping her voice wasn't too croaky. 'I'm up for a challenge.'

'Any further bids for this wonderful lot?' Evie asked, raising her gavel. 'Gabe?'

Tiff stared at Dirk. His expression was positively angelic. She could kill him.

Gabe laughed. 'Two hundred and twenty. It's for a good cause.'

Evie pointed at Dirk. 'Dirk?'

Dirk stayed silent, keeping his gaze on Tiff while she tried to look amused by the whole situation.

'Well, it's a damn sight better than thirty quid and cleaning out the slurry pit,' she joked.

'Going twice!'

'Three hundred.' Dirk's voice was strong and clear.

'Wow. Three hundred. Someone must want

you very badly, dear,' Evie said helpfully.

The crowd laughed and some stared at Dirk. Tiff let out a tinkly laugh but had murder in her heart.

'Gabe?' Evie said.

Tiff's eyes pleaded with Gabe. 'You can make me peel the potatoes,' she said lightly. 'Or do the washing up all day?'

Gabe smiled. 'We have machines for both those things and anyway, I don't want to deprive a mate . . . ' He nodded at Dirk. The audience buzzed like a swarm of bees; Dirk had made it obvious in the most public way that, for whatever reason, he was interested in Tiff. Only Tiff knew that he was out to humiliate her.

Evie banged the gavel. 'Penultimate lot. Tiffany Trescott sold to Mr Dirk Meadows for three hundred pounds.'

With the banging of the gavel and the applause still ringing in her ears, Tiff jumped off the stage and made her way through the crowd to Dirk. She'd no interest in what her Ed Sheeran lot went for any more; she had to find him.

She grabbed his arm. 'Hey, you, what the bloody hell are you playing at?'

'Making a generous donation to the SAR funds.'

'B-but . . . You bid for me! Why? What could you possibly want from me?'

'Er . . . ' His composure wobbled for a second — a moment that sent an electric jolt through her. Already pumped with adrenaline, her legs went wobbly. 'What do you mean?'

'*I mean* I don't know why you bid for me. Is it to humiliate me?'

'If you think I'd do that,' he said quietly, 'you don't know me.'

'Well, as you've just paid to spend a whole day with me, I'll have plenty of time to get to know you, won't I?' Tiff shot back.

'Hmm . . . although I'm not sure there'll be much time for talking . . . '

Her skin prickled and tingled. 'What do you mean? What the hell have you got in mind?'

'That would be telling! I presume you have next Sunday off?'

'Yes . . . '

'Come round to the cottage at seven.'

'Seven a.m. on a Sunday? My God, you do want your pound of flesh.'

He grinned. 'You've got that one right. See you then.'

'Aren't you going to give me a clue?'

'I think it will be a lot more fun if it's a surprise.' A buzzing came from his jeans. 'Sorry. Must go. We've got a shout.'

And with that, Tiff was abandoned on the quayside as the klaxon on the lifeboat station blared out and women and men rushed past her from every direction.

# 10

'Westerly wind four to five. Seas slight to moderate . . . '

Gareth relayed the weather report to a yacht that was on its way into Porthmellow. Sometimes vessels phoned the station on their own dedicated channel to receive the latest local conditions, knowing they'd be up to the minute.

Marina was pleased with his progress; he'd lost some of his excitability and was more professional in his responses to radio calls. He'd almost finished his formal training and was approaching the stage where, if she had no choice, he could be left alone in the station. Solo watching was never ideal, and they always aimed to have two of them, but one was better than none. The day that no one was there was the day when disaster was bound to strike.

Talking of disaster . . . Marina's thoughts drifted to Lachlan and his reaction to the helicopter fly-past. She'd spotted him a few times since the fundraiser but, however much she'd wanted to ask him how he was, there never seemed to be a good moment. The first time, she'd seen him outside Aaron's office in the back streets of Porthmellow when she'd been in her car, and had waved, but he hadn't seen her.

She'd seen him yet again as he'd been jogging towards his cottage. He *definitely* saw her that time but didn't even smile and rushed inside.

She wondered whether to push a note through the door but came to the conclusion he wanted to forget all about the incident.

Apart from Lachlan's meltdown, the fund-raiser had gone well and the Wave Watchers and the lifeboat crew now had some money in the kitty to help them keep going. Funds had been boosted by the addition of Tiff's auction lots. A businessman who was on holiday had forked out a grand for the Ed Sheeran package and, after the event, Tiff's editor friend had come up with two hospitality tickets to an England Test match. They'd sold them on eBay and had raked in another eight hundred pounds.

Then there was Tiff's own personal 'lot'. Marina still broke out in a grin when she recalled the look on her cousin's face the moment Evie's gavel had banged down.

It had taken a stiff G&T and a lot of swear words before Tiff had finally calmed down. Marina wondered what Dirk had in mind: probably nothing, if the truth were known. He most likely wanted to wind up Tiff while making a donation. Still, tongues were wagging all around town. No one could be in any doubt of the chemistry between the two of them, even if it was of the kind that might end in an almighty explosion.

When the relief crew arrived at the lookout station in the shape of Doreen and Trevor, who were retired hoteliers, Marina trudged home. With Tiff out, she sat down with some tea and opened the latest letters from her solicitor discussing her options as the seventh anniversary of Nate's disappearance drew nearer.

Even after so long, reading legal language about her loss felt cold and formal. She felt as if she was hammering the final nail in his coffin and it would be a sad day, not only for her but for his few remaining relatives and friends. Filing the latest papers in a ring binder, she reminded herself that application for the presumption of death wasn't an ending, it was the beginning of the next part of her life.

It didn't make any difference to her vow to never forget him, and her love for him would always be rock solid. Maybe, with everything behind her 'officially', she would also find it easier to look to the future with fresh hope. It was surely what Nate would have wanted, because he'd loved her too . . .

As she had many times before, she resorted to her garden for solace. It was a beautiful evening, with the sun glinting on the harbour far below, where all manner of craft bobbed up and down on the high tide. The evenings were drawing out rapidly and summer was just around the corner. Porthmellow would soon be thronged with tourists, which meant there would be more of a need than ever for the Wave Watchers. It was a constant battle to find enough people, as some had had to give up due to ill health or had moved away. Fresh pairs of eyes were not only welcome but vital.

She tugged some bindweed from the hedge and watered the tubs she'd planted with Tiff, enjoying the fragrance of the honeysuckle growing up the fence. The salty air wasn't the ideal environment for some plants, but others thrived in it, like the clusters of agapanthus which had yet to emerge. By mid-July, their stunning blue-violet heads would burst into flower, giving the garden an exotic air.

She decided to fetch some plant food from the garages and saw Lachlan doubled over outside one of the units. He was in his running kit, breathing heavily and glistening with sweat. He didn't see her at first so she slowed down her approach so as not to startle him.

He straightened up and tapped the FitBit on his wrist. Marina decided to call out to warn him she was around, to avoid startling him. 'Evening,' she said cheerfully, though inside she was very unsure of the reception she might get.

He was still out of puff so she spoke for both of them. 'I've come to fetch some Baby Bio,' she said, in the absence of anything else, and smiled. 'Don't worry about replying.'

'It w-would be h-hard to answer t-that anyway.' His polite smile morphed into a grimace as he regained his breath.

She turned the handle on the garage door. 'I'll leave you to recover,' she said as he waved an apology at her. She walked inside, finding the plastic bottle in less than a minute and exiting, expecting him to have left, but he was still there.

He was upright now, hands on hips. 'Marina? I wanted to apologise for what happened at the fundraiser . . . ' He paused again, whether to get his breath or be cautious, she couldn't decide. 'And for not acknowledging you since then.'

'It's fine. Don't worry.'

'I don't want you to think I'm being an arse or

124

I've been avoiding you. You must have been wondering why I freaked out when that coastguard
helicopter flew over the harbour?'

'First, I don't think you're an arse.'

He smiled though it was more of a grimace.
'That's very generous of you.'

'And you don't have to explain about the
helicopter if it makes things worse for you. Aaron
told me you'd been in an accident. I don't want
to invade your privacy.'

'You've not invaded my privacy.' He faltered.
'You're one of the people who hasn't invaded it.
People are curious, you see, as to how I came by
these . . . ' He touched his cheek fleetingly. The
exertion had made the scars redder and more
livid.

'It's none of my business.'

'But you *have* wondered?'

'No . . . ' She checked herself, sensing that
polite evasion was probably not what Lachlan
was looking for. 'OK. Yes, I have wondered what
happened to you, but you shouldn't feel forced
to tell me or anyone. I know how people can be
if they think someone's an object of curiosity.
The outright stares, the whispers in shops, the
conversations that stop when you walk into the
pub, the pity, spoken and unspoken . . . '

He held her gaze. 'Aye.. The pity. That's the
killer.' His eyes were beautiful, and she thought
she recognised something behind his expression.
It was a knowledge that life could never be
certain again. 'You sound as if you know what
you're talking about,' he added.

'You mean with Nate?'

He nodded. 'Aaron told me a little more about the circumstances. It must have been very hard for you, not having any closure.'

'Thanks . . . it was a long time ago now.' She went on, trying to sound firm but upbeat. 'It's a time I don't want to dwell on.'

'No.' His tone softened. 'I get that . . . Look, I'd love to ask you round so we can talk some more, and show you I can be a normal — well, *partly* normal — human being, but I'm in no fit state at this particular moment.' He wrinkled his nose but Marina didn't think she'd mind *that* much and she wanted to hear more about his background to help her understand him better.

'You don't have to show me you're 'normal'.' She laughed. 'Who is, anyway? I like people who are different.'

'That's good . . . ' He hesitated. 'Maybe another time when I'm fit for company and you don't have your hands full?' There was hope and apprehension in his voice. She liked that. He hadn't assumed she was going to say yes but clearly wanted her to.

'Yes. I'd like that.'

'What about next Sunday lunchtime. If you're free?'

'I have some marking to do early then a Wave Watchers shift but I should be free by half one, if it's not too late?'

'Not too late! I can do a basic roast? Although I ought to warn you, I'm no chef.'

'A basic roast sounds perfect. I'd probably have made do with a sandwich.'

He nodded. 'Great. See you on Sunday, then.'

'Yes. I'll look forward to it.'

Lachlan left and Marina strolled back to the cottage with the plant food, trying to look as if she'd merely had a chat with a neighbour and not been invited to lunch with the first man she'd been truly attracted to since Nate. The way she was already willing the weekend to come, she had to admit that Lachlan McKinnon had most definitely made a big impression on her.

# 11

Tiff rocked up at Dirk's lair early on the Sunday morning, wrinkling her nose at the sky. The weather was a fitting metaphor for the cottage's owner: the clouds could be in a Turner painting, looming over steel-grey seas topped with whitecaps.

She hoped her 'purchaser' hadn't got anything too outdoorsy in mind, like laying paving slabs or creosoting fences.

'I'm here, bright and early as requested,' she trilled when Dirk opened the door. Wearing trackies and a T-shirt and unshaven, he had the rumpled look of someone who had just tumbled out of bed. Tiff tried not to speculate too much and saluted.

'Not sure what my duties are or I'd have brought a mop and bucket, unless, of course, you want to spend the day practising your bow tie knots . . .'

She was met with a growl. 'Oh. Right. You'd better come in.' To say her reception was an anti-climax was an understatement. She'd expected a sarcastic riposte and to be gleefully informed she'd be learning how to operate a mini digger or fillet a kipper. She'd run through so many scenarios over the past few days that nothing seemed too outlandish.

'Coffee?' Dirk asked once she was inside the sitting room.

'Um. Why not? It is *very* early. Are you sure we

have time for sitting around drinking?'

'Yes. There's time. What do you prefer? I have blonde, medium-dark, or Italian.'

Well, she thought, whatever horrors the day had in store, at least it would begin with a decent cup of coffee.

He returned with two mugs and a plate with four croissants, which were fresh from the oven, judging by the delicious aroma. 'Have you had breakfast?'

Tiff didn't like to say her stomach had been churning too much. 'I didn't have time. Headed straight over here, as commanded.'

'It wasn't a command.'

'You did say seven a.m. sharp.'

'Yeah . . . Well, I didn't think you'd take me literally. Look, would you like a croissant or not?' he said, offering the plate.

She reined in her irritation at his apparent lack of enthusiasm. 'Thanks.'

Tiff bit into the warm and crumbly pastry, growing more confused by the minute. She sipped the coffee while Dirk checked his watch before vanishing upstairs to have a shave. She was left alone to finish her breakfast, admire the artwork on his walls and rifle through his collection of jazz and classical music, some of it on vinyl. He certainly had some expensive audio tech, she thought, wondering if she should tell him how impressive his Bose speakers were.

When he returned, clean-shaven and smelling faintly of cologne, she decided to be upfront with him.

'Look, Dirk. I know the auction wasn't that

129

serious and was all about fundraising,' she said politely but firmly. 'However, you have paid three hundred quid for the privilege — or not as the case may be — of having me around for the day. I'd be quite happy to go home and spend the day lying around but you said you had something in mind, so if that wasn't a joke, then can you please let me know what it is?'

He stared at her curiously, as if he was weighing up an intricate piece of marine engineering. She half expected him to scratch his head and reach for a wrench but then he sighed. 'OK,' he said, getting to his feet. 'Come on.'

'Come on, where?'

'Down to the lifeboat station. But don't say you didn't ask for it.'

Flatly refusing to elaborate, Dirk led Tiff down the hill to the harbour. She half regretted goading him into action, but was also fascinated to know what he was up to. When they reached the lifeboat station on Porthmellow quayside, it was a hive of activity. The large all-weather lifeboat was at the top of the ramp inside the boathouse, with a dozen of the crew milling around it. They greeted Dirk cheerfully and seemed to have been expecting Tiff, which was odd when Dirk had had to be forced into taking her down there.

He ushered her into the control room, which was, briefly, empty. It had huge picture windows looking out over the open sea. Waves broke on the slipway and spray spattered the glass.

'So, will you now tell me why I'm here?' she demanded.

'This is a training day,' he said.

'Okayyy . . . so you want me to make the tea or something?' she said, smiling. 'Help out in the lifeboat shop? I'm not above cleaning kitchens and loos either. In fact, I must admit I'm rather relieved. You could have told me you wanted me to volunteer down here anyway — you didn't need to pay three hundred pounds for the privilege! I've got quite a taste for it actually, after helping out Marina and the Wave Watchers.'

'Yes, erm, we *do* need help in the shop . . . ' he muttered.

The coxswain popped her head around the door. Tiff recognised her from the fundraiser but still couldn't believe she was old enough to be in charge of the huge lifeboat. She was a tiny woman, no more than thirty, with a snub nose and freckles, a bit like one of the orphans from *Annie*. 'Are you guys ready to move? Tiff, we need to get you kitted up.'

Dirk hesitated. 'Rachel, we've had a change of plan. It's looking lively out there so I'm not sure this is a great idea.'

'Oh.' Rachel looked confused then smiled. 'No problem, though conditions are pretty good, I thought. The wind's not *too* bad but if not . . . one of the crew can do it. We'll find you something else to do, Tiff.'

She started to walk out but Tiff called after her. 'Wait a minute! What's this about finding someone else to do 'it'. What is 'it'?'

'Doesn't matter now,' Dirk grunted.

'It does to me. What is this thing I was obviously hauled down here to do, and why can't I still do it?'

131

'I thought you'd changed your mind?' Rachel said.

'How can I when I don't even know what I was supposed to do?' She glared at Dirk before smiling sweetly at Rachel. 'Would someone mind putting me out of my misery?'

'Oh,' said Rachel, exchanging a puzzled glance with Dirk who'd subsided into stony silence. 'Well . . . originally I was under the impression that you might like to take part in the drill.'

'Me? I can't sail. I've never been on a boat, unless I had a large G&T in my hand. I'd be a liability.'

'That's exactly what we want!' Rachel declared.

'Dirk?' Tiff lasered him with her eyes.

'I put you forward to be a casualty in a drill,' he said gruffly. 'But seeing the sea conditions, and not having warned you in advance, I didn't think it was fair.'

'Fair?' A wave slapped against the slipway, throwing spray against the window. Tiff shuddered.

'It's a bad idea,' Dirk muttered. 'There's plenty for you to do here, if you want to stay.'

So, he'd assumed she'd chicken out. 'You mean you don't think I'm up to it?' she replied.

'I didn't say that.'

Rachel's face fell, and she sidled to the door, obviously unwilling to be part of their domestic. 'Um. Could you please decide in the next two minutes so we can get ready?' she said.

'No need to decide. I'm up for it!' Tiff declared.

'Wait. You haven't been briefed yet. You don't know what it involves,' Dirk cut in.

'Are you fit and healthy?' Rachel asked. 'You'll have to fill in some forms.'

'Fit as a fiddle,' Tiff declared, regretting her comment about the gin. 'And it would make a great feature for the mag, if it's OK to write about it?' She dared Dirk to object.

'That would be brilliant. We need all the publicity we can get,' Rachel said, beaming. 'Thanks! Now, I'll leave Dirk to brief you and get you to quickly fill in the insurance and safety forms. Then come into the equipment room and we can get you into your survival suit.'

Half an hour later, Tiff held onto her seat inside the cabin for dear life. The doors at the bottom of the slipway were now open to reveal the sea churning, grey and endless. Despite the swell, the coxswain and other crew seemed as chilled as if they were off for a Sunday afternoon picnic. Tiff's knuckles whitened on the edge of the seat and her stomach was a tangled knot. Any moment now, any moment now . . . she felt a hand on her shoulder and the briefest squeeze.

'You'll be fine,' the voice murmured close to her ear. She had just enough time to realise it was Dirk at her side before the lifeboat plunged down the slipway on its nightmarish rollercoaster ride towards the ocean.

'Fu — !'

With a huge boom, the bow hit the waves, spray rising sky high over the boat. For a few horrific moments, Tiff thought they were going to carry on right to the bottom of the harbour.

Then suddenly the bow pointed heavenwards . . . then crashed down again into the surf.

She might have screamed but the noise drowned out her cries.

The lifeboat seemed to steady — though that was a relative term — as it passed the harbour wall and the engine note grew even louder. They were off, hurtling for the horizon, throwing up spray as the vessel cut through the waves. She couldn't believe a boat could go that fast, tearing through the water, up and down, up and down, rearing high when it met a breaker before slapping down on the water.

Tiff sat rigid, gripping the seat, while Rachel, Dirk and a couple of other crew stood in the wheelhouse shouting and laughing.

'Cuppa?' Dirk shouted, miming a drinking sign in case Tiff couldn't hear.

She didn't trust herself to open her mouth in case more than words came out, so she just shook her head.

Tiff had ceased to believe in God a long time ago, but she started to pray. And she hadn't even been thrown overboard yet.

# 12

Since Lachlan's unexpected invitation, Marina had been humming with a mix of excitement, nerves and curiosity about their Sunday lunch.

Tiff had raised her eyebrows and teased her about the 'date' — as expected — and Marina had insisted it *wasn't* a date . . . but on Sunday morning as she shaved her legs and put on lip gloss even she had to admit it kind of *was.*

She'd been due to go to the cottage 'around one-thirty-ish' after doing the first shift at the lookout station with Gareth. She strolled along the coast path, enjoying the late spring sunshine and the bluebells bursting out in the little copse she passed on her route.

She'd barely taken her mug of coffee into the control room when her mobile rang. At first, she thought it was Tiff calling to be rescued from whatever Dirk had planned for her, but saw it was actually Gareth's name flashing up on the screen.

He was very sorry but he couldn't join her because his family's elderly cat was ill. His mum was taking it to the emergency vet and she'd begged Gareth to go along with her for support. Marina wished him all the best and settled down for her watch, knowing she'd be very busy.

It was a cool but breezy day, and many week-end sailors had taken the opportunity to sail their yachts from Porthmellow Harbour around the coast. She spotted numerous craft — fishing trawlers, motor dinghies, dive boats and a wildlife cruiser — bobbing on the waves by the lighthouse. Through the large binoculars she saw what they were looking at: a pod of dolphins playing around in the surf.

At one point, she saw the all-weather lifeboat powering towards Mount's Bay, but she'd been made aware it was on a training day so wasn't concerned. She realised that Dirk would probably be on board and concluded that Tiff must have been let off her 'forfeit' and was either back home or had decamped to the Harbour Coffee Shop for an espresso.

Marina smiled to herself. Tiff was finding some consolations in Cornwall after all . . . With that pleasant thought, she made it halfway through her two-hour watch and was looking forward to her lunch. The sight of so many people out enjoying the spring sunshine and new life bursting out around the station gave her a fresh optimism and buoyancy. On a day like this, anything seemed possible.

She only had forty minutes to go when a call came in from Doreen and Trevor, two of her volunteers.

Twenty minutes later, Marina dialled Lachlan's number with a heavy heart.

'I am so sorry, Lachlan, but I'm going to have to miss our lunch. Both of the volunteers have got sick. They're married and they ate some dodgy prawn cocktail at an anniversary party last night, and I haven't been able to get anyone else at short notice. I daren't leave the station empty on such a sunny Sunday. There are too many people and boats about.'

Having made a quick drink and grabbed the rest of the ginger nuts for consolation, Marina resumed her watch, trying to concentrate on the reason she was at the station. However strong the temptation to go to lunch with Lachlan, this might be the day when someone needed their help.

With so much marine traffic and people wandering along the paths criss-crossing the headland, and others swimming in the cove, she had her work cut out and couldn't feel sorry for herself for long. She even had to turn away a couple of visitors because she couldn't handle showing them around while staying alert. But busy as she was, it was hard not to occasionally think of the roast dinner she was missing, and, most of all, the chance to get to know Lachlan better.

'Hello! Did someone order a takeout?'

Marina turned round. 'Lachlan! I didn't see you.'

He held up a bag. 'I thought you might be in need of some food.'

As he opened up foil parcels, her sense of smell went into overdrive. The packets contained roast chicken and stuffing tucked into floury baps.

'Oh my, they smell wonderful. You didn't have to do that.'

'I couldn't leave you here while I ate.'

'You waited?'

'Of course I did . . . ' He handed her a serviette and a chicken bap. 'There aren't any rules about food in here, are there?'

She smacked her lips. 'Even if there were, I'd be breaking them.'

He pulled a couple of Diet Coke cans from the bag and popped the top. 'I was sure there were rules about beer though, so this is the best I could do.'

She laughed and took a sip of the chilled drink. 'It's better than a fine wine and these rolls are a match for anything Gabe Mathias could rustle up.'

Lachlan laughed. 'In my dreams! But I'm glad you don't mind me bringing Sunday lunch to you as you couldn't get to it. How about I keep you company until relief comes?'

'We could be here together until eight o'clock,' she warned.

He smiled. 'What a hardship that would be.'

Unsure how to respond, Marina tucked into the roast chicken and stuffing rolls with gusto. 'Well, this is delicious,' she said quickly, to fill the silence. 'Whereabouts are you from in Scotland?' she asked, while Lachlan demolished a second roll. 'I think a few of the villagers were hoping you'd turn up in a kilt.'

'Kilts?' he pulled a face. 'Nope. Just nope. If you see a Scot in a kilt during the day they're either on their way to a wedding, on their unsteady way home from a *really* good wedding, employed in the tourist industry, or an American.'

Marina dissolved into laughter.

'I will admit to falling into other Scottish cliches though. I don't drink much unless it's whisky and when a Scot takes their whisky

138

seriously, they take it *seriously*. This one does, anyway. In fact, that's the one thing that I will never ever take with water or anything. No island malt should ever be polluted.'

'That's fine. I don't have any island malts or any malt at all.'

Lachlan smiled. 'Coffee would be fine.'

'It's Tesco basics at the station but we have some decent stuff at home, courtesy of Tiff. If you ever happen to drop by,' she added hastily.

He replied with a smile but there was no time to continue the conversation because she needed to note the three divers who had slipped off the RIB and vanished beneath the water. They must be exploring an old wreck that had foundered on the reef a century before. Two kite surfers had also arrived on the beach to the east of the cove, where a strip of silver sand had been uncovered by the falling tide. They unloaded their gear. Everyone was out today.

She tried to keep an eye on the job, and find out more about Lachlan's role in Aaron's business. Initially they were providing security services for events across the West Country and a few individual clients. Aaron had recently opened an office in Porthmellow and offered Lachlan the opportunity to be his business partner.

'How did you two meet? I thought Aaron was in the army engineering corps and you were in the RAF military police?'

'We were both in a forces mountaineering club. He came up to Fort William for a course and we met on that, did a few more expeditions and became good mates. When he left the army last year, he mentioned he was setting up the business. He didn't know how it would go then, and it wasn't the right time for me.'

'But now is?'

'Being honest, I still don't know. At one time, after the accident, I was in such a dark place that I couldn't even have decided what to have for dinner — that's if I could be bothered to eat at all. I suppose Aaron caught me at the moment when I'd begun to turn a corner.'

Marina realised that she'd turned her corner a long time ago and had been moving forwards ever since. 'I do get the dinner thing. There was a time when I couldn't see the point in cooking a meal, or eating, or breathing — but I couldn't imagine the alternative either. For months after Nate disappeared, I was trapped between living and not living. I'm not saying I wanted to . . . *do* anything drastic — I didn't have the energy — but I couldn't see a reason for almost anything.'

'How did you get through it?'

'God knows. In the beginning, I'd wake up thinking I couldn't spend another minute feeling as bad as I felt, but somehow, the hours and days passed by. My parents and friends were worried about me, so I tried to pretend I was OK for them and eventually I guess I started to believe I was OK myself. Work helped — my students, my colleagues — and after a while, I found a reason to live rather than just exist: the Wave Watchers.'

'That's a very good reason,' he said. 'Aaron told me you've saved at least a dozen lives over the years.'

Marina glanced away in embarrassment. 'Not us personally, but by alerting the coastguard and lifeboats, we like to think we played our part. You know how it is, if you were in the mountain rescue . . . everyone is part of a team. That's what matters.'

'Aye, we all depend on each other to do our jobs . . . ' His tone took a sombre turn. 'You deserve to know what happened to me in Scotland.'

Marina hid her surprise. 'You don't owe me anything, but I'm here for you if you need to talk,' she said gently.

'Now's as good a time, although I'll not want to distract you.'

She smiled. 'I can watch as well as listen. What happened?'

'OK . . . ' He took a breath. 'A couple of years ago, I was involved in a helicopter crash . . . it's why I don't do communities any more, or search and rescue work.' He smiled bitterly. 'Or people in general. Present company excepted of course.'

'You moved here. You do security work. That's in direct contact with the community.'

'Ach, but I stick to the intel in the back room if I can help it. My domain is the admin, IT and planning. Aaron goes out to see the clients and we employ professional personnel to be on the ground. You could call me the office geek. That's what I did in the military police — I was in management after the initial training. I was surprised how much I enjoyed the fundraiser actually, especially your stall.'

'I'm glad you made it.'

141

He paused and smiled. 'I didn't make it to the end, to the auction. I heard I missed a treat.'

'Tiff might not think of it as a treat,' Marina said, relieved to see his sense of humour was intact. 'But keeping away from everyone, or getting involved with a community again must be difficult, especially when it goes against your nature.'

He nodded, staring out to sea.

Marina tried to give him her attention, while noting that the divers had returned to their boat. She was conscious of doing her job while not discouraging Lachlan, now he'd started.

'Getting involved isn't all it's cracked up to be . . . ' He paused and then raised the smaller binoculars he had around his neck. 'Marina, I could be wrong, but isn't that kite surfer a hell of a way out?'

She pulled the large scope to her eyes and focused. 'Yes, I've got her. I think it might be the woman we saw on the beach with a purple kite. She *is* a long way out . . . and she's in the water. It's pretty rough out.'

She watched for a while longer. The kite surfer was trying and failing to haul the sodden kite out of the water so she could get some lift and surf back to shore.

'I had a go at kite surfing once with Aaron in Scotland,' Lachlan said, still with the binoculars to his eyes. 'It was bloody hard work once the kite was wet. We struggled to get going again.'

'Yes. It's easy for people to get very cold and tired, so they can't self-rescue. How long do you think she's been in the water? I'm concerned that she's been struggling for longer than we realise,' she said, glancing at the clock and cursing herself for not focusing on the task in hand.

'It's been over ten minutes since I first noticed so it could have been fifteen or twenty or even more. Plus, weren't there two kite surfers out on the water earlier? Where's the guy who was with her? I can't see him.'

'Nor me,' she said, adrenaline kicking in. 'I'm calling this in.'

While Lachlan kept an eye on the stricken kite surfer, she called the coastguard and resumed her visual search for the woman's companion.

'Look. There, at the far end of the west beach on the rocks. He's dragging his kit out of the sea now. The kite looks trashed.'

'He must have been carried in on the tide.' Marina gave an update on the situation to the coastguard.

Lachlan was on the move. 'I'll go down and see how he is. I can get there quickly. The guy could have hypothermia and I can ask him about the other kite surfer and call you with any info.'

'Are you sure?' she said, alarmed at him getting involved.

'I'll not get into trouble,' he said, pausing at the door.

'Well, be careful going over the rocks to the far beach,' she called after him.

A few minutes later, Marina saw him scrambling over those very rocks. Meanwhile, an update had come through from the coastguard. The big all-weather boat had been diverted from its training session to an incident down the coast so the small inshore lifeboat was being launched from Porthmellow, along with a coastguard helicopter.

She had a quick look to see Lachlan appear, jogging along the beach but Marina daren't take her eyes off the kite surfer for more than a moment. She was clinging onto her kite and at the mercy of the swell. All Marina could do was keep updating the coastguard, and she sighed with relief when, a few minutes later, she saw a black dot in the sky approaching from the west.

Lachlan called her on his mobile. 'I'm with the male casualty. He's sustained a few cuts and bruises from being blown onto the rocks but seems to be in good shape, otherwise. He's far more worried about his girlfriend. She's called Ursula and she's diabetic. He's worried that she's grown very weak.'

'Tell him the helicopter's on its way for her and the lifeboat for him.'

There was no answer but the wind was blowing. 'Lachlan?'

'OK. They'd better be quick,' he said, and rang off.

The inshore craft arrived at the same time as the helicopter and soon, Ursula was being airlifted from the water. It flew off with her to hospital while the inshore lifeboat crew picked her boyfriend up.

An hour after they'd spotted the kite surfers, Marina was still waiting for Lachlan to return to the station and he wasn't answering his phone.

The helicopter and the whole rescue had

144

clearly brought back the trauma of his accident or he wouldn't have made such a rapid exit. Should she call in to the cottage and see how he was, or did he want to be left alone? Her attempts to draw him out of himself and into the community had both backfired so far and she felt guilty. It must have been a very bad accident to have such an effect on him.

At five o' clock, Marina still hadn't heard from him, and the two volunteers who had left a family birthday early, especially to help her, arrived to take over. She was drained and left the hut with mixed feelings. On the one hand, she was relieved that the kite surfers had been rescued, but she was also trying not to think what might have happened if Lachlan hadn't spotted them. Even though it was his visit that had distracted her, she had to focus on the positives: if the station hadn't been there at all, if she hadn't stuck out the watch, if Lachlan hadn't brought it to her attention — things could have been very different.

# 13

'Whoa, steady. Let me give you a hand.'

Tiff grasped Dirk's arm as he and one of the other crew members helped her off the lifeboat as it moored alongside the quay.

'You OK?' He didn't let go of her arm and she didn't push him away until she was safely on the quayside.

'I'm fine. Absolutely fine.' Finally, and unwisely, brushing off his hand, she tottered up the quayside and back towards the station, feeling as if the ground was a giant marshmallow.

'You'll soon have your land legs back,' he said.

'What legs?' Tiff mumbled. 'They don't appear to be working.'

She'd changed — or been helped to change — out of the dry suit by one of the other female members of the crew after her 'dip'.

She convinced herself that would have been OK — just about — if the lifeboat had headed straight back to Porthmellow station as scheduled. Except it hadn't — it had been re-directed to a real 'shout' a few miles out to sea where a yacht's engine had failed and was drifting towards a notorious reef.

Rachel had taken the decision to race immediately to the yacht, with Tiff still on board. Tiff had been briefed and understood the urgent need and had tried not to show how seasick she felt. But by the time they'd reached the yacht and towed it back to port, it was mid-afternoon and she'd thrown up twice.

The crew had been amazing, checking on her and bringing her cups of water, sweets and some seasickness pills which, although a little late, had helped a bit. She hadn't wanted to make life difficult for them, or to take them away from their main task of recovering the yacht, so she'd done her utmost to look cheerful even though she felt like death.

She'd uttered another of many silent prayers as the lifeboat puttered gently into the calm waters of the outer harbour and only now, back on the safety of dry land, did she finally allow herself a small smile that the experience, though horrendous, would make a hell of a good feature — in fact she might even be able to sell it to a national magazine, let alone *Cream of Cornish*, if she could find a strong enough topical slant to it. There was one added angle she could use, of course, but she didn't think Dirk would be happy about it.

'You were awesome!' Rachel trilled. 'The perfect casualty. No matter how many times the crew try to act like a real casualty, they never get it right.'

'Thanks. I aim to please,' Tiff muttered, grateful that a chair was within collapsing distance. 'I can't believe you do this for the love of it.'

'Dirk gets paid. Most full-time mechanics do because we need a trained expert on site at all times.'

'I'd volunteer anyway, even if I wasn't paid,' Dirk said.

'You have to eat, Dirk!' Rachel laughed. 'And you do come out on shouts at all hours as well as your regular duties.'

'What else would I do with myself?' he muttered.

'I can't imagine spending a moment longer than I had to on that . . . thing.' Tiff shuddered, glancing back at the lifeboat. Two of the crew were preparing to take it back to the station where it would be winched onto the launch slipway.

Rachel patted her on the shoulder. 'There's a brew on,' she said. 'Why don't we all have a cuppa and a debrief. You can ask your questions for the feature at the same time? Or if you'd prefer, you can head home and call me when you've recovered?'

Although the dry suit had, as promised, kept her clothes dry despite full immersion, Tiff's hair was stiff with salt and she could taste it on her lips. She did need a shower, but right now, she could barely contemplate getting wet again. She shook her head.

'That's OK, I'd rather do it while it's fresh in my mind,' Tiff said, her journalist's mind clinging onto the sights, sounds, fear and exhilaration like she'd clung onto the crew member who'd swum into the heaving seas to 'rescue' her.

A while later, she was seated in the crew room around the table with a mug of sweet, 'builder's' tea that she normally wouldn't have touched, but which tasted like nectar. She'd set her phone to record and dug out the notebook and pen she always kept in her handbag. Rachel was chatty as ever, more obviously skilled than the others in talking about her role, though a little too 'on message' for Tiff's liking. Others opened up, though everyone was ultra-keen to play down their part, dismissing it with dark humour.

She'd interviewed people who had done 'heroic' acts before — people who'd stayed behind to help the fallen during terrorist attacks, or dragged strangers from burning cars. Almost invariably, they gave the same answers to the question, 'What made *you* step into danger and do something while others stood by?'

Usually still in shock, few could articulate the reasons behind their actions. They'd simply acted 'as anyone else would'. But not many people were as brave as these people — the crew — who *kept* on putting themselves in danger. Every single time they went out.

As a third party, necessarily detached, the one thing she hadn't fully 'got,' that perhaps she now did, was the rock-solid camaraderie, the uniting in a common cause. She'd glimpsed it at the Wave Watchers shifts as well as during her experience today. The sharing of goals, the confidence that your mates and colleagues would always 'have your back' — and perhaps even sacrifice their life for yours, or, more remarkably, a random stranger's. The disparate parts that coalesced as one, like molten lava fusing into solid rock.

They weren't saints. Of course not. There were annoying people, bossy people and pedantic people in the crew and the Wave Watchers. However, when it came to the crunch on a 'shout', they had all become one person, or at least acted as one person with one aim: to save lives.

It didn't take a genius to recognise the contrast between this world and the one she belonged to — or rather, *had* belonged to. But writing and journalism were now part of her DNA. Plus, she knew it wasn't accurate that *all* her former colleagues had deserted her. Two had come up trumps with auction prizes, even though one was too late, and then there was the editor who'd been happy to commission her freelance stories.

The one person she thought had truly mattered — Warner — had not only let her down, but twisted the knife for good measure. The experience had made her even more cynical and distrusting of everyone except her closest family, but today had helped restore her faith in humanity a tiny notch.

When the rest of the crew dispersed, Tiff was left alone in the crew room with Dirk. 'I um . . . should apologise for putting you in a situation where you felt you had to do that,' he said.

'I didn't have to do anything. I can assure you, Dirk, that if I hadn't wanted to, I wouldn't have.' Tiff hid a smile.

'Mind you. You did make a great casualty . . . ' There was a distinct glint in his eye.

'Then I'm glad you had your three hundred quid's worth,' she said.

'Oh, I think it was worth more than that.'

She raised an eyebrow. 'Wow, high praise from Mr Dirk 'n' Stormy.'

He rolled his eyes. 'Look, I think it's my turn to owe you something. Will you come back to the house for something to eat?'

150

The mention of food made Tiff's stomach swim. 'Erm . . . '

'A cup of ginger tea, if a meal is too much?'

Tiff realised that this was her opportunity to get to know Dirk better. She could use his guilty conscience to find out more. 'Well, I can't imagine putting anything solid in my mouth for the foreseeable future but I might manage a ginger tea . . . '

Dirk's eyes narrowed briefly and his lips twitched, whether in a smile or because he was trying to frame a response, she wasn't sure.

He stepped away, seemingly at sea himself. 'Tea it is, then.'

★ ★ ★

It was surprising how quickly she'd recovered, Tiff mused, when Dirk opened his front door and gestured to her to go ahead of him. Her legs still weren't quite steady and she didn't feel like eating just yet, but she was more than ready for ginger tea.

'Make yourself comfortable,' he said, and went out into the small hallway and through to what she assumed was the kitchen, from the sounds of the kettle boiling and cupboards opening and closing.

Left alone, she got up to look at some prints hanging above the fireplace. They were a mix of scenes of Cornwall in all its moods, from sunny to wild, but her heart sank when she saw her reflection in the glass of one stormy seascape. God, what a sight she was! Her hair was wild

151

and stiff with salt, her face pale and devoid of any make-up.

He was back in a few minutes with a tray with mug of herbal tea for her, coffee for himself and a plate of ginger biscuits.

'Try one,' he urged, offering the plate. 'They're Cornish fairings, the sugar and ginger will do you good. It's been a long time since breakfast.'

'Thanks.' She nibbled at the biscuit, deciding to see how her tummy responded before eating more, but the warm tea was soothing and her appetite began to return. She selected another biscuit.

'I can rustle up some proper food, if you want?'

Her stomach rumbled. She couldn't deny she was now hungry, and she wanted to spend more time with Dirk.

'Cheese and mushroom omelette with salad?'

'That sounds good . . . ' she grinned wickedly. 'Though I kind of expected you to put me to work in the galley.'

'I think you've fulfilled your auction duties for the day and besides, you haven't tasted my cooking yet. That might be part of the forfeit.'

She laughed, and glimpsed a smile that told her Dirk had enjoyed making her laugh.

'Join me in the kitchen?' he said, somehow making the request sound absolutely filthy — or was that only in her fevered mind? She doubted that he felt the same crackle of static between them, or that his pulse hammered away when they accidentally touched, or that he also lay awake thinking about her.

152

'Sure,' she said. 'I'll even lend a hand.'

Dirk whipped up the eggs while Tiff grated some Gruyere and chopped up some mushrooms. Eventually, he divided a pretty passable omelette onto two plates, and they ate it at the kitchen table with a salad and some sourdough. The table was positioned in an extension to the rear of the kitchen, which had obviously been recently done, with its bifold doors and roof light flooding the dining area with light. She could see out to the fence between his elderly neighbour's garden and Marina's place.

They chatted about the lifeboat crew while they ate and he seemed to relax and open up when talking about his work. She longed to record him now his guard was down a little, but didn't dare. He'd be bound to clam up immediately if he thought she was going to write about him and she didn't want to do anything that would stem his obvious passion for his vocation. She lapped up every word about the incidents he'd been involved in . . . some funny, some uplifting, some tragic.

'It's the ones you can't save that stay with you . . . ' he said. 'They haunt you.'

Tiff paused, reaching for the salad bowl.

Clarity exploded in her mind as she finally remembered the story the *Herald* had run, previous year. The picture they'd chosen had been taken after a tragic incident at a Thames lifeboat station where Dirk had been working — however, the photo had nothing to do with the story that accompanied it.

The newspaper had chosen it to go with a

piece about Dirk — or rather, about his ex-wife. The *Herald* had published a series of stories on Amira, a successful actress in a long-running medical soap. Dirk's name had been mentioned in some of the articles — and not always in a flattering light.

Tiff's hands were not quite steady as she scooped more salad onto her plate with the wooden servers. Should she stay silent or confess that she'd come across him before?

Should she carry on deceiving him or be honest?

She toyed with her salad until she looked up and found him watching her.

'Do you miss London?' he asked, seemingly oblivious to the turmoil in her mind.

Caught off guard, she answered, 'Do you?'

He held her gaze for a second as the significance of her question sank home. 'Some things,' he said, his eyes narrowing. He'd never told her that he'd lived in London.

Tiff took a leap of faith, not knowing whether it would take her to the bottom of the sea, never to resurface, as far as Dirk was concerned. 'You're talking about what happened with Amira, I suppose?' she murmured.

'Amira?' His expression turned as chilly as the sea she'd been thrown into. 'I suppose she had to come up some time. How long *have* you known I used to be her partner?' he said coldly.

'Your face first rang a bell while I was helping you with the bow tie, but it's taken me until now to realise it was because I'd seen you in the *Herald*. You already know I worked for them, I take it?'

154

'Evie let slip that you worked on the *Herald* before the fundraiser. Marina mentioned it, apparently.' He shook his head. 'Jesus. Is there no hiding place? Why are you people so interested in people's private lives? Is that why you're here now? To dig up more dirt?'

Tiff had expected a reaction, but even she was surprised by the bitterness in his voice. 'If by 'you people' you mean the press, then I won't insult your intelligence by explaining why we're interested,' she declared. 'But on the subject of why I'm here now, you couldn't be more wrong. If you think I put myself up for auction on the off-chance you would buy me, and throw me out of a boat into the Atlantic then, I can promise you, even a cunning hack like me couldn't have arranged *that*.'

'I never thought you did,' Dirk muttered.

'Just to make it clear, I had no idea you even lived in Cornwall, let alone near Marina — and I also didn't arrange to be asked to deliver the leaflets to you or for you to be so crap at tying a bow tie.'

He grunted, which Tiff momentarily took to be an acknowledgement that she might be right, before he murmured, 'Convenient for you, though?'

'I'd say the opposite. I did all I could to avoid you at the auction. You went over the top with your bid. Anyone would think *you* were stalking *me*, not the other way around.'

'That's tosh!'

'Why did you pay so much for me then?' she asked.

'It was for a good cause,' Dirk shot back.

'Oh, of course. The search and rescue volunteers.'

'Actually, I meant it was worth it to see the look on your face.' And he added, raking her body with his intense dark gaze, 'The look on it right now.'

Tiff struggled to regain her composure. 'Well, I guess now we're even. You had your revenge for whatever ills you think I've done you.'

'The ills I think you've done me?' He snorted in derision. 'I'm hardly likely to forget that it was your rag that hounded Amira and me to the point where she couldn't handle it any longer and our marriage broke down.'

# 14

The switch in atmosphere was sudden and sharp. The banter, so sexually charged a few minutes before, had shifted to anger and resentment on Dirk's part, and unease on hers.

'I'm sorry that happened,' she said, deciding that any defence of her former employer was useless. She wasn't sure she could defend the intrusive nature of the press attention he'd received, anyway. It might have been a year ago, but he was clearly still hurting and definitely believed that the press, and specifically her own ex-employer, had had a hand in the break-up. His hostility towards her was now slightly more understandable. However, she hadn't written the stories herself, so it was unfair of him to lay it at her door.

He toyed with his fork. 'Believe me, I was so happy for her when she landed the role in the series. It was what she'd always worked for and she'd gone through hell with all the rejections and knock-backs for years. Even though I knew our lives would probably change a bit, I was thrilled. But I'd no idea *how* drastically our lives would alter, and I wasn't prepared for the attention once she became so well-known.'

'It must have come as a shock after leading a relatively quiet life,' Tiff said. From their brief acquaintance, she knew he was a private man: taciturn, fiercely loyal to his mates and shunned the limelight. It must have been very hard to handle his partner gaining sudden fame, even if he loved her dearly.

'I was astonished — and horrified — but I didn't want to hold her back. I went to some of the parties, but it was difficult. She wanted me to give up being a mechanic at the Thames Lifeboat Station and she said she'd support me so I could attend more events with her and travel abroad when she had to for other roles.'

'That must have been a tough decision,' she offered.

'I thought about it very carefully. I lost sleep over it, but I needed something in my own life too. I couldn't bear the idea of just following her around, even though I loved her. We were struggling to maintain the relationship by then. I thought about doing it. I almost gave in my notice but then that story broke — about the problems we were having. I got home, we had a huge row and I walked out.'

Tiff knew what happened next but waited for him to tell his own side of things.

'Amira went to the papers. She said stuff about us, about me. She later told me her publicist had made her talk to them. He'd told her it would keep her in the public eye and that she could convince me that the journalist had made it all up.'

Tiff pressed her lips together, picturing the conversation between the journalist and Amira's publicist. She winced inwardly. Hearing Dirk's point of view, she felt she was hearing a new perspective — or perhaps, a perspective she'd lost sight of and dismissed over the years.

'The story blew over in days and our lives were fit for the recycling bins before the week was out, but the damage was done. I tried to talk to her and see a way forward but we both knew we'd grown too far apart. She's living with one of the cast members now.' He paused for a second, and Tiff could see the pain in his eyes. 'The worst moment was when Amira was pictured with that actor for the first time. The press hunted me down to get my reaction. They were on the riverbank the night we pulled a young guy from the Thames. He'd been drunk, jumped in and drowned. It made the papers because it happened during the Cricket World Cup and he was in a New Zealand shirt. They used a photo of me after we'd got the poor lad ashore. It had nothing to do with Amira, and there were other pictures of me on the web they could have used.' His voice rose in anger. 'Yet they chose to use the photo at the scene after I'd dragged a dead person from the water! It was obscene.'

'I'm sorry.' Tiff meant it, horrified at the use of such an emotional photo to sell a tabloid break-up story.

'I decided then that my private life was affecting my mates on the crew, and the casualties. Amira made it clear we were over so when I saw a vacancy here, I jumped at the chance to get away.'

Dirk's voice faded. Perhaps he was embarrassed about revealing too much.

'Porthmellow's a long way from London . . . '

159

she prompted, eager to keep the words flowing, dreading that they'd dry up.

'I was born in Cornwall,' he said, frowning as if she should have known that already. 'Up on the north coast. My parents still live up there so when I decided to move away, it was a no-brainer to come back here . . . Closer to them, and as far as possible from the city, as you say.' He looked at Tiff. 'More importantly, as far as possible from Amira and all the crap that surrounded her. It was your newspaper that ran the final story on her — on *us*. It was garbage, most of it, and they called me a tragic lifeboat hero.'

Tiff sucked in a small breath. Now the layers were peeling back. No wonder he'd shown her such animosity. 'I didn't write it, Dirk.'

'Your mate did. Esther Francois.'

'Esther was a colleague, definitely not a mate,' she said, sharply. It was an understatement if anything: Esther Francois was so far from being a 'mate' that she'd urged the editor to sack Tiff.

'You'd have done the story too, if you'd dug it up,' Dirk said. 'Not that there was much truth in the stuff that ended up in print. It was a pack of lies.'

She hesitated. 'Without knowing the circumstances, I don't know what I'd have done presented with the information. Tragic hero is a cliche. I'd probably have tried to dig deeper.'

He breathed out his contempt.

'Look, Dirk, I can't apologise for a story I didn't write. Why don't you tell me more about the true version of events?'

'So you can print it?' he shot back.

160

'No, so I can understand you better.'

His eyes narrowed briefly, he looked at her as if she'd turned into a frog, then he shook his head. 'Now why the hell would you want to do that?'

'Why not? We've got the rest of the day.'

He snatched up his empty plate and put it in the sink. Tiff flinched, certain she'd blown the moment. She was damned by association, but she refused to feel guilty for someone else's article and certainly not Esther bloody Francois' actions. Nor would she apologise for her job, per se.

She took her own plate to where Dirk was standing gripping the edge of the sink. She left the plate on the worktop next to him.

'Tell me more about your side of things, please.'

'Are you really interested in my side?' he said. 'Your friend clearly wasn't interested in it.'

Tiff chose her words carefully, afraid to shatter the moment again.

'Dirk, I am sorry this happened to you. I'm sorry that you split up with Amira, and I'm sorry you think the story in the *Herald* helped to tip her over the edge. Esther is definitely not . . . my friend. I don't like her methods and I like to think I'd have handled it more sensitively, but I am not going to lie to you. I can't say I *wouldn't* have followed it up myself. Journalism is my job, same as fixing the boat is yours. Yours is just noble, that's all.'

'Noble?' He laughed. 'I got a transfer here to get away from London, not for noble reasons. I ran away.'

161

'Then at least we have something in common,' Tiff said lightly. 'Along with let's say . . . a *compulsion* to be honest.'

He laughed. 'Honest? Us . . . yeah . . . ' He turned to look at her, an intensity burning in his eyes. 'Well, if we're being honest — totally honest — I'd tell you, in spite of everything, how much I want to take you to bed . . . but you must already know that?'

'Oh . . . No. I . . . didn't know that.' Her voice was suddenly throaty. 'My God, I *absolutely* didn't know that.'

Even though she was irritated by his accusations, he'd stopped her dead in her tracks with his blunt declaration. She shivered, partly in surprise and partly in lust.

'Are you shocked?' he said.

'Erm . . . shocked isn't quite the word.'

'So . . . I've made a mistake?'

'No . . . I wouldn't call it a mistake either . . . ' She floundered; floored by a directness that had hit her like a missile out of a clear blue sky and made her whole body grow hot and cold with desire.

'Of course, it *would* be a bloody terrible idea,' he went on, cutting the ground from under her yet again. 'I do respect you being honest, but I just don't trust you.'

*Or can't*, she thought. 'Wow. What a fantastic basis for a relationship,' she said coolly. 'You want to take me to bed but you don't like me and you don't trust me. How could I possibly resist?'

'Easily. I'm a grumpy, rude, anti-social bloke who's now insulted you.'

Tiff seethed with indignant anger and at his comments, but a part of her also wanted to rip his clothes off, and she couldn't decide which of those feelings was winning. 'Anyone would think you were deliberately trying to keep me away from you,' she said, putting her finger on his lips. His eyes widened in shock at her touch. His mouth was warm under her fingertips and sent a thrill through her.

'I think you're doing a very good job of being Mr Darcy. Without the gigantic mansion and millions, of course.'

Reluctantly, she lowered her hand, furious with him but dying to feel her lips on his.

'I always thought Darcy was an arse,' Dirk said, holding her gaze. 'Arrogantly jumping to conclusions about people when he didn't know the facts.'

Was he even aware of the irony of his comment? 'There you go, then,' Tiff said sweetly, yet inwardly fuming and glad she hadn't acted on her impulse to kiss him. 'None of us is perfect. Thank you for the lunch and the most absolutely fecking terrifying experience of my life. I'll write up the feature about the crew. Should be in the next month's issue.'

'Wait, Tiff. I didn't mean — '

'Oh, I think you did. I can find my own way out.'

Snatching up her bag, she stormed into the hall. He followed but she flung open the door and marched out. She was pretty sure he was on the doorstep, but she absolutely was not going to look back to check.

What a day. Rarely had she left someone's house so shaken, so unsure of their feelings — or her own. Dirk 'n' Stormy was a very fitting nickname. Not because of his changing moods but because of the turbulence he stirred up in others. Or perhaps, she realised as she reached Marina's place, only in *her*.

# 15

It was several days after the kite surf incident before Marina saw Lachlan in the flesh again. She'd texted him that evening and received a short reply from him saying he'd needed to go home as soon as the lifeboat had taken the male casualty off the beach and asking her if she'd keep him updated on how the kite surfers were. She assumed that the helicopter's arrival had been a trigger for him.

Luckily, she had plenty to distract her at work: exam season was imminent and she encouraged the students to go outside and get some fresh air and sunshine as a break from the stress.

She sat on the grass with her lunch and chatted to a colleague for a while before checking her phone in case Lachlan had messaged her again. His text had given no hint of when — or if — he intended to see her again. What a shame: she was disappointed as they'd been getting on so well and he'd seemed to be opening up to her.

Tiff revealed she'd seen him when she'd been to the post office, but they only exchanged a nod and a 'hi'.

However, when there was still no message the following day, she texted him herself asking how he was. It was Friday and she'd taken the late afternoon shift at the lookout station. In late May, the coast was stunning. The shady banks were smothered in bluebells while the sunny areas popped with yellow gorse, white sea campion and mauve vetch. Pleasure craft joined the fishing vessels in the harbour and the beaches were busy every sunny weekend.

Holiday time for tourists meant more work for the Wave Watchers and the lifeboat crews, but Marina was used to the rhythm of the seasons in the station by now. Fortunately, that day's shift with Gareth was uneventful.

'See you later,' she told Gareth, leaving him to hand over to Doreen and Trevor.

She had plenty of time to go home and change out of her uniform before heading down into town to meet up with some of the Wave Watchers for a drink at the pub. She strolled towards Coastguard Terrace, inhaling the salty sea air and listening to the choughs calling from the cliff edges, and the waves crashing onto the rocks below. Once again, she was struck by the contrast between the beauty and danger of the place. Nate wouldn't have understood that: he was gung-ho about the sea, always telling her not to worry.

An involuntary shudder shook her and when she turned away from the cliff, Lachlan was approaching on the path from the direction of the Lizard. She wondered if he'd slowed at first, having spotted her, but then almost immediately, he jogged towards her.

'Hello, stranger,' she said lightly.

He wrinkled his nose. 'Aye. I have been a stranger . . . Marina, I'm sorry I rushed off after the incident. Once I was sure the casualties were going to be OK, I needed some space. I should have told you straight away, and not disappeared like that. Sometimes a little thing — or a big one — will trigger bad memories and I have to get away. It's probably only a fight or flight thing . . .' He toed the earth. 'Though it always seems to be flight these days.'

'We all need our space from time to time. I know I do. You don't have to explain.'

'It isn't me — running away. It didn't used to be me, anyway . . . perhaps I can't get used to the changes in me. I know other people couldn't.'

Marina left a gap in the conversation, hoping he only needed time to fill it, but he shrugged. 'You don't want to hear about me and my problems.'

'I wouldn't say that. I'm on my way home. Do you want to try me?'

They walked together, chatting, and stopped to look out over the coast. Cornwall was at its finest on this glorious May evening, with the light mellowing and the colours intensifying as the sun sank lower. The sky was a cornflower blue, the breeze whispering through the gorse and carrying its toasted coconut scent.

'It's beautiful,' Lachlan said, standing by her side.

'It is. I do love it.'

'Working up here, sometimes on your own. Does it not bring back unhappy memories?' he asked.

'Sometimes . . . though they are memories now. I made peace with myself a while ago. I accepted that I couldn't change the past, but I could, even in a small way, help to change the future for someone else. That's comforting.'

'I wish I was at that stage.'

Marina found herself wishing he was too, but she understood better than anyone how much time he might need. 'It will come.' She waited for him to speak some more, perhaps unspool his fears and doubts, but he stayed silent — lips pressed together, eyes fixed on some nameless spot out over the waves.

'Scotland must be very beautiful too . . . ' she ventured. 'Can you believe I've never been?'

'What? Ach, you must put that right. It's quieter and wilder; there are far fewer people, which is fine by me. The mountains, glens and lochs have a way of seeping into your soul without you realising it . . . ' He shook his head, a little awkward. 'I'm romanticising. I have to admit the weather is much better here.'

Marina thought he sounded almost lyrical, and she found it endearing. 'We have our moments with the gales and high seas.'

He laughed. 'Aaron's dad loves telling me about the giant waves. They seem to get bigger every time Troy tells the tale.'

Marina smiled. 'Well, those waves can be quite something. A few years ago, in one winter storm, the sea threw shingle over the cliff so high that our kitchen window was broken.'

'That's scary.'

'It was a long night . . . ' She suddenly realised he was only in a running vest and shorts. Not that she wanted him to put more clothes on, but he must be getting cold. Plus she had promised to meet up with her friends in town.

'You must want to get back after your run?'

'I'm in no rush.'

This was promising. 'I said I'd go to the pub with a few mates. It's barbecue night at the Smuggler's Tavern, and Drew's band is playing outside on the quayside. He runs the sailing trust for his day job,' she explained, in case Lachlan didn't know who he was. 'But he's in a folk band too and they're really good. In fact, I was on my way home to change out of my uniform. Would you like to join us?'

He hesitated. 'I'll not say no to a burger and a pint, but I don't want to spoil a party.'

'You won't. There'll be loads of locals there. Everyone turns up and joins in.' She gave him time to refuse, realising that he'd only recently said that he found it hard to join in with community events. At the same time, she realised how very much she wanted him to say yes. 'It's pretty casual but don't feel you have to.'

'OK. Yeah, I'd like that. I need a shower first though or I'll probably clear the whole pub.'

Marina didn't think so. She thought he looked hot in the running gear and wished he hadn't mentioned taking a shower because it was conjuring up images in her mind that she probably ought not to dwell on.

'Great. D'you want to knock on my door when you're ready? Half an hour, enough?'

'It's a deal.'

Back in her cottage, Marina showered, changed into a casual dress and was lacing up her pumps when Lachlan knocked the door. His arrival stirred a tickle of excited nerves in her stomach. He was in cargo shorts, a polo shirt and flip-flops: standard Porthmellow uniform, except that the vast majority of men in the town didn't have a physique that had been honed by swimming in lochs, hiking and climbing. His scars were becoming part of him for Marina. It wasn't that she ceased to notice them; more that her subconscious had accepted them like any other feature of his face and body.

If he was apprehensive about meeting everyone, he didn't show it, although she supposed that could all have been an act for her sake.

There were already a couple of dozen people outside the Smuggler's when they arrived, milling around the tables. On this balmy late May evening, the place was packed with locals and holidaymakers alike, their laughter and chatter ringing out along the quayside. Her nostrils twitched at the smoky tang of food and Lachlan was also hungry after his run, so they headed straight for the barbecue to collect plates of burger and salad. One of the Wave Watchers volunteers had already offered to buy a round, and their drinks were waiting when they joined a group of familiar faces on one of the pub tables.

The sun was warm on her bare arms, and reflections sparkled in the harbour. Porthmellow was on its best behaviour. So far. Marina realised that her arrival with Lachlan was bound to have some people jumping to conclusions about the nature of their relationship. She knew that a handful might even be curious about how he came by his injuries and less than tactful in their reactions.

No one in her group of mates would be that crass, however, and she genuinely enjoyed introducing Lachlan to Sam Lovell and Chloe Farrow from the Food Festival Committee, and to Jude Penberth and Scarlett Latham who shared a cottage on the harbourside. Lachlan already knew Scarlett a little because her older sister, Ellie, was Aaron Carman's partner.

'How's Ellie?' Marina asked Scarlett, noting her absence.

'She's fine. She's nearly four months gone now but she's feeling knackered tonight so she and Aaron decided to stay in.'

Lachlan chuckled. 'Aaron's like a mother hen with Ellie.'

Scarlett laughed. 'Ellie does her own thing. She won't let him wrap her in cotton wool.'

Marina realised that she envied Ellie. She had always wanted to have a family and after Nate had gone, she'd blanked that desire out, for the sake of self-preservation, she supposed.

Lachlan was chatting to Jude and found they shared a love of wild swimming and the great outdoors. Gradually, Marina relaxed. The sun began to slip behind the horizon and cast the harbour in shadow. Everyone pulled on jumpers but the twilight was also the cue for Drew and his musicians to start up.

They played a lively mix of folk and pop, together with the odd Cornish standard, that soon had people singing along, fuelled by plenty of local ale.

'You were right. Drew's band are pretty good,' Lachlan whispered to Marina.

'They're not bad at all,' Marina said, pleased that he was enjoying the music. She decided it was safe to tease him. 'But don't you miss the bagpipes?'

He snorted. 'Bagpipes? Oh God, spare me. I can't stand the things. They give Scotland a bad name, along with tartan trews and tinned shortbread. I never minded a good ceilidh though. We used to have them on the base for the families and I went to my fair share in the town . . . ' Lachlan stopped. Marina guessed that the thought had awakened memories of his previous life — good and bad.

While they listened to the music, the table rang with singing and laughter. Lachlan seemed to be fitting in well. Craig stumbled past them and into the Smuggler's Tavern with a couple of his mates. By the looks of his unsteady walk, he'd already visited some of the other pubs in town beforehand. It wasn't long before he came outside again, a pint in his hand.

The band took a break and Craig lumbered over.

'Evenin', Marina.' He nodded to the others before staring at Lachlan's face. He might simply have been trying to focus but Marina stiffened, dreading him saying anything about Lachlan's scars.

'Lachlan, isn't it?' he slurred. 'You Schottissh, then?'

'Last time I looked,' said Lachlan.

'Not wearing your kilt, though?' He snorted. 'What do you wear under it?'

Oh no, thought Marina, but Lachlan laughed.

'I could tell you, but then I'd have to kill you.' He smiled. 'I'm joking, pal — I don't even own a kilt.'

Craig gave a wobbly salute. 'No offence, mate.'

'None taken,' Lachlan said pleasantly.

He turned to Marina. 'I see you're moving on from Nate,' he said, his voice dripping with sarcasm.

Marina was too shocked to reply but Craig was quickly gone regardless, loudly demanding that one of his mates get the next round in.

'Anyone want another drink?' she piped up. 'It's my turn.'

'I'll come with you,' said Lachlan.

Lachlan took the orders and they ducked under the granite lintel of the door and joined the queue at the bar. It was stuffy after the fresh air of the harbour and her eyes took a few seconds to adjust to the dimly lit interior.

'I'm sorry. Craig's an old buddy of Nate's and he took his death hard,' Marina said.

'Aye. I can see that . . .'

'He's all bluster though,' she added, glossing over the fact she'd been genuinely rattled by Craig.

'It takes more than that to rile me. I'm tougher than I look,' he said. 'Though it's hard on you to have to put up with that sort of stupid comment.'

'Craig was drunk and he's an idiot,' she said, annoyed that Craig had tried to spoil their evening by implying that she ought to be loyal to Nate. 'Let's forget it.'

Marina determined to enjoy the rest of the night, but she was convinced that Lachlan had become quieter since the incident with Craig. By ten, the barbecue had run out of burgers and the band had played their finale. In the twilight, it was also growing cold on the quayside. Marina shivered despite her hoodie and finished her Coke.

They said their farewells and headed back home. Lachlan had left the pub smiling. Marina felt that he seemed to be more comfortable with Porthmellow life than she'd expected, which gave her hope that he might stick around long enough for her to get to know him much better.

Perhaps Craig hadn't got to Lachlan as much as she'd feared.

They walked side by side along the harbour-front, where the lights of houses and restaurants twinkled in the darkening water. It was a warm evening, and there were plenty of people strolling along the waterfront and sitting outside the two pubs. Laughter and Greek music spilled from the balcony of Gabe Mathias's restaurant and delicious aromas wafted into the evening air.

All too soon, they reached her cottage, but he showed no sign of bidding her goodnight. Everywhere was quiet apart from the whisper of the waves on Porthmellow beach, below the cliff.

'Thanks for asking me, tonight. I wasn't sure whether to come at first but I'm glad I did. I really enjoyed it.'

'They're a great bunch, though you were lucky enough to get some of the less weird ones tonight . . . apart from Craig of course.'

'I've already forgotten him,' Lachlan said, which gave her heart. 'I like your mates, but I'll confess the pleasure of the evening was largely down to the company I'm with now.'

A flush rose to her face. She wasn't used to being complimented in this way, but she liked it. She thought for a moment that maybe he was going to ask her to his house for a coffee, or even lean in for a kiss.

A moment later, he'd shoved his hands in his pockets. 'It's work tomorrow,' he said. 'I'd better let you get home.'

'Oh. Yes.' She deflated rapidly.

She left him, cursing herself. She'd read the signals wrong. He had seemed to be moving closer to her — or her to him — but had pulled away at the last moment. They were like kites dancing in the wind, soaring high, almost touching, then diving apart again.

Perhaps it was simply way too soon after Lachlan's accident for him to think of anything beyond friendship. But she couldn't help wondering if Craig's comments about Nate really *did* have something to do with Lachlan's reticence to let her get closer.

Even if she was ready to move on from the past — and from Nate — some people in Porthmellow never would.

# 16

Tiff was enjoying an *affogato* on the terrace of the Net Loft in lieu of her usual Saturday morning cappuccino. The sun blazed down from a blue sky so she was in a sleeveless shift and ballet pumps. On a weekend morning in Porthmellow, there were always plenty of locals around, as well as scores of holidaymakers pottering around the harbour, galleries and cafés. Fishermen were unloading their pots and she recognised some of the townspeople chatting outside the shops. Ellie and Drew were working on the sailing trust trawler; Chloe Farrow was feeding ducks with her granddaughter; Troy was chatting with his old mates on the steps of the Fisherman's Institute. She almost felt part of the scene, part of Porthmellow . . . or perhaps it was becoming part of her . . .

Since their spat about Amira and the newspaper the previous week, she'd barely spoken to Dirk, other than the odd 'hello' or quick exchange around town. She'd lost sleep over it, torn between annoyance at his prejudice and steamy thoughts about his admission that he longed to take her to bed. She supposed their row *had* helped her to understand him better, even if she'd left angry at the injustice of his ideas about journalists. That being said, if his only experience of the press was Esther Francois, she could understand why he might well think that all her ilk were ruthless bitches.

'Uh huh,' she murmured under her breath, laying aside her copy of the *Saturday Post*. She fanned herself with a menu as Dirk made a beeline for the café. Despite it being a hot June day, he was clearly about to launch his own mini thunderstorm on her if his expression was anything to go by. The magazine in his hand was a bit of a giveaway as to the source of his wrath. She would have bet her new pumps on it being the very latest edition of *Cream of Cornish*, which had hit the cafés, hotels and gift shops only that morning.

She coolly sipped her *affogato* and braced herself as he made for her table. He was possibly the only man who could look brooding in a T-shirt and flip-flops, she thought, and noted that his hair was a wild mess, probably a result of too much angsty raking.

Without asking, he sat down opposite her and laid the magazine in front of her. 'I got hold of this,' he said in a low voice, possibly mindful of the glances of several locals who were on the terrace, or watching from the mobile seafood kiosk opposite. 'I'd like a word with you.'

'Only one? Wow. Fine — but first would you mind breathing into my cup?'

His brow furrowed deeply. 'Breathe into your cup? What do you mean?'

'I'd like you to re-freeze my ice-cream, if you don't mind,' she said sweetly. 'You're so frosty this morning, I'm sure you'd have no problem.'

He shook his head. 'You're absolutely — '

'Yes?'

'You're infuriating.' There was a tinge of

amusement in his tone.

Tiff sipped her drink. 'Shouldn't you be tinkering with a propeller or something?'

'I *was* tinkering until someone dropped off a pile of these,' he said, tapping the magazine, 'at the station. Do you know what the rest of the crew are calling me now? Do you have any idea of what you've done?'

She savoured the creamy coffee before replying. 'You read my article about the lifeboat experience, then?'

'Yeah, I read it.'

'And?'

A young waitress arrived. 'Can I get you any thin'?' she said, looking utterly bored.

'No . . . Actually, yes. Espresso, please, Martha,' Dirk replied.

'That all?' Martha smirked.

'I'll have a glass of iced water,' said Tiff, desperate to cool down. 'Please.'

'Still or sparklin'?' said Martha. Tiff had the feeling Martha wasn't one of her greatest fans.

'Sparkling, please.'

After Martha had scrawled their order on her notepad and swept off, Tiff turned her attention to Dirk again.

'So, our 'matter-of-fact demeanour belies a fierce determination to save lives, no matter what the cost to ourselves', does it?' he said, nodding at the article.

'Sorry. Slightly purple prose but, you know . . .'

'Do you really think that about us?'

'Yes, Dirk, actually I do. Sometimes we do write the truth, you know . . . my aim was to give

178

my understanding of why a bunch of volunteers would knowingly risk their lives for strangers.'

'And?'

'You read it. Different reasons, some more obvious than others. The protect-the-herd mentality, where a small community helps each other, knowing it could be them . . . some of the crew have lost loved ones, for some it's simply a generational thing, grandparents in the service in the days when you rowed out in a cork life vest.'

'And me?' Dirk asked.

'I can't quite fathom you, but if I had to bet my life on it, I'd say you enjoy a battle, and the more impossible the odds, the more you want to take on the fight.'

'You can't fight the sea. It'll always win.'

'Ah, but there are many small victories. Every time you pick someone off a lilo, or the rocks, or tow a yacht back to the harbour?'

'It's my job,' he dismissed.

'Yeah. And I was just doing mine,' she replied, determined to stand her ground. Dirk was so close that she felt the hairs on his bare legs tickle her smooth ones under the table, though she wasn't sure he'd noticed. One moment she felt as shivery as if she'd dropped ice down her top, the next as steamy as an espresso. Dirk had that effect on her most of the time these days. 'It was a pretty good piece, though, wasn't it?' she teased.

'I'm not going to massage your ego,' he said.

'Go on, admit it.'

'OK. It was well-written — compelling even — but I can't handle being paraded like this for people's entertainment, even if it will boost the coffers. I'm not a hero. None of us want to be portrayed in that way.'

'At least I was nice. I *did* say you were taciturn rather than bloody rude.' She spoke gently. 'I wanted to portray you honestly. After all, you'd surely hate me turning you into a saint?'

'Too right!' he burst out, then softened his tone too. 'Look . . . it's a good piece. More honest than most, more authentic, but you know I don't like being in the limelight.'

'It's too late now. I'm sure the proposals of marriage will come flooding in when they see that photo.'

He laughed. 'You scuppered any chance of that by making me out to be a miserable sod.'

Martha returned with the drinks. Tiff sipped hers but Dirk left his espresso. 'Aren't you going to drink that?' she asked.

'I didn't really want anything.'

'Why did you order it then?'

'I don't know.' He leaned a little closer, wafting a subtle hint of spicy aftershave in her direction, and triggering a lethal cocktail of hormones that seemed to turn her body to mush. She wondered if heads had turned and tongues were wagging.

'You don't seem to know what you want, Dirk.' Her voice had notched up a pitch. She cooled her palms on the glass.

'I do know one thing I want.'

Before Tiff could reply, the sirens at the lifeboat station went off.

'Oh God. Not now.' Dirk sighed.

Seconds later he was already running towards

the lifeboat house, leaving Tiff stranded at the café and screaming inside with frustration even as she felt a swell of pride that brought a most unexpected lump to her throat. She'd been in Porthmellow barely two months and she was already turning mushy — about Dirk and the town in general.

Tiff groaned. She really ought to guard against it. For now, all she could think of was how close she'd come to finding out what Dirk really wanted.

# 17

The bank holiday week over, Marina was thrust back into the whirlwind of college life, supporting her students during their exams, offering counselling, and attending meetings about the autumn term. Working with young people, helping them achieve their ambitions, had always made her feel alive and valued.

She was also busy with her volunteering because, with summer around the corner, demand for the Wave Watchers' services was greater than ever. People took to the water on any item that floated — and many that didn't — from luxury yachts to kayaks, surfboards to inflatable flamingos. The cliffs were covered with pink thrift, buzzing with bees and walkers hiking along the coast path that ran between the Lizard and Porthmellow.

Now that the evenings were lighter, the lookout was staffed from eight until eight. Marina was grateful that Tiff managed to pop in occasionally, although her own job kept her out long hours.

Lachlan had been back to Scotland for ten days to visit his family, and Marina had missed his presence and even her glimpses of him coming in and out of his cottage. On the bright side, he'd texted her a few times, asking if she'd like to go out for a meal when he returned.

On the Saturday lunchtime she expected him back in Cornwall, she was on watch with Gareth.

It was the warmest day of the year so far, and the windows and doors were flung open to let the air flow through the building. By noon, the cove was a suntrap and peppered with families lazing on the sand, the little ones paddling in the rock pools. A few people were in the sea itself, mostly only wading or splashing around. It was a calm day, but Marina and Gareth still had to be vigilant.

Everything seemed relatively safe until around two p.m., when Gareth piped up, alarmed: 'There's a guy and a teenager in the cove. They seem to be taking a blow-up kayak into the sea.'

Marina winced, thinking immediately of Nate. 'A kayak?' The word always made her chest constrict. 'Haven't they read the signs? It says not to use inflatables of any kind.'

'I think most people ignore it,' Gareth said, dropping his binoculars to speak directly to Marina. 'The weather report says the wind is already strengthening and there's quite a swell outside the lee of the cove.'

'That doesn't sound good. We could do with some lifeguard cover on summer weekends, but the council can't afford it,' she replied, musing for a second. 'I'll pop down and have a word with the kayakers, if you'll be OK on your own?'

Gareth sniffed. 'Of course I will.'

She trotted down to the beach, enjoying the warmth of the sun on her bare arms. The sand was dazzling and the sea turquoise. It looked very inviting, with the spray flying into the air when the waves hit the rocks, and she could see why people were tempted to go for a paddle.

183

Strolling over to the man she assumed to be the father, she fixed her best friendly smile in place, silently noting that he and his son were wearing shorty wetsuits and there was no sign of a buoyancy aid or any safety equipment.

'Hi there!' she called. 'I hope you don't mind but I'm from the lookout station on the cliff. I don't want to spoil your fun but it's not a great idea to launch craft from this spot. It's much windier than it looks, and the tide is going out.'

The middle-aged man took in her uniform and smirked. 'Thank you, my dear. We know you're only trying to help but we know what we're doing. We'll be fine.'

*Dear?* Marina resisted the urge to tell him she wasn't old enough to be anyone's 'dear'.

'This cove can be dangerous,' she said more firmly. 'There are submerged rocks and currents around the headland. It seems calm here but there's a big swell and the surf could easily carry you onto the rocks.'

'We'll consider ourselves warned. You've done your duty now, so you can go back up to your mates,' he said, and turned away from her. 'Jacob, you can leave the wheels up here.' He beckoned to his son. 'I doubt anyone will take them with this lady watching.'

Jacob nodded. He took the kayak off the wheels and dropped them above the tide line.

'We can't mind people's property,' Marina said, boiling with frustration. The father could do what he wanted but she was fuming that he was so blase about putting his teenage son in danger. 'Why don't you put off your kayak trip until

184

you've hired some buoyancy aids from Porthmellow sailing centre?' she said, determined to do her best to stop the man risking his son's life, if not his own. 'Or you could launch from the main beach where they have lifeguard cover? You've no idea what could go wrong out there!' Her voice rose in desperation. 'You can see the waves breaking. They're getting stronger by the minute.'

'We'll think about it next time,' the man snapped, before turning his back on her. 'Jacob! Let's get going!'

With that, he picked up two paddles and marched off towards the water.

'Wait!' Marina said, following him. She didn't care if he was annoyed. She couldn't let him go without trying one more time. If there was the slightest chance she could prevent another tragedy. Another Nate . . .

His son was already in the kayak, as the man pushed it into the surf. It lifted and wobbled as the man tried to climb aboard. 'Wait!' she called again, her feet getting wet in the small wavelets. 'You've no idea how dangerous it is here!'

The father turned his head, a furious look on his face. She thought she heard Jacob say something to him but the man shook his head and they paddled off through the surf towards the open sea.

Tears of frustration stung Marina's eyes. She was breathing heavily and her heart was racing.

She spoke into her radio: 'I t-tried to stop them, Gareth, but it was no use. The father wouldn't listen to me. Please keep an eye on them until I get back!'

Torn between anger and concern, she hurried back up the steps. It was hot work and her blouse stuck to her back. Before she'd reached the station, she realised that she'd probably let her loss of Nate cloud her professionalism. She'd wasted her breath on the father . . . and the likelihood was that they'd be back safe and sound. At least she *had* warned them, and maybe a tiny nugget of her advice had sunk in — though she doubted it.

Marina forced herself to simmer down and try to put the incident into perspective, slightly ashamed about having shouted at the father. Gareth logged the kayakers until they disappeared out of sight, presumably exploring tiny coves and strands further up the coast, which were inaccessible by land. She hoped they didn't disturb the seals which frequently hauled out to rest in one of the coves, or worse, try to get out onto the rocks for a closer look.

They had to come back into range sooner or later and it was almost impossible that she and Gareth would miss them. They remained vigilant, noting the wind had freshened and brought a big swell. Some large clouds came over and Marina couldn't help but think it would be very cold on the water in the short wetsuits.

An hour and a half later, when they hadn't returned, Marina became anxious.

She reported their absence to the coastguard, on the off-chance that someone else might have seen them in difficulties. No reports came in and she tried to relax. She couldn't worry about everyone and all she could do now was ask the incoming Wave Watchers, Trevor and Doreen, to keep an eye out when they turned up.

'*Porthmellow Station. Be advised. Two kayakers have been sighted off Seal Cove. Reports of a person in the water. Porthmellow lifeboat on its way.*'

The radio message made Marina's heart stop momentarily, but she had to stay calm to make her reply. She had no idea who was in the water, the father or son. Either way, that person was in deep trouble. The water was only around twelve degrees this early in the summer and, given their lack of full-length wetsuits, they might have only minutes before hypothermia set in. She shuddered to imagine the fear and panic of both men.

Did Nate feel that fear and panic?

Marina had to summon all her strength to keep calm. She held out her hand. It was trembling.

But she told herself that the lifeboat would do its job, and, five minutes later, she received a call to say that both the boy and his father had been found clinging to the capsized kayak. A few minutes later and it would have been washed onto the rocks. Though the boy was cold, he seemed unharmed, but the crew said they were very concerned about the father.

She took a few soothing breaths, praised Gareth for his vigilance and managed to make it through the rest of the shift, hoping for an update from the lifeboat crew but knowing they probably wouldn't receive any further information on the casualties. You often didn't find out the outcome of a rescue until much later — if at all. However, on the way home, the shock hit her. They could have drowned. They might have drowned without the lookout station. Imagine the boy's mother? What if she'd lost her son and her partner?

She knew all too well how that felt.

She quickened her step, keen to reach home, have a cool shower and calm down.

'Marina!' Lachlan was running towards her. 'What's the matter?'

'Nothing,' she said, with a forced smile.

'You look upset. Are you OK?'

She stopped dead and let out a cry of frustration. 'No, I'm not. Two people, a father and son, almost drowned on my watch. They went off in a bloody inflatable kayak with no life vest or safety equipment. I did everything to stop them going out. They almost died. The man's in a bad way apparently. Oh, hang on . . . ' She pulled her mobile from her pocket, dreading what she might hear.

Her heart thumped crazily as she listened to Dirk's voice. When he'd rung off, she let out a massive sigh of relief.

'The guy's out of danger but it was touch and go. He was a few minutes from giving up and he'd swallowed a lot of water and had hypothermia. Stupid, stupid idiot! Why would you do that? Why be so bloody stupid and risk your life and your son's? Argh.'

Lachlan seemed to reach for her but quickly dropped his arms. 'You did everything you could. You can't save everyone.'

'I let my personal feelings take over but they wouldn't listen. I would have done anything to keep them from getting into trouble, but I just couldn't stop them. I should have tried harder, but I got caught up in what happened to Nate. I shouldn't have let my own life intrude.'

'Why not? Don't be sorry. You tried your best, and you don't have to be 'together' all the time. You're entitled to feel upset when something triggers bad memories, no matter how long it's been . . . time isn't always the great healer they say, is it?'

She took a breath. He seemed to understand her. 'Not always. I was thinking about him a lot today. The weather is so lovely, and he disappeared on what was a sunny day in July — yet a squall blew in very quickly.'

'That can happen in the mountains too,' Lachlan said. 'Conditions change so fast. You can never let down your guard.'

Marina managed a 'hello' to a couple strolling past. It was so British, keeping up the niceties while her heart was in turmoil.

'Shall we find somewhere quieter?' he asked. 'There's a bench near here that's tucked away in the gorse. I saw it when I was running and sometimes I go there if I need some peace. If you want to tell me more about what happened that day,' he added.

She nodded and followed him up a ribbon of a track away from the main coast path. They sat on the granite bench with its pale green coat of lichen. It was slightly elevated and afforded a beautiful view over the sea while shielding them from the coast path below. Marina inhaled the scent of the gorse and pushed her hair from her eyes. Lachlan sat next to her, evidently waiting for her to take the lead.

189

'I wish I *could* tell you what happened,' she began. 'I only know fragments of what took place in the time leading up to his disappearance. He hadn't had the fishing kayak long. It was his new thing; he was hoping to make a bit of extra cash.' She allowed herself a brief, bitter smile. 'He was always looking to make a bit of cash. We'd been married almost two years and, actually, I hadn't known him long before we *were* married. He'd moved to Porthmellow from Newlyn.'

'He was from a fishing background, then?' Lachlan put in.

'His father worked on the trawlers apparently, but Nate had never seen much of him. He kind of abandoned Nate after his mum passed away and Nate was left to his own devices in his teens. He didn't go to sea that often. It's a hard life after all, and many don't take to it, but the fishing kayak . . . well he seemed to enjoy that and went out on it a couple of times a week.'

'So the man knew what he was doing?'

'He thought he did. That was him all over. You might say he was always a glass half full man, even when the glass was obviously almost empty. He was funny, the life and soul. I thought he had a real zest for life when I first met him at a mutual friend's wedding in Porthmellow. He was popular even though he was relatively new here. He was always first to buy a round in the pub, he told a great story, and he'd help people out if he could, but he owed money too. He had debts I didn't know about until after he disappeared.'

Lachlan simply listened, nodding from time to time.

'I shouldn't go on about him . . .'

'I asked. And you obviously still need to get this off your chest,' he said.

'I thought I'd done that long ago. But yes, I understand only too well what it's like to want to walk away from a situation that triggers bad memories,' she said.

A lightbulb flicked on in her mind . . . maybe, she thought, that's what Nate had sought to do: flee from a situation that he found intolerable. She'd always refused to entertain any suggestion by her close family that Nate may have wanted to harm himself, always believed it was a tragic accident, but if his debts and responsibility were getting on top of him, perhaps that's why he went off on his own so often. If that was the case, she wished he'd been able to talk to her. It was too late now.

'I guess I'll never know what really happened, which is why I find stuff like what happened today so difficult. But I've tried to stop asking 'what if'. It's only this milestone and the finality of the legal declaration that's making me focus on it again.'

She paused to collect herself, eyes resting on the panorama of the coast stretched out before her. The pink thrift rippled as one in the breeze and the gorse thrummed with bees.

'You're bound to miss him, despite everything. It's obvious you loved him.' Lachlan spoke softly. He waved away a bee and smiled at her. There was warmth in his smile, but sadness too. Was it sadness for her or himself?

Marina pressed her palms against the cool

granite. 'Life wasn't boring with him, that's for sure. It was a rollercoaster ride. You never knew what he'd do next. He had big ambitions, but no real plan, and he was always getting bored and moving on to the next exciting scheme.' She smiled ruefully at the reminder of their topsy-turvy existence.

'He was going to buy his own trawler, or have a betting shop, or . . . He and I were very different, but opposites attract, I suppose. When we met, I'd not long come out of uni and I was doing my adult teaching certificate while I worked part-time in the Co-Op in Porthmellow.

'By the time we were married, I'd managed to get my first job teaching English at Mount's Bay College. I loved it and we managed to buy a flat in Penzance. Then my grandma passed away and she left me enough extra to put down a deposit on the cottage. It was rundown and ramshackle but we did it up together and made plans, the way you do . . .' She paused.

'Aye.' He didn't elaborate.

Marina wondered if she should stop . . . but it was too late. 'We were young, and I bought into Nate's optimism and the excitement of not knowing where life was heading . . . but as the years went by, I began to realise that that was Nate.' The bees buzzed on the thrift near her feet. 'He was a bit like these bees, flitting from one gaudy flower to the next. That's why I fell for him in the first place I suppose: he seemed fun and ready to take a risk. It was romantic at the start, and so I guess later on I just felt I should stick it out and that things might get better.

Something would come up, as Mr Micawber would say.' She laughed.

'Whit's fir ye'll no go by ye,' he said. 'In other words, if things are meant to happen, they will.'

'Do you believe that? I think you can change your fate.'

'I'm not sure. Before the accident, I thought I was master of my fate, but since then, I'm not so certain.'

His smile was deep and reflected in his eyes. What kind of a man was he before he had the scars? The same as she was? Naive, trusting, never believing anything bad could happen to him? She'd no inkling that there was a cliff edge waiting to collapse beneath her.

'Even when we think we've put the past behind us, some things — some people — stay lodged in our hearts,' he added.

She wasn't sure if he meant Nate, or that someone was still lodged in his own heart. Had he realised how much that person meant to him while he was back in Scotland?

'Let's go home,' she said. 'You've just got back from your trip, and I've had a day and a half.'

He made no mention of the text he'd sent with the dinner invitation and she wasn't in the mood to remind him.

It was frustrating. She wanted to make a fresh start. She was attracted to Lachlan and she thought he liked her. There should be nothing stopping them from taking things beyond friendship, but it felt as if the ghosts of the past were determined to haunt them both.

# 18

Tiff had seen a lot of Dirk in the week or so since their café conversation had been left hanging.

*Saw* being the operative word, because on none of those occasions had she actually spoken to him. Instead, she'd actively tried to avoid Dirk, attempting to cure herself of her craving for him. But every sighting left her more frustrated at her weakness, and more in lust than ever.

The previous day, however, she'd seen him three times: outside the lifeboat station (that was hardly unprecedented), in the post office again, and then, bizarrely, he'd entered a boutique next to the Harbour Café when she was in there taking some details from the owner for an ad feature. Dirk didn't even seem to have noticed her, heading straight to the rear of the shop, where there was a display of what Tiff considered to be vastly overpriced swimwear. What he was doing in the smart ladieswear boutique was anyone's guess. Still, you never know, maybe he really did need some ladies' swimwear. Dirk was full of surprises.

On the Friday evening, almost two weeks after their 'chat' at the café had ended so abruptly, she walked into the Chough Gallery. It was a damp evening and drizzling, so she was grateful to scuttle inside the building, which was tucked away in a warren of streets behind the harbour. She'd been invited to attend an exclusive exhibition by a local artist, and report on it for *Cream of Cornish*. By the time she'd arrived, the room was buzzing with the artist's friends and family, along with some of the gallery's favourite customers, local media and townspeople from the festival organising committee.

She recognised several of the faces and they greeted her like an old friend. Having had no dinner, Tiff discreetly hoovered up as many canapes as she could get away with and sipped her Prosecco. The artist was a lady of at least seventy, renowned for her abstract pastels and oils of the Cornish landscape. Her silver hair was enhanced with rosy tones and she wore a leather jacket that Tiff recognised as vintage Belstaff.

Tiff enjoyed doing the interview with her, vowing to choose a print, even though she still had no idea when she'd ever be able to return to her own flat to hang it. She certainly couldn't keep living off Marina's hospitality — even though she was paying her way, Marina would want her own space sooner or later.

After the artist gave a brief speech, the chatter and Prosecco-chugging resumed, while orders were placed for some of the originals and prints.

Tiff wandered over to one of the paintings, admiring the dreamy take on a low-tide morning at Pedn Vounder beach . . . She adored the view and had made more than one detour to gaze down at the white sands and turquoise waters while in the far west. That was the one she would love for her wall. She wondered if she really did dare indulge in a small print . . . perhaps she could buy one for Marina as a birthday gift.

'I'll admit — that's a stunner.'

She swung round and came face to face with Dirk. He looked smoking hot in a white shirt and black jeans. For a moment, Tiff was stunned herself.

'Um. Yes. It is.' She recovered and waved her glass in his direction. 'Dirk. Is there any reason why I keep bumping into you? Or rather you keep bumping into me?'

'No idea what you're talking about. We live two doors away from each other, if you hadn't forgotten.'

'How could I?' she said in honeyed tones. 'And yet, here's the thing. I can understand why you might have come into the post office when I was there. Twice,' she added. 'Or that your car needed fuel at the exact same time as mine. I can even take the fact that you just happened to be here tonight for this gallery launch. I know you like the arts, albeit you did let slip to me that you hated abstract — '

'I never said I hated it.'

'I think the words: 'I'd rather watch every episode of *Hollyoaks* than waste my time on some of that modern crap' were used.'

'Shh.' He glanced around him. 'I was being ironic.'

She raised an eyebrow while trying not to laugh. 'So, what were you doing in the Quayside Boutique yesterday? Interested in their new range of Kurt Geiger mules? Or was it the Melissa Odabash bikinis that arrived last week?

Anyone would think you'd been stalking me.'

'Erm . . . oh, screw it. I wanted to talk to you.'

'Aha, I see.' She eyed him critically. 'Then why didn't you?'

He opened his mouth to retort then huffed. 'OK. I surrender. I've wanted to talk to you about what happened after the lifeboat drill for ages but I chickened out at the café and again in the boutique.' He paused before going on, almost as if he was plucking up courage. 'Here goes. Do you think you could find it in your heart to forgive what I said to you?'

Tiff raised her eyebrows in genuine surprise. 'Well now. That would depend on whether I actually have a heart, which you strongly implied I didn't.'

'I was harsh, and I made some sweeping assumptions. But I'd like the chance to know you better. To know the real Tiff.'

'You took your time about it. You could have knocked the door or texted. WhatsApp, a call?'

'There never seemed to be a perfect moment. Or I didn't know how to say what I want to say to you. I never know what your reaction's going to be.' He lowered his voice further, struggling to keep the frustration out of it. 'Look, I know I infuriate the hell out of you, but I also *really* like you. You make me laugh, you keep me on my toes, and you make me think. I think about you all the time.'

Tiff suppressed a shiver. A good shiver that made her toes curl in a delicious way. She whispered in his ear, drinking in the wonderful scent of him. 'I never think about you.'

He smiled. 'Of course you don't . . . but I can't get you out of my mind. You're there every moment. Well, not when I'm on a shout, obviously . . . ' He grinned. 'But most of the rest of the time. I would really like it if we could call a truce and simply behave like two adult human beings who want to take things further than a sophisticated playground sparring.'

Her Prosecco glass wobbled. He didn't have to touch her to ignite a fire deep inside her, the words were enough, uttered in that deep, delectable accent.

'I'd love it if we could get out of here now and negotiate a ceasefire.' He was right by her ear. 'Preferably in bed.'

'Mmm . . . ' She couldn't wipe the grin off her face. Dirk's words were the equivalent of warm honey being drizzled over her naked body. God, what was she thinking? She'd gone full-on E L James and what's more she didn't care that people were only feet away. If they'd had the infra-red camera on her, she'd have been glowing white from head to toe. Evie Carman caught her eye and Tiff smiled back.

'Bear with me. I'll see what I can do,' she said, then whispered, 'Meet me outside Gabe's restaurant in five minutes.'

With that, she left him and sashayed over to the artist, thanking her for the invitation and promising to write up the feature, which would appear in the September issue of *Cream of Cornish*. She avoided making further eye contact with Dirk or even looking in his direction. She only hoped he was suffering the molten, naked desire that she was.

She left the gallery and walked onto the quayside, stopping by the Net Loft where she pretended to study the menu board. It could have offered roasted tarantula for all she knew, because her mind was on the delicious prospect of having Dirk Meadows for supper, as a nightcap and for breakfast.

It was actually nearer ten minutes before he joined her.

'What kept you?' she said, curling her fingers so he wouldn't see that they were shaky.

'Evie spoke to me and I didn't like to rush off. I had to put on a good show.' He grinned. 'Why? Thought I'd changed my mind?'

'I was about to go home, actually,' she said haughtily.

'Sure you were.' He grinned. 'My place, I assume?'

'I think so. I love Marina to bits, but this is one occasion I don't want to share.'

She'd never climbed the steps up to the cottages so fast. She hadn't realised she could go that fast, but months of practice had made her fitter than she had been for years. Not to mention she was also fuelled by the desire to rip Dirk's clothes off, and he even gave her a hand once they were out of sight of the gallery.

Out of breath but laughing, they almost fell through the cottage door and into the sitting room. She wasn't sure who pulled who down onto the sofa, but clothes were being ripped off. A shirt button pinged against the hearth and Dirk swore but didn't pause.

'Bloody cuffs,' he said, laughing while trying to

199

pull his shirt off in the semi-darkness.

Tiff dealt with the buttons on his jeans. Once they were free, everything came off or down swiftly and she had his beautiful body against hers, his hands, a little roughened by work, gently exploring her. She closed her eyes and gave him everything.

# 19

Marina had been wrong about Lachlan — she'd wondered if he'd changed his mind about asking her to dinner, but he called her the very next day after their talk with an invitation to Gabe's restaurant later that week.

During the meal, they caught a few curious glances from local people. Marina nodded to a few but she tried to focus on her dinner companion. They talked more about Scotland, about her college job and his new business with Aaron, about the food . . . it was all light and friendly talk, which made a refreshing change from their previous intense conversations.

No one bothered them and it was a relief to simply focus on a relaxed evening out with a friend . . . maybe this was the moment when their relationship might become more?

After their dinner, they strolled up to her cottage and stopped outside. Lachlan surprised her by immediately asking, 'Could I tempt you to a wee dram? Unless it's too late?'

'Well, it's a school night . . . but a very wee one won't do any harm, so why not?' Marina said, more than happy for the evening to go on longer, even if she did have an early lecture in the morning. Being invited inside Lachlan's own place, which must be his sanctuary when the outside world got too much, also felt like a leap forward.

There was no light on in her own cottage as they passed so she concluded Tiff was out and followed Lachlan through the soft green door into his place. She hadn't been inside that particular cottage since it had been sold by the previous owner, a Porthmellow local, and turned into a long-term let. It was one of the smallest in the whole row; a one-bedroom mid-terrace painted the colour of clotted cream.

He showed her into the sitting room, which was neat and tidy. He made her a coffee and fetched a bottle of single malt and two glasses and a small jug of water. Marina had only had a spritzer at the bistro and Lachlan a glass of red wine; they'd stuck to soft drinks after that with a mind on work in the morning, so she didn't think a small one would do any harm now.

He brought out two engraved crystal tumblers that might have been a gift from his comrades in the RAF, but she didn't comment. Leaving the service must have been painful for him — but was it less painful than staying?

'It's very cosy in here,' she said, thinking of the impact Lachlan's appearance had had on her from the moment he'd walked out of the sea like a Scottish Daniel Craig. 'I mean, it's lovely, of course. I haven't been in for years. Er . . . how are you finding it?'

He seemed amused so at least her awkwardness had broken the ice.

'The cottage is big enough . . . some of the neighbours are scary though,' he said, deadpan.

She laughed. 'I see what you mean. Deffo the neighbours from hell.'

He poured a measure of whisky into her glass and offered her a jug of water.

'Thanks,' she said as he added a splash to her tumbler, leaving his own neat.

'What made you choose Porthmellow and this cottage? Was it all because of Aaron?' she asked.

'Mostly . . . his offer came up at the right time. Or at the *wrong* time, because I can't say I was in a happy place at the time he mentioned it. Aaron's a great bloke though. I'd trust him with my life. Once I'd decided to come down here, I wanted to move straight away and this cottage came up for rent at short notice. I'm used to military accommodation, so I don't mind it being small.'

'It looks a lot bigger than I remember it. The previous owner was obsessed with Marvel action figures and memorabilia and they took up every nook and cranny.'

'Really? Wow. I can't imagine it stuffed with Avengers figures.'

'There was a lifesize Incredible Hulk in the kitchen.'

'You're joking?'

'Yes . . . there *were* hundreds of smaller figures though. Mr Rees was a very weird guy. He was only in his thirties, but he used to wear a tweed suit to the pub, complete with a watch on a chain. He was an undertaker . . . the kids used to think this place was haunted.'

'Really? Maybe I should charge people to look round, then,' he said, deadpan.

She laughed, wondering if Lachlan did plan on personalising it in any way, or whether he was content to leave it neutral. It certainly didn't have any trace of his personality yet, but maybe the neatness was a hangover from being in the military. If moving to Porthmellow was wiping the slate clean, this place was the natural embodiment of it.

Then again, it could simply be that he didn't plan on staying long-term.

Pushing away that thought, she focused on enjoying the moment. She was facing the window and the sky outside was indigo blue. Lachlan sat on the sofa, one arm flung along the back, his leg crossed over the other. Marina sank back into the armchair, and let her tensions ebb away. It was the most chilled out she'd seen Lachlan and the most relaxed she'd felt in his company.

He sipped his whisky and a stillness descended between them. Marina sensed he was bracing himself to talk.

'A while back, you asked me what happened back home and why I came here,' he said, his eyes on the amber liquid in his glass. 'The truth is that I was trying to get as far away from the mountains as possible and live a quiet life. Not because of these.' He touched his face. 'I don't care about how I look. I left because of issues that went way more than skin deep. I suppose some of my mates and even my family might call it running away, but I prefer to call it self-preservation. This is my fresh start.'

Marina thought carefully before replying, eager to hear more. 'I'm glad you chose Porthmellow, even if the reasons behind it aren't happy ones.'

'I feel I owe you the full story.'

'You don't owe me anything, Lachlan, but I'm ready to listen.'

'Well, you deserve to hear it . . . ' He managed a small smile. 'When I was in the RAF military police, I was in charge of security on the base. I've grown up in the mountains and loved climbing so it was natural for me to volunteer for the local search and rescue team near the base. In fact, I was acting as leader that day.'

'Was this last winter?' she asked, afraid to shatter the bubble of his confidence.

He sipped his drink. 'Late February last year. The twenty-fifth, to be precise. We were called out on a shout to look for two students who'd climbed Ben Daurrig and hadn't come down to their youth hostel by afternoon. Their mates couldn't raise them, so they alerted the mountain rescue.

'The helicopter picked us up from the base and dropped us above the snowline so we could reach the casualties faster because it was going dark and snowing heavily. We found the students and the helicopter evacuated them to hospital. They were taken off safely and the team started to walk down and I slipped in the dark on the icy path.' He shook his head. 'Stupid, really. Classic error. I'd stopped paying attention after the adrenaline of the rescue was over; I was joking with some of the team and lost my footing. I came off the path and down the mountainside.'

She gasped. 'Oh my God!'

'Fortunately for me, there was a narrow ledge about fifteen feet down which broke my fall and prevented me from ending up at the bottom of a cliff, but I heard the snap, and knew I'd broken my ankle.'

Marina winced.

'I don't mind admitting that I almost passed out with the pain and by then it was snowing hard and Catriona — the medic who was with the team — said we couldn't wait for me to be carried down because conditions were worsening, so she called the helicopter back.'

'It sounds horrendous.'

'I was suffering, but I didn't want the helicopter to come out for me because I knew its crew would be at its limits in that weather. I can't help but think that they only risked it because I was one of their own. I caused them to come back again. If I hadn't slipped, they wouldn't have had to take that risk. Conditions were bad enough on the first rescue, but when they came back they were the worst I'd ever experienced, with massive downdraughts, snow swirling in the high winds and almost no visibility. They should never have taken off again from the base, not for anyone.'

Especially not him? Marina wondered if that was what he meant.

He flexed his fingers, and she noticed the tremor in them. Dredging up bad memories was painful and traumatic, it sucked your energy, but sometimes, you had to get those fears into the open.

'By the time we reached the base, the blizzard was at low level, and the winds were horrific. When we came to land in the valley at the base, a gust caused the pilot to lose control and we hit the ground. I was woozy from the meds, so my recollection's hazy but I remember the impact and the explosion. It felt as if my eardrums had shattered. There were shouts and someone was trying to unclip me from the stretcher . . . ' He gazed into his glass but didn't drink.

He paused so long, she had her doubts about whether he'd continue.

'The next thing I remember I was on my own and crawling through the snow on the tarmac. The ground was freezing, I was soaked, but at my back, was this tremendous heat. I think my clothes were on fire and the smoke was blinding and choking me. There was another explosion and I couldn't crawl any more. I lay there waiting to die.'

He paused and took a breath. 'Next thing I knew, I woke up in the hospital, thrashing about and shouting.'

She hid a shudder. He needed gentle encouragement, not shocked reactions. 'What happened to the others?'

'I only know what I was told because most of that night has vanished. It's a hole, a nothingness, and, no matter how hard I try to remember what happened, I find a vacuum. I must have been unconscious for a time, or I've blanked it out, or both.' He sipped his whisky. 'Three of the crew managed to escape with minor injuries, but not Catriona. She was the one who stayed, undid the straps on the stretcher and helped me to the door. I heard later that she went back to check the pilot had got out safely. I guess in the smoke and chaos, she wasn't sure. The helicopter exploded while she was inside and . . . ' He had to stop. He rested his glass in his palm. 'She died instantly.'

'I'm so very sorry,' Marina murmured.

'She was a fantastic woman; her death was a terrible loss for her family and for all of us. She was engaged to be married to another member of the MRT team . . .'

So, here it was; the deeper grief he'd been hiding all this time and the thing that was keeping him from moving forward. She had been afraid to hear the truth but had needed to. 'I'm very sorry . . . But you can't blame yourself.'

He looked at her as if she'd asked him if the earth travelled around the sun. 'Of course I blame myself. At the end of the day, it was my fault we were in the helicopter at all — my carelessness. If I hadn't fallen, the crew wouldn't have had to come back for me. No one can tell me otherwise, and they *have* tried. Time has gone by and I'll accept it one day, so they tell me.' He met her gaze. 'Maybe I already *am* starting to look at things through new eyes. Like you say, the 'what ifs' are pointless, and they can never bring Catriona back, but I'm only so far down the road.'

'You'll get there . . . or most of the way.'

'Aye.' He knocked back the remains of his whisky. 'Whatever happens in the future, all I know is that I'm finished with the RAF and Mountain Rescue. Once I'd recovered physically, I went back to work, but I couldn't stand being around the base every day. So I ran away.'

Marina had lost the taste for her drink, however nice it was. All her focus was on listening to Lachlan.

'It's very tough to stay in a place that's caused you such heartbreak,' she said.

'And yet you stayed here in Porthmellow. You even chose to open the station overlooking the scene of Nate's disappearance. You didn't run away.'

'That was my way of making sense of what happened. Believe me, some people thought it was the wrong thing to do, macabre even. My parents worried I was fixated on his loss and on that spot in the cove. I probably was — possibly still *am* — but that was my way of dealing with it. Except it wasn't a loss, not really. There was never closure — until I opened the station. Ironically that gave me comfort and helped me to accept that he could never have survived being out in that sea for long.'

He gave a nod of shared understanding that she found comforting. 'There was no chance of Catriona coming back. I knew she'd gone forever. After I returned to the base, every time I saw or heard the helicopters, I'd break out in a sweat and I couldn't face going back to the MRT. Before Christmas, I begged the CO for a medical discharge and eventually, she agreed. So — ' he held out his hands ' — here I am at the other end of the UK. Thanks to Aaron, that is.'

'Are all your family and friends still up in Scotland?' she asked, picking her words carefully, wondering if there *had* been a partner.

'My parents and my sister live in Dumfries. Some of my friends tried to persuade me to stay, but most accepted I wanted to move on. They're used to people passing in and out of their lives, that's part of being in the Services.'

Marina didn't think she'd ever get used to the constant change but didn't say so.

'So, thanks for cutting me some slack . . . ' he said, gazing at her thoughtfully. 'How are you so together? Despite what you've been through, you got up from rock bottom and started the Wave Watchers and you hold down your job at the college. I admire your spirit, Marina.'

'You'll find your own equivalent of the Wave Watchers.'

'Only if I go looking for it. Right now, I just want to keep a low profile.' He laughed bitterly. 'Also known as hiding away from the world.'

'Yet you came to the station to apologise.' And he had chosen her — and tonight — to unburden himself, she thought.

'Aye, you're right — but that's because it's you. Not everyone and anyone. There's a world of difference.'

She laughed. 'You hardly know me.'

'Not yet . . . that's why I asked you here this evening.' He put his empty glass down and leaned forward. 'My instincts are telling me that it was a good idea.'

Marina smiled. 'Mine too . . . '

She was pleased he felt able to open up to her, but she would have to be patient if she wanted to know more.

Her phone pinged with a WhatsApp message and, while Lachlan was in the kitchen, she glanced at it. It was Tiff.

*How are you getting on with Rob Roy? I have*

had *the* most intriguing time with Mr Dirk 'n' Stormy. Tell you more tomorrow.

Marina was surprised to see that it was eleven o'clock.

'Lachlan. I've realised the time. I need to be up early for college in the morning,' she said, getting up as he walked in from the kitchen.

'Eleven?' He glanced at the clock on the wall. 'I'd no idea. I'll not keep you from your bed any longer,' he said.

What a shame, thought Marina, unable to banish the image of Lachlan keeping her in his own bed.

'I've a meeting in Truro first thing too. I'm sorry to have kept you out so late,' he said.

She hoped he'd put her rosy cheeks down to the whisky and the sun. 'You haven't. I've really enjoyed it.'

'Me too. It won't be the last time, I hope?'

'I hope not,' she said, and threw a smile at him as he stood in the doorway to see her off with a promise to call her to arrange 'the next time'. She was buoyed by the optimism of his final statement.

What a day this had been. For the first time, she'd truly begun to understand Lachlan, and, for the first time, she'd seriously begun to think of a man who wasn't Nate as something more than a friend. It felt as if they'd both taken a step forward into a brave new world.

# 20

Tiff woke up in Dirk's bed — again. Since their gallery encounter, they'd made up for lost time by spending almost every night together and there was no sign of the passion wearing off. She thought about him in every spare moment she had and many that she didn't.

Tiff walked her fingers up his torso and rested them on his chest. He really was magnificent — honed but not in a cover model way, with the perfect amount of chest hair. She could even forgive the nipple ring. In fact, it had become a key feature in her fantasies about him, which were extensive and detailed.

Not that he was ever going to know that, of course.

He kissed her. 'You're a health and safety hazard. I dropped a wrench the other day, thinking about what I wanted to do to you this evening.'

She laughed. 'I thought about you while I was having a tour of a clotted-cream factory.'

'I'll take that as a compliment.' Dirk gave her a long deep kiss.

'It was hard to keep a straight face . . . ' Her stomach fluttered. 'It's a shame we can't stay here forever.'

'I'd probably drop dead with exhaustion if we did.'

'Yes.'

He groaned and shifted. 'I have to get up. We open the lifeboat station every Saturday in the summer to get the tourists in . . . '

'I'll come with you, if you like?'

'To the station? You'd be so bored.'

'Try me. I can help. Make tea or something . . . ' The truth was she wanted to spend more time with him and if she had to go down to the lifeboat station to do it, she would.

He thought for a few seconds. 'Well, we always need people to help in the shop while we show visitors round the station.'

'The shop? That sounds easy. I can do that if someone shows me how to work the till.'

'You might regret it,' Dirk said with an arch of the brows.

Tiff laughed. 'I might regret a lot of things, but I really don't mind. Plus, I'm sure it'll be more fun than last time I was at the station, being chucked into the Atlantic!'

Several hours later, she was cursing inside while apologising profusely for not being able to give a young man from Stoke change for a twenty-pound note. She'd put it in the till but let the cash drawer close before fishing out his £9.50 change. Parminder, the retired pharmacist who was helping her in the shop, had gone to 'answer the call of nature' and she'd been alone for ten minutes. She'd barely glimpsed Dirk as he was so tied up in the boathouse itself.

'I need that money for the car park,' the customer grumbled, pointedly looking at his watch. 'My ticket's running out!'

'I'm *terribly* sorry but there's no one around

to help . . . ' Tiff replied, desperately scanning the door through to the station itself. The place was packed with holidaymakers, queuing for tours and asking questions.

Three other people had now joined the queue behind the impatient customer, their baskets full of jigsaws, tea towels and model boats.

Struck by a sudden brainwave, Tiff grabbed her purse from her bag. 'Here you are, I can give you some change.' She managed to fish out some five-pound notes and handed it to him. 'Here you go, forget the extra fifty pence.' She'd have done anything to get rid of him.

'Thanks,' he muttered and stalked off.

Two lavender-haired pensioners, obviously twins, reached the front of the queue, eagerly holding their debit cards up. 'Do you do contactless?' they trilled in unison.

'Um . . . ' Tiff prayed for Parminder to return and almost squealed in delight when he reappeared. In a flash, he'd opened the till to sort out Tiff's impromptu reimbursement of the car park guy.

'Take it as a donation,' she said, simply relieved to have an expert back.

★ ★ ★

'I heard you had a baptism of fire in the shop,' Dirk said later, over a glass of wine on the balcony at The Net Loft restaurant. It was a beautiful evening, with sunlight glinting off the harbour and yacht halyards clanking in the gentle breeze.

214

'Better than a baptism of icy seawater,' Tiff replied, enjoying the evening sun on her bare shoulders. 'Although almost as stressful at times.'

'Parminder told me you'd given someone change out of your own pocket.'

'Only because I was desperate to get rid of him. I couldn't get the bloody till to open.'

He laughed. 'I must admit I'd never have imagined you as a charity shop volunteer when I first saw you.'

'Well, the day you see me in rubber clogs is the day you'll know I'm beyond all hope.'

'I think you'd look good even in rubber clogs,' Dirk murmured.

'Not as good as you would,' Tiff flashed back.

'I'd rather go overboard without a buoyancy aid,' he growled.

She chinked his glass. 'Then we agree on one thing. No clogs.'

She sipped her wine and it was really rather good. The skate wings that arrived, with a lemon butter glaze, were delicious too, and Tiff couldn't even fault the crushed potatoes, despite their associations with queuing on the narrow roads.

Most of all, the company was delicious, and as the sun sank behind them, lighting up the harbour with pink rays, Tiff could imagine how she could stay here forever. She also noticed more than a few sidelong glances, mostly from women. In addition to her London-ness, she'd now added the far greater sin of having 'snared' Dirk Meadows. Except she hadn't snared him, only temporarily invited him into her life.

They lapsed into silence, gazing out over the

boats, and Dirk's hand crept over hers under the table. He squeezed her fingers and it felt so good . . . the electric thrill of his touch . . .

'It's going to be hard . . . ' Dirk said when their espressos arrived.

Tiff raised an eyebrow and laughed. 'I'll pretend you didn't say that.'

'Hard when this ends, I mean. Us.' He frowned. 'You'll go back to London before long, Tiff.'

'Maybe . . . ' She smiled. 'Probably. But that's all the more reason to make the most of now.'

'Keep things casual, you mean? Like they are now? I must admit I'm enjoying the way things are,' he said. 'I hope you're finding the arrangement pleasurable, too?' His eyes sparkled.

'It's an extremely pleasurable 'arrangement',' she murmured. 'Plus it makes things simpler when I do leave,' she added with a smile. 'And when that time comes, we must promise each other there'll be no regrets and no sad faces. Until then, we should make the most of enjoying every moment together.'

He flashed her such a sexy look it almost made her knees buckle. 'Then why are we wasting time here?'

Reminding herself that she still had a lot of exploring to do where Dirk's body was concerned, she finished her cooling coffee in one gulp and reached for her purse, throwing some money down on the table. 'Come on, let's go.'

Dirk added notes from his wallet to her half of the bill and pinned them down with a saucer.

Even as she hurried home, with his arm at her

216

back, Tiff couldn't help reflecting on her words to him. No matter how much she tried to pretend that it was only the sex making her want to spend every moment with him, it wasn't the whole story. She knew too well that if she let herself like him any more than she did, she'd be in trouble. Falling for Dirk would mean a painful exit from Porthmellow when the day surely came.

Hadn't she learned her lesson with Warner — not to get too involved with a man, however appealing? Dirk was no Warner, in fact he was the opposite, not to mention far more gorgeous — but that made him equally as dangerous.

Despite all her vows to keep things casual, she floated up the slope to the cottages in her heels as if she had wings. She didn't need to be reminded of the way she'd trudged up to his house on her first day, expecting a pound-shop Heathcliff. It was impossible not to recognise that, since then, Mr Dirk 'n' Stormy had got under her skin in ways she'd never even dreamed.

# 21

Lachlan stood in the doorway of Marina's cottage, with a leaflet in his hand.

'I picked up this flyer in the village,' he said, handing it to her. 'Some outfit called Stargazey Pie is running an evening cookout called Pie on the Beach.'

'Oh yes, that's Sam Lovell's mobile business. Some of the staff at college were talking about it today. Sounds good. It's at Seaholly Cove, isn't it?' She glanced at the leaflet but was more intrigued by his sudden appearance on her doorstep. It had been a couple of days since their heart to heart at his place and she'd wondered if — when — they might meet up again.

'Yes — this Saturday. You take your own plates and glasses, and chairs or a picnic rug. They dish up the food and you eat under the stars on the sand. There's a menu on their website . . . if you fancy it, that is.'

'Saturday night?' Marina said. 'Oh . . . '

'Is it a problem? If you're busy, we could do something another time . . . '

'No. No . . . Saturday's fine. It's OK.' She smiled. 'More than OK. I'd like that.'

His expression lit up and she realised he'd probably genuinely been unsure of her response. They were still skirting around each other, despite their previous conversations. She did feel that Lachlan was holding back more than her, but perhaps that was because she was further down a path than he was. But the fact he'd invited her to a communal event was a promising sign for a man who said he wanted to 'hide away from the world'. She certainly didn't want to put him off, now he'd decided to venture out.

'Great. I'll book two places and call for you around six so we can walk down together?' he said. 'I'll bring some wine and glasses, shall I?'

'I'll bring the plates and a rug then.'

'Sounds like a plan.' He left, and she heard him whistling softly once he'd gone a few yards. Unable to wipe a silly grin off her face, she went out to the garden to take a few calming breaths.

She looked out to sea. On the Lizard point, the lighthouse was a silhouette in the evening light. There was something that she hadn't told Lachlan and had no intention of revealing in case it shattered the rapport they were building.

Saturday night would be the seventh anniversary of Nate's disappearance — and the day that, legally, he would be officially considered gone forever.

★ ★ ★

Marina told Tiff about the beach date while they were both keeping watch at the lookout station the next evening.

'Wow. Well done. I'm very happy you two finally saw sense. I like Lachlan, even from the few times I've met him . . . I saw him pay for an old lady's shopping in the Co-Op the other day because she'd forgotten her purse.'

219

'What? You didn't say anything before,' Marina said

'Sorry, I must have forgotten. I told him it was a nice thing to do but he brushed it off. He's clearly modest as well as kind hearted . . . ' Tiff's eyes gleamed. 'Although I don't think his chivalry towards elderly ladies is the main part of his attraction, is it?'

'No, I have to admit it isn't.' Marina smiled then her doubts came back. 'I'm looking forward to it in one way but . . . do you think it's a bad idea to go out on a date with another man on a night like that?'

Tiff seemed puzzled. 'A night like . . . oh, I see. That's the anniversary of . . . ' She let the rest of the sentence hang, probably because she didn't want to say the words out loud.

'Of Nate's death. Yes. I haven't told Lachlan. It's not really the sort of thing you want to hear on a date. Especially as we're getting on so well right now.'

'Of course I don't think it's a 'bad idea', my love. If you like Lachlan and you want to have something happy to look forward to on what could be a grim day, then it strikes me as a great idea.'

Marina sighed. 'I'm not sure what my mum and dad will think.'

'Have you told them?'

'Not yet. I haven't told anyone apart from you. I keep wondering if I should be throwing flowers into the sea, dressed in widow's weeds and weeping, instead.'

'Don't you think you've done enough of that

to last a lifetime?' Tiff swept her arm around. 'Who needs flowers when you've got this place as the best memorial Nate could ever have? One that's saved many lives and will go on to save many more. There's even a plaque on the wall outside dedicated to his memory. So you have absolutely nothing to feel guilty about. Plus, I don't think Nate would want you to spend the rest of your life weeping for him, would he?'

'No, I don't think he would,' she replied, though in truth she'd no idea what Nate would have wanted.

'So go out with Lachlan and live your life. You deserve it.'

She nodded and they watched in silence for a few minutes before the radio crackled into life with a message from the coastguard, making them aware that the Porthmellow lifeboat had been called out to a trawler with engine trouble.

Tiff showed a great interest in the message and seemed very keen to be in charge of the powerful binoculars. She was intent on the orange all-weather lifeboat cutting through the waves, throwing up spray on its way to the stricken vessel a few miles up the coast.

'Have you managed to zero in on Dirk yet?' Marina asked.

Tiff pulled her eyes from the scope, blinking. 'The boat's gone out of range and no . . . I don't think I could see him at the helm.'

Marina pointed to the screen on the desk. 'Want to follow him — sorry, it — on the marine radar?'

Tiff wagged a finger. 'Naughty.' She sighed.

'I'm not that desperate . . .'

'Is everything OK between you two?' Marina asked. 'Or is that a stupid question considering you've been at his most of the past week?'

Tiff smirked. 'More than OK I'd say . . . I may as well confess that things have gone quite a way beyond the holding hands stage. In fact, there never was any hand holding. We decided to skip the nursery slopes and go off-piste pretty much straight away.'

Marina giggled. 'You're outrageous.'

She gave a little bow. 'I aim to please . . . but I suppose I'd be lying if I said it was smooth sailing between us. How could it be when Dirk 'n' Stormy meets Tempestuous Tiff? We rub each other up the wrong way from time to time but we're also remarkably similar. We enjoy similar music, most of the same books, our politics are in synch . . .'

'You like him, then?'

'Yes.' Tiff sighed. 'I could like him a lot more if I let myself, but I won't. We've been upfront that things can't go anywhere long-term . . .' She sighed. 'The fact is, there's no future for me and Dirk in Porthmellow. He's made it plain he expects me to return to the evils of London at some point.'

'Have you any plans to go back yet?'

'No, but I can't live off your hospitality forever and I'm still hopeful that when the heat has died down, I can find another job. I might have done a bit of work on the side while I'm here.'

Marina's antenna twitched. 'What do you mean?'

Tiff assumed an innocent look but Marina knew there was no halo. 'I know I said I wouldn't dig anything up on anyone in Porthmellow, and I haven't — not on anyone *you* like anyway. But I did spot an opportunity in the St Austell area recently that was too good to miss.'

'St Austell? Oh God, what have you been up to?'

'A tip-off about a councillor who used to be involved in a lifeboat crew until he was asked to leave. I heard via a solicitor who knows him; she's one of *Cream of Cornish's* ad clients . . . I pursued the story and it turns out he's been harassing women — *including* this lawyer. They haven't wanted to say anything because the councillor's firm was one of their clients. It's a tangled web, but she put me in touch with more women he's alleged to have hassled, and he's been suspended. I felt duty bound to mention it to a contact in London.'

Marina blew out a breath. 'Wow. I've been at fundraisers with that guy. I thought he was creepy but I'd no idea he was such a shit.'

'Dirk seemed shocked. He only knew the man slightly but he was disgusted. He said 'the bastard deserved everything he got',' and he wished he'd known about it before.'

'That's good, isn't it?'

'Yes, but . . . he didn't say anything explicitly, but I think it reminded him what my job is and that in spite of everything, I love doing it — if I'm ever allowed back.' She paused, letting her eyes rest on the horizon as if, Marina thought, the answers to anything concerning Dirk could be found in the deep blue depths.

'Which only reinforces the fact that he and I both know I won't be here forever,' she resumed. 'I love Porthmellow and I could — if I let myself and was extremely foolish — fall very hard for Dirk. Despite his reputation, you know yourself that there's a kind, loving guy under that craggy, moody exterior: a man who wants to trust someone but refuses to ever open up a chink of vulnerability ever again. I even think he rather likes me, and we're certainly compatible when no words are required.' Tiff smiled. 'But as for committing to anything longterm, or letting myself fall any deeper, I can't let that happen.'

'Oh, Tiff. This all sounds so bleak.'

'Not at all. It's merely self-preservation. I'll admit when I go back to my wicked ways in London, I'll miss Porthmellow, I'll be heart-broken to leave you and I guess it will sting a bit to say goodbye to Dirk . . . ' She heaved a sigh. 'But I have to survive, financially and career wise. I can't imagine settling down here, fixing Dirk's dinner every night when he comes home from the station, smelling of engine oil and shouting 'Hi, honey, I'm home!' '

Marina could hardly reply for giggles at Tiff's version of an American housewife.

'That's rubbish! Dirk would never expect you to do that. It's like something from the 1950s and, anyway, you can't cook.'

Tiff nodded. 'Good point — and, actually, when he smells of anything, it's either salt water or Creed . . . anyway, I digress. I can't see a way for us to be together long-term.'

After that Tiff changed the subject and Marina backed off. Tiff was a grown-up and, after all, she had her own love life to focus on and Nate's anniversary to get through. Hopefully, the evening at the beach would go some way to helping her put the past behind her for good.

# 22

The evening sun broke through the clouds as Marina and Lachlan strolled around the coast path from Porthmellow and down into Seaholly Cove for the Pie on the Beach event. There were around a hundred people booked in, and Sam had told Marina that she'd had to turn more away.

The van was parked at the end of the track right above the cove and Marina could have found her way by the delicious smells emanating from it alone. People had already set up their camping chairs and picnic rugs as the tide was going out and the sun sinking lower in the sky.

Lachlan spread the rug on the sand a little way from the busiest part of the beach and Marina unloaded the plates and cutlery from the picnic set. They joined the queue for the van, where Sam and her assistants were dishing up the pies, accompanied by large helpings of salads.

Marina recognised many of the faces in the queue and on the beach: Scarlett and her boyfriend, Jude Penberth, Gareth and several of the other Wave Watchers. She'd known most of the towns-people for years, but there were some newcomers who would never have met Nate, or perhaps not even known that he had existed at all.

She'd found the day more difficult than she'd expected, rising early to do some work before spending the late morning and afternoon at the

226

lookout station. After her shift, she'd walked down to the cove and spent some time thinking about her husband, shedding a few quiet tears.

The anniversary had been on her mind for a long time and she had been struggling to decide what she was going to do that day. She'd actively tried *not* to have plans, but to go about her business and maybe spend the evening quietly at home, or visit her parents — perhaps stay overnight and take Tiff with her. In fact, she'd spent the late afternoon with Tiff, as Tiff had insisted on taking her up to the Porthmellow Hotel for tea and they'd chatted together until it was time to meet Lachlan.

Marina was grateful that Lachlan had helped her to make up her mind, but while she was relieved, she still questioned if she should have accepted. Did it matter that she'd be out with him on such a night? Should she feel guilty about it?

Too late now. She hadn't wanted to burst his bubble once he'd found the courage to ask her out and maybe it was the best thing she could do on such a momentous day: spend an evening with a special friend surrounded by her Porthmellow mates. Of all the nights since Nate had gone, this should be a moment for looking ahead not back.

Now, Marina chatted to friends and fellow Wave Watchers, introducing Lachlan to those who hadn't met him yet. They chatted with a Scottish colleague from the college who reminisced about the area where Lachlan had been stationed, whilst Marina exchanged hellos with some of her students.

The two of them lounged on their rug on the sand amid the other feasters once they had their food. The pie and salad were delicious, and they washed them down with local beer. Afterwards, they made room for the puds on offer: crunchy pavlovas with mountains of strawberries, or apple pies topped with caramel sauce and clotted cream.

They shared each other's puddings, and when Drew's band set up, the atmosphere on the beach started to buzz. The evening was still fine and warm, and the lively music soon had people clapping and singing along.

Eventually the band took a break. Marina stretched her legs while Lachlan popped to the gents and the bar. She revelled in the fuzzy feeling of pleasure that came from being in his company. They'd laughed and chatted all evening, and she was sure he was having a great time too. She was so glad she'd accepted his invitation and not stayed inside on her own, or even gone to see her parents, much as she loved them. Tonight had really 'taken her out of herself', as her mum had suggested it would when she'd finally told them her plans. Sometimes, mothers were right . . .

She was exchanging a few words with Jude and Scarlett when a less welcome face came into view. She'd seen Craig from a distance earlier, but he'd seemed happy enough to spend the evening near to the bar, with his wife and children. Judging by his flushed face, he'd had more than a few and was now making a beeline for her. Marina's heart sank a little watching him weave his way over, knocking over someone's wine bottle and crushing a plastic plate on the way.

'Evenin', Marina. Surprised to see you here tonight,' he said, breathing beer fumes at her.

'Really? Half the town is here.'

'Wouldn't have thought you'd want to spend your evening like this.'

Her stomach flipped. 'Like what, Craig?'

'Out partying. With your new bloke.'

'Partying?' She laughed but grew cold with unease. 'I'd hardly say this was partying — and anyway, you're here too.' The last thing she wanted tonight was a confrontation.

'Yeah, but I ain't the grieving widow.'

Marina bit back an angry retort. 'Look, Craig. I appreciate that you were Nate's friend and you're upset, but you have no right to tell me what I should feel or do. I think you should go back to your family.'

Marina was rattled and upset but she refused to let Craig see that. Craig's wife was staring at them anxiously, and Marina felt a bit sorry for her.

'What would Nate think?'

'I don't know because, however much I wish he wasn't gone, he is. He's not coming home, and we all need to move on.'

'Well, I can see that's what *you've* done.' He curled his lip.

At that moment, Lachlan returned with a couple of beers. 'Hi there.'

Marina cringed. This altercation was the last thing she wanted to happen when they'd been having such a lovely time.

'They ran out of Doom Bar, so I got a lager.'

'Hello, Lachlan,' said Craig. Even though

229

Lachlan was six feet, Craig was a giant and towered over him. 'I'm a good mate of Nate's. That's Marina's husband, if you didn't know.'

Marina was annoyed but tried to sound as pleasant and neutral as possible. 'Of course Lachlan knows,' she said. 'Your Hayley's waving at you.'

Craig ignored her. 'Do you know what tonight is?' he asked. 'It's a very special night. A very *significant* night.'

'Craig, leave it.' Marina was trying to shut things down, aware that Lachlan was bristling by her side.

Craig's eyes flicked from Marina to Lachlan. 'You haven't told him, have you?' he slurred. 'I guessed as much.'

Her heart sank as Lachlan was stung into a response. 'Look, pal, I don't know what you're getting at here but now's not the time. Why don't you go back to your family?'

'I will, but first I'm going to tell you. Nate went missing seven years ago today. That's seven years since he drowned trying to make a living for his family.' He stabbed a finger at Marina. 'That's you, Marina, and yet you're here with another man as if you'd forgotten Nate even existed.'

'I haven't forgotten Nate and I never will, but seven years is a long time,' she snapped, growing angry.

Lachlan cut in, his tone silky. 'You don't have to justify yourself to this guy, Marina. I'm sorry for your loss, Craig, and I appreciate you're still upset, but Marina's life is none of your business.'

'Upset?' Craig laughed but his eyes blazed

230

with rage. 'You have no fecking idea how I feel, mate.'

Marina was aware that people had started to gawp at them, and she was ready to pack up and leave. She felt sick watching Lachlan and Craig square up against one another. Craig was big, but drunk and unsteady. She knew who'd come off worse if things kicked off.

Luckily, Craig's wife and kids came to Marina's side before anything could.

'Come on, Dad. A seagull might steal your pudding,' the youngest trilled.

'You'll not want that to happen,' said Lachlan with a smile for the girl.

Hayley Illogan linked her arm through her husband's, probably to stop him from falling over. 'Come on, love,' she said, exchanging a desperate look with Marina.

Craig seemed about to say something but then smiled at his daughter and ruffled her hair. 'I'd better do as my missus says.' He shot an accusing look at Marina, but still allowed himself to be shepherded away. His wife glanced over her shoulder, mouthing 'sorry'.

When they were out of earshot, Marina breathed a huge sigh of relief, although she was still mortified that Craig had caused a scene and dragged Lachlan into it.

'I'm so sorry. Craig's obviously worked up about tonight. He's out of order, though,' she said trying to defuse the situation. 'The situation's not helped by the fact that he likes a drink or ten.'

'Don't worry about me ... the guy's upset

231

and he's clearly had a few too many. Bad combination. I'm more worried about you. Honestly, I had no idea that tonight was the anniversary of Nate's disappearance or I'd never have put you in this position by asking you out.'

'You didn't know it was a . . . ' She paused, still trying to get her breath back from the encounter with Craig. 'A landmark day. I could have refused to come out, stayed home and wallowed in misery and self-pity, but I wanted to be here, with you and with my friends, and I'm really glad you asked me.'

'I'm happy you said yes, but why didn't you warn me?'

'Why would I spoil the evening by telling you? When all's said and done, it's only a date on the calendar. One more day further on from the worst day of my life. That's something to be happy about. I loved Nate, but I'd started to rebuild my life a long time before you came to Porthmellow.'

His fingers brushed hers, lingering against her. She knew he wanted to hold her but felt it was wrong to do so in a public place. She was grateful for his discretion and yet filled with sadness too. They shouldn't feel held back by what people thought — but now wasn't the right moment. 'If you're sure you're OK.'

The band started their second set and they sat back down on the rug. The music was upbeat, and some people got up to dance on the sand as the sun went down and the sky was ablaze with crimson, orange and purple. Lachlan's hand was close to hers, but he made no attempt to hold it or slip his arm around her like some of the other couples. Craig's comments were obviously playing on his mind. They stayed a while longer, but as twilight fell, she shivered. Drew's band were playing a ballad.

'Shall we go home after this one?' Lachlan whispered in her ear.

'Yes, it's getting cold and I'd like to walk home over the coast path before it's too dark to be safe. We don't want to end up being rescued, do we?'

'No.'

She realised what she'd said. 'Oops. Sorry.'

'Don't worry about it.' Smiling, he held out a hand and his warm fingers closed around hers to pull her up from the sand. He held onto her longer than necessary and they exchanged a glance. She longed for more of that contact; it had been so very long since she'd felt that jolt of pleasure and need when a man had touched her.

After packing away, they walked back around the headland, down into the town. Marina was lost in her thoughts of the past and the future.

'It's natural to be sad on a day like this. It's OK to go easy on yourself.'

'Did you?' She glanced up. 'Go easy on yourself, I mean.'

'Not often enough but I'm learning to. Coming here to Porthmellow has reminded me that you can't run away from your problems. I have bad days still, but the good times are beginning to outweigh the tough.'

Marina dared to hope that she'd helped with his recovery, even in the short time he'd known her. They passed a fishing boat in the harbour: the one that Nate had crewed with Craig, on and off. Marina could understand why his friend had been upset but that gave him no right to confront her and make her feel guilty about seeing Lachlan. Not that she was seeing him yet, not 'officially'.

'I'm glad you've made peace with yourself,' Lachlan said when they reached the lane where their row of cottages was situated.

'I have. Thanks for talking to me about all this,' Marina replied.

Lachlan's eyes glinted in the darkness and his voice was soft. 'Good friends can talk about anything, I hope.'

'Yes. They can,' she said

'Good night for now. Thank you for this evening.' He leaned in and kissed her cheek, but it went no further.

She let herself into the cottage, wondering if his interpretation of friends was the same as hers.

# 23

June ended with a heatwave, so Tiff had resorted to a floaty dress from one of the local boutiques. She'd almost considered flip-flops but checked herself in time. Instead, she purchased a pair of strappy low-heeled sandals that were cool but smart enough for work.

The car was sizzling every time she got into it after one of her client visits and she'd bought a fan for her desk in the eaves of the office. Every time she caught herself longing for the air-conditioned tower that housed the *Herald*, she glanced out of the window and saw the harbour bustling with masts, and the sea sparkling in the distance.

In the time it used to take to reach the coffee area at the London newspaper office, she could skip outside and buy an ice-cream from the quayside kiosk. Come to think of it . . . Tiff picked up her bag and trotted out onto the harbourside.

The lure of an ice-cold treat was too much to resist, and she joined the queue at the kiosk. When her turn came, she felt very virtuous when she refused the clotted cream and chocolate flake and took a lick of the vanilla cone. The ice-cream was made at a local farm and, on this red-hot day, it tasted like nectar. Murmuring hello to a couple of people she recognised, Tiff started to walk slowly back to the office, savouring her single scoop.

Suddenly, she felt a rush of wind and wings brushed her face.

She let out a scream as her cone was snatched from her hand by a seagull the size of a pterodactyl. It flew off to a rooftop and swallowed the ice-cream whole, while other birds dived in to pick at the scraps of broken cone at her feet.

'You little — !' Tiff shook her fist at the thieving gull but cut off the expletive because the quayside was busy with visitors, several of whom were staring and laughing.

Tiff wasn't so amused. Her dress was now splattered with melted ice-cream and the sticky mess oozed down her legs and onto her sandals.

A familiar figure jogged up. It was Lachlan.

'Don't you dare laugh!' she warned, seeing the grin on his face.

'I wouldn't dream of it.' He set his mouth in a solemn line and Tiff finally grinned. 'Sorry about your ice-cream.'

'I should have been more careful. We don't have vicious gulls in London. A few vultures, maybe . . .'

He smiled again. His face, even damaged, was very handsome and he'd caught the sun since he'd been here, which made him look much healthier. Tiff hadn't spoken to him much herself but she could see why Marina liked him so much. She was also aware of how frustrated her cousin was at the lack of any progress beyond friendship. She'd related some of what had gone on at the Pie on the Beach event over dinner a few nights ago.

He held out a handkerchief.

'Thanks,' Tiff said, wiping herself down with it. 'I'm afraid you won't want it back.'

'It's fine. Can I get you another ice-cream?' he asked.

'I'm not sure me and that cone are meant to be.'

'Go on. I need cooling down myself. I'm not used to the heat, you know, coming from the Highlands,' he added.

She laughed, and a thought occurred to her. They hadn't chatted much, so it would be nice to have the opportunity — as well as suss out why he was holding back from Marina. 'OK,' she said. 'As long as you act as seagull bouncer.'

They queued again, chatting about how busy the town had become in the past few weeks. Once they had the ice-creams, Lachlan suggested they stand under the porch of the Institute to eat them.

'If you stand with your back to a wall, they can't attack from behind,' he said. 'Although there's always the possibility of a frontal assault.'

She laughed. 'Thank you for the security tip. How's business, by the way?'

'Not bad. We're building up bookings. In fact, we signed a contract at a big visitor attraction only this morning and we're recruiting more freelance staff. That should keep us busy for the next year.'

'You're planning on staying in Porthmellow, then?' she said, before licking her ice-cream innocently.

'I'd like to give it a go, yes. What about you?' he said.

His directness reminded Tiff that he'd been a military policeman. 'My plans aren't as fixed as that. The honest answer is I don't know . . .'

He nodded and she took the plunge. 'I can think of at least one person who'll be pleased you're staying longer,' she said, hoping she hadn't gone too far. Marina would probably kill her but what she didn't know wouldn't hurt her.

Lachlan didn't pretend not to know that she meant Marina. He didn't look at her, but said quietly, 'You think so?'

'I do. She's had a very tough time, but I think you know that already.'

He nodded. 'We have spoken of it. It's hard to lose someone you care about . . . someone you loved. It must be even harder when you've been left in limbo as Marina has. We had a guy go missing from the base once, for weeks. We found his body eventually, on a remote part of Ben Daurrig. I was part of the mountain rescue team who recovered the body. Seems as if he fell, but we'll never know the full story. Marina hasn't even had a body to bury, no closure of any kind.'

'Yes, it's been very hard for her, although she did accept Nate was dead a long time ago,' Tiff said.

'She must still miss him keenly.'

'She did — does — but . . . I don't want to be disloyal to her or Nate but he wasn't a saint. Far from it,' Tiff ventured, hoping she hadn't crossed a line.

'I gathered that and yet . . . he *was* her first love, her husband, and to have him so cruelly taken from her . . . '

238

'Of course, she grieved for him but . . . it was a long time ago.'

Lachlan turned to her. 'Even so the memories must be raw, especially at this time.'

Tiff thought he was almost daring her to contradict him and play Devil's advocate, which must mean he'd been holding back because he thought Marina was still in love with Nate. 'Marina's strong and even stronger after what she's been through,' she said, before adding, 'She deserves a new shot at life, at *every* aspect of it.'

Lachlan's lips twisted as if he was framing a reply.

'Aye . . . ' he murmured. The clock tower struck three. 'I'd best be on my way to the office again. I told Aaron I'd only popped out for a breath of air.'

'Me too,' said Tiff. 'Thanks for the ice-cream and the seagull security advice.'

'Thanks for your advice too,' Lachlan said.

'I hadn't realised I'd dished any out,' she said lightly.

He gave a wry smile. 'Either way, you've helped me.'

'I hope so. I only want Marina to be happy and step into the light again. She's lived in Nate's shadow, in so many ways, for far too long.'

Lachlan answered with a brief incline of the head before stepping from under the porch into the sunshine.

As she headed back to the office by way of the cottage to change her dress, Tiff hoped she hadn't gone too far with her comments, although she doubted Marina would ever hear about their conversation because Lachlan struck her as nothing if not discreet. She was self-aware enough to realise that she might also take some of her own advice. She'd implied to Lachlan that he should waste no time in letting Marina know how he really felt.

Did the same apply to her? Should she admit that she was falling for Dirk far more than she'd ever expected?

She pulled out her phone to text him, and realised he'd beaten her to it.

*Can you call me asap?*

She could do better than that, she thought, making a detour to the lifeboat station. He was sitting at the desk in the crew room, a tabloid newspaper spread in front of him.

'You've seen this, of course,' he said, the moment she got through the door.

'Seen what?' She put her bag on the table and closed the door behind her.

He tapped the paper. 'This.' He passed it to her and frowned at her. 'What happened to your dress?' he said.

'Seagull versus ice-cream,' she muttered, realising she still hadn't changed, though it was now hardly the main focus of her attention. 'I haven't seen this,' she said, glancing at the newspaper with a prickle of foreboding. 'Why?'

He folded his arms. 'Read it.'

Tiff picked up the paper, and read the piece with an increasing sense of horror.

Amira had given a feature to the *Herald* about her new relationship with another actor from the medical soap she was starring in.

She scanned the copy, rolling her eyes and muttering to herself.

### RESCUED BY LOVE
*My heart has finally healed, says Amira*
*A Herald exclusive by Esther Francois*

*Soap superstar, Amira Choudhury, has finally broken her silence about her 'agonising journey back to love' after her split with partner, Dirk Meadows.*

*After enduring 'months of misery', she's found love again.*

*And it's her hunky Medics co-star Marc Rayburn who's helping to heal the wounds.*

*Amira says she was left 'in pieces' after the end of her marriage to lifeboat mechanic Dirk, adding that while devoted to his job, he suffered from mood swings and 'jealous sulks' that strained their relationship to breaking point.*

*'Things between Dirk and me had been going downhill for a long time. He said he supported my career but he wasn't willing to compromise. In the end I made the terrible choice: Dirk or my future. I chose to be free.'*

*Amira claims that Dirk became 'consumed' by his job as a mechanic at a Thames lifeboat station.*

*'Obviously I was proud of the good work he did there, but it affected him badly. He made it clear that our lives came second.*

241

When I landed the role in Medics and started to be recognised in the street, he'd try to hurry us away and then retreat into his shell.'

Amira struggles to hold back tears when she talks about those painful times.

'It was clear Dirk didn't like people wanting to talk to me,' she said. 'We were spending more time apart and things came to a head when I offered to support him so he could give up his job. He walked out and that was the night I decided to make a clean break.

'I was devastated, but I had to do it for both our sakes. I felt like I'd cut off a limb, but it was essential to my recovery. It's taken months to get over the split from Dirk, but Marc has made me see that there's love out there for me.'

Judging by the happiness radiating from Amira when she talks about Marc, Amira clearly thinks she might finally have turned a corner . . . Has she found the best cure for her heartbreak?

'God, give me strength!' Tiff said, with a snort of contempt. 'I can't take much more. This is even worse than I expected.'

'You could say that,' Dirk murmured darkly.

She read on, groaning in derision and muttering. It was typical of Esther's style, loaded with cheesy cliches, and littered with typos that the sub hadn't picked up on — which suggested the story had been slotted into the first edition with indecent haste. Tiff might have done a happy dance of glee at the terrible writing and errors, if she hadn't been annoyed on Dirk's behalf.

She threw down the tabloid. 'You do know that Amira might not even have said any of this? It could have been cooked up by her publicist or her words were taken out of context. There's even a possibility Esther paraphrased them or made them up herself. She's done it before.'

Dirk sighed. 'Thanks for trying to soften the blow but we both know she did say this — or something like it.'

'I'm sorry it's upset you. It's a shitty piece of journalism. The *Herald* is going further downhill.'

'Is that all you care about? The quality of the prose?'

'Are you implying I don't care about the effect on you?'

'I think you should read to the end,' he said.

'I don't know if I can bear to. It's such rubbish.'

He folded his arms. 'Read the rest.'

There was something in his tone, a downbeat edge almost of defeat, that made the hairs on the back of her neck stand on end. She picked up the paper again and read the next few paragraphs to herself.

*'Dirk and I went our separate ways and I can accept that but I must admit I was heartbroken when I heard he was seeing someone else in Cornwall.*

243

'I cried for a whole night, but then I thought: this is the wake-up call I need. I deserved love too. I realised I'd been holding back from opening up to Marc because I was clinging to the past. Finding out my ex had moved on so quickly made my decision and I phoned Marc there and then and poured out my heart. We started dating a week later and I know it sounds like such a cliche, but now we're blissfully happy.'

Tiff swallowed hard. Oh God, no . . .
'Well?' he asked.
'I — I am a little lost for words. The woman they mention you're with — '
'Who do you think they mean?' he murmured.
'I've only been here a couple of months. How can they know we're — '
'Yes. *How?* Did you tell Esther we were seeing each other?' he said ominously.
She gasped. 'What? No, I bloody didn't! How could you think that?'
'I can think anything lately. Anything at all, where the press is concerned.'
'Well, I didn't tell her. She could have found out from anyone in Porthmellow with a few calls. I don't want to be in vile Esther's tawdry pieces of crap. I'd never reveal anything to her — least of all about someone I cared about.'
'Cared about?'
Tiff bit back an angry reply. 'Yes. Cared about.'
He gawped. 'I thought you only wanted to sleep with me until you got a better offer in London.'

244

Stinging from his comment, she unleashed both barrels. It was so unjust. She cared about him more than he ever imagined. 'That is so far beneath you, Dirk. So far below the man I thought I was getting to know.' She dropped the newspaper on the desk table. 'If that's what you really believe then there's no point in me staying here or seeing you again.'

He shook his head. 'You know how well we get on. You know how much I liked — *like* — you but I can't take that leap of faith. Not after what happened to Amira, not with someone — someone I . . . '

'Someone you *what?*' Her eyes blazed at him.

Rachel popped her head around the door. 'Tiff? Dirk? Everything OK?'

'Yes, thanks, Rachel. Everything's perfect! I was just going.'

Without a backward glance, Tiff marched onto the quayside and along the harbour, not quite sure where she was going. For the first time since she'd left London, she was on the verge of tears. Dirk was hurt and upset, she knew that — she didn't blame him — but there was no reason to take it out on her, or assume she'd betrayed his trust by telling Esther about their private life.

She was angry at the injustice of his comments, but that wasn't what had made her want to cry. It was the way he'd lashed out so strongly. Despite saying he was over Amira he was clearly still raw at losing her and that had cut Tiff to the bone. She'd let herself be vulnerable again in a way she'd vowed she never would. Her and Dirk were never going to work

245

— it was an impossible romantic fantasy and she had to crush it and face reality. People like her weren't cut out for 'true love' — if it existed at all.

# 24

*In memory of Nathan Hudson*
*Forever in our hearts*
*From his loving wife, Marina,*
*and the people of Porthmellow*

Marina frowned at the plaque on the outside of the station and rubbed at it with her sleeve. There were few materials it could have been made of that would survive the elements so they'd raised the extra cash for a bronze one, but even that was spattered with mud and salt.

She'd fetched a stool to stand on and was rubbing hard at the grime but the plaque really needed unscrewing and taking down for a proper clean. She'd ask Trevor if he'd do it when he came on shift. He was a kind soul and Marina didn't feel she could bear to see it come down.

Marina heard whistling.

'Hi, it's me,' Lachlan called cheerfully, then added, 'Oh. I'm sorry.'

Heart sinking, Marina stepped down, the cloth still in her hand. 'It's weathered . . .' she said. Why did he have to come across her at this moment?

'I'm intruding. I'll leave.'

'Lachlan! Wait!' She grabbed his arm and he swung round. 'You're not intruding. Please don't walk away.'

He glanced at the plaque and at her. 'I don't want to go.'

247

'Then stay . . . come inside?'

He followed her into the lookout. 'I came to ask you something . . . after we talked at the beach night, I've been thinking about you — about us.'

The cloth was still in her hands. 'I think about us too. Please don't think I don't just because you found me here, with Nate's plaque. Because that's *all* it is; a sign on a wall — a memorial to him — but not a *shrine*. You understand me? Please don't let it hold you back from saying what you feel.'

'How I feel? I — ' He didn't finish his sentence but reached for her and drew her closer to his body. She went more than willingly and a moment later, they were kissing each other. It was gentle and warm; the first kiss she'd had in however long. Kissing Lachlan felt as natural as breathing.

Yet it *was* strange, touching another man, skin on skin, his mouth on hers as they explored each other. She'd stepped into a new world — a strange and wonderful land — that was as thrilling as it was unknown.

The kiss ended but they stayed entwined, her head against his shoulder, cheek against the soft cotton of his T-shirt. She was enjoying the moment, enjoying the scent of freshly washed clothes, the touch of his hands resting lightly on her waist. She felt that sunshine had broken through into her world of semi-shadows, and it was the sunshine of a new morning when the day stretches ahead, ready to be filled with good things . . . happy things.

Lachlan pulled back. 'Wow, that was a surprise,' he murmured. 'To both of us. I didn't plan for it to happen . . . perhaps it shouldn't have?'

'No, it absolutely should have. I wanted it to happen. Lachlan, that comment you made about us being friends after the picnic . . . It was a lovely thing to say but I have to admit that I'd been wondering — *hoping* — that lately, we might be something more?'

'I want that too. I've wanted to kiss you for weeks but I don't want to push you. I've held back because of Nate, especially as this is a sensitive time for you and you've so much on your plate with the legal stuff. I don't want to come blundering in and make life even harder.'

'You haven't blundered in.' She smiled. 'And it *is* a tough time, but it's a turning point too. That's why I didn't want to spoil our evening at the beach picnic by telling you. But Craig had to stomp in . . .'

'It was a shock to find out that night was the anniversary, I'll admit.' He picked up her hand. 'Marina, you must know I care about you. You've brought me out of my shell, even when I didn't want to be dragged out of it.'

She winced. 'I haven't meant to bully you.'

'I needed a kick up the arse.' He rubbed her hand. 'And I can't think of anyone I'd rather did the kicking.'

'That's nice!' she said, through laughter. 'I've had to come out of my shell since Nate died, so perhaps I go over the top.'

'No. No you're just what I needed,' he said. 'I

wish I'd said this sooner and not spent so many nights fretting about whether I should tell you how I feel.'

'I'm really glad you did,' she said, before adding, a little shyly, 'And about what just happened . . . '

His eyes lit up in pleasure. 'Then let's do it again. Properly.' He leaned in to kiss her.

'Yoo hoo!'

They sprang apart.

'It's Trevor and Doreen!' Marina hissed. Lachlan turned away and picked up the binoculars but his shoulders were shaking with suppressed laughter. Marina wasn't so blase; the last thing she wanted was to be caught in a passionate kiss while on duty.

'Hello!' she said, far too blithely. 'Lachlan was just visiting.'

'Hi there,' said Lachlan, nodding a hello to the couple who exchanged knowing glances, much to Marina's horror. Had they guessed they'd interrupted something? Even if Lachlan was poker-faced, Marina's fiery cheeks might have given them a clue.

Lachlan said his goodbyes and Marina did the handover to the couple. When she went outside, she found him waiting for her on the path above the station.

'I got your text!' she said. 'I almost gave the game away by grinning like an idiot.'

'I thought I'd let you know I was out here. I think we were rudely interrupted. Shall we go to our bench?' he said.

Our bench. She liked the sound of that,

although there was still a possibility they'd be seen by prying eyes. She led the way into the gorse and they sat down. At high summer, the scents were heady and butterflies joined the bees buzzing around them. The path was busy with walkers and families so there was no way she could resume the kiss, however much she longed to.

'There's no hiding place,' Lachlan said.

She nodded vigorously. 'No . . . ' A daring thought struck her. 'I can't help thinking we should get away from Porthmellow completely,' she said.

'For a day, do you mean?' he asked, then shared a look that thrilled her. 'Or longer?'

'Longer if you want to. Maybe . . . ' She was thinking on the hoof, becoming more daring. 'We should find somewhere without any memories or history. Somewhere new to both of us.'

He considered for a few seconds. 'I'd love to. I can't stay away from the new business for long, but I'm sure Aaron could spare me for a few days over a long weekend. He won't mind.'

'I have a free Friday and Monday coming up, and I can rearrange my Wave Watchers shifts.'

'Did you have anywhere in mind?' he asked.

She remembered the ad in Tiff's magazine. 'There is somewhere, actually. It's not far away and they might have a last-minute vacancy. Tiff was invited to a new set of luxury cottages that have only opened this week on the Isles of Scilly, but she couldn't spare the time. They were coastguard houses and they're on St Agnes, the most remote island. The views are to die for and

251

I've always wanted to go to the Scillies.'

'Remote sounds perfect.' He quickly kissed her again. 'If you can bear to be stuck with me alone.'

'I think it's exactly what we need and . . . ' Her brain worked overtime. 'We can get there by boat, so shall I look into it? Tiff says the owners are keen for visitors and I could report back to Tiff so she can write about it.'

'I'll check it's OK with Aaron. We could go early on the Friday and come back Monday evening, maybe? Have the whole four days to relax?'

'Sounds great. I'll ask Tiff how I go about booking it.'

'And I'll call Aaron as soon as I get home and we'll take it from there.'

They walked home, chatting about the week-end plans like kids. The kiss had been thrilling but, somehow, it felt too soon for anything else — or perhaps they were both waiting to get away from prying eyes and bad memories. But if this break came off, she was well aware that four days meant four nights too.

# 25

'You sound happy.'

Marina glanced up, a little startled to hear Tiff's voice. She'd expected her to be out with Dirk — or *in* with Dirk.

It was a sultry afternoon and Marina had been deadheading the geraniums to encourage them to flower again. She'd also been humming to herself, possibly more loudly than she'd intended. She'd been humming a lot over the past few days and felt her life was finally blossoming as promisingly as her garden. 'Yeah. I am.'

'You look glowing, too,' Tiff said.

Marina laughed, a little embarrassed. 'Probably because I forgot to put any sun cream on before I came out.'

'It's nothing to do with the sun, as you well know. You've been like this since you decided to go on this weekend away. He's good for you and, judging by the smile on his face whenever you're around, you're even better for him.'

'I hope so. I daren't let myself believe that things could go so well.'

Tiff flopped onto the garden bench. 'You deserve it.'

'Can't remember when I last had a weekend break like this. As a . . . couple, I mean. I've been on a few hols with work colleagues and training weekends with the Wave Watchers but, ahem, this isn't quite the same.' She laughed nervously.

253

'Have you heard back from the Lighthouse Cottage Company yet?' Tiff asked, kicking off her pistachio-coloured lace-up pumps. Marina didn't think she'd seen her cousin in pumps since they were kids.

'We're waiting for a confirmation but we've booked our ferry tickets. I suggested taking the boat because of . . . well, you can guess why I didn't ask him to go by air.'

Tiff's nose wrinkled in horror. 'Good idea. I've seen those so-called aircraft take off from Land's End. They're like toy planes.'

Marina stripped off her gloves, happy to abandon the gardening now Tiff was home. 'I must admit I'm nervous, but that has nothing to do with the trip itself.'

'As long as it doesn't turn out like a Bridget Jones minibreak, you'll be fine.'

'I hope not. Wasn't it all ruined when they got home to find Daniel Cleaver's girlfriend naked in the bath?'

Tiff nodded. 'Personally, I've always been more of a Cleaver fan than a Mark Darcy one. You're not really worried about this trip, are you? Dirty weekends are meant to be fun.' Tiff raised an eyebrow.

'It's not a dirty weekend . . . I'm sure nothing like that will . . . happen,' she said, yet she was unable to keep the smile from her voice at the thought of things moving to a new physical level with Lachlan.

Tiff reached forward and patted her arm. 'Go on, you'd be disappointed if it didn't! Oh, Marina, it'll be fine. I'm sure. *More* than fine.

Lachlan seems like one of the good guys, you fancy each other and you deserve an amazing time. Try to stop worrying.'

'You're right and it should be idyllic. Hope so, anyway.' Marina went into the kitchen and brought chilled lemonade outside with a dish of tortilla chips. There had been a few more kisses between her and Lachlan but nothing else yet . . . and she was more certain than ever that they both needed to get away from past associations, somewhere fresh and new.

'Dare I ask how things are going with Dirk?' she said, sitting down at the table again.

'I wouldn't go there if I were you.' Tiff grabbed a handful of chips.

'I'm sorry. I should have asked you sooner — I thought you seemed quiet and you haven't mentioned him for a while. I've been so wrapped up in my own little world.'

'I'm glad you haven't. Dirk and I have had a tiny falling-out.'

'What over?'

'The *Herald* ran a story about Amira — his ex — and her new boyfriend and how she was having a wonderful time getting over Dirk and his moods.'

Marina groaned. 'Oh God, I bet that went down like a lead balloon.'

'You could say that, but that wasn't the worst of it. The story mentioned me in a roundabout way, and Dirk accused me of telling the *Herald* we were seeing each other.'

'No!' Marina was genuinely shocked. 'How could he do that? You wouldn't do that!'

'Thank you for the defence. You're right, I wouldn't do it and I didn't tell them. They could have found out in numerous ways, but Dirk jumped to the conclusion it was me.'

'Does he still believe that?' Marina was amazed and fuming on Tiff's behalf. Dirk was an idiot; she'd thought that the two of them were finally building a real rapport but this showed otherwise.

'He back-pedalled a little but I was so furious that I walked out.'

'Have you seen him since?'

'He has messaged me, asking to meet, but I've ignored it. Haven't seen him for over a week now. Like all fireworks, we appear to have enjoyed a spectacular display and then fizzled out.' She grinned. 'And at least I'm now able to get my beauty sleep. Now, don't worry about me. You worry about this trip. I hope you've no intention of packing those 'sensible' knickers I saw in the laundry basket. Trust me, it won't end well . . . '

\* \* \*

A few days before their trip, Marina invited Lachlan round for dinner while Tiff went to a Pilates class at the community centre. She said she'd probably go to the pub with some of the other women afterwards so they had the place to themselves.

A warmth stole into her cheeks at the thought she might not have quite so much sleep over their weekend away, if they took things further than kisses.

Lachlan brought their plates through and sat

256

down but didn't even pick up his knife and fork. 'It's no good. I can't wait any longer. I want to tell you something.'

'Oh? What?' She readied herself. Lachlan seemed twitchy. What was about to happen?

'I've got a bit of a surprise. I hope you won't be disappointed . . . there's a slight change of plan for our trip.'

'Oh . . . I see,' she said, readying herself for disappointment. Was he going to say the whole thing was off? Was that why he'd spent a while on her iPad and gone quiet before dinner?

'We're not going to Scilly on the boat,' he said, with a smile.

'Oh no! Have they had to cancel?' she said.

'No. We're going by air.'

'What? But we've booked the *Scillonian* tickets already.'

'We had . . . but I rebooked them earlier and upgraded to Skybus. They're all part of the same company and they managed to squeeze us onto an early morning flight. It'll be much faster and give us more time on the islands to relax. Don't worry, I'm paying for the upgrade,' he added, possibly seeing her jaw drop in amazement.

'No. I'll pay for my share. I don't mind at all and I'd love to fly but . . . how will you handle it? I thought you wanted to sail?'

'I want to fly, Marina. I need to try and get back to the way I was or at least regain some confidence. I'll be honest and say that I *am* bricking it but I need to do this. And besides,' he added with a smile, 'you'll be there to hold my hand, won't you?'

257

No wonder he'd seemed on edge, she thought. It was a bold and unexpected step. Wow. 'Yes, of course! This is . . . very brave of you.'

'Brave?' His brow creased and she worried she'd said the wrong thing. 'It's not brave,' he said. 'Brave is flying out in dangerous conditions to save a stranger or going into battle.'

'You *are* going into battle. You're facing up to very real fears when your instincts are screaming at you not to. I understand a little of what it's like to decide to re-engage with your fears, to decide to come back to the world instead of hiding away. I respect that and I'll help you in any way I can.'

He looked at her with what she thought for a second were eyes glistening with tears but then he reached for her. 'Better toughen up, hadn't I? If I'm to live up to you.'

'I don't expect a 'tough guy' or a 'hero'. I'm happy to have a kind, decent man who's pre-pared to face up to life, even when it gets difficult. You don't need to prove anything to me.' And one she fancied like mad too, of course.

'Ah, but I want to and I'm going to do my very best to show you what I was — what I can be.'

She didn't argue any longer and after they'd eaten, they wandered down to Porthmellow Beach with a bottle of wine and some glasses. Lachlan put his arm around her and they drank their wine, watching the waves break softly on the sand. There were still people strolling, walking their dogs and watching the sunset. She'd missed this so much: the pleasures of sharing a meal

258

with someone special in her little back garden or walking on the beach on a summer's evening.

Most of all, she was touched that Lachlan was ready to set his fears aside for her sake and to try to move on. She'd missed that most of all: someone doing something for her, not out of pity, but because — dare she even think it — she was special to them. It was a heady feeling, and one she was rapidly becoming addicted to . . . one that would be even harder to lose, second time around. And no amount of reminding herself to live in the moment could stop her from hoping it would go on forever.

# 26

Wrinkling her nose, Tiff scrutinised herself in her bedroom mirror. She hadn't worn a swimsuit for years and the designer one she'd brought from London was black with a plunge front and a gold chain. She'd once thought it sophisticated and had lain around the odd spa pool in it, sipping a cocktail. Here it seemed more 'Marbs' than Cornwall so she purchased a new one with a discreet flower print in the mid-season sale at the boutique.

She'd had to go up a size as a result of Marina's great cooking and being too polite to refuse free goodies from the clients — not to mention being ravenous from all the walking and step climbing around Porthmellow. She also had a 'farmer's tan' from wandering around in short sleeves, plus freckles and a very pink nose despite slathering herself in SPF moisturiser. That was the least of her worries.

She was hardly in the beach mood, but Marina had been keen to make the most of the light, warm evenings and suggested they have an evening swim, so she'd agreed to go.

She hadn't heard from Dirk for well over a week and she was still lightly simmering. She'd even wondered if maybe it was time she thought about moving on from Porthmellow, even though it had wormed its way into her soul. But it quickly transpired that jobs weren't lying around like pebbles on the beach, so she'd have to stay put for now, keep her hand in with the freelance stories and wait for an opportunity.

She was considering whether there was time for a quick once-over with the tinted body lotion before Marina came back when there was a loud rap on the door.

Swearing to herself, she lifted a corner of the curtain to see Dirk on the doorstep. Her heart rate sped up.

'Hello?' he called.

She shouted through the open window. 'I won't be a minute.'

'I can't stay. Could you let me in?' he called up at her.

'Um. Is it urgent?'

'Yes.'

'Hang on.' She grabbed a robe from the back of the door, tied it tightly and padded downstairs in her bare feet.

Tiff pulled open the door. Dirk loomed on the doorstep but she looked down at him from the added height given by the step. 'You said it was urgent,' she said haughtily.

'It is. I'm here to apologise. I was too harsh and I'm sorry.' His words rushed out in a torrent.

'And rude,' she said.

Dirk looked solemnly back up at her. 'Yes, I was rude.'

Tiff kept him on the doorstep. 'And arrogant and unfair.'

'If you say so . . .'

Clutching the robe tighter, she raised her eyebrows.

'OK, yes, I was arrogant, rude, harsh and unfair. Plus, any other adjective you want to throw at me,' he said. 'And that's why I've come to eat humble pie and offer an olive branch.'

Tiff was enjoying herself immensely, especially the idea of Dirk eating humble pie, but her curiosity was piqued by his last comment. 'What olive branch would that be? I don't see any flowers or chocolates.'

'I'm not a flowery kind of guy . . . my olive branch is of a different kind. Are you free on Friday evening?'

She held her chin. 'Hmm. Well, I was thinking of taking up Troy Carman's invitation to go mackerel fishing with him but if you're saying you have a more tempting offer, I might be persuaded to change my plans.'

The truth was, that although she'd made light of Dirk's lack of trust in her to Marina, she was more hurt than she'd ever let on. She was more worried about the fact that she was bothered by what he thought at all. Their relationship was meant to be one of 'no strings sex' but that wasn't working out how she'd hoped, which wasn't Dirk's fault, to be fair. She'd been determined for things to stay casual, but she hadn't bargained for the strength of her feelings.

Dirk swore softly. 'Has anyone ever told you that you are the most infuriating and frustrating woman on the planet?'

'Frequently. So what *is* this olive branch?'

He grinned. 'You'll just have to wait and see.'

262

# 27

Marina refused to say what kind of knickers she'd packed, even to Tiff, but she had popped into the M&S at Hayle the day before their trip. Before she knew it, it was time to go. Marina could sense that Lachlan was on edge but wasn't sure if she should ask him if he was OK or try to distract him. So, it was with a mixture of excitement and slight apprehension that she waited with him in the departure lounge at Land's End airport on a scorching July Friday morning.

She enjoyed flying, although she'd only done it a few times, on the occasional holiday abroad with her parents and on a backpacking adventure to the Far East with student friends immediately after her degree. She and Nate hadn't flown anywhere at all.

She assumed Lachlan was a veteran of many types of aircraft, but this morning, you'd think he was the most nervous of first-timers. It was totally understandable and there was really nothing she could do about it.

Perhaps, she thought, when she saw the six-seater prop plane parked right outside the departure lounge, it might have been better to have chosen a bigger aircraft for Lachlan's first time back in the air. This one had to be 'trimmed' or balanced, and that meant all the passengers and their luggage had to be weighed on a baggage scale when they checked in. Although Marina was fascinated by watching the planes taking off and landing so close to the windows, she was worried about Lachlan.

There was also a helicopter service to and from the isles and at one point one of the helicopters owned by Trinity House, the organisation that looked after the lighthouses around the coast, took off from right outside the lounge windows.

'OK?' she asked, squeezing his hand. 'I'm here for you.'

He took a breath. 'Is it too early for a wee dram?'

She smiled. 'I don't think they've opened the bar yet. Should have brought a hip flask,' she added.

'Why didn't I think of that?'

He settled for a herbal tea and the passengers for their flight were summoned to a safety briefing in the terminal, because there was no room for a demonstration in the plane itself.

He sat ramrod straight throughout, and, in his defence, Marina had to admit even she was a little freaked out by the talk of ditching in the sea and how to remove the aircraft windows. The moment it was over, Lachlan sprang up from his seat, looking white.

'I'll be back in a minute,' he said, and strode off towards the gents.

The airport staff called for the passengers to assemble by the door to the runway, but there was still no sign of Lachlan. Marina hurried over to the loo, pacing up and down, half-fearing a call from the car park to say he couldn't go through with the flight after all.

She let out an inner sigh of relief when he emerged from the gents. His face was pale and his hair damp as if he'd had to splash his face with water. She suspected he might even have thrown up.

'How are you doing?' she murmured when he joined her.

'Not great,' he said. 'But I'm going through with this no matter what.' He grasped her hand tightly. 'I don't think I'd even have made it this far without you.'

There was another call for passengers. 'It's now or never,' she said, with her other hand on his arm.

His expression was that of a man being led to the scaffold. Marina was proud of him for trying to overcome his fears but wondered if they'd actually make it onto the aircraft.

*Calling passengers McKinnon and Hudson. Please go to the gate now.*

Tiny beads of perspiration glistened on his forehead.

'Then it has to be now,' he said.

They walked hand in hand out onto the breezy airfield. Up close the plane was even tinier than she'd dreamed and they had to duck under its wings to climb up the steps.

It was cosy inside the cabin, and that was putting it mildly. Lachlan followed her in and had to bend low to reach his seat. Marina tried not to think that this scrap of metal and the pilot, whom she recognised as a graduate of her college, was all that was keeping her from the

265

same fate as Nate. She only hoped that the pilot had calmed down since the days he'd almost been thrown off his degree course for riding a shopping trolley through the campus and crashing into the principal's Lexus.

'Oh hello, Mrs Hudson. Lovely to see you again,' he said cheerfully, greeting each passenger as they squeezed into their seats.

'You know the pilot?' Lachlan asked, looking greener than ever. 'He looks about twelve.'

'He was a very responsible student,' she lied. 'And much older than he looks.'

She decided not to share her real knowledge with Lachlan, especially when the first officer reiterated how to remove the windows in the event of an emergency before 'Captain Stokes' wished them a pleasant flight and took control of their lives.

When Lachlan pulled out a pair of dark sunglasses and put them on, Marina guessed he was trying to blot out his surroundings. His shoulders were rigid, his palms flat on his knees when the ground crew waved the plane onto the airstrip. She took his hand while the plane taxied along, its engines a dull rumble before they roared into full life. His grip on her fingers tightened as the plane hurtled down the runway. She saw his lips move, whether in a prayer or a curse, she didn't know and, in a few seconds, the ground fell away.

Cornwall was a patchwork of green fields and brown moorland and a minute later, they were climbing steeply out over the sea towards the Longships lighthouse. Lachlan stayed upright, staring straight ahead behind the safety of his shades. She could only imagine the fear in his eyes but his face was almost as white as the foam on the sea, hundreds of feet below.

She had to gently release his grip to avoid having her fingers crushed.

'Jesus. I'm sorry,' he said.

'It's fine . . . ' She placed her hand over his. 'And you did it. OK?' she said, close to his ear.

He nodded, lifting his aviators a fraction to show her that his eyes were tightly shut. At least he had a sense of humour, even when he was clearly terrified. Holding his hand, she wondered if he'd see anything of their flight as the plane left Cornwall behind. Within a few minutes, scores of tiny islands set around a turquoise lagoon came into view.

She was proud that he'd even made it there as they came in to land, and he let out an audible gasp when the plane flew low over the cliff and onto the runway at St Mary's.

The fact that he'd been willing to face his fears to make this trip, for her, caused her heart to soar. Whether they made it home again was another matter, but at least for the next few days they could forget the past and focus on getting to know each other a whole lot better.

# 28

'Wow. Just wow.' Tiff shook her head. 'When you said you were taking me to the theatre, I'll admit I didn't have this in mind.'

Tiff caught her breath at the panorama in front of her. A dozen words flew into her head but none were adequate to describe the view over the theatre hewn into the cliff side, with its epic backdrop of the ocean, white sands and dramatic cliffs.

When he'd picked her up from the cottage, Dirk had given no clue whatsoever as to where they were going and refused her pleas for a hint on what to wear. The result was that she was in ballet pumps, a dress and cardigan. Luckily it was a fine, mild evening.

She hadn't realised their destination until they'd turned down the steep twisting lane that led to Porthcurno, but had kept the guess to herself, enjoying Dirk's look of satisfaction.

Now, they were at the theatre, looking down at the incredible sight in front of them. She'd heard of the Minack, of course, and seen numerous photos in the magazine, even driven past the end of the road that led to it. She'd often wondered if online pictures showing its amphitheatre with a backdrop of the lagoon of Pedn Vounder were heavily Photoshopped.

Surely the experience couldn't actually live up to the pictures and the hype.

It could. Oh, how it could.

The theatre itself, and the setting, knocked any West End venue out of the park. In fact, she concluded, it was the most spectacular outdoor performance space she'd ever been to, anywhere in the country.

'It's not the Albert Hall, I'll admit,' said Dirk solemnly.

'No. It's *far* more fun than that. They don't have seagulls flying around in the Albert Hall or . . .' Tiff sniffed the air. 'The scent of pasties.'

'No need for pasties! I brought a picnic. Shall we buy our seats?'

It turned out he meant it literally, and shortly after, clutching plastic cushions, they carefully made their way down the steep terraces to a spot halfway between the stage and the café.

The show, a student production of *Much Ado About Nothing*, was fun, if a little creaky at the seams. The performers were young and although talented, hadn't yet blossomed to RSC levels, but she loved it. The fiery relationship between Beatrice and Benedick wasn't lost on her either, though she'd no idea if Dirk had noticed the similarities.

The wind blew, drowning out a few lines, and a passing shower meant she had to deploy the hooded waterproof she'd bought and would not have been seen dead in in London.

But after the shower passed, the evening sun broke through to give a glorious sunset, setting the pink granite aglow. After dark, the theatre was even more spectacular. The sky changed from teal to indigo, with the jagged ridge of the Logan Rock silhouetted behind the performers.

Tiff found herself clapping and cheering along with the audience in a way she never would in London. Was it the change of venue, she wondered, or was it her that had changed? Was a slightly less cynical and weary Tiff emerging? A different Tiff to the woman who'd tottered up the steps to Dirk's cottage all those months before?

Possibly . . . but that didn't alter the fact that she must leave one day — mustn't she? That prospect seemed very bleak with Dirk by her side, driving through the dark lanes east to Porthmellow.

She closed her eyes and she allowed fresh and even more dangerous thoughts to intrude into her mind. If she stayed in Cornwall, she'd never be able to have the career or lifestyle she cherished and still missed. Then again, maybe she could stay, she could try to make it work, if she found enough freelance work and perhaps got a senior job on a bigger regional . . . but those were hard to come by these days.

And she was ignoring the biggest reason for not staying: Dirk himself. Even if Tiff allowed herself to envisage a future in Cornwall, she was almost certain that Dirk wasn't thinking the same. They'd both agreed to a casual relationship that would inevitably end. She'd told herself there were to be no regrets when they parted, and yet on this beautiful evening, with him beside her, even the unimaginable seemed possible.

'Whoa!'

Her eyes flew open as the car jolted her. Dirk had turned off the road onto a stony track that ran perilously close to the edge of the sea.

270

'Dirk. Forgive me, but this doesn't appear to be a road . . . ' She risked a quick glance through the window. 'Plus I hate to mention it but there seems to be a cliff drop next to the car.'

He patted her arm. 'Relax.'

'I would find it easier to relax if you kept both hands on the wheel, please.'

'We're almost here,' he said, slowing.

White foam of breakers flashed in the darkness out of the passenger window. 'Here, where? We could be in the sea at this rate!'

The car lurched to a halt and he grinned in the darkness. 'Won't be long,' he said, leaving the door open and strolling to a white-painted barrier a few feet in front.

Tiff called to him out of the open door. 'What are you doing?'

'Perk of the job.' He used some kind of key thing to undo the barrier, which swung upwards. He jumped back into the car, bumped it under the barrier and locked it behind them.

She shook her head in disbelief. 'I feel as if I've been kidnapped by you,' she said.

'Is that a bad thing?'

'Depends what you have in mind.'

'Something good, I hope.'

His response thrilled her, making her tingle from top to toe. She hugged herself to stem a shiver of sheer lust. Shortly afterwards, the car stopped at the top of a short but very steep track at the top of a tiny cove. The moon came out, illuminating the cove and a little hut, a bit like a beach chalet, adorned with lifebelts, fishing creels and ropes.

271

'Far as we go,' he said.

'What's that?'

'Fisherman's Mission hut.'

'You're not going to . . . in there? I hope they don't have CCTV!'

He rolled his eyes. 'As if they could afford it. No. Come on.'

She joined him on the slipway and he picked up a bundle from the boot, before taking her hand and walking her down the steep slipway.

He threw the blanket on the beach.

'What if we get cut off?'

'Lucky you're with someone from the lifeboats, then.'

The moon was full out and the stars shining brightly. Everything was silvered, burnished: the sand, the rocks, the sea breaking on the cove. She felt as if she was almost the first person to discover it.

He held her and leaned down to kiss her. Under the stars, with the waves crashing onto the beach, they made love in true movie style. It was enough, Tiff thought, as Dirk kissed his way down her body, to make the most hardened cynic believe in happy endings. Even her?

As they sat together on the sand under the moonlight, it was impossible *not* to imagine more nights such as this, together with Dirk — nights that went on and on, that involved sharing their lives. They had so much in common, and not only their interests and pleasures and the sex. They'd both known what it was like to love and to lose that love; they also knew how rare it was to fall in love so deeply and

272

that there might not be many more chances to feel that intensely again.

It was past midnight and the tide was starting to go out, the wet rocks glistening under the silver moonlight. Dirk insisted on wrapping the rug around Tiff and then sat with his arm around her as the waves lapped the shoreline. He kissed her neck and a sense of deep happiness filled her, a sense of peace . . . It might have been a post-sex mellowness but she'd never felt so safe, or so content.

The beauty of this isolated place brought words to her lips. 'Slowly, silently, now the moon . . .' she began.

Dirk supplied the next line. 'Walks the night in her silver shoon . . . '

She turned to him in amazement. 'You know the poem?'

'Don't sound so surprised. I learned it at school.'

Tiff smiled in delight. 'It's my favourite. This place reminds me of it.'

'Yes. When the moon glints on the rocks, I've thought that too.'

'Ah. You've brought people here before?' she said, her spirits sinking a little.

'For a rescue once, for fishing a couple of times. For what we've just done . . . you're the first.'

She laughed. 'I'd like to believe that.'

'Then believe it because it's true. Do me the credit of trusting me.'

She turned to look at him. 'Not until you do the same for me.'

He nodded. 'Look, I'm sorry for what I said about your job. I let the past cloud my judgement. I made the mistake of assuming you were part of a group of people and indistinguishable from them, rather than an individual in your own right.'

'I did the same when I first arrived. Assumed, I mean, about Porthmellow, about you. I've been surprised by the place and you and most of all by myself.'

He kissed her, and then said, 'And I'm amazed by you. You mesmerise me. I can't keep away from you and I want to keep looking at you and listening to you. I want to know what's behind the shell, and strip back the layers one by one . . .'

'I think you already did that,' she said, her voice was light but she was trembling a little, astonished by the frankness of his comments.

'What happened to you in London?' he asked. 'I mean, what really happened to you? You can tell me. I know what it's like to bury pain, and hide it behind a mask. Mine happens to be an uglier mask. Yours is glittering, but as fragile.'

'Has anyone ever told you you should have my job?' she said softly. 'Your way with words.'

'I want to know the real Tiff.'

Could she share that person with anyone? Could she make herself that exposed and vulnerable? 'I'm not sure who she is.'

'Try me.' He kissed her very softly. The gentle touch was like turning a key that released her pent-up emotions, regrets, hopes, fears.

Before she knew it, the secret she'd never

274

thought she'd share with him came pouring out. 'I was very badly burned by a man I loved, and who I thought loved me. That's what happened.' She looked into his eyes. 'So now you know that hard-nosed, savvy Tiff has a heart that's as fragile as any other human being's.'

His arms tightened around her. 'I never thought you didn't.'

'Really? You could have fooled me.'

'I . . . I've been angry and wounded myself. I misjudged you. Please tell me more about what happened. About this man — this bastard — who hurt you.'

'You know all that needs to be said, other than I trusted him and thought he might be 'the one'.' She laughed bitterly. 'That's the worst thing. I ought to have known better. He made me feel like a fool and, while he was at it, he got me the sack from a job I loved. He took away everything: my work, my home, and my self-respect.'

'And your trust in other people?'

'Yes . . . I guess that's why I now find it even harder to let myself get too close to anyone else again — in a romantic way, I mean.' She looked into Dirk's face, feeling the tears trickling down her face. 'That's my tale of woe.'

Dirk wiped away her tears with his thumb. 'I'm so sorry,' he said and touched his forehead to hers. Far from comforting her, it unleashed the floodgates.

She wiped her face. How disgusting. Snivelling was so not her.

'It's OK to be human,' he said. 'I felt the same way since I split with Amira and, unlike you, I've no charm or energy to put on a front. I'm just a miserable bastard and recent experience has made me worse. We were even planning to have a family, you know, before we split up.'

So, Dirk and Amira had been trying for a child. He must have wanted a family; he probably still did. Tonight had been wonderful and terrible too. She'd let her guard down and she now felt as if she'd revealed her most personal secret — flung it at Dirk like a nuclear missile. What if he thought she was trying to emotionally blackmail him?

Or worse, that she was trying to say she wanted to stay with him and . . . and . . . what?

She didn't know what she wanted any more.

She hugged the blanket around her. 'Can we go home, please? It's bloody freezing out here and very late.'

He hesitated, obviously confused and troubled by the switchback to the 'old' buttoned-up, brittle woman. 'Yes, but you can talk some more if you want.'

She got up, dragging the blanket with her, sand flying into the air. She was on the verge of tears again and panicking at showing any more emotion in case it unleashed a torrent. 'I think we both know I've already said far too much.'

It was time to go, before she told him her other secret, the one she'd now admitted to herself: she'd fallen in love with him.

# 29

Marina and Lachlan strolled along the beach after dinner in their Scilly cottage situated above a tiny cove on the far west on St Agnes. It had taken a boat ride from St Mary's to get there and they'd spent the day strolling the coast path and hunkering down at the one and only pub.

After a day of bright sun, the evening sky was tinged with rose gold and fiery orange while wavelets whispered onto the sand. All the visitors had gone and she and Lachlan were alone on the beach together. She was brimming with hope and happiness.

A helicopter flew over, heading back to the mainland after a visit to the Bishop Rock lighthouse. Lachlan stopped and shaded his eyes to watch it fly past.

'OK?' Marina asked.

He turned to her. 'Yes, I think I am.'

'Thank you for coming here. What you did today — facing your fears — was no small thing.'

'I'm glad I made it, but without the incentive of having you by my side, I never could have even considered it. I've always felt the accident didn't just rob me of my job in the RAF, but of my confidence — of my reason for being.'

'I do understand,' she said.

'I couldn't face going back to the MRT, even though they offered to find me a role away from the sharp edge — manning the phones, looking after the kit and giving talks. I felt that if I couldn't offer my whole self, then there was no point being involved at all.'

'Do you think that by denying yourself any contact with the team and leaving your job . . . do you think you might have been punishing yourself for what happened to Catriona — even if it wasn't your fault in any way?' she asked.

'Possibly. It was more that I felt everything I loved and believed in — all my certainties in life — had been shattered. Obviously, my physical recovery took a long time, and it's still on-going. The mental side of things will take even longer and that hit me much harder than I'd ever expected. I was grieving for Cat, and feeling guilty, and both of those things still apply.' He grimaced. 'Sorry, this weekend was meant to be a break for us both.'

'It's the space you need to think and talk. I don't mind.'

They strolled hand in hand in silence for a while. Lachlan was staring at the horizon and seemed to be on another planet.

'Earth to Lachlan?'

He turned to her. 'Yes.' He smiled. 'Sorry. Miles away. There's a bottle of champagne in the fridge with our name on it that we haven't drunk yet.'

'Why don't we have it out here?' she suggested.

'OK. I'll nip in and get it.'

He returned with the bottle, two glasses and a rug, which he laid in the dunes. With no one else around, they kissed and cuddled close, watching the sun sink lower.

'You know this is the furthest most westerly edge of Britain. There's nothing between us and America but rocks and the lighthouse,' she said. 'In ancient days, it really would have been the edge of the world for the people living here.'

'It reminds me of the Western Isles,' Lachlan replied. 'Only warmer.'

She laughed.

'Even though I'm almost a thousand miles from 'home', I feel I belong here in Cornwall, and Porthmellow,' he went on. 'It's ironic that when I first arrived, I was determined to keep as far away from people as possible. It was nothing to do with the scars. Yes, some people do judge people on how they look and they're disturbed by it initially, but that's their problem and if they can't get over it fast, then they're not people I want to know.

'The truth is that I didn't want to engage with people, full stop. I thought I could stay in the background at the office, only communicating through a screen.'

'You'd have been better off going to London if you wanted to avoid people.'

He chuckled. 'You're right, but I knew Aaron, I felt comfortable with him and I trusted him. Cornwall was literally the other end of the country. I didn't expect to be drawn into the community as I have. I fought against it.'

Marina's eyes widened. 'Really? I hadn't noticed.'

He grimaced. 'I'm sorry. I was an idiot.'

'Oh, I wouldn't go *quite* that far.'

He narrowed his eyes at her then smiled ruefully. 'I've realised over the past few months

279

that I can't stop myself caring about other folk. I tried my hardest but it hasn't worked. Most of all, I can't stop myself caring about you.'

Wow. Now he'd taken the wind out of *her* sails. She listened intently, willing him to say more.

'I don't know what the future holds . . . ' he went on after a pause. 'But I can only see it in Porthmellow. You might be stuck with me.'

'I learned not to look too far ahead a long time ago,' Marina said carefully. 'But I'm happy you want to stick around and found a way to be comfortable with us. Porthmellow isn't for everyone but I think it's great that you're giving it a chance.'

He turned his head to her, his eyes demanding an answer to the main part of his statement. 'And you? Are you happy to give me a chance?'

Marina's heart beat a little faster. 'You know I am. More than happy. Like you, I can never take the future for granted again but, since you've arrived, and we've grown close, I've started to look a little further . . . and I'm excited to see where this takes us.'

'Yes . . . ' He slipped his arm around her waist and she rested her head on his shoulder, drinking in the glory of the endless view over sea and sky, wishing the weekend could go on forever.

They lapsed into a silence that felt the opposite of awkward. It was so natural to simply sit there, with his arm around her, enjoying his presence, the awe-inspiring beauty and sense of isolation from all the pressures of the world.

She would approach the new season with fresh

energy this year. She'd grown used to her own company in front of the fire on a dark evening. No storm bothered her after the one she'd weathered over the past years. She was independent, had good friends, colleagues, students and Tiff and she finally had closure in emotional — and soon legal — terms.

However, it would be lovely to have someone to share the sofa with in the evening — and her bed with at night. She certainly hadn't known Lachlan long enough to think of moving in together but he was only a few steps away and despite her hints about living for the moment, she couldn't drown out the desire and hope that they would have much longer than the next few months to enjoy. She was thinking of autumn and winter too, Christmas . . . and beyond?

'Marina?'

His voice was soft. 'Hmm.'

'This may be too soon and you can say no if you like but . . . I'd like to join the Wave Watchers.' He smiled. 'If you'll have me.'

She took her head from his shoulder to look in his face. 'Of course we'll have you. I think you'd be great, but are you sure you're ready?'

'No, but it would be another step back into the life I once had, or rather the life I want to live. Like I said, I tried to stay away from the community but I found it impossible. Someone made me look at my life, and the way I was living it, in a new way.'

The sun had gone now, leaving the sky deepest indigo and the breeze freshened as night fell, so Lachlan tightened his arm around her shoulders to try and keep her warm. She carried her shoes, revelling in the damp sand under her toes on the way back to their cottage. It was as if all her senses were heightened; she hadn't felt so alive, deep in her skin and bones, for a long time . . . or perhaps ever. This intensity of living wasn't from a time before Nate disappeared, it was completely new, and she couldn't compare it with the past. They hurried home, went straight to bed, making love in the pure darkness here at the edge of the world.

For the first time, she felt she could let go of the guilt that came in admitting that her life was more deeply joyful this evening than, perhaps, it had ever been with Nate.

# 30

'Hi Tiffany, I'm ho-oome!'

Trying not to giggle, Marina trilled out the greeting as she unlocked the door to the cottage. Tiff would be bound to walk out of the sitting room, ready with a 'Don't you dare use that name!' remark.

Still buoyed by the happiness of her break with Lachlan, Marina left her case by the bottom of the stairs. Maybe Tiff was in the garden. Or upstairs with Dirk.

'Helloooooo!' she shouted again, ready to make a rapid escape to the garden herself if the pair of them really were in bed. She doubted it — their liaisons were almost exclusively kept to Dirk's place — but Tiff might have invited him for an away match while Marina had been in Scilly. She was home slightly earlier than planned, having been put on the flight immediately before the scheduled one.

Thuds on the stairs almost confirmed her worst fears, but it was only Tiff with her hair in a towel and green gloop on her face.

'I'd kiss you but I don't want you getting avocado facemask all over you. You look fantastic. How was it — or need I ask?'

'Well, it was . . . wonderful, actually.' Marina burst into a grin. 'How about you?'

'Oh, it's been . . . interesting. Let me wash this off and we can tell each other everything.'

Marina wasn't sure she wanted to tell Tiff everything, and she was certain that Tiff was holding back some of the events that had passed between her and Dirk. Still, she felt buoyed by happiness and Tiff seemed to have made things up with Dirk for now. She couldn't ask for more.

She felt sure her life was on an upward curve. Lachlan was good for her, and she hoped she was good for him. Their blossoming relationship would make it easier to go through with the legal necessities around ending her marriage to Nate and, finally, closing the door on a dark time of her life, forever.

★  ★  ★

Over the next few weeks, Lachlan was as good as his word, joining her for his first official shift at the lookout station and signing up for the training course. In the meantime, Marina and some of the other Wave Watchers helped to supervise him, although with his military background and training, he was already very familiar with search and rescue routines, radio operation and procedures.

Marina felt he'd taken a giant leap forward in being able to return to this kind of environment. She really did think she'd helped him and was quietly pleased she'd persisted in trying to bring him into the community, and that she'd found the courage to reach out to him personally.

He spent many nights at the cottage, which suited Tiff too, because she spent as many at Dirk's — though when they were both there, Marina was pleased to see they got on well.

'Hi there.' Lachlan leaned down to kiss her one evening when he came round for dinner. 'Busy?' Marina had been busy all afternoon, emailing her solicitor and preparing a lecture for the coming term, but while dinner was cooking, she'd broken off for a much happier duty — writing a Facebook review of the lighthouse cottages.

'I was . . . but I'm now writing a post about how fantastic our stay was on St Agnes. Do you want to see it while I finish dinner?'

'Do you *really* want me to see what you've written about our weekend?' He raised an eyebrow and she was reminded of their days — and nights in bed — on the island.

'I haven't gone into too much detail!' She laughed. 'Here, you can see for yourself while I serve up the pasta.'

Leaving him with the iPad, she drained the linguine and added it to the white wine and garlic sauce, before tipping two portions into chunky bowls. Just in time, she rescued the garlic bread from the oven and put it into a basket.

When she returned, he was sitting at the dining table staring at the iPad. His expression wasn't what she expected: slightly stunned rather than pleased or amused.

'Everything OK?' she said, putting a bowl in front of him. 'I haven't revealed anything I shouldn't have?'

He closed the case on the iPad and pushed it away, the smile back on his face. 'It's great. Love the bit about the 'exciting activities' on offer, though I don't think that what we did was quite what the guide book had in mind.'

285

'No . . . it was much more fun, though.'

He smiled again and inhaled the steam from the bowl. 'This smells good.'

'Hope so, I got the mussels and prawns from the harbour fishmonger this morning.'

He poured some chilled wine left over from the sauce into her glass and topped up his own. Marina chattered away about more memories of their trip, hoping they could visit again. Lachlan hmmed in the right places and smiled but, from time to time, he seemed not to have heard what she'd said.

At one point, he paused, with a hank of linguine around his fork.

'Is dinner OK?' she asked, half amused, half wondering what planet he was on.

'Oh, aye. It's great.' He popped the pasta into his mouth.

After dinner, they took the rest of the bottle out onto the terrace and sat quietly in the evening sun.

'I went to see the solicitor earlier,' Marina said, feeling that they'd relaxed.

She'd got his attention again finally. 'Oh aye?'

'Mmm. I should have the legal declaration in a couple of weeks.' An unexpected lump rose to her throat.

Lachlan squeezed her hand. 'So soon?' he said.

'Well, it has been a long time coming . . . '

'Aye. It must feel like a lifetime and yet now, so . . . strange.'

'It is. Every time I visit the lawyer or sign something, I tell myself it's a positive step but it still feels like . . . ' She was about to say a betrayal of Nate, but stopped just in time. 'A weird thing to do.' She kissed him quickly and got up. 'I'll get us a coffee. I need perking up.'

When she returned with the coffees, Lachlan was speaking to someone on his phone but he ended the call. 'Aaron,' he said, and smiled broadly, accepting the mug.

They sat down and she thought he looked tired, with dark smudges under his eyes. Well, they had been burning the midnight oil, she supposed, with a thrill of delight. Maybe it also had something to do with the extra work he was putting in in Aaron's business, and the Wave Watchers shifts.

'Are you still OK with the coastguard coming to assess you on Saturday?' she asked. 'It's a bit of a pain but you can move on to the next stage of the training when she's given you the certificate.'

'*If* she gives me the certificate,' he quipped.

'Of course she will.'

His smile faded quickly. 'Don't worry, I'm used to assessments. Or rather I was. It's been a while.'

'You'll smash it,' she said, hoping he wouldn't lose any more sleep over the test. He'd already made giant strides from the day she met him, when he could hardly bear to talk to her. It would be a huge pity if he went back into his shell again, for him and for her.

★  ★  ★

Shaking her head, the coastguard assessor glanced at her watch. 'I'm afraid I can't hang on much longer, Marina. I've another assessment to do in St Ives, so if Mr McKinnon doesn't arrive in the next five minutes, I'll have to cancel.'

Marina tried not to panic. She'd been at the station for over an hour already, and had agreed to meet Lachlan for his assessment. She'd spoken to him only the afternoon before, when he'd been about to head off to Plymouth for a meeting. He'd warned her he'd be late back that evening, but never mentioned anything that might make him miss the test.

'I'm sure he'll be here any second,' she said, though she was clutching at straws by now. 'I'll try to get hold of him again.' She called his mobile but, once again, it went straight to his answerphone. A text and WhatsApp had also failed to get a response. What if something had happened to him? An accident? Or perhaps he'd had a last minute panic attack at the idea of being tested, and couldn't face telling her.

'I'm sorry but I can't reach him. It's not like him to miss something this important,' she said.

The assessor's lips twisted. 'Well, we'll have to rearrange it for another time. I do have to go, Marina,' she added in a softer tone.

'It's OK. I understand, and I can only apologise for wasting your time.'

'Let me know when he's ready. We'll work something out.'

With a sinking heart, Marina saw the assessor out and sat down in the control room, feeling completely deflated. It was hard not to feel let down by Lachlan, but anxiety over where he was and what he might be going through eclipsed her disappointment.

She thought about calling Aaron and asking him if he knew anything, but she didn't want Lachlan to think she'd been checking up on him and, if he had got cold feet, he might be embarrassed by other people knowing.

She picked up the binoculars and tried to focus on her job but she felt she was scanning the sea for Lachlan and wondering where he was . . . It must be something serious; he'd known the assessment was today, so it couldn't be a misunderstanding. Her stomach clenched hard. What if he never answered her calls? What if she never saw him again?

The terrible feeling of helplessness and loss that had overwhelmed her all those years ago flooded back. She scrabbled for perspective, but the fear of losing Lachlan the way she'd lost Nate overwhelmed her. She dropped the binoculars on the counter and covered her face in her hands in despair.

'Marina?'

Lachlan stood in the doorway to the control room.

Marina let out all her fears and anger. 'Where the hell have you been?' she cried. 'I had the assessor here for ages. They had to go and I had no idea what had happened to you! Why didn't you reply to my messages? Answer my calls! If you'd bottled it, all you had to do was tell me.'

He took the onslaught without a word and it

was then she saw his face: drawn, the eyes dark with lack of sleep.

'Lachlan? What's wrong?'

He didn't answer, but she saw him swallow hard. His lack of reply had done nothing to allay her fears. In fact, she felt even more anxious.

'Will you sit down, please?' he said, so softly she could barely hear.

Her body turned cold with dread. 'Sit down? Why? What's the matter?'

'This is the hardest thing I've ever had to do and there's no easy way of saying it that will ease the shock. It's not about me, it's Nate. He's alive.'

# 31

Marina stared at him, wondering if he'd had a meltdown. 'Is this some kind of sick joke?'

'No. It's not a joke. You know I'd never joke about something like this. Nate's alive. He's living in South Africa.'

She shook her head. 'I don't know what's made you think he's alive, or who's convinced you he is, but they're wrong and they need to understand that.' Her voice rose as the shock of his statement turned to anger. Who could think such a cruel thing, and convince Lachlan enough to force him into telling her? It was ridiculous and she wanted to know who they were.

'I'm certain it's him,' he said.

'Well, it's not.' She clung onto her composure by the thinnest thread, convinced he'd been duped in some way. 'He drowned seven years ago off the cove. Where are you getting this information from?'

'I'm afraid it's true. I can show you some photos of him right now.'

'I don't believe you.' She reached for the counter top, feeling light-headed.

'Will you sit next to me and take a look?'

She didn't want to look. She didn't want to be here. He had to be wrong. And she was angry too. 'You must be mistaken.'

She glanced at a photo he'd pulled up on his iPad. It showed a man with blond hair and a beard standing outside a bar. There was an auburn-haired woman next to him in a white bikini. Marina's heart was in her mouth. The bearded blond man . . . it couldn't be. It was impossible. It had to be a doppelganger! Everyone had one somewhere, didn't they? 'No. That's not Nate. It's just someone who looks like him.'

'What about this one then?' he asked, scrolling down to a shot of the same blond man laughing with two other people, an older man and the same redhead, this time with a ponytail and a wiggle dress. She shook her head. 'Nope. It must be a coincidence, a lookalike,' she insisted, yet her heart was pounding at the uncanny resemblance. Even the way he grinned at the camera, so sure of himself, reminded her of her husband. Her *dead* husband. A wave of anger swept over her. 'Lachlan, this isn't funny. In fact, it's pretty horrible and I don't know why you're doing it.'

'Please, sit down.'

A hand on her elbow guided her onto the swivel chair and despite her indignation, she found herself sinking onto it. What Lachlan was saying was impossible. It was ridiculous . . . a sick joke. The radio crackled with a message, but she ignored it.

'I'm sorry, but I have no choice. I wanted to wait until we were at home but I couldn't hold back any longer. What about this man?' he asked again, pointing to a face on the screen.

Marina glanced at the third picture and her heart almost stopped. It was the blond man, minus the beard. He was handsome, no doubt, in a rakish way. This time, he was squinting into the sun and had the same half-smile on his face, showing the slightly crooked front tooth that had always irked her husband. The one he said he'd damaged jumping off the harbour when he was a kid. The one she'd always liked because it added character to his features.

Her anger was swept away by shock and she started shaking. 'No,' she cried. 'No. No. No, it *can't* be Nate.'

'I'm afraid it is him. I've already spoken to the police in Stellenbosch. He's been living there under an assumed name for at least the past five years, although he's now probably under investigation for entering the country illegally. We're — *they're* — not sure where he was before he moved to the area.'

Marina put her head in her hands. She didn't need to look at the photo again, or the date. It had been posted only a year ago. It was Nate, no matter how hard she tried to deny it, and how much she wanted it to be his doppelganger. Even if she'd convinced herself of that, Lachlan was piling on evidence she couldn't ignore.

'I'm so very sorry to have to tell you this, Marina. It must be devastating.' His voice came from inches away and when she prised her fingers apart, he was there, kneeling on the floor by her side.

She stared at him. 'I can't believe it. I don't understand . . . When did you find out about this?'

'For certain . . . yesterday morning but I've had my suspicions for a few days.'

'Days? What? So, you've been investigating him — us — that long? Why didn't you tell me immediately?' she wailed, knowing she was wildly conflicted. Even in her shock, she knew she meant: why did you tell me at all?

'I didn't want to believe what I'd found at first. It was only a hunch and, in fact, even when I had the very first inkling he wasn't dead, I dismissed it as impossible. I didn't want him to be alive and I certainly didn't want to tell you that he was . . . ' He had to look away from her for a few seconds but, finally, he met her eyes again. 'When we were having dinner and you asked me to look at your review of our weekend away on Facebook, a notification popped up and the banner dropped down and it said 'Nate Hudson is alive'. And . . . God help me, I opened it. I'm sorry, I shouldn't have, but I did.'

'Oh my God. But why didn't you tell me?'

'It was a message from a woman who claimed to be living with a man she thought was Nate. I . . . we were having such a great time together. I was so happy and you seemed to be too. I thought it was a troll and a malicious hoax and . . . I didn't want it to upset you so I deleted it.'

'You read my messages and you *deleted* one?'

'I admit, it was a terrible thing to do, but I genuinely wanted to protect you . . . and also — ' he closed his eyes '- honestly, I didn't *want* it to be Nate. I convinced myself it was malicious and I tried to ignore it, but I couldn't, could I? No matter how much I didn't want him to come back, I *had* to follow it up, and then you told me about the visit to your solicitor. I knew then that I had to make certain, for everyone's sake — for yours most of all. If this woman's claims came to nothing, I thought I could dismiss it and you'd never know and she'd leave you alone.'

She let out a howl of anguish. She felt like she was being ripped in two. 'How could you do this?' she cried, so horrified that he'd lied to her, and unwilling to even process the even more awful possibility that Nate really was alive and had put her through years of hell.

'I couldn't help myself. I care for you. More than that, I love you. It was wrong of me — beyond wrong — to look at that alert, but it was impulse, a bad impulse, and now I can't undo the past or its consequences. It's not a hoax. This woman lives in Stellenbosch and when I got home, I checked her profile and her friends. There was a man. He looked like Nate in some ways though he had a different name. I've spent a lot of time since digging around and I started to form the opinion that Nate really might be alive . . . '

*Form the opinion.* It sounded so cold, as if he was talking about a case involving strangers, not ripping her life to shreds with his truth.

'This woman who contacted you,' she said, each word feeling like a hot coal in her mouth, 'is she his girlfriend?'

'Yes. She lives with him at a vineyard, which she owns with her parents. For one reason and another, she came to believe — or perhaps accept — that he wasn't who he said he was. I think he might have been borrowing money from the business — '

'Oh, Jesus.' That sounded so much like Nate that Marina felt sick. 'A *vineyard*?'

'Yes. It's a small-scale operation apparently but they must make a living from it.'

'But Nate didn't — doesn't — know anything about wine making. He never even drank it. He said it was all like gnat's piss. He only ever drank beer.' She was aware how bizarre her statement was: worrying about stupid stuff like that when she was going through the biggest betrayal imaginable. Was hers a normal reaction? Who knew? There was no normal any more. No one to ask who'd been through the same experience.

The world was full of grieving widows, but who on earth had had their husband come back to life?

In this new and terrible world, everything was possible and nothing was unimaginable.

'So, why did she try and contact me now?' she asked, shaking with shock.

'She claims she couldn't hold back her suspicions any longer. She said she found an old photo in his wallet, and a business card of a pub in Porthmellow. It led her to you, eventually.'

Marina was sickened. Everything Nate had done, or was doing, was a lie. His whole life was a fabrication. His love for her. Everything.

'Have you actually spoken to . . . to *her?*'

'Not by phone, but my contact in South Africa has. Once I knew for certain that Nate was alive and had it confirmed by the police over there, I knew I couldn't rob you of the opportunity to know everything that I do. The only decision I could make was to tell you before you see your solicitor.'

'Oh God. I — I — I can't — I don't know

what to say. I'm — ' What could she say? That the man she'd mourned, grieved for, screamed and cried over, wished was safe and well . . . was after all?

'I don't know what to think. How I *should* think? I don't want him to be dead. I'm relieved he's alive but what he's done to me is — it's . . . ' She put her face in her hands. Her world was out of control, spinning. She yelled at the air, she screamed out her pain, not really knowing who she was screaming at: Nate, the cruelty of fate, Lachlan, herself, anything and anyone because there was no anchor she could cling to — only chaos. She was glad he wasn't dead, and she was angry at him for not being dead, and horrified at herself for being angry . . . She didn't feel human, more like a raging animal trapped in a cage.

Lachlan was by her side, his hand resting on her back. She didn't have the strength to move it. She barely had the strength to breathe.

He handed her a box of tissues and she dried her face but couldn't stem the tears.

'Do you want me to call anyone? Tiff? Your mum? A doctor?'

'I don't need a doctor. I need . . . Oh God, I don't know what I need. I don't know what I feel.'

'There's no precedent for this, no plan or guide. Nothing I can say or do. It's out of anyone's experience and I'm so bitterly sorry that you had to hear it from me.'

'Then *why* did you make the decision to rake up the past and drop this huge fucking enormous bomb into my life!' She drew in a huge juddering breath, dimly aware that she was angry at the wrong person but unable to help herself. The normal rules were gone. Only this raw and terrified essence of herself was left. 'Oh God, please don't tell me he's married someone else . . . ' She felt sick. 'Does he have a family . . . kids?'

'The woman said not. And they're not married,' Lachlan told her.

Marina felt as if her heart had been rent in two, as if the life she'd carefully, painfully reconstructed had been torn apart all over again. She'd accepted Nate was dead, grieved for him, always given him the benefit of the doubt. That was the narrative she'd written for him. He'd drowned in a tragic accident that day seven years before off Porthmellow Cove. He was far from perfect, and she'd always known deep down that he might have had his secrets . . . ones she perhaps hadn't *wanted* to know about . . . but this?

'How could he have let me think he was dead? How could he have let me go through that pain? All the time he was living somewhere else, making a new life for himself. How could anyone be so cruel and so callous?'

'I don't know, Marina. Some people are . . . They just are. I don't know his reasons. Only he knows them. Honestly, I'm gutted to be the cause of re-opening this pain.'

'I wish you hadn't. I really wish you hadn't!'

Her cry was met with silence. Did he wish the same? Hot tears trickled down her cheeks and she tasted salt on her lips. She dragged her hand across her face and forced herself to ask the questions she had to ask, while knowing the answers could only bring more pain.

'Have you told the British police?'

'Not yet. I wanted to be sure it was him first . . . and to tell you, to warn you. You had the right to be the first to know. Like I say, I didn't want to believe it either. The last thing on earth I'd ever want to do is hurt you. Yet that's the job that's fallen to me: to tell you this news..'

'But . . . but . . . ' the questions flew in at her like harpies, attacking her all at once and scrambling all sense. This man — who she'd only let into her life a few months ago yet who she had trusted so readily — had ripped that wound open, overturned all those certainties, crashed into her past life without her asking.

She felt broken . . . and that the trust she'd placed in Lachlan had also been damaged. It felt as if it was beyond repair.

'Please go.'

He got up. 'I didn't mean to hurt you, but I had to tell you this. There was no way I couldn't, once I'd found out the truth.'

'I didn't want the truth. I had the truth. *My* truth. Now you tell me that my husband lied to me, cheated on me, let me think he was *dead*. That he has another partner and another life.' She gasped. 'Oh God . . . Just go. *Go*.'

'OK. I'll go, but I'm not moving from my place until I can see you again. I'll be here when you want to talk to me, or cry on me, or hit me. I'm sorry about this. It's a terrible shock but

299

once I knew, I couldn't *un-know* it. I had to make sure it was true. It would have been wicked to keep silent. I will always be here for you, Marina. Believe that.'

After he'd left, she stood for a while, her arms wrapped tightly around herself. She was frozen. She heard people on the coast path, kids shouting on the beach, the gulls screeching, life going on around her like a movie in which she played no part.

She knew that she was in shock, but all the ways she helped others to deal with it had failed her.

She had to turn over every stone, see what horrors crawled out, but that meant looking at the photos, seeing Nate's new life, the one he'd left her for so cruelly, so selfishly. It might even mean talking to him . . . seeing him again. Her stomach clenched and she felt very hot and light-headed.

She rushed to the cloakroom and threw up.

# 32

Tiff was home late. She'd spent her Saturday afternoon interviewing an author at an arts festival in St Ives, after which she'd met Dirk and they'd gone to a classical concert. Dirk wasn't on call but when they'd neared Porthmellow, he'd been paged to join another lifeboat crew on a difficult shout. She'd leapt out of the Land Rover outside the station and walked up from the harbour alone as twilight fell.

'Hello!' she called, walking through the cottage sitting room to the kitchen. 'I could murder a nice cup of tea.'

Marina was slumped in a chair at the table, her face streaked with mascara, a box of tissues in front of her. Tiff's first thought was that she and Lachlan had had a huge dust-up, or that there'd been an accident. Her stomach turned over.

She dropped her bag on the floor and rushed over. 'Marina? What's happened?'

Marina sat like a zombie. 'I can't even tell you.'

Tiff was horrified by the state she was in. 'For God's sake, what's the matter, love?'

Marina stared at her. 'It's Nate . . . he's alive.'

Tiff had seen and heard many things in her time — shocking, upsetting, impossible — but none had caused her to grab hold of a chair for support. She'd been ready for bad news but this was way beyond her imagination.

She kept one hand on the chair, wondering if Marina had been in an accident after all, and was in shock. 'Nate? He can't be.'

'He *is*,' she cried. 'Lachlan saw a Facebook message from a woman who wanted to contact me. She's been living with Nate and was suspicious about who he really was.'

Tiff was still so gobsmacked that her cogs were turning more slowly than usual. 'Wait . . . What?'

'It's true. Nate lied and let me — and everyone who cared about him — think he was dead. He let me go through all that pain because — well, God knows why, but it's probably to do with money. I didn't want to think the worst of him. I never thought he would do that, but Lachlan's saying he has more debts in South Africa . . . and a partner.' Tiff recoiled at the anger in her cousin's voice.

'Jesus. Don't say he's married this woman?'

'No, but he does live with her. Lachlan says she owns a vineyard.'

Tiff took a second to process the onslaught of news, picking up on Marina's last statement. 'Hold on a minute . . . did you ask Lachlan to investigate this?'

'No. I didn't. I had no idea what he was doing or I'd have — God, I don't know what I'd have done. I wish I didn't know in so many ways, but it's too late. No one can ever put the genie back in the bottle.'

'And Lachlan did all this without your permission?' Tiff repeated. 'He read your messages and went searching for Nate even though you and he thought he was dead?'

'He says he thought the first message was a hoax and he didn't want to upset me.' Marina was aware how that sounded and she was still angry but . . .

Tiff's eyebrows shot up. 'That's quite a leap, from curiosity to investigating this woman and Nate.'

'He was in the RAF military police, Tiff, and once he had his suspicions, I don't think he could help himself. I'm not happy about it but that's not my concern right now! Lachlan checked out the photos of Nate on this woman's page and he thought the guy looked like Nate, albeit he's changed his appearance. I've seen the photos of him. He's dyed his hair and grown a beard but it's him.' Her voice wobbled.

Tiff put her arm around Marina. 'God, Marina, I'm so sorry. This is absolutely horrifying.'

'I can't believe it myself. I don't know how to deal with it. I feel as if I'm drowning.'

'No wonder,' said Tiff, handing Marina a tissue while trying to tease out more details of what exactly Lachlan had discovered. While she made a cup of tea and comforted Marina as best she could, Tiff's brain skipped rapidly on from the shock of the revelation to its likely consequences. The police would have to be informed, of course, but she was sure Marina knew that.

However, inevitably the media would also find out and then . . . God help her.

They might find out even sooner than the police . . . but it would not be from Tiff herself. This was devastating for Marina and Tiff would never betray her.

However, many people would.

She sat down at the table with her mug. 'Marina, my love, who else knows about this? Apart from Lachlan?'

Marina stared into her drink. 'I'm not sure.'

'He must have spoken to contacts in South Africa, and here, maybe?'

'Yes, a few, I think . . . I hadn't thought about it too much. I was so angry with Lachlan, I sent him away.'

Tiff persisted gently but firmly. 'This woman who messaged you in the first place. Does she now know exactly who Nate really is?'

'I think she's worked it out quite a bit and she'll definitely find out for certain once the South African police contact her. She'll have a shock too.' Marina lifted her eyes and the desolation in her face almost made Tiff burst into tears. 'Please tell me this can't be real. This morning, I thought he was dead. Now, I'm finding he has a partner, a mistress. I can't even comprehend it.'

'No wonder. It's horrendous. I can't comprehend it either.' Tiff rested her hand on Marina's shoulder before continuing gently. 'So, what happens now? What about the presumption of death and the dissolution that was going through the court? Have you had chance to speak to your solicitor yet?'

'No, but I'll have to very soon. We'll have to stop the process. God knows, I don't want Nate to have died,' Marina said. 'I loved him, but now I know he's done this to me, I'm so angry with him. I feel as if he's a stranger who's come into my life and destroyed it.'

'Of course you're angry with him, my love. That's perfectly understandable. I'll do anything I can to help you . . . ' An idea was already forming in Tiff's mind and it wasn't a pleasant one and now was definitely not the time to broach it with Marina. 'You call your lawyer and then let's try to make a plan, or at least think of a way of trying to cope with what might happen next. I presume Lachlan wants to help?'

'Yes. That's the other thing about this whole horrendous mess. He'd do anything to help but I feel that things can't be the same between us ever again. However much I try to tell myself I *had* to know and that it's better that I do, I can't help blaming Lachlan for bringing this trouble back into *my* life. I can try to ignore it or deny it, but nothing can change the fact that I'm still Nate's wife.'

★ ★ ★

Marina's solicitor came out urgently on the Sunday afternoon to offer advice, the situation being so serious. Tiff was invited to listen in and, although she didn't want to intrude, she hoped she could help Marina by being fully informed of the facts.

Tiff took on the job of phoning Marina's parents with the news. Hearing them gasp in shock and Marina's mum burst into tears, she almost wept herself. After they'd had a few minutes to take it in, she then handed over the phone so Marina could talk to them herself.

They arranged to come over the next day.

After an exhausting day, Marina finally fell asleep in her clothes, on the sofa. Tiff covered her with a throw, deciding it was better to let her sleep while she could. Tiff went to bed herself but lay awake long into the night, dreading the conversation she needed to have in the morning, but knowing it had to be confronted for Marina's sake.

Still rubbing sleep from her eyes, she wandered into the kitchen as dawn broke. Marina was sitting at the table, a cup of black coffee in front of her. It was barely light outside and the wind was howling off the sea.

Marina's eyes were red and puffy. 'I won't ask how you are, but did you get much sleep?' Tiff asked.

'Some. Thanks for staying with me and covering me up last night. I woke around five and knew I'd never drop off again so I decided to get up. There's coffee in the machine. I'm trying to wake my brain up.'

'Me too.' Tiff poured herself a cup of coffee and sat down at the table.

Marina cradled her mug. 'It's a good job it's still the holidays and I don't have to go into work.'

'You'd have to phone in sick, anyway, my love.'

'What would I say to them? My dead husband isn't dead any more so I won't be in today? I'm sure my boss has heard some wacky excuses for being off work but even she'd struggle with that one.'

Sensing her opportunity, Tiff steeled herself

306

for the news she had to deliver with a good glug of her coffee. 'She'll have to believe it. Let's face it, you are going to have to tell people that Nate's alive.'

'How can I do that when I can't even accept it myself? What do I say when they tell me I must be overjoyed? How do I tell them what I feel when I don't know myself?'

'You'll work it out. *We'll* work it out.'

'Not that it's any of their business,' Marina declared.

'In an ideal world, no. It's no one's concern but yours and Nate's, and your close family and whoever else he's misled and cheated . . . but this isn't an ideal world. It's a shitty world, where for every good, kind person with your interests at heart, there will be one who wants to use the situation to their advantage.'

'What do you mean?'

'That this news is bound to find its way into the open sooner or later.' Tiff sighed. 'Much sooner, probably.'

Marina's hand flew to her mouth. Tiff felt as if she was dealing one cruel blow on top of another. Yet she had to step in now, for Marina's sake.

'This isn't going to help, but I have to say it. The press are going to have a field day with this story.'

'It's not a story. It's happening to *me*.'

'I know, my love . . .' she said, more soothingly. 'But the South African police and various contacts of Lachlan's have already been alerted. The police can't keep a lid on it for long and even if they did, Nate's connections in

South Africa will find out and start to talk.'

'Oh God. Do you think they'd go to the press?'

'I'd love to be wrong but I can't lie to you. If this woman has been deceived and fleeced by Nate, then she's not going to baulk at selling her story, is she? And I'm sure he has other friends, business associates, enemies . . . even if Porthmellow rallies around and refuses to talk to the media, these strangers have no loyalty to you. They'll be angry and they'll see no reason why they shouldn't make a quick buck. And I promise you, the news outlets will be queuing up to offer the cheque.' Tiff stopped, not adding her biggest fear: that Nate himself might sell his story.

'How bad will it be? Will it fizzle out?'

'Eventually, but for a few days it'll be pretty huge and it'll rear its head again if he comes back here. You can imagine the headlines: 'Kayak man comes back to life'. I'm afraid it's going to be on the front pages of every newspaper, on the telly and all over the Internet and social media. People will have their opinions and I advise you now to avoid them like the plague. I'm so sorry, my lovely, but you're going to need to brace yourself and be very, very strong over the next few months.'

Marina's expression of utter bewilderment was heartbreaking but Tiff had to be strong herself to help her cousin in any way she could. On this occasion, it might mean going against every instinct and doing the very thing that seemed harshest.

'I hadn't thought about all the media attention,' Marina murmured. 'I've been so bound up in taking in the fact he's still alive . . . the media coverage was bad enough when he went missing . . . although then, I was grateful that people were looking for him. But *this*, this is horrendous.'

'I'll deal with the media, when it comes to it. I'll write the story. I know that sounds callous and hard, but if I don't do it, someone else will. Give me the exclusive and I'll do my best to put forward your side of things. I can't stop other people from writing what they want, but at least you know you can trust me.'

'I want to go back to not knowing. I wish Lachlan had never looked for Nate. I'm relieved he's not dead or hurt . . . but why did I have to know?'

Tiff rubbed Marina's hand. 'You'll get through this, I promise you.' She sighed. 'I suppose you could look at it another way. If he'd kept it to himself, how would you have felt?'

'I don't know.'

'Maybe you think that now, but you won't always. Come here.'

Tiff leaned forward and hugged her. Marina had been a rock to her in her darkest hour and now she owed it to her cousin to be the same.

Her auntie and uncle arrived shortly afterwards and Tiff spent the rest of the day handing out tissues, making tea and finding out as much as she could, always aware of the clock ticking.

Marina needed time to let her initial shock and anger abate before they told the authorities and all hell broke loose.

# 33

Marina didn't know how she would have coped if Tiff hadn't gone with her to the police station to report that Nate had been found. As she wasn't reporting him for committing a crime, the police could do nothing but take enough details to alert the South African police to conduct a welfare check on the person suspected of being Nate. They confirmed he was perfectly within his rights to go off and live his life elsewhere, so long as he wasn't doing it to commit a crime.

On the journey home from the police station, familiar sights like St Michael's Mount seemed alien. She felt as if she couldn't even take a rock or a stone for granted, and every time she looked, she feared it might not be there. She knew she was still in shock and tried to tell herself that it was OK to feel this sense of total disorientation. No one could help because no one had ever been through a remotely similar experience.

Back at the cottage, Tiff put a mug of tea in front of her that she didn't really want. 'This is the hardest part,' she said. 'I'll not say it's going to get easier but you've taken the first step. How are you doing?'

'Part of me wants to pretend he's still dead. I spent so many days, months and years wishing he'd come back and now he could, I don't want him to. I need to know why but I don't want to know why.'

'That's understandable, my love.'

'I also can't stop thinking about Lachlan. I know it isn't his fault. I can understand and forgive him for checking out the message, and I realise now that even if he hadn't, one day there might have been a slip-up or Nate might have decided to come back anyway . . . But I can't cope with a new relationship at the moment. I feel as if I've crawled to the top of a mountain and been knocked back down again. This time, not because Nate's dead, but because he's been found.'

Tiff patted her hand. 'No wonder you're at sixes and sevens after such a betrayal.'

'Yes. And I know Lachlan's a good man, but I'm not sure I can believe in anyone ever again.'

'You will,' she said firmly.

'Do you think so?'

'One day . . . ' Tiff murmured. 'Give yourself time.'

A short time later, Tiff left her to her thoughts while she popped down to her office in town. Life had to go on, Marina realised, but alone in the cottage, with all its associations, many of them now tainted, she felt the walls were closing in on her. Even the waves crashing on the beach below and the gulls' cries added to her melancholy, rather than soothing her as they usually did.

She had to get out of the house, so she walked along the coastal path. Even though it was a sunny day, she pulled the hood of her sweatshirt up, feeling like a fugitive herself. She rested on the cliff a little way below the lookout station, a few hundred yards away on one of the narrow paths that had been formed by walkers exploring a collapse of the cliff from years before. It was now thick with gorse and bracken, but no amount of warning signs prevented people from using it to reach the beach below.

The watchers on shift — Trevor and Doreen — could probably see her. In fact, if they were doing their job correctly, they *would* see her, but they were good people and they'd take her excuse that she had personal reasons for not going on shift at face value.

She kept walking and then sat for a while at a bench above the station, and the cove, looking down at the place where she'd last seen Nate. She'd watched him launch on that Saturday morning and had then gone home to do the washing, clean the cottage and do some marking.

She'd expected him home after lunch and he'd never come back.

It was still almost impossible to believe that he was now thousands of miles away living a different life.

By now *he'd* know that she knew he was alive. He must do, the South African police would surely have been in touch?

Was he shocked when they called him? Would he try to deny it? Who would he tell? His partner already knew or had guessed . . . what about any friends he had?

Did he have any conscience at all about it? A shred of guilt? Would he try to contact her by phone or email — or even return to the UK? She presumed he was within his rights to return.

At least she didn't have to tell his cousins and uncle. The local police had said they'd do that.

So now she had this brief window before the news got out, as it surely would. Tiff had been cruel to be kind in warning her and she'd discussed it with Lachlan too. The calls from the press, the reporters and cameras would land at any moment.

She'd had to tell her boss at work, in case they hounded her colleagues, and she knew she'd also have to tell her fellow Wave Watchers, the neighbours, Dirk, Troy and Evie . . . all of whom she could rely on. Beyond that close circle, she realised that her most private, personal agony was about to become public property and she couldn't do a thing about it.

She got home to find Tiff back and waiting in the window, watching for her. She had the door open before Marina reached the step and practically hauled her inside. 'Brace yourself,' she said. 'I'm afraid it's started.'

★ ★ ★

Tiff had warned her it would be bad, but she must have sugared the pill, because Marina was horrified at the intense interest in her life over the next week or so. Her own story was soon due to appear in the *Post*, but before it did, there was a piece from Nate's girlfriend. She was bemoaning how he'd lied to her and betrayed her and insisting she'd no idea that Marina existed.

Reporters knocked on neighbours' doors — though no one told them anything — waited

313

outside for her and took photos of the cottage, of Lachlan and of Tiff. The press delved into everything, raking it over endlessly. It trended on social media, made the local news, the national radio and was even discussed on a lunchtime talk show. Marina tried to keep away from the Internet as much as she could but it was impossible to avoid all the coverage.

Tiff had brokered a deal with the *Post*, a rival newspaper to her previous employer, and managed to negotiate an increase in the fee.

'I don't want a fee,' Marina protested, but Tiff had insisted.

'You're having one, you should take it. I'll have mine and I'll give it to the Wave Watchers. And Porthmellow Lifeboat Station,' she added with a wry smile.

'I never thought of that. We need the station roof repairing before winter sets in.'

'Then use it,' Tiff said firmly. 'If you can extract even the smallest bit of good out of this horrendous experience, you should take it. Now is the time to play dirty, my love, even if it goes against every scrap of your nature.'

Marina no longer knew what her 'nature' truly was. She'd been through so many emotions lately, some of them involving a lot of hate and anger, and that had scared her. 'Has Nate said anything about me publicly in the press?' she asked.

'Not yet, but he must be under enormous pressure to give his story,' Tiff said. 'Unless his lawyers have told him to keep his mouth shut while he's still under investigation by the police . . . ' She peered at Marina. 'Do you want to speak to him?'

'No! I never want to hear from him again. I don't know what I'd say if I did.' There was a knock on the door. 'Will they ever stop?'

'Eventually. You'd better hope for some major political turmoil.'

'That's not likely to happen, is it?' Marina said, dragging up a scrap of grim humour from the depths.

Tiff patted her arm. 'That's the spirit. The attention will fizzle out, I promise. Now all you need to do is decide if you want to contact Nate . . .'

'Easy then,' Marina murmured, wondering if the nightmare would ever end.

# 34

With a huge sigh, Tiff flopped onto Dirk's sofa.

She closed her eyes and breathed deeply, trying to ease the tension in her shoulders and neck. It was Sunday, and she'd hardly slept so her eyes were propped up on matchsticks after writing and rewriting Marina's story dozens of times. She'd filed it earlier that morning and it was due to appear later in the week.

Marina had gone to stay with her parents and Tiff was glad her cousin had got out of the cauldron of Porthmellow for a while.

She'd taken no pleasure in writing the feature, which had been the most difficult she'd ever done. She'd lain awake most of the night, hoping she'd got the balance between giving her perspective and writing a story that would pass muster with the editor. She'd even shown it to Marina, something she'd never done before, and done her best to incorporate her amendments. Writing it was horrendous but she took a certain grim satisfaction in using her skills to shine a shaft of light on the darkest situation.

She knew Marina would be asked time and again if she was pleased that Nate had been found, and for a while, her every nuance of emotion would be picked over by the vultures like herself, and the millions on the Internet.

She opened her eyes to find Dirk putting two gin and tonics on the table. The simple pleasure of him making her a drink brought tears to her eyes. It was probably only due to her lack of sleep, but she was definitely teetering on the edge. She could get used to this kind of treatment: the everyday little kindnesses, someone to share the highs and lows of life with, to feel loved by and love in return.

'Thanks,' she said, taking the glass and trying to get a grip on her emotions. Ironically, she felt Marina's troubles had brought her closer to Dirk.

He sat at one end of the sofa and she swung her feet up into his lap. He inclined his glass towards a newspaper on the coffee table. 'I've seen the crap they're digging up about Nate in the papers. Poor Marina.'

'Yes . . . and you ought to know, that there's another big story about to appear. The *Post* will be publishing an exclusive interview, giving Marina's side of the story.'

'Did you write it?'

'If I hadn't done it, someone else would,' she said.

'I'm glad you did, and I understand why you wanted to. I'm not judging you, Tiff.'

'Thanks.' She blew him a kiss, touched by his understanding. 'It's the one way I can help her. I've been desperate to get it right for Marina's sake. I don't think I realised how hard it would be and I did wonder if I was the right person to tell her story.'

'No wonder you're shattered if you put your heart and soul into it,' he said, and sighed. 'Imagine being the subject of it.'

317

Tiff nodded. It was the first time she'd ever felt so drained by a story. It was a new feeling. She sipped her gin. 'Writing it has given me a better insight into the hell Marina was — and is — going through.'

'She must be having a crap time and she doesn't deserve it. I feel deeply sorry for her. I wouldn't pretend to know what she's going through, though I understand how it feels to be at the centre of a media storm.'

Tiff was heartened by his empathy. 'You could tell her that when you see her. She needs her friends and neighbours to give her some sense of normality and kindness.'

His tone darkened. 'I'll chuck those leeches in the sea if I see them bothering her!'

She had to smile. 'A very noble sentiment but perhaps not the best way of avoiding further publicity. Besides, have you forgotten I'm one of the 'leeches' myself?'

'No, you're not. You're doing the story for Marina's sake and this is what you do.'

'Yes, it's what I do,' she said wearily.

He nodded. 'Let's have a drink. I made a cassoulet for dinner. I've been hoarding a good bottle of Crozes Hermitages and now seems as good a time as any.'

Tiff sat down to the meal and the excellent wine. It was great to have someone cook for her but she felt very low. It might be only that she was wrung out emotionally and physically, or that the days were shortening, although she couldn't deny she was apprehensive about the reaction to her article and the effect on Marina.

She'd hate it if the story made things worse, not better.

★　★　★

The following day, Tiff's exclusive appeared in the *Post*. By eleven a.m. that morning, she'd had to stop the car in an Asda car park on her way to do an ad feature on the tenth anniversary of World of Hot Tubs in Falmouth, because her phone had been going crazy.

There were calls and messages from several editors, including Yvette Buttler, the editor-in-chief of the *Post* itself. She knew what they might be about, and although she'd expected some reaction to the story, she had never anticipated this. Tiff phoned Yvette back and found herself with an offer of a job covering maternity leave for their features editor, with a view to a permanent position at the newspaper if all went well.

'Call me when you've had chance to think about it,' Yvette said, which really meant that Tiff should snatch her hand off.

She drove home, pleased for once that she was stuck behind a potato lorry, as it gave her time to think.

How ironic it was. What a shitty world this could be at times. She'd been desperate for a break in London, but she never would have wished things to happen this way. Now she'd profited from Marina's misfortune and felt sick to her stomach. She pulled up in the parking spot next to Marina's garage, laid her head on

319

the headrest and prayed for forgiveness.

Everything she'd wanted, hoped for, a mere six months ago was hers: a dream job, a chance to return to London, and the vindication.

Redemption and reward were laid out in front of her. All she had to do was take them.

She took a deep breath and called Yvette back.

# 35

There was a hint of yellow in the trees when Marina returned home from her parents' house the Saturday after her story had been published. A few leaves were floating in the harbour and had piled up on the slipway. September had crept up on Porthmellow while she'd been dealing with the turmoil in her own life.

Normally at this time of year, she'd have been in college to prepare for the new term but, instead, she'd been on compassionate leave dealing with the fallout of the past. She'd decided to stay with her parents when the article appeared to avoid any more press attention, and to her huge relief, there were no longer any photographers or reporters hanging around her house.

She'd not spoken with Lachlan while she'd been away. They'd withdrawn from each other, like the tides ebbing away; clearly, he'd taken her at her word to give her space. She'd like to say she was ready to move in his direction, but that wasn't yet true.

She was still overwhelmed by the shock of finding Nate and the fact that Lachlan had interfered — however well intentioned his actions were. She was still in survival mode. The past few days of hiding away had made her feel that her life had been snatched away again, and she felt she needed to claw back a semblance of normality.

Steeling herself, she decided to go into town and have a coffee at the Harbour Café, a familiar environment. Most of the customers were holiday-makers, pensioners or people in walking boots. She recognised a couple of faces, including Drew and Chloe who smiled and then went back to their coffees. Ellie Latham was working behind the counter and insisted on making her a free flat white, while discreetly asking how she was.

Ellie's sister, Scarlett, came in with her boyfriend, Jude, and they sat at the table next to Marina and started chatting to her about the next Solstice Festival, which was coming up in December. She guessed they were trying to avoid bringing up the elephant in the room and she appreciated it, even though it was hard to concentrate on 'normal' life or even see beyond the end of the week — let alone to Christmas and a new year.

After her coffee, she forced herself to go to the supermarket, pleased to have survived her first hour in Porthmellow. It was more difficult than the coffee shop and she felt eyes burning into her back. Some were familiar faces who glanced at her and forced smiles when they caught her eye, quickly going back to extravagantly examining cereal packets and carrots. Others were locals she knew only by sight, and they were not so shy in openly staring. She wondered if they might even have followed her inside the shop to confirm she was who they'd thought, or might be messaging their friends.

She carried on shopping, putting stuff in her basket without really caring what it was. Ready meals, tins, who cared? She wanted to get home. While the press attention had abated, the other issues associated with Nate's discovery had not.

The police had been in touch but Nate's disappearance was now a matter for the South African authorities. They were investigating how he'd entered the country and there was a strong possibility that he could be arrested and even jailed. Marina didn't want that to happen but she couldn't see how it could be avoided. She was drained and exhausted.

Her solicitor was dealing with all the legal issues, but that meant a constant stream of emails, calls and letters to deal with, each one hammering home the bizarre and awful reality of the situation. It had been horrible to even have to answer questions about whether she'd known Nate was alive. She'd had to break the news to so many people now, and every conversation had been hard in its own way. Even when she had a moment of peace, the biggest, most terrible question of all pecked away at her.

*Why?*

Why had Nate done this to her?

What had she done to him to make him leave?

'Hello.'

A familiar voice reached her and she was filled with relief to see Dirk's face looming over the other side of a bread display.

He joined her in a quiet corner. 'I needn't ask how you are?' he said in a low voice.

She had to smile. 'Do I look that bad?'

'No, but you've been staring at that packet for a while.'

Marina realised she was holding a bag of *pain au chocolat*. She dropped them into her basket, figuring that any food in the cottage was better than nothing.

'Thanks for the support you've given me since Nate . . . . since he was found.'

'It was a pleasure.' He grimaced. 'You know what I mean. I'm only sorry you're having to deal with this shitstorm. I hate to use a cliche but, in this case, it's warranted. This will blow over, I promise.'

'I hope so. To be honest, it's already dying down a bit.'

He nodded. 'I — um — had a taste of it myself after Amira left. Nothing like this, but it was still crap. We never asked for it.' Dirk glared at a young woman who was openly staring at Marina, a phone in her hand.

'Don't even think about it,' he growled, and the woman hastily shoved her phone in her bag and scuttled off. 'Vultures,' he muttered.

'Thanks for coming over. I do appreciate it, Dirk.'

'Any time.' He smiled and Marina was struck by the expression in his eyes. He was a beautiful man, almost sculptural in his handsomeness. Too austere for her taste, but she could see why Tiff had fallen so hard for him. She wondered if Dirk felt the same way.

Marina walked home and escaped into her garden. The tubs were still in bloom but some were past their best so she dead headed the faded flowers then made a cuppa and sat on her bench. She ought to tackle the Wave Watchers rota for the next week, which was tricky now that she wasn't doing any shifts.

She hadn't been up to the station since Lachlan had broken the news about Nate. The volunteers had rallied round, doing extra stints or manning the station solo, and one former member had even come down from Wales for a few days specially to help out, but she knew they couldn't go on like this for long.

Tiff came home to find her back indoors, with the laptop, juggling with the rota. She held up a paper bag and a delicious aroma filled the sitting room. 'I come bearing gifts. I was passing the Stargazey Pie van and Sam Lovell insisted on giving me free pies.'

Marina's appetite wasn't great but she was very touched by Sam's kindness. There were some solid gold people in Porthmellow, some of whom you could trust with your life. 'That's great. I haven't had time to cook. Again.'

Tiff fetched plates and Marina unearthed a tub of coleslaw she must have bought from the shop earlier.

'You look worn out, my love. Is that more stuff to do with Nate?' She pointed to the computer after they'd eaten.

'No. It's the Wave Watchers rota. I'm struggling to fill it.'

'I can keep you company if you want to go. I'm slightly less than useless now,' Tiff said.

'That's kind but it's not your usefulness I'm worried about.'

Tiff nodded but Marina could tell she was bemused. Marina couldn't tell her the truth: that

Nate's reappearance and betrayal and her own guilt and shame meant that right now she wasn't sure she could ever go back to the Wave Watchers.

'Have you seen Lachlan since you got back from your mum's?' Tiff asked.

'No . . . and I don't want to.' Unable to face talking about her feelings towards Lachlan, she quickly switched the conversation to Tiff. 'How are you and Dirk? You must have been spending a lot of time away from him with all my stuff going on.'

'Oh, we're fine. He's busy too. He went on some course at the lifeboats HQ. Something about saving lives and engines.'

Marina frowned. 'You normally know exactly what he's up to. You know you care, really.'

'Do I?' she said, shrugging.

'Yes.'

'Well, we both have our own lives, don't we? We managed perfectly well before I came to Porthmellow. It'll do him good to spend some time away from me.'

★ ★ ★

On Monday Marina phoned her boss and said she wanted to go back to work. She started to do some of her college admin from home when the house phone rang out. The handset showed a London number and she was going to ignore it but decided to answer it, in case it was related to Nate.

Tiff arrived home around four, so Marina let

326

her settle down with a coffee before telling her about the call.

'I had a phone call this afternoon from the editor of the *Post*. Yvette Buttler?'

'What?' Tiff rolled her eyes. 'I *told* them not to hassle you and to do everything through me. I'm so sorry.'

'Don't get worked up. It was you she wanted, she asked if you could call her. Is it about the story?'

'Ooh, I'm not sure. Could be . . .'

Abandoning her coffee, Tiff took her mobile outside to make her call. Marina heard dull snatches of conversation for a few minutes, then silence. However, it was a further ten minutes or so before Tiff came back into the sitting room, looking a little shell-shocked.

'What's going on? Are you OK?' Marina asked.

'Yes, but I need to tell you something, and you must promise not to be angry or try to persuade me to change my mind.'

'Why would I do that? What does this call have to do with me?'

'Yvette showed faith in me even when things were bad — she was the one who provided the auction tickets. She's offered me a job as features editor after our story appeared. It's maternity cover but it might become something permanent.'

Marina sat up straight. 'That's fantastic news.'

'It is but I'm not going to take it.'

'What? You're joking! Why ever not?'

Tiff pouted. 'I'm not leaving until the worst of this has blown over.'

327

'Oh no,' Marina wagged her finger, and not in jest. 'You're not giving up this chance for me. I don't need mollycoddling. You *have* to take it.'

'Yvette will wait.' Tiff set her jaw. 'She'll give me another chance as soon as one comes up.'

'Tiffany Trescott. I will *never* forgive you if you don't do this . . . unless you want to stay for other reasons too. Like Dirk . . . Does he know about this yet?'

'Of course not. He wouldn't want me to stay here either, but that's what I intend to do.'

'Don't you think you should give him the chance to say how he feels?' Marina asked, in despair at Tiff's stubbornness.

'I don't think that would be a good idea for either of us, but I will tell him *if* and when I decide to leave. I'm certainly not leaving you until the interest has died down and I'm certain you'll be OK.' Tiff folded her arms and Marina saw the pout melt into a rueful smile. 'You can't change my mind. I won't leave you.'

'Oh Tiff, you can't do any more, and I have the Wave Watchers, and plenty of friends and neighbours. They offered to stay with me in shifts and keep a guard at the door to get rid of the press — although they seem to have gone now anyway.'

'And . . . you haven't mentioned Lachlan?' Tiff said.

'Perhaps I can't handle anything more at the moment. I can't see a way forward.'

'You will do, once you can breathe again.'

Marina was touched but wracked with guilt that her cousin had turned down her big chance.

The fallout from Nate's actions had spread like ripples in a pool, affecting those she cared for most, from Lachlan to Tiff. Would it ever end?

# 36

'How did today go?' Tiff asked, accepting the cool beer Marina handed her. It was Marina's first day back at college.

Marina joined her on the garden bench. 'OK,' she said. 'Obviously the students were curious and a few of the younger ones asked me questions, but most of the new ones were too terrified to speak or only interested in talking to their mates.' She smiled. 'I'll take a self-obsessed teenager over a nosy colleague any day.'

'I'm glad you felt you could go back to work . . . ' Tiff rested her own bottle on the arm of the bench. 'Have you given any more thought to going back to the Wave Watchers?' she said.

'That's much more difficult.'

'Why?'

She sighed. 'Because I feel like a fraud, and that I've betrayed people's trust.'

'Oh, my love, why would you think that?' Tiff exclaimed.

'Because the station — the whole Wave Watchers project — was built on a terrible lie. All that effort, all that energy that I threw into starting the Wave Watchers . . . People sympathised with me, I played on their sympathy and good nature. On their pity. They gave their time and their money to re-open the station, for my sake, when all along . . . ' She raised her eyes to the sky in shame. 'That plaque on the wall dedicating the hut to Nate's memory. The thought of even seeing it makes me feel sick with guilt.'

'Listen to me,' Tiff said sternly. 'You didn't know any of that. Nate was dead, in your eyes. Your feelings were genuine and no one will think otherwise. And besides, they didn't do it only for you and Nate. They did it for their loved ones, for the community, for themselves. They knew it would save lives and it has. For God's sake, don't let Nate steal this Wave Watchers from you along with everything else he's taken.'

The passion in Tiff's voice moved Marina, but she still felt desolate.

'Everything you're saying is right, but I can't help it. What's happened has shaken everything I believed in: love, this community, myself. Now I don't know if I can ever go back.'

# 37

Tiff had just walked out of a luxury apartment development when her mobile rang. On seeing Yvette's number, she was a little surprised. After all, she'd turned down the job twice. Perhaps she was calling in connection with more freelance work.

'Tiff. Hello. Yvette here. I have to tell you that your cousin called me this morning and told me that I mustn't let you turn this job down.'

Tiff couldn't stop her squeak of amazement. 'What? I had no idea! Marina did that?'

'Clearly she has your interests at heart. Would you consider changing your mind?'

'I — I'd need to think about it,' Tiff said, still taken aback by Marina's intervention and Yvette renewing her offer. She must be very keen to work with Tiff.

'OK, but please, let me have your answer asap, because I really need a features ed. We're busy, and going to be busier. And, Tiff, before you go — I have to tell you something else you might be interested in . . . '

It was dusk by the time she arrived home and she went straight round to Dirk's. He answered the door in a dark blue sweater and jeans, his hair wind-blown, his cheeks shaded by stubble. He was magnificent and wild, like the land he lived in — and as impossible to leave.

As soon as they were in the sitting room, he

kissed her, leaving her reeling with lust and guilt. She had to tell him about the job offer; she owed him total honesty.

'Wow,' she said.

He grinned. 'I needed that. I've been on a shout all afternoon. Some guy stole a rowing dinghy from the harbour and tried to get to France for some cheap wine. He lost an oar. We got him a moment before it was swamped.'

Tiff rolled her eyes. 'What is wrong with people?'

'This one was pissed. He didn't want to come aboard even though he was sinking but we told him it was happy hour at the Smuggler's and to save his booze cruise for another day.'

She raised an eyebrow. 'Is that standard casualty procedure? If so, I'm not sure you'll ever get a job as a hostage negotiator.'

'It made him leave the boat and saved his life. The paramedics picked him up at the quay.'

She smiled and kissed him. She knew that behind the dark humour, these incidents bothered Dirk far more than he let on.

'You look tired too,' he said.

'Thanks.'

'But still very hot.'

'That's better. Actually, I am a bit knackered. I've been doing a couple of stints at the lookout station while Marina is taking a break, not that I'm much use. I had to endure an hour with Bryony Cronk today and if that's not deserving of the highest honour, I don't know what is. You know her, I suppose?' Tiff said, rolling her eyes. Bryony ran a dog-grooming parlour in the village and had her own unruly Rottweiler constantly in tow, although with her booming voice and blunt opinions, Tiff considered Bryony to be far scarier than her dog.

He chuckled. 'I heard Bryony had decided to join the Wave Watchers. I agree, spending any length of time with her deserves a medal.' He smiled to himself again.

'What's up?' she asked.

'The idea of you spending your precious time in a coast watch station with someone like Bryony, out of the goodness of your heart . . . you've come a long way from the Tiff who first knocked on my door.'

'Firstly, I only do it for Marina. Secondly, you overestimate the goodness in my heart.'

'I don't think so,' he said, so gently that her skin tingled. She wished he wouldn't say such nice things to her; every kind word would make it so much harder to leave him.

'I'd say the jury's out on that,' she said lightly, dread weighing her down. He was right in one way; she'd never have dreamed that she'd become so involved in Porthmellow life and she wasn't simply stepping in to help Marina. She'd begun to understand how no community, particularly a tiny one pitted against the elements, survived without pulling together. If that sounded cheesy, she couldn't help it. It was true.

But the satisfaction she felt in helping out her cousin and the townspeople was overshadowed by her guilt over what she had to tell Dirk. Now here he was, leg crossed over his thigh, his arm flung over the back of the sofa. He looked tired but at ease, unsuspecting. Oh God . . .

Her stomach was doing backflips while she sipped the mug of coffee he'd made her. She teetered on the very edge of not telling him about Yvette's revelations. Why did life have to throw these bloody great boulders in your way and, just as you'd found a new path, roll them away and reveal yet another route? She decided to start with the easier of the two.

'If you've been out saving lives, I take it you won't have seen the news?' she said.

He frowned. 'No. Why? Don't tell me something else has happened to Marina?'

'No, thank God. It's about my ex, Warner. There was a short piece on the BBC news channel. He's been sacked by the government. Misconduct in a public office. Turns out he was fiddling his expenses and claiming cash for employing a girlfriend. Not me, obviously.'

Dirk swore. 'Is nothing enough for some people? Why do they have to be greedy as well as bastards?'

'I don't know. Some get into a bubble. Knowing Warner, he was simply arrogant enough to assume he wouldn't get caught. He had this attitude that he could get away with anything . . . shaft anyone. Actually, I found out about it this morning. An editor friend called me to warn me the news was about to break.'

'I'm relieved he's finally been rumbled. How was he caught?'

'An undercover team had been investigating him and they handed over their findings to the police. What I find most amusing is that it was the old expenses fiddle that got him in the end.

He's done much worse, but I'm sure a lot of stones will be turned over now he's been caught out. He has plenty of enemies. We'll see what comes crawling out.'

'I'm assuming you had no idea of the kind of man he was?'

'Do you need to ask that?' She was a little hurt.

'No. I'm sorry I did. He must have hidden his real nature well.'

'He fooled me. My pride was hurt and it still is. I'm angry with myself that I fell for someone who I thought . . . ' She still felt the sting of betrayal. 'Who I thought would never use me like he did.'

'I know that,' he said gently.

'Even so, I'm not sure how I was so taken in, and yet I was.'

'You're as human as the rest of us. Don't think you're not. People always amaze me. The strongest will clutch at a drowning relative to save themselves; the smallest, oldest, seemingly the frailest will show enormous strength . . . '

'Really?'

'Yes, but we don't use that in our PR.' His brief smile melted away. 'How do you feel about this . . . finally being vindicated?'

'It's . . . hard to say. I suppose I should be doing a dance and whooping but I don't feel like doing that as much as I might have once expected.' Tiff could not deny that she'd thought she loved Warner back then, and she couldn't openly revel in his misfortune . . . but she wasn't sad for him either.

But she knew too that the real reason behind her sadness was sitting right in front of her. She hadn't known that tearing herself away from Dirk would have hurt so much. That a pound-shop Heathcliff was the man she loved. She was also painfully aware that she was only putting off the moment when she had to confess all to Dirk. 'My contact is the editor of the *Post*. She didn't only call me to warn me that Warner had been dropped in it. She had something else to tell me.'

Realisation flickered in his eyes. He'd guessed . . . 'Somehow I had a feeling you might say that,' he murmured.

'She also offered me a job.'

He waited before replying, measuring his words. 'I see. Is this because you're now back in favour?'

'I wouldn't put it like that; this editor — Yvette — told me at the time that she thought I'd been done an injustice. She believed I'd been set up, but there was no proof so she couldn't justify taking on a disgraced reporter, not to mention she didn't have a job for me. She has tried to help along the way; she's the one who's been running my freelance stories and, as you know, she came up with the auction lot.'

'Yours is a world I will never understand.'

Goosebumps popped up on Tiff's arms. He'd hit the nail on the head. The gulf between their worlds was huge and about to widen. She could see no way of bridging it.

'Is the job offer anything to do with the exclusive about Marina?' he asked.

337

'That played its part, I'm not going to lie to you, but if you think for one moment that's why I did it, then you aren't the man I thought you were.'

'What man is that, Tiff?' He fixed her with those dark eyes that made her shiver with lust. They were also eyes that let her know there was no hiding from him.

She held up her palms. 'No, no. I'm not feeding your ego . . .'

'It would make a change.' His smile was chilly but his expression softened quickly. 'You'd be a fool not to accept it.'

'Then I'm a fool.' She laughed. 'I'm not sure I can accept it.'

'Why?' he burst out.

'Because . . . ' Tiff faltered. 'Because Marina needs me.'

'This is your big chance to go back.'

*Yes, but at what cost?*

'It's not quite as simple as that . . . ' she murmured, unable to frame her feelings in words. Seeing Dirk now, feeling that their relationship had moved to a new level, she suspected that he was the reason she'd told Yvette she still needed a little more time to think over the renewed offer. How ironic it was that the door back to her old life — a *better* version of her old life — had opened again, right at the moment when she'd felt that she and Dirk had a glimmer of a chance at making a go of things.

'You know I'll miss you,' Dirk said, so gently that she could hardly bear it. 'But I'd never hold you back. You'd despise me if I tried.'

'Despise?' She smiled, but her heart ached. 'That's not quite the word I'd use.'

'You wouldn't respect me if I asked you to stay. Which I both want and absolutely don't. If you really need to be here for Marina's sake, that's different.'

Was it? She cared for Marina, she cared for Dirk. In different ways, of course, but each equally as powerful. The pull of Porthmellow had become stronger by the day, a little bit at a time, carrying her away from the shore until she was so far out, she wasn't sure she could get back.

'Actually, it was Marina who told Yvette I should take the job. I'd turned it down once.'

'And you should take it.' He looked into her eyes. 'Be all that you could and should be, for my sake.'

Tiff saw his expression and she realised, finally, that he probably was right. Why was it so very hard to do the thing she'd vowed from the start — have no regrets? Was he secretly feeling as sad as her at the possibility she actually might leave soon?

The worst thing was she'd probably never know now . . .

She fought back tears, and placed her finger on his mouth, feeling its warmth. 'Please, would it be OK,' she managed, 'if we avoided the issue for now and had knicker-ripping, hot and sweaty sex?'

His audible intake of breath told her that her diversion tactic had worked.

'Hmm. Let me think . . . '

His eyes darkened with passion and Tiff's own

body tautened with desire. He leaned in closer and she felt his breath against her as his lips brushed the tender skin of her neck. How could she ever leave . . . would it be so very bad to stay and experience this every day?

'Dirk!'

Her shriek of delighted surprise pierced the air as, without warning, he swept her up in his arms and dropped her onto the Chesterfield. Even as she was getting her breath back, he was pulling his sweater and T-shirt off in one go and wasting no time in delivering on her request.

# 38

After more soul searching, Marina decided to start formal divorce proceedings from Nate. Her lawyer pointed out that it was the natural step, given that she'd applied to dissolve the marriage anyway. However, that was when she'd accepted he was gone and that the dissolution was a conclusion to a process she'd had seven years to grow used to — divorce brought a whole new load of emotional baggage. At least it should go through quickly, as Nate had so clearly deserted her, behaved unreasonably, committed adultery . . . He ticked every box, her solicitor had said in an attempt at grim humour.

Without her Wave Watchers shifts, she'd thrown herself into her college work, and now the new term had begun she had more than enough to occupy her. Yet even with a few weeks away from the station, she still felt as if she'd cut off a limb: she missed it so much — the camaraderie, the sense of purpose and company. However, she still couldn't face going back, and the longer she stayed away, the harder it was to even contemplate a return. The thought of walking into the station, built on a sham, made her feel ill.

One Saturday morning, after Tiff had stayed overnight at Dirk's, she had the cottage to herself. The face she saw in the mirror when she went into the bathroom was gaunt and pale.

She needed to sort herself out, so she showered, put on some make-up and dug out a new top she hadn't even worn from the wardrobe. Her Wave Watchers uniform, the blouses and trousers, still hung in the same place they had for weeks. She wondered if she'd ever have use for them again.

A knock on the door took her out of her thoughts. Hoping it wasn't anyone from the press, she went downstairs to unlock it. The moment she opened it a chorus of voices rang out.

'*Surprise!*'

The lane was blocked by a crowd of people. There was Gareth, Trevor and Doreen plus half a dozen other members of the Wave Watchers. Rachel and several of the lifeboat crew had also joined the throng, along with Troy, Evie and Aaron Carman. She spotted the harbourmaster, the guy who ran the diving school, a woman from the sailing centre, several sea cadets in their uniforms and half a dozen local fishermen, some still in their yellow waders. One of them was Craig Illogan, arms folded.

Tiff stood at the rear of the group with Dirk, both smiling.

'What?'

Marina covered her mouth with her hands.

Gareth stepped forward. 'We've come to persuade you to come back to work at the lookout station, boss,' he said.

'And we won't take no for an answer until you agree,' Trevor and Doreen piped up in unison.

'We need you,' everyone chorused.

342

'We *all* need you,' Dirk called.

'The people of Porthmellow need you,' the harbourmaster spoke up. 'The holidaymakers, the sailors, the kite surfers and the divers . . .'

' . . . the daft buggers who set sail in leaky dinghies, three sheets to the wind,' said Troy.

Craig stepped forward. 'And the fishermen,' he said. 'Thanks, Marina.'

'Thank you, Craig,' Marina managed, although her throat was almost too full to speak. It must have been devastating for him to discover that Nate had also willingly chosen to put him, a mate, through hell.

'And us.' A teenager emerged from the crowd with a huge bunch of flowers, followed by his parents. Marina recognised him as Jacob, the boy who had been rescued from the kayak. 'Thanks for saving me and my dad,' he said shyly, handing over the bouquet.

'And for saving my life too,' his mother added. 'The lifeboat crew told us that you were the ones who tried to warn my husband and spotted that he and Jacob were missing. Please keep doing what you're doing, even when it seems tough. It does matter, it does save lives, and we can never thank you enough.'

'I've made a donation and so has my company,' the man said. 'It can never be enough but thank you from us all.'

Marina was going to reply but instead she could only burst into tears and let people hug her and shake her hand, one by one. She'd half hoped Lachlan might have appeared, but she'd told him in no uncertain terms that she needed a

343

break, so why would he come?

Focusing on those who were there, she spoke up, her voice breaking. 'Thank you so much. I'm more touched than you could ever know. I'm too choked up to say much but I promise I *will* come back to Wave Watchers as soon as I can,' she said. 'I mean it. Thank you.'

Satisfied, the throng began to leave and the street was empty again, save Tiff who followed Marina into the cottage. 'I hope you didn't mind the surprise,' she said.

'No,' Marina said, still wiping her eyes. 'Did you organise it?'

'Me. No? I knew about it, but I didn't arrange it.'

'Who did then?'

'I'm not sure . . . Dirk told me about it. Maybe one of the lifeboat crew or Gareth or Trevor and Doreen?' Tiff shrugged. 'Does it matter? The only important thing is that it's made you think about returning to the Wave Watchers. Will you?'

Marina nodded. 'Yes, I think I will.' She thought about the crowd of people who'd spared their precious time to come to her doorstep and let her know how much the Wave Watchers meant to them and smiled. 'After what just happened, how could I let my friends and neighbours down?'

Tiff patted her arm. 'That's the spirit. Now, shall I make you a nice strong coffee and then help you write an email to the Wave Watchers saying you're going back?'

Marina laughed. 'I won't say no to the coffee but you don't need to supervise me. I promise I'll message them now.' While Tiff put the kettle on, Marina opened her laptop, but she couldn't help thinking that someone had organised this morning's gathering, and, despite her protestations, it surely had to have been Tiff. Had Lachlan not heard about it? Or did he know and had taken her at her word and kept his distance? If so, she had only herself to blame.

# 39

Summer felt like a distant memory when Tiff called into the Harbour Café for an espresso. The autumn landscape was as beautiful as ever, with the trees tinged with russet and the holiday crowds thinning. Even the increased potato-lorry traffic struck her as a charming quirk of country life.

She'd called Yvette the morning after she'd got home from Dirk's and finally accepted the job.

Yvette had shocked her by asking if she could start work within the next two weeks. Tiff had been in tears when she'd broken the news to Marina, but her cousin was supportive as ever. She'd given notice at *Cream of Cornish* and spent her final couple of weeks with a fresh enthusiasm for the job, now that it was ending.

She spoke to Ellie Latham who was working behind the counter. Her bump was large now. 'How long to go?' Tiff asked her.

'Only a month or so. I finish work this week actually and I'm ready for a break. The usual, dark roast espresso?'

Tiff smiled. 'You know me too well.'

'You're becoming a regular. You've really settled in here, haven't you?' Ellie asked.

'Yes,' said Tiff, her insides twisting with guilt. 'I'll admit, I never expected it to be this interesting or fun.'

'Porthmellow gets under your skin like that,'

Ellie said, making the coffee.

Tiff chatted for a little while longer before taking her coffee over to a quiet corner. She couldn't bear to tell Ellie — or anyone — that she was leaving.

After a few words with Ellie's boss, and Drew and Chloe, who'd popped in with Drew's son and Chloe's granddaughter, Tiff finished her coffee and escaped onto the quayside. She'd had no idea how hard it would be to leave these people behind. They'd been strangers when she'd first rocked up and she'd found many of the locals 'quirky', to say the least, but now she felt she was abandoning friends.

She should have told Dirk immediately so she could say goodbye properly to everyone. How could she say that she'd decided to leave, and how would he react?

Were they both lying to themselves as well as each other? She stopped for a few moments to contemplate the harbour, which was bustling with fishermen landing their catches on this weekday morning. Seagulls squabbled around the boats, fighting over a scrap of fish on the cobbles. That was where she'd almost broken her heel, where Evie and Troy had come to her rescue.

She knew she couldn't leave without saying goodbye to them — or at least calling in. She popped into the florist's and left with a pink rose in a pot. The climb up to the Carmans' was steep, but at least she wasn't gasping this time.

Evie pulled open the door and smiled broadly. 'Hello, Tiff. This is a surprise.'

'I have the morning off,' Tiff said. 'And I

brought you this.' She handed it over.

'That's beautiful . . . ' Evie frowned in puzzlement, but beckoned Tiff inside. 'What have I done to deserve it?'

'Oh, nothing in particular . . . though I wanted to thank you for being so supportive to Marina these past few weeks.'

'Thank you, but you didn't need to buy me a gift.' Evie inhaled the scent of the roses. 'Though it is a beautiful plant. Look at this, Troy!' Evie called.

Troy appeared from the kitchen, a tea towel in his hands. 'That's very nice. What's the occasion?' he asked.

Tiff shrugged. 'It's a thank you for looking after Marina and generally making me welcome.'

Troy laughed. 'Well, I must confess I never thought you'd fit in here. Thought you'd be off within a week, back to the bright lights,' Troy said. 'You proved me wrong, maid.'

Tiff laughed but felt queasy with shame. 'Thanks, Troy, and double thanks for calling me a 'maid'.' It was the least appropriate epithet she'd ever heard in connection with herself, especially of late, but it was funny. 'I can't stay, I'm afraid — '

'Eh, wait a minute. I've something for you and Marina myself.'

He scuttled off, leaving Evie to shrug in confusion, but Troy soon returned with a large plastic bag. 'Here. Have these mackerel for your dinner. I caught them myself last week, and I've had them in our freezer.'

'Oh, thank you, Troy. I don't know what to say,' Tiff said.

'They'll be tasty with some fried potatoes and gooseberry sauce. Hang on, I'll fetch a pot that Evie made last week.'

'Yes, do,' Evie said. 'It's not bad, if I say so myself.'

Tiff was going to refuse but Troy was off and she put the pot in her handbag.

'Thank you for this. Thank you for everything.' She hugged Evie.

Evie looked her in the eyes. 'That sounds very final, my love,' she murmured.

'I . . . I'd better go before I embarrass myself,' she said, clutching the frozen mackerel to her chest.

'There's no shame in a few tears when you leave good friends,' Evie said quietly.

'What do you mean about leaving?' Troy asked.

'Nothing, Troy. Nothing to bother you,' Evie said, brushing Tiff's fingers with hers.

She knew. Evie knew. Tiff's throat was clogged with emotion. 'Take care, and thanks for the fish,' she murmured, her eyes stinging.

Evie patted her arm and Tiff hurried out of the door towards Marina's before she burst into girly sobs. She wondered if anyone would ever call her a 'maid' again. Not likely, in London. She really must write about the characters down here, maybe send a photographer to get some shots of Troy's weather-beaten face . . . if she could ever bear to be reminded of such an emotionally charged time. Perhaps it would be too dangerous.

She would have wiped away her tears but her arms were full of fish so she let them flow. Better let them out now than when she took her leave

349

of Dirk. Better let herself wallow so she could stiffen her spine for the ordeal to come.

'I come bearing gifts,' she said, walking into the cottage to find Marina at the kitchen table hunched over her laptop. 'Mackerel with gooseberry sauce for supper?'

'Where did you get that?'

'Troy and Evie Carman.' She handed over the mackerel.

Marina opened the paper. 'Hmm. It will need to defrost and I'll have to prepare it but it should be delicious.'

'You know how to gut a fish?'

'Of course I do. I was a fisherman's wife, you know. Still am . . .'

Tiff sat down. 'How was your day? Any more news on Nate?'

'No. I'm meeting my solicitor. The divorce is going ahead but it'll take a lot longer now, of course. I've got to be patient and Nate will have to be involved.'

'Will you have to speak to him?'

'I hope not . . . I can't face him, Tiff. Why should I have to see him after what he's done to me?'

Tiff held her tongue. How could she say whether it might be cathartic for Marina to confront Nate? She wasn't in that position, thank God. She saw it as her duty to listen and give a few gentle prompts if she thought they might help.

'I'll stay a few days longer if you want me to.'

'No. Mum and Dad aren't far if I need them. You must go.'

350

If saying goodbye to the locals had been hard, the worst was still to come. Tiff rang Dirk's doorbell the following evening. She'd put off the dirty deed long enough and even considered running away without saying goodbye.

It would be so much cleaner to simply walk out of his life without looking back, but she'd never been one to shirk away from a hard job and she wasn't going to start now.

No matter how painful, or how much it would cost, she owed it to him above all people to be honest.

'Hi,' he said, kissing her. She allowed her lips to linger, savouring every second of his touch, his scent, his presence.

Dvorak's 'Largo' was playing in the sitting room, its poignant strains piercing her heart. Anyone would have thought he knew why she was there. She almost faltered but braced herself.

'Can I get you a coffee?' he asked.

'No, thanks . . . ' She took a little breath. 'Dirk. There's no easy way of saying this. I'm going back to London.'

He nodded almost immediately. 'Of course you are.'

'What do you mean, 'of course'?'

'Of course you're going. You told me you were almost from the moment we met.'

'So you're not bothered about it?'

He shook his head and looked at the floor, before meeting her eyes again. 'I'm not surprised.'

'Right. OK.' He'd avoided answering as skilfully as any politician. She probably shouldn't have asked. Why did she ask? Why should she care what he thought when his response would make no difference to her plans?

'When?' he asked.

'Tomorrow. I'm going to visit my parents and then move back into my flat. The newspaper wants me to start work the week after next and I thought there was no reason to hang around.'

Pain flickered in his eyes.

'I didn't mean it like that,' she corrected quickly. 'I meant . . . oh God, Dirk, I can't stand a long goodbye. It'll only be more painful for both of us. Do you understand what I'm saying? I have to go as soon as I can, or I might never leave at all.'

'Tiff . . . ' he began carefully. 'You always made it clear that one day you'd go home. I can't expect you to give up your career to stay here and I don't want you to. We both know your job means everything to you and I told you I fully supported you taking Yvette's offer.'

'Everything? Yes, of course it does. Thanks for reminding me.'

He frowned, picking up on the bitter edge in her tone, which was born of sadness and desperation. 'Am I missing something here?' he said. 'Is there something I should be saying that I'm not? Begging you to stay here with me? Pleading with you not to leave? Because if that's what you want, I can't do it. For my sake, but more importantly, for yours. You would go crazy here, and you'd resent me for it. You deserve the best from life, Tiff, and that means doing the job you love in the place you love.'

'Well, hey. Thanks for taking care of my welfare,' she said.

Dirk said nothing but he wouldn't look away. 'I do care. You know that without me saying it.'

'Sure I do. I'm sorry. This is exactly the kind of scene I didn't want to create. It's exactly what we both said we wouldn't do right back when this started.'

'What did we say we wouldn't do, Tiff? Remind me. It was a long time ago.'

*Get emotionally embroiled. Care too much about each other. Fall completely in love with the right man at the wrong time.*

None of those things reached her lips, of course. They would only have made the situation far worse and tipped her over the edge.

'It seems like only yesterday to me,' she said lightly. 'It's been a blast, Dirk. An education — ' she allowed a wicked smile to hide her real pain ' — in so many ways, but I think we should say goodbye now and have done with it.'

'If that's what you want. You do know London's not the moon? I could come and see you. You could even come and see me.'

'True . . . and maybe we should do that.'

'So why do I see fear in your eyes? Why don't you think it's a good idea?'

She decided to be honest with him, if only to close down the conversation so she could get out of his sight faster. 'I . . . I'd hate to see us — what we have — fizzle out over the next few months, a year if we're lucky. You belong here and I belong there.' How could she really tell him that she didn't want to be hurt and disappointed all over again and this time by someone she deeply cared about? 'Be realistic. Long distance relationships don't work. You know that.' She smiled at him. 'Besides, I don't want you to feel you have to be a monk while I'm not around.'

'Do you actually mean you don't want to behave like a nun when I'm not around?'

She burst out laughing. After Dirk, she couldn't imagine ever sleeping with anyone else; ever becoming close to someone again; ever loving again. The realisation hit her, rose up from her chest and choked her.

She dug her nails in her palm, trying to drown out the clamour that screamed that she loved him. Loved him in a way she had never loved any man. She knew then that everything she'd felt for Warner had been straw in the wind.

But he was right about her job meaning everything. Absobloody — lutely right. She couldn't stay.

Not even another minute.

'Don't make this any harder than it is. Why face the messy awkward pain of saying 'goodbye'? We're not ones for that kind of slushy, emotional stuff. We've both been there, done that and we didn't want to do it again. I don't . . . I can't.'

'Just let me say one thing. I won't ask you to stay *because* I care about you, not because I don't. I've never wanted you to be anyone but yourself, it just took me longer than it should have to realise that you being you is what makes me . . . what makes me like and care for you so much. Do you actually want me to get down on my knees and beg you to stay?'

'I don't want you to beg me.'

'The press pressure was the tipping point in my marriage to Amira, but I knew in my heart it was already over by then. She'd been moving away from me for a long time. More accurately, we'd both been moving in different directions. Deep down, though, I didn't want to admit it for a long time, she'd grown out of me. She needed to spread her wings — I wanted things to stay the same.'

Tiff was astonished at his outpouring. No way was she going to stop him now, not that she could.

He paced the room.

'I said I'd compromise: that I could handle her working away, and that I'd go to all the glitzy events with her. I told her I'd do anything she wanted, but I think she could sense that my heart wasn't in it or that I'd never be able to deal with it. When she finally told me she was leaving me, I lost it. Just lost it.' He stopped. Tiff wondered what the hell was coming.

'I pleaded with her. Told her I couldn't live without her. Told her she couldn't live without me.' He groaned. 'Jesus, the arrogance of it. The stupidity. It was all pointless, of course, because she'd already made up her mind and knew that the split was the right thing for both of us. It was what she needed and what I needed. The only possible solution.'

Tiff knew when to speak and when to simply let someone pour out their raw emotions and she wasn't about to stem the flow. She couldn't imagine this proud, strong man begging anyone for anything. She'd no doubt that he was baring his soul for the first time, and to her. She was moved . . . and she felt responsible, holding this precious secret in her hands.

'I'm ashamed I made Amira feel guilty for pursuing her dream for even a second. I'm ashamed I put her in that position by begging her to stay. She left anyway, thank God. Of course, it took a while for me to realise how wrong my actions were. It was a few weeks after she left that I decided to come down here, and months before I had any kind of clarity. I learned something else too. I will never beg anyone else to stay in my life, never try to tie them down, no matter how much I want to be with them, or how much I care. Which is why I want you to go back to London and take this job. Not because I don't care about you more than you'd probably ever believe, but precisely because I do.'

'Oh, Dirk. Don't do this.'

'Don't do what? The right thing?' He laughed. 'Don't go all mushy on me now. That's what I like about you. You don't do mushy. I'm very proud of you, even though you drive me insane at times. Now, forget I ever said any of that stuff about Amira. I already regret telling you.'

'Enough. Don't say any more. This is too painful. It's worse than I even expected; I can't stay any longer.'

'Wait, Tiff.'

'No. I d-don't think so. Bye, Dirk. Have a good life.'

She fled out of his cottage, leaving the door open behind her. Thank God she wasn't wearing those stupid heels like when she'd arrived or she'd have tripped over on the lane. She practically ran back to Marina's, not risking a glance behind, and slammed the door behind her.

What if he came after her?

Oh God, she couldn't see him again or her resolve might wobble. She'd definitely make a fool of herself.

But the knock at the door never came.

She tried to look forward to her new opportunity. Not many people got a second chance, especially not one this good. She should embrace it; soon she'd be sucked into her crazy, manic life again and Dirk and Porthmellow and the pain of leaving him would surely fade away . . .

But he was wrong about one thing: she didn't love her career more than him. If it were that simple, she'd be able to walk away from this — from him — without feeling that she'd left her soul behind.

# 40

Even though Tiff had barely been gone for a week, Marina missed her more than she'd ever expected. The house felt as if it knew a vibrant soul had departed from it — which it had. Another part of her life was missing too. The gap left by Lachlan was proving impossible to fill. The fact he lived a few doors away and she inevitably saw him, made things worse. Yet she was still handling the legal fallout — not to mention the emotional betrayal. She was grateful to have a busy term at college to throw herself into, with colleagues to support her, and she could distract herself with the Wave Watchers again, now that she'd resumed her duties.

It had been strange walking into the station a couple of weeks earlier, after so long away. She'd soon picked up the operational side of things but, somehow, being there didn't feel quite the same.

The wooden hut seemed particularly isolated on this late September afternoon on the very cusp of autumn. It should have been a turning point for her and yet, with Nate back in her life — however far away and uninvited — and Lachlan out of it, she was still in limbo. She was alone waiting for Gareth to arrive, but he was running late as his moped wouldn't start, so she steeled herself for the shift, trying to focus on all the good reasons why she'd opened the station and not the sham that she now felt its foundations had been built on.

She'd be fine on her own and she didn't mind a little time to collect her thoughts. It was a gusty day, with leaden clouds constantly chasing patches of blue across the sky. One moment the sun would light up the whitecaps on the sea, the next the ocean would be plunged into angry shadow. It was typical of the kind of weather Porthmellow experienced as autumn set in. She watched as fishing vessels battled the swell, and on the horizon, a tanker made its way along the shipping lanes of the Channel.

Marina had been on watch for half an hour when Gareth called, breathless.

'I'm sorry! I'm still stuck. My moped's out of action. I'll have to get a lift off Mum when she comes back from my nan's but I'll be an hour at least.'

'It's OK. Don't worry,' Marina said, soothing him. 'It's not worth you coming for half a shift. Doreen and Trevor will almost be here by the time you make it. I can manage until they get here.'

'I don't like letting you down on a busy weekend. Can you get someone else to help?' Gareth sounded genuinely upset. 'What about Lachlan? He's the closest.'

'Lachlan? I — I'm not sure . . . he's probably busy and I'm not sure he's up to doing any Wave Watchers shifts at the moment . . . '

'Why not? I'm sure he'd come down in an emergency. After all, it was him who organised the visit to your cottage — '

'What?'

'Yes. It was Lachlan's idea.' Gareth paused. 'It was meant to be a surprise at the time. He didn't want you to think he was taking the credit for arranging it. We all promised not to say, but I thought by now you'd have found out.'

'Yes, of course. I'd . . . kind of worked it out.' Marina covered her shock with a laugh. 'You go and sort out your moped and I'll see you on your next shift.'

She rang off, reeling. So it was Lachlan who'd been behind the visit. Tiff must have known. So must Dirk and everyone, yet they'd all kept quiet. Her heart sank at the same time as she felt choked with emotion. It was just like him. Quiet, unassuming . . . yet he must care about her very much. He knew her so well and knew what she needed, perhaps in this instance, even more than she did herself.

She had to talk to him and apologise, explain and see him again. She reached for her phone, but the radio receiver flared into life. Her own concerns would have to wait a while. The call was from a yacht whose skipper was wondering about the worsening local weather conditions and asking if he should seek shelter in Porthmellow Harbour for the night.

Marina relayed her report and he thanked her and signed off. She was about to put the radio down when a voice came from behind her.

'Hello, babe.'

She spun round, and the radio clattered onto the desk.

'Nate.'

He stepped forward. 'I didn't mean to frighten you.'

Carefully, because her hands were shaking, she replaced the radio handset in its usual place. 'You haven't frightened me.'

'It must be like seeing a ghost.'

'I've never believed in ghosts, Nate.' *How could he stand there, so blase — so flippant? As if the past seven years — and all the horrific uncertainty he'd put her through — had never happened?*

'I'm sorry I came here but I thought you wouldn't answer my calls and once I knew I was coming home, it was better to see you face to face.'

Her jaw dropped. *Home? This isn't your home any more. You left it in the cruellest way.*

He was so different physically, much bulkier, with dyed blond hair, a goatee and a deep tan. He didn't even *sound* Cornish any more, his burr almost eclipsed by a South African accent. He was a stranger, an impostor, but he was still her husband, still the man she had once loved. He took her breath away — but not for the reason that he once had.

'H-how did you get to the UK? I thought you were dealing with the South African police.'

'I was, I am, but they decided it was cheaper and less trouble to kick me out.'

'Why have you come here?'

'I wanted to explain.'

'Explain?! How can you explain how you put me through years of agony? How you lied to me, cheated and betrayed me? And — ' Marina's

361

focus switched to his sudden appearance in the station '- how did you know I was at the station?'

'I knew about this place. I have done for a while. I saw what you were doing online, on your website. I saw the plaque to my memory . . . ' He swallowed hard. 'I know you won't believe me and it will sound pathetic but I *am* truly sorry for what I put you through.' Were those tears in his eyes? Were they real? Once she would have comforted him but now she could never believe anything he did ever again.

Marina gripped the binoculars to try to stop her hands from shaking. 'I started this place *because* of you,' she said. 'Hundreds of people — your family, friends and neighbours — gave time and money they couldn't afford so that we could open this place, in your name!'

'Are you saying you wish I *was* dead?'

The injustice of his words stung her. 'How could you say that?' She had to take a breath before she could go on. 'Oh Nate, of course I'm relieved you're safe and not dead. I loved you once, but I wish — I wish you hadn't taken the path you did. Why not simply leave me? That would have hurt like hell but I'd have had to accept it. If you had problems, we could have talked it over.'

He scuffed the floor with his boot. 'I don't know. I've asked myself the same thing and had no real answer. Honestly, I wasn't thinking straight at the time and once I'd done it, it was hard to come back from. Once I heard people were searching for me, I couldn't face coming home, even if I was tempted. What excuse could

I have given? You'd have hated me.'

Marina gasped. 'Have you even the slightest idea what you did to me by staying away and letting me think you'd drowned? By letting me think how you must have suffered and been terrified? That almost broke me. What do you think that did to me and everyone who knew you?'

'Not everyone. Some must have been glad to see the back of me, and others would have only been upset to have been cheated out of their money.

'I'm not a good man, Marina. I never have been. I did love you. You probably won't believe me, and I don't deserve your trust. For a while, when we were together, I like to think I was half decent. When we met and got married, I made a vow to myself that I could be strong and live a 'normal life' but . . . you must have realised I was never cut out for settling down and the daily grind. I never had a good role model, what with never really knowing my dad and Ma passing away while I was still a lad. That's still no excuse, I suppose, for what I put you through.'

'No. It's not.'

'The thing is, babe, I knew you were strong and you'd survive.'

His selfishness made her feel physically sick. 'My God, Nate. I almost didn't! There were a few times, the darkest times of my life, when I wondered if it would be easier to follow you. You almost broke me — in fact, you *did* break me — and it has taken years to put myself back together. This place helped me but lately, I've even had to force myself to come back here. It's only because of — ' She stopped herself from blurting out Lachlan's name. 'Because of Tiff and my friends that I'm here today. Now you simply stroll in here as if nothing has happened. You have *no* right to walk back in here, or into my life.'

'I'm sorry. I regret what I've done. I had to come back to tell you my side of the story. God, Marina, if I could turn back the clock.'

He reached for her but she stepped away behind a chair.

'Don't you dare! You can never touch me again.'

His eyes glinted, whether in anger or hurt, she wasn't sure. For the first time in her life she felt briefly afraid of being alone in the station.

To her relief, he shrugged and nodded. He moved a few feet away and ran his hands over the radar equipment. 'I can understand why you're so angry. I owed money, I'd let people down, I was worried that some of them would come after me . . . after you. It felt cleaner to just vanish.'

After her? How could he have known they wouldn't still pursue her after he'd gone? Or now . . .

'So I took the kayak out and let everyone think I'd be back within a couple of hours. No explanations. I didn't have much of a plan other than to get to SA and get a job. This guy said he could get me a new identity, but it came at a price, so I borrowed some money. I knew I would never have to pay it back.'

She wished she could throw him out, but now he was here, she had to know every last detail, no

364

matter how much it cost to hear it. 'How the hell did you come across someone who could get you a new identity?'

'I asked around in the pubs in Newlyn and Falmouth. I found someone on a fishing boat in Newlyn — some Russian passing through — and he got me a passport and a new ID. Then I came up with the kayaking plan: I thought it would mean you could get a divorce and be rid of me.'

'Rid of you? I never asked for that. I never made you feel I wanted to be rid of you. Don't put that on me.' She was shouting. She was dimly aware that she hadn't been doing her duty and watching. But she couldn't take her eyes off Nate.

'After I ran away, I suppose I could have told you I was OK, but the longer I stayed away, the worse it seemed. I felt guilty and ashamed. In the end, I figured you'd have got over me and met someone else. I am sorry I left. I regret the debts I left you with, but I couldn't pay them off. I knew you had a good job and you'd be OK, but I guess it was tough on you at first.'

*Not as tough as thinking you were dead*, she wanted to scream, but she let him carry on, shocked at the glibness of his explanation, at the planning, the deception.

'It was hard for me too when I first got to Jo'burg. I found some bar work and then moved to work at a vineyard in Stellenbosch and worked my way up to manager . . . ' he said.

'Is that where you met your new partner?' Marina said acidly.

'Yes. That was a couple of years ago now. Not straight away.'

365

'Oh well, that's OK then,' Marina snapped, but Nate seemed immune to the irony.

'How much did she know about me?'

'I said we were divorced.'

Marina was speechless at his sheer audacity. The ease with which he'd lied again and again, not only to her but to everyone he came into contact with, was mind blowing. She'd never known him at all, not *ever*.

'Stef is my girlfriend and business associate, or so I thought until she started asking me questions I didn't want to answer. I think her parents tried to turn her against me because I wanted to expand the business. Stef didn't like the way I was investing money. It turns out she was checking up on me behind my back — she found a card from a pub in my wallet and a photo of us up here on the cliff.

'I'd kept the picture among a load of others . . . sentimental reasons, I suppose. It had your name on it. You'd written on the back, 'with love from Marina'. I should have thrown it out but . . . ' He shrugged. 'I *did* love you,' he said, his tone desperate. 'I still do, in my way, but it was my undoing. Stef used the card to track you down to Porthmellow on Facebook. You must have had the shock of your life when she contacted you.'

'That's the thing, Nate,' Marina said, astonished that he could claim to love her after the agony he'd caused. 'I didn't see the message. Lachlan read it and he went looking for you.'

'Lachlan?' His eyes widened. 'You let some bloke read your private messages?' he said contemptuously.

'Lachlan's a friend,' she said, wishing she hadn't told him and wary of his reaction; this stranger she'd once shared her life with. 'A close friend. He was in the RAF police.'

He blew out a breath. 'Well, well. Military, eh? So he's one of the guys who've been hunting me down. I didn't know you knew him . . . ' He stared at her. 'So, you haven't been *that* lonely. I'm glad you've found a consolation.'

'He isn't a consolation!' she shot back, then saw that she'd played right into Nate's hands. Defending Lachlan was only revealing her real feelings. 'He's a good friend and what he does, or I do, is none of your business,' she declared.

'He's the one who's ruined my life. Ruined yours too, because if he hadn't gone looking for me, you'd still have been living in blissful ignorance.' Nate's voice was a whine of self-entitlement. 'Do you want a guy like that in your life? Spying on you, controlling you? I might have done a terrible thing but I don't want you to be taken in by this stranger.'

Marina's anger, born of deep hurt, threatened to engulf her. 'No. *You're* the stranger, Nate. You've forfeited the right to know anything about me or my friends. In fact, I think you should leave right now.'

'OK. OK. I'm sorry to have upset you, but don't be like this. I have more to say.'

'I don't want to hear it. I don't want to see you again, and don't even think of trying to get back in the cottage or I'll call the police.'

'I won't. Chill out!' He held up his hands. 'Jesus, I haven't come back to ask for anything. I don't want the house or your money. I'm not going to stick around . . .'

She almost fainted with relief that he wasn't going to ask to stay with her, not that she'd ever have let him near her home. What a terrible feeling to hold towards the man she'd once loved and now . . . pitied.

'I know you won't believe me, but all I came for was to explain and ask for your forgiveness.'

Marina stared at him, open-mouthed.

'Can't you grant me that before I go?' he said, softly, the way he used to when he wanted her to bail him out. It used to work. His eyes were full of hurt. 'Or do you hate me that much?'

'I don't hate you, Nate. I never have and you can leave with my sincere wish that you'll realise what you've done and that your life takes a different turn from these past few years. I don't hold out much hope of that but I can never wish you ill.' A feeling of resigned sadness filled her as never before, like ice freezing her veins and making her numb to him. Until this moment, she'd been clinging to the last gossamer-thin thread of love for him. She hadn't wanted to finally let it go, but now it had snapped.

She owed him absolutely nothing. 'As for forgiveness,' she said. 'I can't give you that. Not today, and maybe not ever.'

He curled his lip, anger glittering in his eyes. Marina wasn't worried he might do something violent but she was afraid that her own feelings might spill over.

At first, he made no signs of moving, so Marina gestured towards the door.

'If that's what you really want.'

'I'm sorry, Nate, but it is.' She was going to call for help on the radio if he didn't leave soon, but he turned on his heel and walked out without another word. She heard his boots on the steps and waited for him to reach the bottom before she moved herself. She quickly turned the key to lock the station door in case he came back. How ridiculous was that? Locking the door on her own husband?

She leaned on the counter in the staff area, taking some deep breaths to find some calm. The wind had freshened and howled around the station. She couldn't afford to be off watch for much longer.

She spotted a boat among the waves some way up the coast, by the lighthouse. It was the yacht that called her earlier to check on the weather. It was perilously close to the rocks below the lighthouse. No skipper in their right mind would venture so close, but there was no sign of anyone on deck . . .

She tried to raise the skipper on the emergency channel but got no answer so she picked up her marine radio.

'Falmouth Coastguard. Have you had an SOS call from a yacht off Porthmellow Bay?' She gave the coordinates. 'I'm concerned she's very close to some rocks. She may have engine trouble or be without a crew.'

The coastguard came back to her and confirmed they'd heard nothing.

'She's only a few hundred metres from the reef. She looks like she's drifting without any engine power. I can't raise the skipper but I know he's aboard because he called me earlier to get a weather report.'

A few minutes later, the coastguard told her that Porthmellow lifeboat was on a shout towing a trawler taking on water thirteen miles out so they'd asked for the smaller inshore lifeboat to attend the call.

Relieved that help was on its way, but alarmed at how much the yacht had drifted, Marina kept her eyes glued to the vessel. Try as she might, it was impossible to banish her encounter with Nate from her mind.

Her phone rang and she snatched it up.

'Marina. It's Nate. No, don't ring off! I'm in the cove. I'm cut off by the tide.'

'What?'

'I'm in big trouble here. Can you call the lifeboat out to me?'

She took seconds to register what he was asking. 'Are you really cut off or is this some kind of game?'

'I'm not lying. I don't have long before the beach is covered and I can't climb the cliff. Marina, help me!'

'I'll try but the Atlantic class is out at sea rescuing a sinking trawler and the inshore boat is on its way to a yacht. Where exactly are you?'

'I managed to climb the rocks at the far side of the next cove.'

'Why the hell are you even over there with the tide coming in?'

'Does it matter? I just went off after I left you. I didn't care where I went. I was angry and I wasn't thinking. Christ!' She heard a crash.

'What was that?'

'A feckin' huge wave. It's coming in fast. The cove will be swamped in no time and I can't get any higher up the cliff.'

'OK, stay where you are. I'll get help to you from the coastguard or one of the other lifeboat stations.'

'Hurry. I won't last long.'

Marina shivered. Had Nate deliberately put himself in danger to get her attention? No, surely it wasn't possible . . . and anyway it didn't matter. He needed her help like anyone else.

'Oh my God. I have to go. I can't hold on and — '

There was another huge crash and then nothing.

'Nate? Nate, can you hear me? Nate!' she called.

The line went dead. He must have dropped his phone, or far worse, been swept into the sea.

# 41

Marina had just enough presence of mind to call the coastguard before dashing out of the station and down the steps to the beach. She prayed Trevor and Doreen would arrive soon and pick up on what was happening, but there was no time to lose.

She'd tried to reach Nate again by mobile while she ran across the sand towards the rocks that separated her cove from the one where he was stranded. Her lungs were bursting and her legs burning by the time she reached them. There was still no answer from him and she was forced to put her phone in her pocket in order to make her way between the slippery pools.

She'd done everything wrong, broken every rule by leaving the station but she didn't care. Nate might have minutes — seconds — and no matter how she felt about him, she couldn't leave him alone, even though she had no idea of what she'd do when she got there.

She managed to climb up high enough to reach a vantage point over into the next cove. There was no use going any further because even if she scrambled down the other side, she'd have to swim across the cove to get to him, or he'd have to swim to her.

At first there was no sign of him and she feared he'd already gone into the sea, but then she saw a movement on a rocky ledge above the water. Nate was wedged in a small crevice against the rocks. He waved at her and she signalled back at him with her arms. Every few seconds, the waves crashed against the base of the cliffs, throwing up spray that all but obscured him. He had maybe ten minutes before he would be swept into the sea by a big enough breaker.

She reached for her radio to call the coast-guard again and her stomach knotted in dread.

She'd left it behind in the station.

Her scream of frustration was swallowed by a large wave thudding into the rocks below her own feet. Cold droplets spattered her face. She was safe in her position — for now — but she couldn't stay there forever for risk of being cut off herself. She wedged herself between two rocks, and took out her mobile, fumbling because her fingers were wet and cold, and the adrenaline was coursing through her.

Nate had inched up to an even narrower ledge but waves were breaking over him. He pressed further into the cleft in the rocks. She tried to call the coastguard but then saw something that made her grip the rocks tighter. 'Oh God. No.'

It was Lachlan.

He was at the top of the cliff, around thirty feet above Nate. He waved his arms at her and moments later, lowered himself over the edge. She could see he was in running gear, just a vest and shorts with no protection from the rock face.

Marina shouted, even though he couldn't possibly hear her. 'No. No, don't do it.'

Even if he could hear, she suspected he wouldn't take a bit of notice — like the day he'd gone swimming in the cove right in front of her.

'You idiot. You stupid bloody idiot . . . I can't lose you too.'

Lachlan climbed down to a small outcrop, around ten feet above Nate.

Marina saw Nate look upwards. He must have panicked because he tried to reach for Lachlan, grabbing for his ankle, missing, his arm flailing . . .

Thrown off balance, he lost his footing and slipped off the ledge backwards. He rolled onto a rock platform a few feet below, which the retreating surf had momentarily uncovered.

'Nate!'

Marina's scream was drowned by the thunder of the surf.

Nate raised his head, seemed about to get up before the next wave, almost gently, broke over him and rolled him into the water.

He bobbed in the surf, one arm thrown up, before he disappeared under.

Marina summoned all her training. Nate was drowning — this time right in front of her eyes — and she could only do one thing. She called the coastguard on her mobile for an update, trying to stay calm.

They said a helicopter was on its way but it would be ten minutes.

Ten minutes. It was an age.

Nate didn't have an age.

The coastguard operator knew her and ordered her not to move, to hold on and to try to make Lachlan stay out of the water, but it was too late. He was on the platform where Nate had been, pulling off his trainers and moments later, slipped into the sea.

Marina spotted Nate again, above the water, his arm aloft, tossed around like driftwood in the swell. At least he was still alive, which meant there was hope — but for how much longer?

Lachlan battled his way to Nate, fighting the heaving seas to reach him, at one moment further away, the next lifted almost within touching distance. A minute passed by, then two, and Lachlan was next to Nate. They seemed to fight for a few seconds as Nate grabbed his rescuer. Lachlan managed to turn him over onto his back, holding his head above the water.

How long could they hang on? How long before one or both of them succumbed to the cold water or exhaustion or were dashed against the rocks?

'Hold on!' she screamed until her throat was raw, with no hope they could hear her. 'They're coming.' She waved at the sky even though there was no sign or sound of the helicopter yet.

A huge wave broke below the outcrop she clung to, its spray wetting her fleece and hair. A glance behind showed surf boiling over the path she'd taken to reach her vantage point. She was already cut off but she didn't care. She clung on, willing Lachlan to hold onto Nate, willing them both to stay alive, but knowing that no one could win a battle with the sea for long.

Her clothes were soaked, her hands numb and her throat raw when she heard the whump whump of the coastguard helicopter in the distance.

She waved her hand. 'They're coming!' she shouted.

She wrapped her arms around a rock when the helicopter approached and hovered over her head. The downdraught felt as if she was standing in the teeth of a gale and made the water in the cove ripple outwards like a maelstrom. In seconds, a winchman descended from the helicopter towards the water, waving his arm to manoeuvre closer to the two men.

He took Nate up with him first, leaving Lachlan alone, tossed by the surf. Marina watched as Nate was hauled inside the helicopter and she wept with relief. Nate was inside, perhaps not safe, but he had a chance.

Now for Lachlan. She searched for him in the water as the winchman descended again. But as she watched, a huge wave — bigger than any before — rolled into the cove, picked up Lachlan and crashed against the cliffs.

When the boiling foam retreated, there was nothing.

# 42

In her deepest, darkest moments, in the blackness of night, Marina would admit, only to herself, that she'd occasionally longed to vanish beneath the waves. In the weeks and months after Nate had gone, when she'd finally come to realise he must be dead, those thoughts had crept into her mind.

Now again, seeing the swirling water around the cliff, the helicopter hovering above, but no sign of Lachlan, she thought of joining him in the sea.

The helicopter and winchman edged closer to the cliffs behind the cove. The crew must be able to see something she couldn't . . . She screamed out in hope, begging the sea to let Lachlan live.

The winchman was almost touching the rocks, the rotors were perilously close . . . and then she saw why. Lachlan had been propelled by the waves back onto the ledge where Nate had fallen. He seemed to cling onto to the rocks but a backwash of surf tore him off and flung him back into the water yet again.

The helicopter backed off, dragging the winchman through the whitecaps. He was feet above the surf, metres away from Lachlan, then feet again. He reached him but it was clear he couldn't get a hold of him.

The winchman tried again and they were on top of each other, but Lachlan was flailing. Was

Lachlan too scared to go with the winchman? Too terrified to allow himself to be winched up?

The winchman hugged Lachlan and put a strap around him while the water bubbled and boiled. Marina was terrified they'd both be swept away or the helicopter would be blown against the cliffs. They were so close to saving him, but she daren't let herself hope until they were safely inside the helicopter . . .

Suddenly there was daylight between the waves and the two men, and they were being pulled upwards above the rolling seas. They spiralled upwards, like marionettes in a deadly dance, while the helicopter flew away from the cliffs and hovered above the heaving sea.

She held on tight, soaked by the sea, shaking with the cold and adrenaline, but weeping with relief when she saw the winchman and Lachlan vanish inside the aircraft, which was already speeding off. In half a minute, she was left alone, with only the roar of wind and sea.

She laid her cheek against the rocks and uttered a silent prayer.

'Marina!'

There was shouting from behind her, in the cove beneath the lookout station. The inshore lifeboat bobbed in the waves and two of its crew were climbing up to her. 'Stay there!' they ordered, waving at her frantically. 'We're coming to get you.'

Rachel was at the helm, keeping the small RIB away from the rocks as two of the crew reached her. 'You're going to have to come into the water with us,' they warned.

Marina didn't care. She only wanted to know that the man she'd loved once, and the one she did now, would be OK.

They helped her down and waded with her the few feet through the water to the RIB. She was shaking uncontrollably, despite the coats they laid over her.

'Is Nate alive? Is Lachlan OK?' she kept asking all the way back to Porthmellow Harbour, but no one had an answer for her.

She went through a thousand agonies until they reached the lifeboat station, where Dirk, now back from the trawler tow, had news from the hospital. Lachlan was OK, apart from a few cuts and bruises apparently.

Hearing Lachlan was safe, Marina sobbed in relief while Dirk drove her to the hospital and told her what little he knew about Nate's condition. It had been touch and go but he was alive and conscious. He'd been treated for hypothermia and he'd swallowed a lot of water.

She was told to wait outside A&E and asked the nurse in charge, who she knew slightly, how Lachlan was, desperate to see him. She hadn't dared to text him while he was undergoing treatment.

'He was released,' the nurse said. 'I think he's gone home.'

'Already?'

'He had a few cuts and bruises and naturally he was very cold, but otherwise he's been extremely lucky. He's a tough cookie.'

'I know that,' Marina replied, her shoulders sinking in relief despite the disappointment she felt on hearing that he'd gone when she wanted to see him and thank him — and hold him to make sure he really was OK. She had an urgent need to see with her own eyes that he was alive and well. Nothing else would satisfy her.

She reached for her phone to text him but the doctor came out of the side room.

'You can see your husband now, Mrs Hudson,' he said.

'He's not my husband,' Marina replied. 'But I still want to see him.'

Nate was sitting up in bed. His tanned face was bruised but other than that he seemed OK.

'That was a close call,' he said.

Marina kept her distance; afraid he might reach for her. 'You could say that.'

'Thank you for coming to rescue me. That bloke who pulled me out said you'd almost been cut off yourself.'

'Don't thank me. That bloke who pulled you out is Lachlan. He risked his life for you. For God's sake, Nate, you both almost died!'

'I know . . .' he said defensively. 'I didn't do it deliberately.'

'Really? I don't know what to believe any more. I only know that if one — or both — of you had been killed, I'd never have been able to go on.'

'This Lachlan. I heard him in the helicopter, asking after you. He was begging the crew to make sure you were safe. You're even closer than I thought?' Nate asked.

'Yes, we're close.' She held Nate's gaze. 'He's one of a kind. In fact, I love him.'

380

His mouth fell open and he let out a breath. 'I knew it. I *knew* you wouldn't be on your own for long.'

'For long? It's taken seven years to find someone I care about again,' she said, almost adding 'the way I cared about you'.

'What will you do?' he asked.

'What I started to do a long time ago: move on with my life — a life that, however much I once wished otherwise, you're no longer part of, Nate. I'm pleased you're alive and you're not hurt. I would never wish that on you — even though you hurt me so much I thought I wouldn't survive.'

He avoided her eye.

'I want you to know that I loved you once and, because of that, I hope you come to understand what you've done to me and the other people who cared about you is unforgiveable. I don't hold out much hope of you changing, but stranger things have happened.'

He looked at her as if she'd taken leave of her senses. 'Babe, I know you want to make a clean break with me, but are you sure that's the right thing for us?'

'Us? What *us*? There is no us. Your part in my life is over forever. I say this with no malice, but because it's true. I never want to see you or speak to you again.'

She walked to the door. 'Goodbye, Nate.'

'Wait, Marina!' He climbed off the bed. 'Don't end things like this. Babe!'

She didn't turn around again. She kept on walking with her head held high, away from Nate and out into the gathering twilight.

She didn't call Lachlan — what she had to say had to be said face to face, so she took a taxi straight to the cottage and rapped on his door.

As soon as he opened it, her words rushed out. 'Lachlan! I thought you'd be at the hospital, but you weren't there. The staff told me you were OK and you'd been released but you didn't contact me, and I was about to phone you when the doctor called me in to see Nate . . . Oh no, your face is cut.'

He listened to her doorstep tirade until she ran out of breath.

'It's only a scratch,' he said, his voice hoarse with weariness. 'You'd better come inside.'

'I didn't bother you because I assumed you had enough to worry about with Nate,' he said, once they were in the sitting room. 'How's he doing?'

'He'll live. I have to tell you that he . . . he came up to the lookout station and had it out with me. I didn't invite him.'

'Jesus Christ, I might have known. He was moaning about something in the helicopter but I thought he was delirious and then they put him on oxygen. You mean he actually confronted you in there?'

'He wanted to explain why he disappeared.'

'Explain? That man is — ' Lachlan clammed up. 'No, I'll not say what I think he is. It's not right.'

'You can't say anything about him I haven't thought myself. I told him to leave and he marched off. Turns out he ended up in the cove and got cut off. I'm not sure if he did it on purpose to get my attention or sympathy. I hope not; it so nearly lost me both him and you. I'll never forgive him for that . . . And you! Don't you ever do that to me again!'

'I had no choice, Marina,' he said simply.

'You did have a choice. You might have been killed too. You almost *were*.' She shuddered at the memory of her sheer terror of watching him vanish in the surf.

'I was out for a run . . . No, I was out hoping to see *you*. I've jogged past the station many times lately, hoping to see you and talk to you again. I've never found the courage to come in or knock your door because you rightly wanted me to keep away. But today, when I saw Nate from the coast path and you perched on the rocks, I recognised him and I was terrified you'd do something crazy like trying to jump in to save him.'

'No. I wouldn't . . . ' said Marina, trying to process the fact that Lachlan had been trying to see her and make his peace with her. She longed for peace. 'There's no way I'd ever dare go into that sea,' she said. *Not for Nate . . .*

'How could I have known?' he said. 'All I saw was a man in trouble and his wife who might risk everything to help him. I'd have done the same for anyone but especially for Nate — you loved him once. He wouldn't have lasted a minute longer. I didn't plan it. I could see what was happening in front of my eyes and I reacted instinctively.'

'What if I'd lost you?' She took his arms, still unable to believe he'd escaped and was here with her. 'How could I live with myself if you'd sacrificed yourself for Nate?'

'I really thought you might have gone in to save him.'

'I might have jumped in to save *you*.'

His eyes widened in shock. 'How can I deserve that? You shared a life with him whereas I turned up a few months ago, invaded your privacy and brought the world down on you. What right do I have to think I can overturn your feelings for Nate? I wouldn't even try . . . even though I wanted to. I want to now.'

'Listen to me,' she said, burning with a need to let him know how precious he was to her. 'These past few weeks since we found Nate have been almost as hard as when I lost him because in finding him, I felt I lost you too. I've been so embroiled in the fallout and so confused about how I feel about Nate reappearing — the guilt, the relief, the anger — that I pushed you away and made you feel part of it was your fault. I haven't meant it.

'And I know you were the one who organised half the town to come and persuade me to rejoin the Wave Watchers. It was exactly what I needed. It made me realise that I had to try to get my life back again. Thank you, and I'm sorry I had no idea.'

'I wanted to help you in the best way I could, and encourage you to carry on with the thing that's given you purpose but I didn't want you to think I was trying to interfere . . . ' He held her gently in his arms as if she might shatter if he applied any pressure. 'Just like I didn't know if you might want to see Nate again. Or what would happen when you did. No matter what he did, he's still your husband and . . . you have every right to love him, or even make a go of it.'

'Why would you think I'd want that?' she said.

He touched her forehead with his. She held onto him, trembling at how close she'd come to losing him.

'I didn't want to be the consolation prize you settled for because the love of your life was dead,' he whispered. 'That's why I was always wary, deep down, even before Nate was found. It's why I agonised over whether to tell you my suspicions or keep quiet because, God forgive me, I convinced myself you were better off without him and things were going well between us. I'd found someone again after thinking I never would.'

He kissed her and the joy of having him back filled her heart almost to bursting.

When their kiss ended, she rested her fingers lightly on his jaw, feeling his beautiful flesh under her fingers. 'You couldn't wait to get out of my sight when I first came to warn you in the cove.' She smiled.

'Yeah well, I couldn't wait to get out of anyone's sight. I didn't want to be here at all, or anywhere. I didn't feel I belonged, but now I do. I love you, Marina. There, I've said it.'

She whispered it back. 'I love you too. I love you and I'm going nowhere.'

# 43

## London

### Two weeks later

'Settle down, everyone. Let's welcome our new features editor, Tiff Trescott, to the *Post*.'

Yvette Buttler's Geordie accent cut through the chatter around the boardroom table. It was Tiff's first editorial meeting at the *Post*. The other department editors murmured their welcomes and Tiff smiled her thanks. She knew a few of them personally and the rest by reputation; she trusted some and had the measure of the others. She'd survive.

Yvette peered at Tiff over the specs she kept on a gold chain. 'Just so everyone here is forewarned, I hear you can be a bloody difficult woman.'

Tiff smiled at the murmurs of amusement in the room. 'I do try,' she replied.

Yvette's eyes gleamed. 'I'm pleased to hear it because I can be a bloody difficult woman too. In fact, I think we're going to rub along well together. Right, let's hear what delights you all have in store for tomorrow's edition,' Yvette said, sweeping the room in one glance. 'Go on, astound me.'

Tiff's nerves eased a little. It was a new job in a tough business, but it was the second chance she'd doubted she'd get and she was going to make sure she didn't waste it. Yet, when she stopped racing around and allowed herself a moment to dwell, she couldn't help thinking that it had come at a great cost, and that there would be no second chance with that.

Hours later, Yvonne called Tiff into her office. She had a proof page of the next day's 'Female' section on her desk.

'Are you sure you want this to go out, Tiff?' she asked.

Tiff's eyes flicked over the proofs of her feature. She hid her nervousness with a smile. 'It's a bit late for that, isn't it?'

Yvette nodded. 'True. It was a rhetorical question.'

'Is the story that bad?' Tiff asked, her light tone hiding the beating of her pulse.

'It's good, Tiff. It's very good . . . ' Yvette met her eye. 'Though I'll admit it's unexpected.'

'Unexpected in what way?'

Yvette pushed the feature forward. 'Unexpected as in a surprise, fresh, from the heart.'

Tiff laughed. 'I bet you didn't know I had a heart.'

'Oh, I did. I have one too — a very bruised and battered one — but in this business, particularly as a woman, I've worked very hard to hide it and I know you have too.'

Tiff shrugged. 'Hmm. Well, I think I've blown that myth out of the water, haven't I?'

★ ★ ★

387

A few days later, Tiff lay back on the teal velvet chaise longue in her flat. Miraculously, it had survived the attentions of the tenant, who'd had a cat. Tiff had vaguely known the man, and hadn't the heart to separate him from his beloved pet, so had agreed to allow him to rent her home. However, the whole place had had to be de-furred according to the letting agent. Tiff didn't mind too much. She half wondered if she should get a cat herself for company, but decided it wouldn't be fair to have a pet when her new role meant she was out much of the time. Even when she wasn't at work, she was socialising with colleagues and contacts. Since she'd been back in London, a constant stream of invitations to parties and events popped up in her inbox every day, but she delegated a lot of them to junior colleagues or she'd have been knackered and pickled.

She lay back on the chaise longue.

'Alexa, play 'Ride of the Valkyries',' she instructed the Echo she'd bought herself on her return home.

Well, it was as far from Dvorak as she could imagine, and she needed a rousing tune to stiffen her spine and raise her spirits.

She closed her eyes and tried to enjoy the music, and embrace the solitude after a day of constant noise in the busy newsroom. Even though she had her own office, most people kept their doors open and the chatter and phones ringing had been a shock after the peace of Cornwall. She'd been reminded of her first day as a reporter, way back in the day, when she'd

388

been amazed that anyone could ever focus on their own work amid the din and distraction.

The music thundered out but Tiff's mind was still three hundred miles away in Porthmellow. Her life there seemed a distant memory now. She'd been anxious about leaving her cousin, especially with the situation with Nate not finally resolved, but she was in regular touch with her and expected a visit from Marina within the next few weeks. Most of all, she felt confident that Marina had good friends around her, and now she had Lachlan at her side. He was a good man, like Dirk . . . Marina would be fine.

For the umpteenth time, she made a conscious effort to remind herself how happy she was, how it was all for the best, and to dismiss Dirk from her mind.

Weren't you supposed to emerge from an experience like hers by having learned some lessons?

If the purpose of her fall from grace was to persuade her to give up being a journalist and settle down to a life of embroidery in front of the fire, it was never going to happen.

Dirk had recognised that. She was never going to change her love for her career, and why should she?

Had she emerged from it as a nicer person? She didn't know, but what she had taken from Porthmellow — from Marina and the locals and above all from Dirk — was that she could still love someone, with her whole heart.

He'd reminded her that she was a decent human being. You had to make hard decisions in her job — in his too — but he'd never wanted her to be anyone but herself. She knew that he hadn't even tried to persuade her to stay because he cared about her.

Should she have given him the chance by agreeing to see him? The signs weren't pointing in that direction. He texted her and she'd WhatsApped him a few times in the past few weeks, but that was their only contact. Light-hearted stuff about London and Porthmellow . . . nothing heavy. The relationship, from his side at least, seemed to be already dying.

She lay back again, having deliberately put her phone in the bedroom out of reach. If Elvis came back to life, if Lord Lucan was found working in a pasty shop in Porthmellow, it would have to pass her by for the next fifteen minutes while she tried to calm her thoughts.

Ten had gone by before she heard it ringing, and she dashed into the bedroom to answer it.

'Tiff. Why aren't you answering your phone?'

'Because I'm trying to have a bloody life, that's why,' she tossed back. 'What I could say is 'Dirk, why are you calling me?''

'Because I want to know if I have the right flat.'

'What do you mean 'the right flat'?'

'Look out of your window.'

'What?'

Her stomach was doing an Olympic floor routine when she rushed to the window and flicked the blinds open. Dirk was standing by the wheelie bin under the orange streetlight. He spotted her and waved.

'What is this? A Richard Curtis movie?' she said, unable to stop her heart from racing.

'I don't have a bunch of cards declaring my true feelings for you, if that's what you mean,' he said tersely. 'Can you please open the front door before I get arrested for stalking?'

She pressed the buzzer to give him access and thirty seconds later he was walking into her sitting room. 'What are you doing here?' she asked.

'Nice to see you too,' he shot back.

In a black reefer coat and jeans, he filled the small space. He was even more heart-stoppingly handsome than in her wildest dreams and there had been many of them since she'd walked out of his cottage.

'I can't cope with you out of context,' she said, in wonderment at his presence.

He frowned. She loved him frowning. She'd got it so bad . . . 'What's that supposed to mean?' he asked

'It just feels strange you being out of Cornwall,' she said. 'It's hard to process that you're here now.'

He arched an eyebrow. 'Would it help if I had a box of pasties with me?'

'I don't think so.' She laughed, but what she'd told him was absolutely true. She simply couldn't believe he was here in her flat, all her fantasies turned to flesh and blood. However, the shock and awe were fading rapidly to be replaced by the same fear that had driven her to make a clean break with him in the first place.

'Dirk. It's wonderful to see you, naturally, but why are you here at all?'

'I want to talk to you face to face. I read this.' He thrust a copy of the newspaper at her. 'Is it anything to do with me or am I making a massive dick of myself?'

Tiff shook her head before touching the lapel of his coat. 'Oh Dirk, how many other people have I left a piece of my soul with?'

His smile was the widest she'd ever seen and he started to read from the newspaper.

She put her hands over her ears. 'Oh, don't. Don't, please.'

He ignored her.

## THE END OF THE WORLD
*Tiffany Trescott on how being in exile saved her life — and broke her heart again*

*I was sent into exile earlier this year. Against my will, I was despatched to the end of the world — otherwise known as the Cornish harbour town of Porthmellow. A brush with high politics ended in disaster. I lost my job, my reputation, my partner and my home.*

*But I found my self-esteem — and at the risk of turning into a pound shop Pollyanna, I realised what truly mattered to me.*

*If you're looking for a happy ending, there is and there isn't one.*

*The fact I'm writing this piece, back in the offices of the Post, tells you that I clawed back some part of what I thought I'd lost forever. My career — being a journalist and hopefully a teller of truth does matter a great deal to me. Losing my job on a bleak day at the end of winter was like having my heart ripped out and fed to the crows.*

*It felt like my soul had been torn away although I now realise I didn't know how much pain I was in until I lost all the other things. I chose not to share that loss for a long time, but if I really do believe in telling truth, I must shine a light on that pain now.*

*I don't know if I'll get another chance at love. I'd like to think so. The past few months have shown me it's fine to dream other dreams . . .*

*I don't need a partner to be happy, successful or fulfilled.*

*And yet . . . I left something elemental behind in that little town at the edge of the world. I'm not going to say who it was, but if that person is reading this, I want them to know that they will always be with me, wherever I go. A piece of granite lodged in my heart. A grain of sand that I will never be able to remove.*

Finally, he stopped and dropped the paper on the table. Gently, he removed her hands from her ears. 'Granite? Sand?'

'It sounds ridiculous now you say it out loud.'

'Ridiculous?' His gaze was intense, a search-light that she couldn't hide from and didn't want to. 'So, did you mean it?' he demanded. 'Do you?'

'Of course I do!'

He kissed her and she kissed him back, drinking him in deep until she thought she might bruise his lips or hers or both.

393

'Wow.'

'Yeah, well, it's been a long time.'

Gently, he pulled her down next to him on the sofa. 'I have something to say that can't be said over the phone and I knew that if I tried to write it down, you might dismiss me or misunderstand. The only way is to tell you . . . I've been for a job interview up here.'

'In London?'

'Don't look so surprised. There are four lifeboat stations along the Thames alone, plus the ones along the coast in Essex and Kent. There's a place for a full-time mechanic come up at Gravesend so I applied and got an interview. I've come from there now.'

'That's, um . . . that's intriguing . . .' Tiff dared not acknowledge what she hoped and feared he meant in almost equal measure. 'How do you think it went?'

He shook his head. 'Pretty good. They were interested because I used to work at the City station, obviously, and I've a lot of experience of the river and the class of vessels they operate.'

'That sounds positive,' she said.

'I think so. I'm optimistic about the job, but what I came here to ask you was how you feel about it? About me, moving back to London? If I get it.'

'You know you'll get it, Dirk. They'd be crazy to turn you down.'

'You turned me down.'

'You didn't ask me,' she said. 'You refused to ask me to stay.'

'Well, I am now. I'm asking you, if I get this

job — and even if I don't — will you let me back into your life? Not in the half-arsed way we were going about it in Porthmellow, but properly. Like grown-up people do. Committed people.'

'We'd have to be committed to do this,' she said lightly, but Dirk was unsmiling.

'Tiff, be serious for once — take off the armour and answer the question. God knows, that's what you always want from other people, isn't it? I'm here telling you that I love you and I want us to be together and I'm prepared — happy — to do whatever it takes to make sure that happens.'

'You have no idea how much I want this to work, but I can't ask you to do this for me, make these big changes in your life.'

'What if I want to? We can work it out. I like Porthmellow but I'm not wedded to it in the way some of the crew are. Before things went wrong with Amira, I loved London and I still miss it. You've reminded me of what I enjoyed about it: the buzz, the vibrancy, the unpredictability.' He smiled. 'I've got a mate who's going to work in the States for a year and he says I can have his flat. It's on the river.'

Tiff was overwhelmed that he would make such a sacrifice for her. 'How can I deprive Porthmellow of one of its finest?'

He burst out laughing. 'I'll miss my friends and neighbours, but there's a few in town who'll be glad to see the back of me and my moods. No more Mr Dirk 'n' Stormy — I know what they call me.' He looked down at her. 'They'll survive, but I'm not sure I will without you.'

'M — ' A strangled squeak came out.

'Aren't you going to say anything?' he asked, doubt creeping into his voice. 'Have I got this badly wrong? I can withdraw my application.'

'No!' She hadn't meant to say it so loudly. 'No. I'm . . . simply lost for words.'

'That'll be a first.'

And trying not to cry, she thought. Trying very hard and failing.

She didn't have an answer but he did. He kissed her gently, almost tentatively, a kiss that showed her he had no idea of what her verdict would be.

'Is it too much?' he murmured, holding her around the waist.

She shook her head. 'No one's ever done anything like this for me before. No one has ever offered to give up so much for my sake. I can't quite handle it.'

'Then let it be a first. Let it happen and see where it takes us. After all,' he said with a gleam in his eye, 'we can always change our minds.'

'No. That's just it. I *won't* want to change my mind if you do this and come to London with me. I won't want you to change your mind.' There she'd said it: opened herself up completely to this man she'd never sought out, never expected to find at the end of England, in that tiny quirky town.

'Then, I promise I won't change my mind if you don't.' He crossed his heart.

'How can you know that?' she said.

'My good opinion once lost is lost forever. Didn't Darcy say that?'

Tiff laughed, carried away on a tide of euphoria. 'You said Darcy was an arse.'

'In some ways. Not in others. He was able to admit he was wrong and grovel, I'll give him that.'

'True.'

'I'll take the job then and, if I don't get it, I'll keep looking and applying until I do. We have that much in common. We're both stubborn, and if we want something, we carry on with bloody-minded determination until we get it.'

She laughed. 'We'll drive each other insane,' she said, as if it was the most wonderful thing in the world.

'I hope so because personally I couldn't live with someone safe and steady. I'm not cut out for peace and harmony. I like the excitement. I also happen to love you.'

She sighed. 'I suppose there's no point denying I feel the same.'

'None at all,' he said, holding her tightly. 'None whatsoever.'

# Epilogue

The scent of the sea and the cries of choughs filled the air as Marina walked along the path towards the lookout station. Russet bracken brushed her jeans and the bushes had been stripped of their leaves by the gales that had torn through Porthmellow that week.

October was racing by and the nights shortening, but on this early evening the sun was orange as it sank to the horizon. The post lady had brought some mail that morning — a card from Tiff, a happy card, simply to say thank you and tell her how thrilled she was that Dirk was applying for a job in London. No one knew but Dirk and Marina, nor would they until he'd secured the job and put his cottage on the market. She'd miss him as a friend and neighbour but she was delighted for Tiff, and for Dirk.

Along with the card and some legal papers, there had also been a letter. It was one sheet in a white envelope, postmarked from Liverpool.

She knew the handwriting but hadn't opened it until now. It felt like a letter to read under an open sky, with a fresh wind blowing; a letter to read in a place where she could put all that happened, for good and ill, into perspective — a place where she could feel at one with the home she loved, yet remind herself of how inconsequential her troubles were when set against the magnitude of sea and sky.

She made her way into the heathland, to the 'hidden' bench, and took the paper out.

Dear Marina,

*I don't expect you to forgive me, but I thought if I sent an actual letter, it had more chance of being read.*

*I've moved to Liverpool and I hope to stay here, find a job and try to turn over a new leaf, as they say. I've had the papers from the solicitor and won't contest the divorce, not that I'd be able to after what I've done to you.*

*No matter what you think, I swear I did love you. You probably won't believe me. I don't deserve you to. As I said, I'm not a decent man. I might have been once for a moment or two, when we were together. The thing is, I'm weak — but you are strong.*

*I hope you'll be happy with Lachlan. He seems OK to me and I'll always be grateful he saved my life.*

*So, be happy, Marina, and try to think of me without too much bitterness and anger.*

'I won't. I don't, Nate,' she murmured.

*You won't hear from me again and don't worry, I'll be OK, just as I know you will be fine.*

*With love,*
*Nate*

399

She read the letter again and wiped away a tear.

In that moment, she knew it would be the last she ever shed over Nate.

She got up and retraced her steps through the gorse to the main coast path. A narrow track ran off it directly towards the cliff edge itself. Marina followed it and stopped a few feet from the edge, pausing to listen to the waves crashing a hundred feet below. Out to sea, a fishing boat bobbed off the island where Nate had last been sighted seven years ago.

She took a deep breath and looked into the horizon, at the magenta clouds and the setting sun. She stepped closer to the edge where the turf had cracked and the rock was crumbling. The seagulls circled high above the cove below. The October wind plucked at her hair as she recalled the vow she'd made after Nate had first vanished.

Silently she made another vow about love — but it was the future and Lachlan in her thoughts this time. She held out her palm with the sheet of paper balanced on it, and waited. By the time she'd let out a long breath, a gust plucked the paper from her and carried it over the cliff, whirling it higher and carrying it out to sea until it was a speck suspended high above the waves.

She didn't know where it went next. She'd turned around, with the sea at her back, striding back towards the lookout station.

'Marina!'

Lachlan climbed over a stile and jogged along

the path towards her.

'Marina! I didn't know where you'd gone. You weren't in when I got home. I let myself in with the key and then I got your text to say you'd come out here.'

'No need to worry. I needed some fresh air. I'm fine.'

'Good. Great. I thought it was that.' She knew by the strength of his embrace and relief in his eyes that he had been concerned. She kissed him.

'You don't have to worry about me now.'

She smiled, determined to never look back again and to live with hope and for this moment, and for the man holding her even tighter against him. In that moment, she truly knew he would always be there, for as long as the waves crashed onto the shore in the cove.

# Acknowledgements

With huge thanks to Moira Briggs for her help with Lachlan, and to Colin Taylor for his legal and policing advice. Thanks to Sarah Bennet for her suggestions on Lachlan's background and to Angie for her insight into college life.

To Tiff from Radio Cornwall, I've never met you but your name alone inspired a character who I love and hope my readers have loved too.

As ever, my group of friends, including Janice, Sarah, Jules, Rachel, Bella, Nell and Liz, have been there for me through thick and thin, often on an hourly basis.

This past few years have seen Team Avon get my books into the hands of more and more readers, which is no mean feat and makes me happier than I can say! I want to also thank Sabah Khan and Ellie Pilcher of Avon, and all the book bloggers who spread the word about my stories far and wide.

My editor, Tilda McDonald, has been amazing, stepping into the shoes of Rachel Faulkner-Willcocks who was enthusiastic about the idea of the Wave Watchers from day one. Thank you, Tilda, for being happy to withstand the barrage of excited emails and for your insightful editing advice.

I'd also like to thank my copy editor, Jo Gledhill.

To the volunteers of the RNLI and the

National Coastwatch Institution, I salute your inspiring work, which helps to keep us safe around our coastlines.

Finally, my family are the rock on which everything I do is founded. John, Charlotte, James, my parents and Charles: I love you — first, last and always.

We do hope that you have enjoyed reading this large print book.

Did you know that all of our titles are available for purchase?

We publish a wide range of high quality large print books including:
**Romances, Mysteries, Classics**
**General Fiction**
**Non Fiction and Westerns**

Special interest titles available in large print are:
**The Little Oxford Dictionary**
**Music Book**
**Song Book**
**Hymn Book**
**Service Book**

Also available from us courtesy of Oxford University Press:
**Young Readers' Dictionary**
**(large print edition)**
**Young Readers' Thesaurus**
**(large print edition)**

For further information or a free brochure, please contact us at:
**Ulverscroft Large Print Books Ltd.,**
**The Green, Bradgate Road, Anstey,**
**Leicester, LE7 7FU, England.**
**Tel:** (00 44) 0116 236 4325
**Fax:** (00 44) 0116 234 0205

*Other titles published by Ulverscroft:*

## A PERFECT CORNISH CHRISTMAS
### Phillipa Ashley

After last Christmas revealed a shocking family secret, Scarlett's hardly feeling merry and bright. All she wants this festive season is to know who her real father is . . . So Scarlett heads to the little Cornish town of Porthmellow, where she believes the truth of her birth is hidden. She just didn't bargain on being drawn into the Christmas festival preparations — or meeting Jude Penberth, whose charm threatens to complicate life further. Everything comes to a head at Porthmellow's Christmas Festival . . . But can Scarlett have the perfect Christmas this year, or are there more surprises on the way?

# A PERFECT CORNISH SUMMER

## Phillipa Ashley

Summer is on the horizon, and the people of Porthmellow are eagerly awaiting the annual food festival. For Sam Lovell, organising the festival is one of the highlights of her year, providing a much-needed distraction from the drama in her family life (and distinct lack of it in her love life). When Gabe Mathias, a popular chef and former local, agrees to headline the weekend after the star booking unexpectedly cancels, Sam should be delighted. But Gabe is the last person Sam was expecting to see. They haven't spoken in eleven years, when their relationship imploded after Gabe made a choice with far-reaching consequences. Can they put aside their differences for the summer? Or will Gabe's return change Sam's quiet coastal life in ways she never imagined?